RESURRECTION

Other titles by S. Usher Evans

THE RAZIA SERIES
Double Life
Alliances
Conviction
Fusion

Empath

THE MADION WAR TRILOGY
The Island
The Chasm
The Union

THE LEXIE CARRIGAN CHRONICLES
Spells and Sorcery
Magic and Mayhem
Dawn and Devilry
Illusion and Indemnity

THE PRINCESS VIGILANTE SERIES
The City of Veils
The Veil of Ashes
The Veil of Trust
The Queen of Veils

RESURRECTION

DEMON FALL TRILOGY

Book Two

S. USHER EVANS

Sun's Golden Ray Publishing

Pensacola, FL

DEMON SPRING TRILOGY
Resurgence
Revival
Redemption

DEMON FALL TRILOGY
Reawakening
Resurrection
Reclamation

ISBN-13: 978-1945438431

Demon Art by Ashley Gonzales, Zeefa Studio
Line Editing by Danielle Fine, By Definition Editing

Sun's Golden Ray Publishing
Pensacola, FL
www.sgr-pub.com

For ordering information, please visit
www.sgr-pub.com/orders

DEDICATION

To MJS
You and this book grew in my heart
November 2020

CONTENTS

DEMONOLOGY

The following is a brief introduction to the five kinds of demons found in the human world. The International Coalition for Demon Management (ICDM) is charged with protecting humans from unwanted demonic transformation, but we can't do it alone.

Learn the signs of demonic coercion and don't become a victim.

ATHTAR

First Seen: 1500 BC, Syria
Magical Element: Void
Original Sin: Pride
Original Demon: Bael

The oldest and rarest demons, Athtars live in the Underworld and appear during Demon Spring. They have the ability to manipulate time and space. If you encounter an athtar demon, seek shelter as quickly as possible, and alert your local US Division office. NOTE: With the death of Bael in the Great Demon War, athtars are thought to be extinct.

ELOKO

First Seen: 400 AD, Democratic Republic of the Congo
Magical Element: Earth
Original Sin: Envy
Original Demon: Biloko

Eloko demons use the sound of a bell to hypnotize their victims into a false sense of security. If you think an eloko is trying to coerce you, stomp your feet or clap your hands to disrupt the magic, then run away.

KAPPA

First Seen: 600 BC, Japan
Magical Element: Water
Original Sin: Greed
Original Demon: Mizuchi

Kappas mostly live near water, and will create an illusion of a house or structure. When the victim enters the illusion, it will break and the human will be drawn underwater, given the option to transform or drown. When near bodies of water, familiarize yourself with existing structures, and watch for others coming in and out.

LILIN

First Seen: 200 AD, Germany
Magical Element: Air
Original Sin: Lust
Original Demon: Freyja

Lilins use a mixture of pheromones and glamour (illusion) to lure humans into sexual intercourse, then transformation. If you think a lilin is trying to coerce you, pinch yourself or think of something unsettling, then run away.

NOX

First Seen: 1500 AD, Mexico
Magical Element: Fire
Original Sin: Anger
Original Demon: Mot and Xo

Nox demons use the human's innate fear of demons to construct terrifying nightmares, and the human agrees to transform to cease them. To combat a nox demon, take a deep breath and remind yourself it's only a vision.

PROTECT YOURSELF

If you encounter any demon or supposed demon, contact your local US Division of the International Coalition for Demon Management right away to report the incident.

UNITED STATES DIVISION
INTERNATIONAL COALITION FOR DEMON MANAGEMENT

#demonspring

CHAPTER ONE

Cam Macarro couldn't stop staring at her love, Lotan, prince of the nox demons, inhaling the cold tacos that Abeula had left out for them. In fact, Cam was almost afraid to blink. If she did, she might realize this was all a dream, perhaps the last panic-induced fantasy before her blood left her body and her spirit ventured to wherever they went after death. Because that was infinitely more believable.

She, Jack, and Lotan had just been rescued by a newly rejuvenated Anya, who had *somehow* managed to discover that the demonic athtar magic was still around and also *somehow* managed to absorb it for herself. She was now the most powerful demon in the entire world, able to wield time and space, and had retrieved the imprisoned trio from the clutches of the noxes who'd betrayed Lotan and put them in Cam's grandmother's kitchen.

"Okay, you have to stop looking at me," Lotan said, putting down the half-eaten taco. "I promise you, I'm fine." He flashed his wrists at her. "Look, no scabs. Nox magic healed me."

"I..." Cam started, rubbing her face. "How is any of this possible? Bael's magic was... How did she... What the shit is going on?"

"I have absolutely no idea, my love," Lotan said. "But I assume we will all find out in due time. I don't even know if Anya knows what happened." He took another bite and moaned. "Cam, this is the best pork I've had in my entire life."

And that was saying something, considering he was born over five hundred years before. "I'll be sure to tell abuela that you enjoyed it," Cam said with a half-smile. "But really... I'm still in shock, I think."

"Well, eat up," Lotan said, pushing the plate of food toward her. "And we'll go to bed. I'm sure everything will seem less... shocking in the morning."

The kitchen door opened, and Jackson Grenard, Cam's best friend, partner, and almost-death buddy, walked in, a concerned and confused look on his face.

"Where's Anya?" Cam asked.

"Out there, I guess," Jack said, sinking into the chair.

Cam pursed her lips. "What did you do?"

"Me? Nothing," Jack said. "Anya's the one who—"

"Who what?" Cam asked, tilting her head to the side. "Saved all our asses?"

Jack snorted. "Took Bael's power. Became a demon again."

"And why is that such a bad thing?" Cam asked.

"Yes," Lotan said, grabbing the last taco on the plate and chowing down. "It sol' a lo' of our pro'lems."

"Or creates a mountain of new ones," Jack said. "We have no idea what that magic is going to do to her. If she's the belu, then—"

"Is she the belu?" Lotan asked, after swallowing. "Was she actually touched by God?"

"She said she took Bael's powers," Cam said. "Does that make her a belu?"

"Good question."

Cam nearly jumped out of her skin. Anya stood in the kitchen, her power filling the room. Her eyes, formerly a beautiful mossy green, were now emeralds, shining behind thick, dark lashes. Her skin had darkened to a beautiful, smooth bronze, as if she'd just spent a week on the beaches of her native Syria. Even her nails were long and sharp, unlike Cam's jagged edges.

"It's okay," Anya said with a nervous half-smile that didn't meet her eyes. "I'm still me."

Cam hadn't realized she'd been gripping a napkin and released it, forcing herself to relax and smile. "Thank you, Anya. I don't know... Thank you for coming for us."

She took the chair next to Jack without looking at him. "I'm glad I got there in time."

Cam glanced between the two of them—Jack looking like he wanted to walk out of the room and Anya holding herself so tightly she might implode. Their communication issues hadn't been resolved with her newfound powers, it seemed. They'd need to hash it out eventually, but Cam wasn't the one to make them do it.

"Why don't you tell us what happened, Anya?" Lotan said, saving them all from the awkward silence. "And how you came into...this."

Anya licked her lips. "After Jack left in Lisbon, I..." She swallowed, casting a nervous look around. "Diogo found me. I asked him if he'd help me, and he said he would...but not the way I wanted. He had a portal."

"Wait—a portal?" Lotan said, sitting upright. "An athtar portal? Between the human world and Underworld?"

Anya nodded. "He made his own. All athtars could, apparently."

"Huh." Lotan rubbed his chin. "Sorry, please continue."

"We landed in Ath-kur, and we had to walk... We passed the battlefield," she said with yet another half-glance at Jack. "The land was very unstable. Earthquakes and mist. He took me to a large crack in the earth that we climbed down. There was..." She furrowed her brow. "I don't know how to explain it. It was Bael's magic—just without Bael. It felt familiar, like him, but it wasn't him."

"How did you take it?" Lotan asked, leaning on the table.

"I think...." She hesitated, glancing at Jack, and Cam could practically hear the calculations in her mind. She was trying to massage the truth so Jack wouldn't freak.

"You can tell us the truth," Cam offered, gently. "We won't be mad." She caught the gaze of the only person whose opinion Anya really cared about. "Right, Jack?"

"Right," Jack said.

But Anya stayed silent for another long moment, chewing on the inside of her cheek. "I think it was waiting for me," she whispered finally. "Bael's magic wanted me to take it."

Jack's brows went to his forehead, and he looked at Cam as if to say "I told you so," but she ignored him. "What do you mean? Was the magic sentient or something?"

She shrugged. "I don't know how to explain it. But Diogo tried to take the magic and it didn't let him."

"But Bael let you take it," Jack said.

"It's not..." Anya cleared her throat. "He's dead."

Jack caught her in his gaze. "His power clearly wasn't."

"And I don't know what that means," Anya said, her gaze desperate for him to believe her. "But I know that I'm still myself."

"This is fascinating," Lotan said, clearly ignorant of the tension brewing. "Bael is dead, but his magic remained in Athkur and another person was able to absorb it. I wonder if that means... If I gave up my power, could someone else take it?"

"We'd have to make sure it's not Yaotl," Cam said. "Speaking of... what the hell are we going to do about him?" She sat back. "I guess Anya could—"

"No." Lotan's tone was firm. "He's gone astray, but we can't kill him."

"He was going to kill me," Cam said with a glare.

"And two wrongs don't make a right, my love," Lotan said.

She pursed her lips at him. "Lotan. Yaotl has his eyes on world domination. At this moment, he's making alliances with demons in every corner. He plans to take control and perhaps eradicate ICDM. Clearly, we need to do something about that."

"And I will," Lotan said with a half-smile. "But killing him isn't the answer. And if my goal is to reclaim my pack, I have to do it without assistance. They won't take kindly to the noxslayer stepping in."

"Then what will you do?" Cam asked, a little nervously.

"For now, nothing," Lotan said.

"Nothing?" Jack said with a look. "So you want to let him continue to find allies? He was trying to overthrow ICDM and put the humans in chains."

"My educated guess is that once the demonic folk find out there's a new athtar in town, they might be less inclined to listen to a nox who's merely powerful." Lotan looked at Anya. "I assume you plan to announce yourself to the belus."

Anya's mouth parted, and she hesitated just long enough to pique Cam's suspicions. "Eventually, yes, but I don't want to be the kind of belu who goes around threatening people to bend them to my will."

Jack snorted, and Cam kicked him under the table.

"But your presence will be as much of a deterrent to Yaotl's plans as we can ask for," Lotan said. "Which means that in the interim, I can continue work on my experiments. It might be beneficial to see the crevasse where you found your magic in Ath-kur, Anya. If you want to take me there."

"Oh, uh..." Anya cleared her throat. "Ath-kur is...not the same as you remember."

"What do you mean?" Cam asked.

She smiled, as if she had a secret. "I can make the world any way I want. So I made it... I recreated it into something better. I would love to show you." She turned to Jack, her hesitation clear on her face. "If you'll come with me."

But Jack just looked at Cam. "What do you think?"

The adrenaline of almost dying was leaving her blood, and exhaustion was settling in. She had been in Lisbon yesterday, today, had nearly lost her life, and tonight, was just too tired to deal with Anya's newfound powers, as well as all the other chaos left unresolved in this world.

"Can we go tomorrow?" Cam asked. "I just...I think I need to stay put in one place tonight. My brain can't absorb any more information."

"Sure," Anya said with a firm smile.

"Shall we go to bed?" Lotan asked. To his credit, he kept the question innocent.

"You go ahead," Cam said, squeezing his hand. "I'll be there in a minute. I need to get some air."

The moon was full tonight, and Cam couldn't stop looking at it. She'd never been so close to death before, at least a death she couldn't fight her way out of, and it put things in perspective

—made her appreciate these beautiful moments more.

"You should be with your prince." Juana, Cam's grandmother, left her bedroom to join Cam on the veranda.

"I will," Cam replied. "But first, I need to know... Was María really going to leave me?"

It had been a revelation from Jack that Cam's great-aunt, a Councilmember for the ICDM, had given the order to let Cam die at the hands of the noxes who'd kidnapped her. María was always willing to sacrifice for the greater good, but this one, in particular, stung.

Juana's old face, so familiar and warm, hardened. "I do not know the particulars. But it seems to me...your Jack was ready to kill every nox in existence to get you back, and he was doing it alone."

Cam sighed, leaning on the railing. "When the nox magicked me, I saw María telling me she knew everything. About Lotan, and me turning athtar, and she was firing me." Cam chuckled. "And all I felt was relief."

"I bet the nox didn't like that," Juana said.

Cam shook her head, refusing to think of what he'd shown her instead. "I love my job, but I love Lotan more. Does that make me..." She stared at the moon. "I never thought I'd be one of those people who'd give up the perfect job for love."

"Jobs come and go, but your prince is once in a lifetime," Juana said softly. "Like your abuelo, God rest his soul. He was the only man to keep me on my toes and change my mind about anything. I would've given up your job for him." She sniffed.

"But I also wouldn't have taken your job. You have your father in you."

Cam shook her head. "Do you think mama and papa would be mad at me?"

"I think they just want you to be happy, Camilla. And that man makes you happy." She patted Cam on the butt. "Now get in there and enjoy him, or else I might go in your place."

Cam snorted. "Hands off my prince, Abuela."

She cackled and waddled toward the kitchen, presumably to tell Anya to go to bed. And Cam turned to walk back to the bedroom where she'd find her prince.

She opened the door to the dark room slowly. The small twin Cam always slept in already had a body in it.

"Plenty of room for you," came a soft voice. "Come, my love. I miss you."

Cam unstuck her feet and padded over to the bed. Climbing in, she realized just how little room there was for the two of them. Lotan's broad shoulders and long legs took up most of the space, and she had to lie on her side just to fit. But as she decided this wasn't going to work, Lotan draped an arm over her and pulled her close.

"We can make do," he whispered, his breath tickling her ear. "And make love. But in the morning, mmkay?"

She smiled; he must've been exhausted. She settled, relishing this moment of peace. Perhaps Juana was right—this man did make her happy. Even here, uncomfortable as she was, and knowing she would get very little sleep on the edge of the bed, there was nowhere she would rather have been. And with that thought, and the knowledge that everyone she cared about was safe tonight, she allowed herself to relax into the arms of her demon prince.

CHAPTER TWO

Jack tossed and turned, his dreams plagued by visions of noxes firing guns at his head and Anya begging him not to hate her. He woke up feeling just as poorly as he had the night before, only now he had to face another day. Rolling onto his back, he replayed the conversations with Anya over and over, looking for any sign that the woman he cared for was gone. But she was just herself—and the only thing keeping him from marching down the hall and taking her was his own fear.

But it was potent, so he just showered quickly and followed the scent of fried eggs and bacon to the kitchen. To his surprise, Lotan was the one with the skillet and apron, hovering around and making breakfast for an amused Cam and Juana. Anya was nowhere to be found, which Jack actually found rather... disappointing.

"Morning, sleepyhead," Cam said. "You're right on time.

Lotan is impressing us with his ability to make chilaquiles."

"It's what my lady requested," he said with a cheesy grin.

"Tortillas are burning," Juana said, sitting back.

"Shit," Lotan said, dashing over to a smoking pan and lowering the heat. "Well, they'll be a little extra crispy."

"You shouldn't torture him like this," Jack said, settling in the empty seat. "The man's been through enough."

"He insisted," Cam said with a haughty look as Juana stood to help Lotan with the pan of eggs. "How about you? Have any good conversations last night?"

Jack didn't feel like answering the question. "Where is Anya?"

"No clue. But I assume she comes and goes as she pleases these days," Cam said. "What with being able to cross the entire universe in the blink of an eye."

Jack nodded. Cam seemed to have accepted Anya's transformation without hesitation, which made sense, considering that she'd been an athtar herself for a brief period.

"Are you still mad at her?" Cam asked. "Because if you are, you should probably get over it. She was athtar when you met her, and you still managed to fall for her. So I don't understand why you've suddenly got this stick up your ass."

A hum of energy made the hair on Jack's neck stand up and as he turned around, Anya appeared in the room. She gave Jack a half-smile, which he didn't return.

"Well, I have to say, it's nice to know you're coming," Cam said.

"How?" Anya said, taking the empty chair.

"You aren't exactly subtle about your magical presence," Lotan said, putting a plate of burnt food in front of her. "But you're amongst friends, so it doesn't really matter."

She looked down at the food and made a face. "What's wrong with it?"

"It's great," Cam said, swallowing hard. "Thanks, Lotan. Now please let me help clean up."

"I told you I'd be doing all of it," he said with a look. "Just sit there and eat."

"Mm, delicious," Cam said, forcing the food into her mouth.

The sizzling sound drew down to a low rumble, and Lotan's movements slowed with them. Anya's eyes glowed darker, but her smile was genuine. She'd slowed time except for herself, Cam, and Jack.

"Do you want me to get us some real food?" she asked, pushing the burnt tortilla around the plate. "This is inedible."

"It would break his heart, though," Cam said with a tut. "Let's all power through, kids. He tried so hard."

"Anya, you can't just..." Jack began but then stopped. He couldn't tell her to stop using her powers, especially for something as innocuous as having a private conversation to spare Lotan's feelings. But the ease in which she'd reacquainted herself with this magic unnerved him.

"Can't what?" she asked.

"Nothing," Jack said, shaking his head. "But Lotan's

weirding me out. Can we get back to real time?"

Lotan had turned to bring his plate to the table, and the sight of him slowly walking with a proud grin on his face was strange indeed.

Cam made a sound and softened, putting her face in her hand. "Look at that big dummy. Yeah, let's get back to him."

The world sped up and before Jack could say anything, Lotan was seated with them, ready to dig into the meal he'd made.

He took a bite and winced. "This is abysmal."

"It's great, honey," Cam said, taking another bite and daring the other two to say a word. Wisely, neither Jack nor Anya responded.

After breakfast, which Jack and Cam cleaned up, despite Lotan's protests, Anya seemed eager to get to Ath-kur. Jack had no bag to speak of, and neither did Cam, so the only thing left were goodbyes with Juana. Cam's grandmother gave them big hugs each, and made Cam promise to call her parents and give them a heads up as to her next move.

"Perhaps leaving out that you were kidnapped," Juana said with a smile.

Before any of them could answer, Juana faded from view and Jack braced himself for his arrival in the Underworld. But they didn't land there—at least not that he could feel. They were in a library, dimly lit by candles and gas lanterns. He caught Cam's similarly confused look.

"Where—"

"My lady." A man appeared in a blur, and immediately bowed his head. An athtar—Diogo. "It is an honor to have you in my home again."

Diogo seemed like an old soul—and not just because he was transformed in 1755. He wore a tweed jacket with leather elbow patches, and a plaid shirt that was in style sometime around the time Jack was born. The spectacles perched on his nose gave him a professorial look, as did the rows and rows of books that lined his expansive library. Even Lotan looked impressed, walking over to a nearby stack to get a closer look.

"Diogo, these are my companions," Anya said. "Cam Macarro, Jack Grenard, and—"

"Lotan," Diogo said with a small nod. "I'm glad to see you are well. My lady was very worried for you."

He smiled. "Thank you for helping her."

"She's my belu. I would do anything for her," Diogo said.

Jack furrowed his brow. "She's only been your belu for a few hours. And from what I hear, she's not really your belu."

"You have not been a demon, so you don't understand," Diogo said with a warm smile. "My connection with Lady Anat is as strong as it was with Bael. My power comes from her, and I'm grateful for it."

That didn't give Jack any warm fuzzies, but with a look from Cam, he decided to let it go. "Then we're happy to count you as an ally."

"My lady, how may I serve you?" Diogo asked, bowing to

Anya.

"We simply need the portal," Anya said. "I wouldn't have disturbed you, but I wanted to introduce my friends formally."

"You have never disturbed me, and never will. It is always an honor to have you here."

How much of this was a show for the all-powerful demon beside him? Anya's smile lacked the usual hubris of Bael's, though. Still, for a demon who hadn't wanted anything to do with them before, Diogo was certainly kissing their ass now.

"Shall we?" Anya said.

Before any of them could answer, the ground slipped beneath their feet once again. The burned eggs came back with a vengeance as Jack was flung from the normal to the abnormal. His entire being was being torn apart, the pressure outside his body fighting against that inside, and neither side was winning. His chest constricted so tightly that it was hard to suck in more than small gasps.

"Just breathe," Anya said, pressing her hand to his chest. "It'll pass in a moment."

He opened his eyes to a bright blue sky surrounded by tall trees. Familiar trees. Redwoods.

"Where are we?" He was supposed to be in the Underworld, not on his mountain in Washington.

"Don't worry about that now, just focus on coming back to yourself." Anya's face appeared in his line of sight, and her warm hand touched his cheek, grounding him to reality. He also didn't think it would be gentlemanly to vomit in her face, so he swallowed what was about to come up as he took deep, gulping breaths.

"I'm sorry, I don't think I can fix that," she said softly. "Cam?"

"Gonna be fine," she grunted from somewhere far away. "Just after—" She, clearly, was not concerned about upchucking the breakfast Lotan had made.

Jack slowly pushed himself up, still unsure what he was looking at. Because if he believed his eyes, he was in Seattle, staring at his house. But that was impossible—they were in the Underworld.

"Anya, what's going on?" Jack asked. "Where are we?"

"Ath-kur," she said, helping him to his feet. "My version of it."

He shook his head slowly. "What does that mean?"

She wore an enigmatic smile, looking pleased with herself. "I can't really explain it, but...there's this innate knowledge I have now. This intimate feeling that this world is mine to do with what I want. And I wanted...this." She gestured toward the house. "Do you want to see it?"

Jack took a hesitant step forward then forced himself to continue. Anya opened the door to the foyer, with the long lines of dark pine flooring leading into the living room. Everything was exactly the same as he remembered it, right down to the arrangement of the furniture and the dining room. If he ignored the nauseated feeling in the pit of his stomach, he could almost believe that he was home.

"This looks familiar," Cam said with a smile to Jack.

"Where will I be able to work?" Lotan asked. "This room looks too nice for me to be making a mess."

"Follow me," Anya said, gesturing him toward what was a broom closet in their house in Seattle, but here appeared to be a stairwell. As soon as the door closed behind them, Cam wheeled on Jack with a grin on her face.

"So...this is real interesting," she said.

"What is?"

"She could build anything she wanted and she chose to build *your* house in Seattle. Down to the shade of the flooring. I think that's something, Jack."

"She's already made it clear what she wants," Jack said. "The problem is me."

Cam sighed. "Well? Out with it. What's wrong now?"

"I don't know. I just feel like... I feel like there's something." Jack walked to the window. "I'm trying to be okay with her and these powers, but Diogo is acting like she's Bael, and she's able to do things at the drop of a hat and—"

"If you want my opinion," Cam said, joining him. "And you do, because you're asking me about it. I think..." She seemed to consider her words. "Do you think maybe you're just looking for something to go wrong?"

"What's that supposed to mean?"

"It means that... Every time you guys get somewhere in your relationship, when both of you are at the same place emotionally, *something* happens. So now that Anya's pretty much back to her old self, ready to start a relationship with you, you're backpedaling as fast as you can. I think you're just trying to guard yourself."

Jack blinked at her. "That's...astute of you."

"Speaking from experience," she said. "I'm not saying you should jump in, and maybe you can't yet. But you have to at least try. She's trying." Cam gestured to the house around them. "Meet her halfway. You both obviously care about each other. While you're waiting for the shoe to drop, you might as well enjoy what you have."

"This shoe, Cam, it's going to drop hard," Jack said.

"And you've survived harder falls," Cam said. "Besides that, you can't know how this ends. Maybe Lotan unlocks the secret to demonic powers and maybe Anya decides it's better to stay human and be with you. But she can't make that call unless *you* pull this stick out of your ass and talk to her."

CHAPTER THREE

Anya led Lotan down a short staircase, lost in her own thoughts. She'd hoped Jack would give her some hint about what was in his mind, and if he was angry with her, even though he'd sworn he wasn't. She'd returned to Ath-kur, to this home, to make it perfect for him—and for Cam and Lotan, too. Something to prove to Jack that she wasn't the monster he suspected. And perhaps to prove to herself that what had happened with María was just...a fluke.

She could barely stand to think about it—and how easy it had been to succumb to her emotions. She'd never had this much control over literally *everything*. There was no one holding her leash now, no one keeping an eye on her. She could destroy the world if she had a mind to.

Not that she did. But it was intoxicating. And dangerous—her mistake with Cam's great-aunt was one she wasn't hoping to repeat.

"What do you suppose they're talking about back there?" Lotan asked, drawing her attention back to him.

"Us, probably," Anya said, clearing her throat. "Cam seems to have settled down."

"Was she worried for me?" Lotan asked with something of a boyish grin.

Anya rolled her eyes. "I'm not talking about that. I'm talking about..." She didn't quite know how to explain it. "She's not as nervous to express herself."

"She's never nervous to express herself," Lotan said with a chuckle. "But I know what you're saying. She's been much... freer with her expressions of affection." He sighed with a content smile. "It's been nice."

Wonder what that's like? Anya tried to bury that jealous voice in her mind as she reached the bottom of the stairs. She opened the door to a large, expansive room with absolutely nothing in it —white walls and white floors that extended as far as the eye could see.

"I wasn't quite sure what you needed, so it's kind of a blank slate," she said with a small shrug.

"You weren't kidding," Lotan said with a bewildered look. "I confess... I don't know anything about this world manipulation thing you suddenly have. Is it... How does it work? Do you think I have it as well?"

"If you'd like me to accompany you to the noxlands, we can find out," Anya said.

He made a noise. "Not yet."

"Why are you afraid to go back there?"

"I'm not afraid."

"Aren't you?" Anya asked, without a hint of malice. "They've disrespected you. You are their leader. You need to show them what happens to insubordinate underlings."

"They were never mine, Anya," Lotan said with a soft sigh. "Most of them had lived a hundred lifetimes before I showed up. I'm merely their connection to my mother's magic. Yaotl has made my place in the world exceptionally clear to me."

Anya could hear the pain in his words. "And yet, here you are, looking for a way to keep them connected to their magic. You would be within your rights to rid yourself of it and see what happens."

"I would be," Lotan replied. "But that's not… I don't think that's what my mother would've wanted."

Anya had doubts about that. The only reason Yaotl and the rest of his band of traitors had their powers in the first place was because Bael had "gifted" them to Xo and Mot. Xo had initially refused the gift, but after Bael had ordered Anya to slaughter them, she capitulated. It wasn't until after Xo's death that those noxes even returned to the human world to grow their numbers. As far as Anya knew, Xo had no interest in preying on humans the way the others did.

But Lotan, only five when his parents had been taken from him, might've been fed a different story. And Anya knew from experience it was difficult to break someone from a long-held reality.

Luckily, Lotan was otherwise distracted with the table Anya had conjured for him. "Would it be possible to return to my home in Mexico City? I have some notes and papers I would like to retrieve—and some clothes, as well, unless you were able to conjure those."

"I could, but we can make a quick trip," Anya said.

Cam's voice echoed behind them. "Whoa."

Cam and Jack had ventured down the stairs, craning their necks at the world Anya had built for them. Anya's gaze landed on Jack, hoping to see something other than disdain and distance. He seemed bewildered now; that was something of an improvement.

"Lotan would like to retrieve some items from his home," Anya said. "Would either of you like to accompany us?"

"I'm still nauseated from our arrival," Cam said with a firm shake of her head. "But I wouldn't say no if you grabbed some stuff from my apartment in Shanghai." As Lotan grinned, she narrowed her eyes. "Sensible underwear only, please."

"Jack?" Anya asked.

"How long are we planning on staying here?" he said, slowly lowering his gaze to her.

"As long as it takes," Lotan said. "I want to complete my research and become human. Then we'll figure the rest out."

"What does that entail, exactly?" Jack asked, crossing his arms over his chest.

"I'm currently testing theories on the talismans, and how

their proximity affects the demon magic," Lotan said. "A process that'll be made much easier with a human assistant."

"I can answer that one for you," Cam said, narrowing her eyes. "You put a talisman on your body, and it hurts. Next theory."

He smiled. "Maybe Jack would be a better assistant, on second thought." He looked to Anya. "And perhaps even our fair belu athtar can lend a hand if needed. Knowing Bael's magic existed after his death is a game-changer, to be sure. There's so much we don't know, even now."

"We can stay here as long as we need," Anya said. "Anything we need, I can get for us back in the human world. It would be easier for me to go."

Jack released a sigh, clearly sensing he'd been outnumbered. "Fine. Grab me a couple things. And my whetstone."

Anya and Lotan, unbothered by the Underworld-to-human world transition, stepped through the portal and stopped first at Cam's apartment. Anya had never been there before, but it was a nice size, though sparsely decorated. Lotan found a suitcase in the closet and began dumping the contents of Cam's drawers into them, while also grabbing her hanging clothes and tossing them on top.

"Are you taking everything?" Anya asked.

"I don't expect she'll return to this place," Lotan said. "Not after what ICDM did to her. I would be surprised if she stayed with the organization for much longer." He glanced in her direction. "You should probably plan to take what you need from Seattle as well. It doesn't sound like our human counterparts want to make the journey often."

It didn't sound like Jack wanted to stay at all, but only was because Cam was. Anya had hoped once she'd come back to herself, they could finally begin to be together and not just cohabitate. But these powers seem to have pushed him farther away. Taking them had been borne from desperation—

"Why lie? You wanted it."

She paused, closing her eyes to clear that voice from her mind. It felt like Bael's whispers, but instead of his deep, gravelly voice, the timbre was more of her own. She'd hoped it would fade, or at least that she could exert some control over it. But it was still there, whispering truths and goading her on.

"I'm not the one who sent you to María's office. That was all you."

She'd merely lost control; she hadn't meant it. Besides that, María deserved to know that she couldn't abandon her family anymore. She'd made the choice to leave Cam to die, the same way she'd left Jack's first wife. And Anya merely…

She opened her eyes to the dark city below. "Jack doesn't seem pleased that I've taken this magic at all."

"I think he's being cautious," Lotan said. "I can't say I blame the man. He spent weeks being tortured at the hand of the last owner of that power. But he shouldn't be worried. You seem the same taciturn athtar you were before." He flashed her a grin. "Though perhaps you hate me less than you used to."

"I have no reason to hate you, and never did, it seems," Anya replied softly. "Besides that, it's you who should hate me."

"Believe me, I've tried," Lotan said, pulling a pair of black lacy underwear from the pile and grinning devilishly. "But they say I have too much of my father in me to hate anyone. Perhaps it's because I understand why you thought you had to seek revenge."

"I was lied to," Anya said, staring out at the city. A cruel irony that Bael's lies continued to haunt her after his death—even Diogo had seen past them. "You know, you might ask Diogo for his help. He knows more about the demonic magic than even I did."

"A man after my own heart," Lotan said. "I caught a glimpse of his library. I'm jealous."

Anya wore half a smile. Even at this distance, if she concentrated, she could feel Diogo's joy. He was reading something, sipping an espresso. She could practically taste the coffee on her tongue.

"He is yours to do with what you wish. If the nox wants his library, he would hand it over without a second thought if you told him to."

She shook herself, sweeping the voice from her thoughts. "Hush."

"Anya?"

She looked up at the nox prince, bringing herself back to the here and now. "What?"

"I asked if you could see anything else I needed to grab," he said. "I'm not really sure what Cam packs in her overnight bag."

"Not much," Anya said, finally turning away from the window. "Lotan, can I ask you a question?"

"Mm." He'd leaned his whole weight on the suitcase, trying to latch it closed. There were still piles of clothes scattered around the place, but he seemed to have given up packing them.

"Do you ever hear your parents?"

He stopped, catching her gaze in the window. "What do you mean?"

"Do you...ever hear their voices in your mind?" Anya whispered. "Like they're still with you?"

Slowly, he shook his head, leaving Cam's suitcase on the bed and joining her by the window. "No. Why?"

"No reason," she said, shaking her head. "Let's hit Seattle then your place and get back."

CHAPTER FOUR

It had certainly been a strange couple of days for Lotan. In his wildest dreams, he never thought he'd be taking up residence in a newly rebuilt Ath-kur with the new belu athtar, her on-again-off-again boyfriend, and the love of Lotan's life, the latter of whom was currently curled up in the space next to him, dreaming. Then again, a few days ago, he was furiously trying to figure how he could end his miserable life to spite the noxes who'd captured him.

Cam made a noise and rolled over violently, nearly throwing an elbow in his face, then settled against him, the tension line on her brow fading. She'd barely let him out of her sight, and he was happy to occupy her in every way he could think of. But Lotan couldn't quite follow her into dreamland, not when there was so much weighing on him.

He'd been coy about his plans for Yaotl and the noxes,

because the truth was, he had no plan. After losing his own father so early in life, Yaotl had been something of a stand-in for Lotan. The elder nox had taught Lotan everything about life—how to shave, how to hold a sword. How to speak to a girl. How to address a crowd. How to lead, how to be strong. It was on Yaotl's knee that Lotan had sat when he'd been told his parents were gone. These memories weighed heavily on his mind, even as he'd sat in captivity. Because he'd been raised by Yaotl, he knew his mind—understood the intentions. And because he was his father's son, he couldn't shake his affection for the man who'd taken everything from him.

Even now, Lotan lacked the gumption to march into the noxlands and take what was supposedly his. All he wanted was to rid himself of this demonic curse and the yoke of being responsible for those who didn't care for him and live out the rest of his days with his perfect Cam—while not leaving the noxes who still had good in their hearts without their one link to his mother.

But first, he'd have to figure out that demonic riddance part. Carefully, he slipped from the bedroom and found the pants he'd tossed on the floor. Then he padded out of the room, closing the door behind him.

The house was silent, and if he ignored the athtar magic pressing against his own innate magic, he could forget he wasn't in Jack's house in Seattle. He'd been here once, during a Christmas when he'd surprised Cam with a flight home to see her parents with a stop to see her best friend. He hadn't exactly been allowed to go *with* her to Christmas, but the time had been magical all the same.

He opened the door to his basement laboratory. Much like the rest of the house, Anya had done her best to recreate what she'd seen of his setup in Mexico City. It had remained blessedly untouched since his capture.

Turning on the lamp over the large drawing table, he plucked his notes from the stack where he'd left them and refreshed his memory. Much of what he had was random thoughts, wild hairs that he would investigate. So far, nothing had come from his efforts except more frustration.

He grabbed a pen and scribbled on a new line. *Bael's power existed after his death.*

What that meant, Lotan had no clue. Bael's power could've remained because he'd had a child with Anat, the same way Lotan held his mother's power after her death, but that child had been dead for five hundred years. Unless that connection was still there, even *in* death. But how did that work? What was the science behind it? Lotan didn't know any of it.

There was one person who might. The kappa belu, Mizuchi, had lost his life in the Great Demon War, and his line of turtle-looking water demons had retained their powers, the same way the noxes had after Lotan's mother's death. But Tabiko, his right hand, wasn't talking—especially not to Lotan.

And if he wrote a letter now, how would it make its way to Kappanchi? Lotan no longer had a suite of noxes at his beck and call. He had no one, save a couple of humans and the belu athtar. An odd little family, but one that he felt more protective of than the noxes who'd raised him. Even quiet, taciturn, calculating Anya. There was much she wasn't sharing, and while that was cause for concern, Lotan had faith that between Cam and Jack, her tongue would loosen.

But he was daydreaming. And if he was going to be away from his bed, he might as well try to get some work done.

On the table behind him, a black leather briefcase sat waiting for him. He approached it much like a human might a bomb, putting on thick gloves and walking to the table with slow, deliberate steps. Keeping his distance, he unhooked the snaps on the leather and the case popped open, revealing a pile of metal coins.

Nox talismans.

The magic in Lotan's bones reacted to the collection; he'd sensed it the moment he walked into the room. He'd been somewhat obsessed with these talismans since finding out about them from Cam last year, but the damn things were so potent he could barely stand to be in the same room with them.

He took a deep breath, girding himself for the pain that was to come. And as sweat broke out on his forehead, he reached into the box and grabbed one.

"Son of a bitch!"He dropped the coin immediately. It landed on the metal floor with an innocent clang.

Lotan growled, pulling off his glove and inspecting the bright red welt that had appeared on his fingertips. His demon healing was already mending the wound, but the presence of the talismans made it take a little longer. He counted the seconds until the injury was completely gone. Forty-five.

He jotted down his finding next to the list of ten other readings from past experiments, all within the same time, give or take a few seconds.

With another deep breath, he readied himself again, clocked on the timer, and reached in to grab two coins. This time, he was ready for the pain, gritting his teeth even as his eyes watered. The talismans felt like fire spreading through his veins, like every inch of him was being torn apart.

Spots filled his vision, but he braced himself against the table. He just needed to hang on a few more seconds. For science. For Cam. For—

"Nope."

He dropped the coins and staggered away, cursing in every language he could think of. This time, his fingers had split open, and deep rivers of red flowed down to his wrists. Lotan hit the timer again and waited for the magic to do its thing. Two minutes and five seconds, this time, for the pain in his body to fully subside.

He jotted down his thoughts and observations and sat back down in his chair to give himself a break. In some way, this felt a bit like insanity—doing the same thing over and over and hoping for a different result. Cam wasn't too far off in her estimation that the talismans just hurt him, but there had to be something. Some way to use them to free him from this demonic curse.

Or else he didn't know what he'd do.

He dismissed that desperate thought and braced himself for another effort. This time, three. And he'd hang on until he couldn't anymore.

"Lotan! Lotan!"

Someone was shaking him awake, and when he opened his eyes, he thought it might be an angel. His angel, to be exact.

"I'm sorry," he said, his mouth barely working. "Did I fall asleep?"

"What the hell is wrong with you?" Anya was here too, and she looked pissed. "You nearly died."

"What were you trying to accomplish?" Jack as well. The whole gang. He must've...

He groaned as he sat up and his head swam. The last thing he remembered was taking three talismans then perhaps... Perhaps falling over. Had he fallen still holding onto the talismans? He glanced at his hand and swallowed hard. It was black—not just dead but decaying. There was a stench about it, too, one that told him he'd been holding onto that talisman for several hours. He couldn't even feel it.

No, he could. His nox magic was moving into the skin, knitting it back together, regrowing the tissue and reconnecting the nerves.

"Lotan, answer me," Cam said, fury in her gaze. "What the actual fuck were you thinking?"

"I was experimenting," Lotan said simply, forcing a smile

onto his face. "And clearly, the experiment was a failure."

"Do *not* pull that shit again," Cam said, pointing her finger in his face. "Do you hear me? You aren't allowed to experiment by yourself."

"Yes, ma'am," Lotan said with a deferential nod.

"Seriously," Anya said, her Mother Athtar on full display. "It's a good thing we found you when we did. This...whatever you're doing with the talismans, let it go. You'll end up dead."

"Not likely," Lotan said, looking at his hand, already turning purple with the influx of new blood. "Hasn't killed me yet. But fascinating nonetheless."

Cam swore under her breath and stormed out, slamming the door behind her.

Jack just smiled and put his hands in his pockets. "At least act like you aren't going to do it again, man. For all our sakes."

"And don't," Anya said, walking to his research and reading it. "This...this is just wasted time. It only serves to hurt yourself. The talismans can be used to kill and ward humans against magic. That's it. Trying to use it to cleave the magic from your veins won't work."

"How do you know?" Lotan asked.

"Based on your research, I'd say you do too," Anya said. "You've run this experiment twenty times and had the same result."

"Not exactly the same," Lotan said, pushing himself to stand with his good hand. "But perhaps you're right. I wonder if there's a way we can separate my human body from my magic without killing my human body."

"That sounds like a bad idea," Jack said.

"Besides that, magic doesn't work that way. It's fused inside your bones, in your blood," Anya said, looking through the papers. "When the soul leaves the body, when the head is severed and there's no hope of survival, the magic is released into the ether and all that's left is the human remains."

"There must be a way," Lotan said, falling back into his thoughts. "But perhaps I've been looking at this wrong. Perhaps instead of killing the magic in my body, it's about killing the human part first, but not really killing it." He flashed Jack a smile. "Do you know CPR?"

"Let's not do that either," Jack said, looking at Anya, who seemed deep in thought. "Right, Anya? Let's not get a defibrillator."

"Wouldn't work anyway," she said, almost off-handedly. "The demonic healing would kick in. It always does, unless—"

"Unless the head is severed from the body," Lotan finished, finding his chair and sitting down in it. His hand was now a bright pink, like he was healing from a bad sunburn. "And there's no coming back from that."

"Not usually," Jack said.

"Perhaps Cam will do us all a favor and kill me," Lotan said with a smile.

"Don't joke about that," Jack said. "Because she will if she finds you down here doing this shit again."

His hand fully healed, Lotan decided to tempt fate once more and find his furious soulmate.

"My love?" Lotan said, opening the door to their shared bedroom.

"Don't talk to me."

Even from the other side of the room, he could see that her whole body was stick straight with tension. She was the bomb now, but he couldn't stay away.

"I'm sorry I worried you," he said, sliding his hands over her shoulders.

She smacked them away. "Don't."

"My love—"

"I *just* got you back, you stupid dick," she said, whirling on him with tears in her eyes. "And you just... You just... How can you care so little for your own safety like that?"

"Because I know I'm safe," Lotan said, showing her his hand. "Because no matter what I've tried, I can't seem to untangle this demonic magic."

"And what happens when you do and you bleed to death?" But she took his hand, running her fingers along the new skin. "God damn, I thought you were dead. I've never..."

Lotan kissed her forehead gently. "I'm sorry I scared you."

"Just...have a partner or something," she said, the anger melting from her eyes. "Who knows how long you had that talisman on you?"

"Five hours and three minutes," Lotan said with a cheeky smile. She glared at him and he flashed her a smile. "The timer was still going when you roused me."

"Well, now you know that five hours and three minutes is long enough for you to almost lose your arm," Cam said.

Lotan slid his hand across her hips, grabbing her rear as he pulled her close. "I've still got the other one."

"I'm not laughing," she said, but even her stubborn nature was no match for his featherlight kisses on her cheek. "Lotan, I'm not..."

His free hand found the front of her pants and slipped beneath the waistband. "You're not what?"

"I'm still mad at you," Cam said, though her eyelids fluttered as he found his favorite spot. "And don't think you can just... *do* that and I won't be mad at you anymore."

He removed his hand. "Then what can I do to make it up to you?"

She turned to him. "Promise me you won't play with talismans anymore."

"I promise," he said. "If it makes you feel better, I can't seem to permanently injure myself, no matter what I try. And yet, every day I get older."

"You have to have some other avenue of research," Cam replied. "Maybe ICDM has something that can help you?"

"Are you still considering yourself an employee?" he asked.

"Until my ID no longer works, I suppose," Cam said. "Would it be wildly out of character for me to want to quit?"

He smiled. "No. Not in this case. I'll let you know if I suspect a personality transplant, though." He wrapped his arms around her and pulled her close. "Another option that has so far not borne fruit is to ask the Kappas what they know about it. Mizuchi's line continued after his death, after all."

"Seems like that might've been your first option," Cam replied.

"Yes, except they haven't exactly been answering my letters."

"Then we can go there," Cam said. "Tabiko is familiar with us at least. She'll give us an audience."

He nodded, and those wandering fingers dipped between her legs again. "Perhaps with your assistance, I might be more successful. You have a way with people."

"Stop trying to butter me up." She closed her eyes and released a small moan. "I'm still mad at you."

"I wouldn't expect anything less."

CHAPTER FIVE

"Kappanchi?" Anya looked like Cam had asked her to eat a pile of shit.

"Yeah, it shouldn't be a problem, should it?" Cam asked.

"No," Anya said, shaking her head. "But I don't think I'll go with you. Best for me to stay put and continue working on things here."

Cam didn't buy that for one minute; Anya had been staring off into space when Cam found her. But perhaps she wanted some alone time with Jack to sort out their relationship.

"I guess... Can we get a ride, at least? I don't fancy traveling through Liley, as much as I'd like to see Freyja."

Anya smiled. "I'm sure she'll be popping by eventually."

"Still." Cam squirmed a little. "If memory serves, it takes a few days to get here and there. Might be faster if you just took us."

"I don't think I need to go," Anya said, not quite meeting her gaze. "But perhaps I might have something else..."

She turned fully to Cam and held out her hand, concentrating as her eyes grew black. A tear appeared in her hand, almost like a miniature portal. But instead of growing, it remained as it was—palm-sized.

"What is that?" Cam asked, after a moment.

"Your own car," Anya said, her eyes returning to normal. "I think." She held out her hand to Cam, who didn't move. "It should be stable. I hope."

"That doesn't give me much confidence," Cam said, hesitantly holding out her own hand. But to her surprise, the portal slid from Anya's hand into her own. It weighed as much as a piece of paper. Cam gripped it with two fingers, mesmerized as the portal flickered and sparked but remained steady.

"You should be able to use that to go anywhere," Anya said, smiling and looking proud of herself. "Kappanchi or even the human world, should you want to return there."

"How do I use it?" Cam asked.

"Just tell it what you want," Anya said, her green eyes darkening a little.

"Siri, take me to Kappanchi." Cam smirked.

To her surprise, the portal flickered and jumped from her hand, growing wide enough to walk through. Kappanchi, all swamplands and gray skies, was visible on the other side.

"Wow," Cam said. "Siri, close portal."

The portal shrank and fell to the ground, and Cam picked it

up.

"You can just tell it what to do," Anya said. "It's not an iPhone."

"You said this could take me back to the human world?" Cam said. "Will I still want to hurl?"

"I can try to make it less nauseating, but no promises." She brightened. "But on the other hand, if you keep it open to the human world, your phone might work."

"Yay, internet," Cam said. "That would help with the research." She folded the portal in half and stuck it in her back pocket. "This thing is wild, Anya. You...you really have some strange powers now."

"I feel like I've just scratched the surface," Anya said, looking at her hands. "That there's this whole universe of possibility that was denied to me for so long because I just...believed Bael." Her smile faded. "I wish I'd been more curious like Diogo."

"Don't start that again," Cam said. "You have all the time you need to learn now, don't you?"

She nodded, glancing up at Cam. "Do you think Jack is angry with me for becoming athtar? He seems...distant."

"I think he's trying to figure out what it all means," Cam said. "Give him a little time. He'll come around, like he always does." She tilted her head to the side. "Are you sure you don't want to go to Kappanchi with us?"

Anya's smile was firm. "I'm sure. Good luck."

"Amazing."

Lotan jumped back and forth through the portal a few times, moving between Kappanchi and Ath-kur with ease.

Cam grinned at his unabashed curiosity, but had to step in as he poked the edges of the portal.

"Don't lose a finger, please," Cam said, grabbing him by the arm and pulling him into the kappa land fully.

"Yes, Mother," Lotan said, placing his hand on top of hers. "Such a lovely day for a stroll."

They walked, arm-in-arm, toward the small village in the distance. Cam had been relatively clear in her directions to the portal—to take her to Tabiko, but not inside the village. And it seemed to have worked so far.

"So I could tell this portal to take me anywhere," Lotan said. "I could have it drop me off in the middle of the noxlands, if I wanted."

"Do you want that?" Cam asked. "Or are we still avoiding responsibilities?"

"Ssh," Lotan said, shaking his head. "Don't ruin our walk."

Cam laughed, but then movement caught her eye. A crowd had gathered—kappas, grotesque creatures that looked like a cross between a turtle and a frog. Each of them had a dip in the top of their head holding water—and all of them bore spears and swords, pointed at Cam and Lotan.

"Whoa," Cam said, holding up her hands. "We come in peace."

"Please, friends," Lotan said, throwing a protective arm in front of Cam. "We mean no harm. I'm just seeking an audience with Tabiko."

"Is it true you have allied yourself with the athtar monster, Anat?" the kappa growled.

"Monster?" Lotan said as he and Cam shared a look of confusion.

"Fuck me, what did she do?" Cam said with a small groan. "May we please speak with Tabiko? Just to smooth things over."

The kappa who appeared to be in charge gave them a once-over then pulled back his sword. "We will announce your presence. Stay here."

He waddled away, and Cam sighed loudly, shaking her head. "We have been here one day. What could she have done in that time?"

"A lot," Lotan said. "She can stop time, remember?" He took Cam's hand and squeezed. "Let's get the facts before we jump to conclusions."

The kappa returned and made a noise, beckoning them forward. His fellow soldiers lowered their blades and stepped back, but no one seemed relaxed.

"This doesn't bode well for us," Lotan said quietly.

"To be fair, it's not that unexpected. Tabiko has hated Anya for centuries," Cam said. "As Anya was responsible for the death of her wife."

"Well, isn't that great."

Cam's stomach was in knots by the time the kappa opened the flap to a small grassy hut, revealing a woman seated at a desk. She had a cup of smoking liquid; from the scent on the air, it was tea. Her green skin was smooth, and her long, black hair was braided down the side of her head. She gazed up at them with sharp, black eyes, and there was very little friendliness in them.

"Tabiko," Lotan said, bowing at the hip. "It's a pleasure to see you again."

"I wish I could say the same," she said, crossing her arms over her chest. "What do you want?"

"First, a little enlightenment," Lotan said, inching closer but stopping at her cold glare. "I was under the impression we were on good terms. We fought side-by-side in the Great Demon War."

"We were allies toward a united cause, nothing more," Tabiko said shortly. "The kappas owe the noxes nothing. You owe us nothing in return."

"Not even friendship?" Lotan asked with a smile that withered under the kappa's frosty gaze. "Very well. I would then ask if we could strike up a deal—something you need or want in exchange for a little information."

"Fine," Tabiko said. "I want your athtar belu to agree *never* to set foot in my lands again."

"Why?" Cam said then added, "If you don't mind my asking, this seems a little brusque."

"She threatened one of my spawn," Tabiko said. "Stormed in here a few days ago like she owned the place and demanded Doroteia's head on a platter."

Cam closed her eyes and let out a long, deep sigh. "Damn it, Anya."

"I don't understand," Lotan said, looking between Tabiko and Cam. "Who is Doroteia?"

"She's the kappa who betrayed us in Lisbon," Cam said. "The one who told Anya she'd set up a meeting with Diogo, but instead sent Mazatl to...well." She tossed her hand in the air. "You know the rest."

"So...perhaps Anya's in the right?" Lotan said, looking back to Tabiko, whose gaze had darkened considerably, so he coughed and shook his head. "No, she's not. Absolutely not. Shouldn't have set foot here."

"I do not doubt that she has a grievance," Tabiko said. "But to walk in here and demand from me, the Sewanin—"

"Sewanin..." Cam furrowed her brow, looking at Lotan.

"Caregiver," he said. "To the magic?"

She cleared her throat. "The point is that my kappas look to me to protect them, to show leadership." She gripped her hands. "I do not know nor care how she managed to regain her athtar powers, but if she returns to this land, we will be ready. My kappas have inscribed the athtar symbol on their weapons. They seemed to be effective before."

Lotan licked his lips. "May I be the first to offer our sincere apologies for the behavior of our friend Anya?"

Tabiko said nothing.

"Then we'll get her to apologize," Lotan said to a slightly interested look from the kappa. "If we do, would you be willing to discuss something with us?"

"Depends," Tabiko said, raising her brow. "On what the

subject of that discussion is."

"How Mizuchi was able to continue his line after his death," Lotan said.

Tabiko just stared at him, amused. "I would've thought it would've been obvious, especially to you."

Lotan leaned forward, smiling in such a way that his dimples popped up. Cam should've warned him that his male charms wouldn't work on Tabiko. "I'm not asking for any other reason than a selfish one. I would like to understand how to keep my noxes connected to their magic should I discover a way to release myself from this curse."

"And why would you want to do that?" Tabiko asked then looked at Cam. "For her?"

"I'm aging," Lotan said simply. "And if I'm going to one day grow old and die, I'd prefer it be on my own terms." He glanced at Cam with a warm smile. "And with the person I want."

Tabiko sighed. "I'm afraid I can't help you, Lotan. But feel free to let Anat know she can go to hell, if it serves your needs."

CHAPTER SIX

Jack reached down and picked up a pine cone, staring at it and trying to remind himself that nothing he was seeing was real. He'd been out walking for a few hours, trying to clear his mind and digest this new reality. He'd gone to bed and tossed and turned again, unable to keep his own worries from crowding his attention. Worries about Anya, about what Cam had said, about staying here in this place. Lingering fears the nox had given him that he couldn't quite shake.

He'd gotten up early and found Lotan in the basement half-dead. He'd removed the talisman and called for help, and Anya had arrived in a blur, Cam showing a few moments later. Jack had never seen her look so terrified, and had a feeling Lotan had his work cut out for him in getting her to forgive him.

Anya had become engrossed in Lotan's work, so Jack left her and headed out to explore this...not-his-mountain mountain. It felt good to stretch his legs and move after his long night, and to explore how far he could go in this world—a far cry from the prison he'd been stuck in before. Bael had prevented him from seeing further than the window of his castle, save for the moments he was allowed to have dinner with the belu athtar and the lilin masquerading as his dead wife.

That he was in the same physical plane blew his mind.

He climbed over a rock and took in a deep breath of the cool air. Anya'd even recreated that perfect scent of decaying leaves and that particular cold, wet feeling that lingered on every surface. He kept having to remind himself that all of this had come from the wellspring of demonic magic now standing between them.

"What's so bad about her becoming athtar?"

Jack still didn't have an answer to that question, other than the unsettled worry in his stomach.

As before, the sensation of her approaching magic raised the hair on his neck, and he turned to find her standing behind him.

"Felt you coming," Jack said with a half-smile. "How are things back at the house? Have the lovebirds made up yet?"

"And then some," Anya said, coming to stand next to him. "They actually left on an errand to Kappanchi."

"Oh?" Jack frowned. "Where's that?"

She smiled. "Just keep going this way another couple of days until you reach Liley then another week or so until you cross the border into Kappanchi. You'll know you're there when you hit the swamplands." She glanced at him coyly. "Or just hop into an athtar portal and you're there in a second."

"Convenient," Jack said. "Is that a thing? Athtar portals?"

"I just came up with them," Anya said, holding out her hand and showing Jack the small portal. "Cam gave me the idea, actually."

"Looks a little small," Jack said.

"It grows when you want to use it," she said, sliding the portal carefully into Jack's hand. "But I wanted you to..." She licked her lips. "It's... Well, if you want to go back to the human world, just tell it and it'll open for you. The pressure change will still happen. Haven't figured out how to make that go away fully. But I'll keep working on it. That way you can... You can come and go as you please." She spoke without looking at him, and there was a nervous underpinning to the tone of her voice.

"What's wrong?"

Her green eyes met his, surprise in them. "What?"

"You're talking like..." Jack put the portal down on the rock next to him. "What's bugging you?"

"I just..." She gazed out onto the world beyond. "Nothing."

Jack watched her, unable to read the conflicted look on her face. She was still holding back, and he couldn't quite figure out why. Then again, he hadn't given her any signs that he was willing to talk. So he took a deep breath and decided to offer an olive branch.

"Will you show me how to use it?" he asked, picking up the portal between his thumb and index finger.

"Just tell it where you want to go and it'll take you there," Anya said, leaning in a little closer. "Cam was thinking she'd leave it pointed at the human world so she'd be able to pick up a cell signal."

"Smart," Jack said. "Er…human world, please. For internet."

The portal flickered, and the phone in Jack's pocket began to buzz uncontrollably. He pulled it out and watched as three days' worth of notifications appeared on his phone.

"That's useful," Jack said. "Thank you."

"I—" An email arrived, marked important, from Frank. Jack frowned as he opened it.

Jackie -

We need to talk. Please call me at your earliest convenience.

Jack frowned and turned the phone over in his hand. The last time he saw Frank, Jack was storming out of the Mexican Division offices when they refused to help Cam. Something about this email made him think it wasn't about that, though.

"You can tell the portal to take you to him," Anya said softly. "As long as you come back."

"Why wouldn't I?" Jack said with a curious look—but by the time the words had left his mouth, she was gone.

Anya's portal did nothing to stop the pressure change between worlds, and Jack had to take a few minutes in an alley emptying his stomach and getting himself right. Once his brain stopped spinning, Jack dialed his grandfather's cell and waited.

"Jackie?"

"Grandfather," he said, watching the ICDM building across the street. "Do you have time to talk?"

"For you, absolutely."

"Great. I'll be there in a second."

"Wait... Where are you?"

Jack smiled, looking down at the portal in his hand. "Nearby." He pulled the phone away from his head and nodded to the portal. "Take me to his office."

The portal shimmered and grew, revealing the interior of Frank's office and his bewildered grandfather seated behind his desk. Jack stepped through and grabbed the portal, shaking it out to reduce it to its normal size and sticking it in his back pocket.

"What in all things good is going on?" Frank said, leaning back in his chair.

"We have some things to catch up on," Jack said, crossing the room to Frank's wet bar in the corner. "Namely—"

"Your Anya has regained her athtar powers," Frank said, though he didn't sound enthusiastic about the idea.

"How'd you know?" Jack asked.

"She paid María a visit," Frank said.

Jack stilled then turned slowly. "And?"

"She's fine, but shaken up," Frank said, his gaze heavy. "Your Anya wasn't too pleased about the Council's decision regarding Cam."

Jack swore under his breath and took a long sip of whiskey. Like her great-niece, María was a hard woman to unnerve. "What did Anya do?"

"María swears she did nothing," Frank said. "But I don't believe her. There were threats, of course. An order to cease operations, of course."

This was that shoe he'd been afraid of. "Great. So she's been lying to me."

"Why don't you start from the beginning?" Frank said, helping himself to the second glass Jack had poured. "Spare no detail."

Jack told his grandfather everything he knew, from Anya appearing in Mexico City and saving Lotan, to how Ath-kur looked now, and Anya's weird behavior. But as he described Anya, it was hard to square the timid, nervous woman with someone who would threaten María García and actually shake her up.

"We are in a very precarious position, my boy," Frank said. "Since Bael's death, we have set in motion wheels that are hard to stop. While Anya might own Bael's powers, she has always struck me as a much different person." He smiled. "I don't think Anya will be threatening to kill thousands if we don't do what she says."

"Probably not," Jack said. "But she's still uncontrollable."

"Maybe not. You, Jack, have some kind of power over her. Whether it's through your relationship or friendship or whatever you want to call it." Frank smiled at him. "I think you might be able to sway her one way or another."

Jack took another sip of whiskey, not liking the direction this conversation was going. "So you want me to manipulate her?"

"Not in so many words," Frank said. "I see it more as keeping her tethered to what humanity she still has. She'll be careful with human life as long as she still values it. And you can help us make sure that happens. You're merely reminding her of who she is."

"Was this why you called me?" Jack said, a little disgusted. "So I can babysit her and report back?"

Frank shrugged. "You're the only one who can."

"I don't want to be in the middle of this," Jack said, putting the now-empty glass down. "I don't even want to be in Ath-kur right now, but Cam and Lotan need my help. And Anya..." He sighed. "I don't even know where to begin with her."

"Humanity needs you to figure it out," Frank said, slapping him on the shoulder. "So I suggest you get on it."

Jack didn't feel like venturing back to Ath-kur immediately, not with his stomach still in knots, and not when he wasn't sure he could face Anya without arousing suspicion. Instead, he used his portal to transport himself home to Seattle. Immediately, he frowned—the floors were scratched, and there was a giant hole in the side where the nox had taken Anya. More annoyingly, the heat had been on all this time, spewing out to the frigid mountain beyond. His power bill was probably through the roof.

After shutting off the heat, Jack turned the couch over and

sat down, staring at nothing. Eventually, he'd have to go back to Ath-kur and face Anya. Try to navigate the tricky waters he suddenly found himself in. He felt stuck between what felt right in his heart and what his head was telling him, compounded by his unease around her. He had no clue what was going on in her mind, and now, finding out she was already lying to him, made him uneasy.

To his face, she seemed eager, timid, excited—not at all the monster who'd done some unspeakable act to María.

His phone lit up with Cam's face, and he frowned, walking over and picking it up.

"Hey, Jack," came her clear voice on the other side. "Where are you?"

"I'm in Seattle grabbing a few things," Jack said. "What's up?"

"Did you know that Anya went to Kappanchi to find Doroteia and threaten her?"

Jack groaned. More and more secrets. "Did you know that she also paid your aunt a visit and threatened her?"

Cam swore and released a long sigh. "What the hell are we going to do with her?"

"Well, Frank wants me to seduce her so she doesn't start murdering humanity," Jack said.

"I mean…"

"Cam!" Jack barked. "That's not what I'm going to do."

"Not seduce, but she does *desperately* want your approval," Cam said. "So much so that I think if you exerted a little pressure—"

"No way. I'm not doing that to her. Not again." Jack stared at the gaping hole in the side of the house. "She's suffered enough manipulation."

His partner was quiet on the other end. "We're in a weird spot, Jack. I don't want to hurt her, but she can't hurt others. And I don't...man, I don't think she wants to hurt others, either. I think she's confused and a little overwhelmed. I wouldn't call it manipulation, more like guidance." She paused again. "I'll help, too, but you're the only one she's got eyes for right now."

"This isn't what I signed up for," Jack said.

"You signed up for this the moment you left with her in Atlanta, Jackie," Cam said, her voice taking on a warm tone. "You care about her. Or else you wouldn't be wrestling with this."

Jack turned away from the gaping hole in the home he'd bought for her almost a year ago. He did care about her. But things were so much more complicated now. "Anything you need from the human world while I'm here?"

"A bottle of tequila, please. The good stuff. I have a feeling we're all going to need a drink."

CHAPTER SEVEN

Anya buried her head in her hands, shame threatening to drown her.

She knew exactly what Jack and Frank had spoken about, just as she'd known what Cam and Lotan would find in Kappanchi. Her mistakes hadn't stayed hidden for very long, and this utopia she'd built for her friends and loved ones had crumbled before she'd even had a chance to spend one joyful night.

Jack hadn't come back after visiting his grandfather; he'd gone straight to Seattle—she wasn't trying to spy on him, but the portal was built from her magic, so she knew, at least, where it was being pointed to. Anya tried not to overthink what that meant, but she couldn't stop ruminating. It was as bad as when Bael would give her the silent treatment and she'd lie awake for weeks fearing what would come next.

Her pulse spiked as Cam's portal activated, drawing a connection from Kappanchi back to the house. Anya wasn't ready to face their wrath—but where could she go?

The connection with Diogo was clear as day. He was in his library, deep in thought. She didn't want to disturb him, but there seemed no one else in this world who could take her mind off her troubles.

She appeared and he looked up, jumping to his feet and bowing deep. "My lady. Such a pleasure to see you again."

"You as well," Anya said, wishing she sounded at least a little more enthusiastic as she chewed on her thumb distractedly. "How are things?"

"Things are excellent, as they always are." His brow furrowed and he closed the book. "Are you well? You seem uneasy."

She stopped gnawing on her thumbnail and turned to him. "Do you think Bael was a monster before he was touched by God, or do you think he became one?"

His confused look deepened. "I'm not quite sure how to answer that."

"I mean, do you think he was a bad person when God found him?" Anya resumed her pacing and thumb-chewing. "Or do you think the demonic magic warped his sense of right and wrong? The humans say it's evil, so maybe. But Freyja and Mizuchi, they never seemed like him. They weren't mad with power, at least."

"My lady." Diogo had appeared in front of her and placed his hand on her shoulder. "Please, take a breath."

She looked at him, unable to hide her true fear. "Am I destined to become like him? Has it already started?"

"Let me make you some tea." He was a blur and had tea ready for her at his small dining room table. "Have a seat."

She moved herself across the room and plopped down in the chair, taking the steaming cup of tea and inhaling the scent. "Thank you."

"To answer your question, I don't believe any of us really know," he said, helping himself to a cube of sugar. "And if anyone *would* know, it would be the person who spent thousands of years by his side. If you aren't sure, then..."

"But he lied to me," Anya said. "Every day, every single word out of his mouth was a lie."

Diogo shrugged. "Perhaps that's your answer. Why are you so concerned with Bael's behavior?"

"Because I feel like..." Anya exhaled and stirred her tea absentmindedly. "I feel like I'm losing my mind. All I want is to do good things, to be better than Bael was. But I can't... It seems like I just keep screwing it up. I've never felt so unsettled before."

"But?"

She looked at him. "But I also can't stop using this magic. I have this need to know everything there is about it. I want to go deeper. Look." She created a small portal in her hand. "I gave one to Cam and Jack. They can use this to travel anywhere in the world. Bael never did anything like this."

"Bael never thought to," Diogo replied. "He was a very

uncreative soul, if we're being honest. He wanted to know just enough to stay in control and had very little interest in anything beyond that. For him, simply being able to manipulate time and space was enough."

"I want to learn everything," Anya said, looking at her hand. "But at the same time, I'm afraid if I continue down this road, if I keep expanding my knowledge, I might go too far. I'm worried learning more will turn me *into* Bael."

"I think there is untapped magic in your veins," Diogo said. "This portal magic is only the beginning. If you set your mind to discovering all there is, you might find yourself more in control."

"But what if I end up losing it?" Anya said, jumping to her feet and leaving the cup of tea behind. "Diogo, I went to Kappanchi and threatened Doroteia, told Tabiko to her face that she'd better hand her over or else I'd kill everyone in their village. Then I..." Anya swallowed, the guilt coming up from her stomach. "I hurt Cam's aunt."

"The Councilwoman?" Diogo said with a frown. "Why?"

"I was angry that she didn't help Cam," Anya said. "And that she and the rest of ICDM were planning to start decimating the demon populations in cities around the globe. I told her that if she didn't halt those plans, I'd do something drastic." She rubbed her face. "Like Bael."

"The methods may be similar, but the intentions couldn't be farther apart," Diogo said.

"Who cares what my intentions were if everyone fears me as they feared him?" Anya said. "If I hurt people—"

"Fear doesn't equate to hurt," Diogo said. "Fear keeps people in line, and perhaps some fear is healthy to prevent them from harming themselves."

"But who am I to say what's right?" Anya said. "Maybe I should just stay out of things. Let them start a civil war between demons and humans." She winced. "God, I can't even stomach that."

"Then don't," Diogo said. "You have the power to make the world behave, and unlike Bael, you seem to have the world's best interests at heart. If putting fear into a few people's hearts means that millions more can live peaceful lives then so be it."

But Anya couldn't square that sort of thinking. Bael had made her life miserable with that logic, and she couldn't bring herself to perpetuate it on someone else.

Jack used the portal, arriving back in Ath-kur, and Anya knew she couldn't hide forever.

"Thanks for the advice," Anya said, feeling much like a lamb to slaughter. "I'll think about it."

When Anya stepped into the living room, Jack, Cam, and Lotan were hard at work in the kitchen—or rather, Lotan was hard at work making food, and the other two were enjoying a bottle of wine and laughing at his attempts. But the echo of laughter faded when they noticed Anya standing there.

Cam was the first to recover. "Where'd you go?" she asked with an almost too-cheery smile.

"Uh... To speak with Diogo," Anya said. "How were your

respective trips?"

"Unfulfilling," Lotan said, using a spatula to scrape the meat that had stuck onto the skillet. "Tabiko is unwilling to share kappa secrets unless we provide her something in return, and our fair Sewanin needs nothing at the moment."

"She's calling herself the caregiver?" Anya asked, allowing a little disbelief to slip into her voice. "That seems a little presumptive."

"She also happened to mention that you showed up and threatened to kill everyone in her village if she didn't hand over Doroteia," Cam said, leveling a piercing look at her.

"Cam, I thought we weren't going to mention that?" Jack muttered under his breath.

"I changed my mind. There's enough pussyfooting around this house these days." Cam sat back and crossed her arms over her chest. "And you also paid a visit to my aunt."

Anya's mouth opened and closed as she struggled to come up with an excuse for what she'd done, but all she had was dread.

"Well?" Cam said. "What do you have to say for yourself?"

"Nothing," Anya said, sinking down into the chair. "Nothing except...I'm sorry. I'm not sure what came over me." She waited, staring at her hands for the continued lecture, but it didn't come.

"I get it," Cam said, softer than Anya had hoped. "You had new powers and you had some scores to settle. But you running off and fucking things up doesn't help anyone, and it definitely doesn't scream teamwork. We're still a team, remember?"

Anya nodded, giving her a sideways look. "What did I fuck up?"

"Tabiko says if you set foot on her lands, and by extension, if *we* set foot on her lands again, she'll have our guts for garters," Cam said. "So we can't ask her how Mizuchi managed to continue his line. That's now a dead end for Lotan."

"Unless you feel like apologizing," Lotan said.

"Doroteia should first," Anya snapped.

"Whatever," Cam said. "And as for María—"

"I understand if what I did was unforgivable," Anya said, the words tumbling from her mouth. "And I would take it back if I could."

"She's a tough ol' broad." Cam grinned. "And maybe I'm not mad you sought her out on my behalf. But you can't go back to ICDM and threaten them. You aren't Bael, and you told us you wanted to be better. So be better."

Anya nodded. "I will, I promise."

"There." Cam turned to the two men. "Was that so hard? Now let's…" She grimaced at the food. "Let's get takeout."

"It's on me," Anya said, taking a step forward. "It's the least I can do."

An hour later, the foursome sat around the living room with full bellies. Anya had taken the opportunity to retrieve the food, picking a spot on Cam's recommendation and bringing it back piping hot. She'd also grabbed a case of good beer, which improved the general mood even further. No more was said of

Anya's fuckup, and for that, she was grateful. Leave it to Cam to bluntly break the ice and make things better.

Anya nursed the beer and kept glancing at Jack. She was burning to know what else Frank had spoken to him about, because he was barely acknowledging her. But cowardice kept her tongue, and she took another small sip of her drink.

"So...what do you want to do tomorrow?" Cam asked Lotan, who'd draped a lazy arm over her shoulder. "And don't say throw more talismans at yourself."

"Clearly, that's not the way forward," Lotan replied. "And since our overtures to the kappas must go on the back burner for now, my other options are limited. We could reach out to Freyja or Biloko—Freyja, I'm sure, would like to see you, Anya."

"I'm surprised she hasn't shown up yet," Anya said with a quiet smile. "She did like to visit."

"I don't know if you need a jolt of lilin magic," Cam said, poking Lotan's thigh. "You're already too handsy."

As if proving a point, he reached behind her and she squealed, nearly losing her drink. Jack laughed and got out of the way, and for a brief second caught Anya's eye. But he looked away before she could read it.

"There is a third option," Lotan said. "We could venture into the Nullius."

"What's that?" Jack asked at the same time Anya and Cam vehemently said, "Absolutely not."

"It's the center of the Underworld," Cam said. "I went there as a demon and nearly died. You, my love, would most assuredly die."

"But you also said there were talismans inscribed on the rocks," he said. "Perhaps we should pull that thread more."

"Or perhaps you should stay away from there," Anya said, giving him a dirty look. "It's not a place for demons."

"Cam and I could go," Jack said, again missing her eyes when he looked at her. "We're not demons. I'm sure we could just wander there and come back, hm? At least take some photos and show you what we've found."

"No way," Anya said. "It's far too dangerous—especially for humans."

"But it wouldn't be," Cam said. "We wouldn't be affected by whatever anti-demonic magic is there."

"Do you believe it's anti-demonic magic?" Jack asked.

"I don't know what else to call it," Cam said. "But it does stand to reason that if we aren't demonic, whatever magic is there won't affect us."

"That could work," Lotan said, his leisurely gaze resting on Anya. "If Mother Athtar gives her blessing."

Anya chewed her lip. Cam had a point that the danger was more toward demons than humans, but she still didn't like the idea. The Nullius was always something to be avoided.

"I can't control what you do or don't do," she said, finally.

"Then it's settled—Cam and I will go in the morning," Jack said.

"You're going to have to walk," Anya replied. "There's no way my portal magic will work there."

"You could grab us a car?" Cam said to Anya. "Maybe one of those dune buggies? Or a Land Rover?" She waved her hand. "You know what? Surprise me."

"Expensive tastes," Jack muttered.

"Lotan's paying for it, right?" She fluttered her lashes at him.

"Whatever my lady wants, she will get," Lotan said, pulling her close.

Anya had to look away as they started getting handsy with each other. For a moment, she caught Jack's eye and he actually smiled at her. But it was gone before she could say anything about it.

CHAPTER EIGHT

Lotan woke with a smile on his face, and not just because he and Cam had spent the evening wrapped in each others' arms. He had often thought about the Nullius, but being demonic himself, he'd never been able to get very far into it. It was a land of unanswered questions, and he couldn't wait to hear what Cam and Jack found.

Soon after breakfast, Anya arrived with a Land Rover, as promised, as well as more supplies that Jack and Cam might need in the desert. It didn't escape Lotan's notice that Anya tried to catch Jack's gaze and he continued to purposefully miss it. Perhaps even this trip to the Nullius was a way to avoid the conversation they so desperately needed to have. They certainly hadn't talked the night before, and it was getting somewhat awkward for them to dance around each other.

"Don't go too far without keeping track of where you are,"

Anya said to Cam, who was checking their supplies. "We won't be there to pull you out if you get lost."

Cam waved her off. "I don't expect we'll be gone for long. Hopefully just an hour or two. I don't think we'll get as disoriented, what with us being human and all."

"It's still a desert," Anya said. "Keep an eye on the sun and that should help you get where you want to go."

"Yes, Mother." Cam nudged her and looked at Lotan. "And you two stay out of trouble while we're gone."

"Absolutely not," Lotan said with a cheesy grin.

"I mean it." Cam poked him in the chest. "No more talisman experimentations, mmkay?"

"I promise." He took her hand and kissed it, hoping the memory of the night before was playing in her mind. Having her around all the time was bringing out the more experimental side of his lovemaking, and she was a willing partner.

"Let's go," Jack barked from the driver's side. "You two had enough of that last night. And next time, keep it down, will you?"

He gave Cam one final, long, languishing kiss, and she climbed into the passenger side and gave Anya a thumbs-up. "Posh. It's perfect. Exactly what I wanted when rolling through the desert. Luxury and leather seats."

"Just don't run out of gas," Anya replied, turning to open a portal. Beyond the shimmering rim was the Nullius. Even from a distance, the distinct pull of the No Man's Land made Lotan's stomach turn. He was glad they were going and not him.

"This is as close as I can get you," Anya said, also looking somewhat green. "Once you cross back into Ath-kur, I'll know and send for you."

"Thanks," Cam said, before looking ahead. "Gun it, partner!"

Jack hit the gas and the car zoomed through the portal, which closed behind them, leaving Anya and Lotan alone in front of the house.

"There they go," she said, sounding a little forlorn.

"We are unattended," Lotan replied. "What kind of trouble should we get into?"

"Didn't I just hear you promise Cam you wouldn't?" Anya asked, gazing at him slyly.

"Well, what Cam doesn't know won't hurt her," Lotan replied. "I'd like to try again with those talismans, if I can. Perhaps even—"

"Lotan." Anya turned to look at him face-on. "Hurting yourself repeatedly isn't going to solve this problem. Try something else."

"Like?"

"You could always try asking God," Anya said.

"That's ridiculous."

She smiled. "It's how I got pregnant."

Lotan gave her a side-look. There was a tinge of sadness in her amusement, as if even the memory of conceiving her child was fraught with danger. And knowing Bael, it probably was.

"I confess, I've never put much stock in the theory that some all-powerful deity came down and blessed five people with this magic," Lotan said. "Don't share that with the believers, though."

"Wouldn't dream of it," Anya said.

"I've often wondered how my mother managed it after thousands of years," Lotan said. "If she simply decided she wanted a child or if it happened by accident or..."

"However it happened, I know that she loved you," Anya said softly. "And once you were there, she wanted nothing more than to..." Her brow furrowed.

"What?" Lotan asked.

"Someone's come onto Ath-kur," she said slowly, her eyes growing black as she used her Sight, probably to check the boundary.

"Jack and Cam back already?" Lotan asked, hopefully.

She shook her head. "This is on the border with Elonsi." Her frown deepened. "Yaotl. He's requesting an audience with... you."

"Oh." Lotan swallowed. "He's traveled a long way to speak with me."

"I doubt he's got your number," Anya replied, her eyes returning to normal. "I can expel him if you want."

"No. I suppose I should deal with this problem," Lotan said with a shake of his head. "I've been avoiding it long enough. Would you mind bringing me there?"

"Not at all."

Anya opened a portal, revealing the edge of Ath-kur. Yaotl's magic filtered through the hole, settling Lotan's nerves on edge. Yaotl was alone, at least, which made him somewhat less concerned. But Lotan wasn't so much afraid of the man as what he'd come to discuss.

"He's a little way over there," Anya said, nodding to the darkness. "Right on the border. I thought you might want to make an entrance instead of—"

"You are kind," Lotan said with a firm smile. "I'm sure I'll hear an earful about relying on the noxslayer's magic." He cleared his throat. "If I might ask another favor..."

"Depends what it is."

"If you could give me a little privacy," Lotan said. "As much as I appreciate your assistance, this is nox business. And it wouldn't be right to have an athtar interloper." He paused and forced a smile onto his face. "I promise I won't get kidnapped again."

She studied him, clearly having a different opinion on the matter. "I'll keep an eye on the border. If you cross it—"

"You can come rescue me," Lotan said with a smile. "I suppose Mother Athtars don't change their spots, do they?"

She shook her head. "Just go, you idiot."

The leaves crunched under Lotan's black shoes, fallen from the tall trees Anya had conjured. Lotan couldn't believe how quickly she'd turned this land into the place of her heart, and how thoroughly she'd put her thumbprint on every inch of it. It made him burn with curiosity to explore his own abilities in the noxlands—but not enough to want to return there.

He entered the clearing where Yaotl was waiting. The other nox had perched on a large, mossy stone and seemed lost in thought. His face was unchanged from Lotan's earliest memories, a beautiful man with sharp cheekbones and dark, calculating eyes. His style had evolved over the years as he integrated with the humans; he now favored the look of an Italian model. Dark suits, dark shirts, and enough hair product in his tight ponytail to protect against a head injury.

Yaotl looked up when he heard Lotan's footsteps, and his tight smile set Lotan on edge. There were no other noxes around, but Lotan still stopped a healthy distance away. Yaotl was a proud man, and his hubris was as essential to him as Bael's had been. But Lotan doubted Yaotl was here to simply taunt him. He had better things to do than that.

"What do you want?" Lotan asked.

Yaotl stood, brushing the dirt from his pants. "So glad you could join me. Is your athtar friend floating nearby?"

"I asked for privacy, and she obliged," Lotan said, eyeing the other nox as he walked closer. But despite his reservations, he stayed put.

"Do you trust her?" Yaotl asked, now within striking distance.

"More than you."

Yaotl tutted. "Is that any way to treat me, boy?"

"Considering you had me imprisoned, yes," Lotan said.

"And now? Hiding behind the belu athtar, abdicating your

responsibilities?" He shook his head. "These are troubling developments, Lotan. I was sure I'd raised you better than this."

"I felt your disappointment while I was languishing in my own blood," Lotan replied dryly.

"You did that to yourself, boy," Yaotl said. "I provided bandages, and a warm body to apply them. Or did you forget?"

Something about Yaotl's insinuation irked Lotan. "What do you want? I don't have all day."

"Don't you?" Yaotl asked. "You're in the land time forgot. If your athtar wanted, I'm sure she could make your human's life last forever. So why do you continue experimenting?"

Lotan clicked his tongue against the roof of his mouth. "How did you know that?"

"I have my sources," he said. "I've been making my own alliances, too."

"So I've seen. Are you still planning on toppling the human ICDM or have you given up on that particular dream?" Lotan asked.

"Will you continue your experimentations?" Yaotl countered. "Putting this pack you proclaim to love in danger?"

"There's clearly a way for this magic to exist after the belu has left this world," Lotan said. "The athtars figured it out, the kappas, too. Why not the noxes?"

"Because you are not touched by God," Yaotl said, baring his teeth. "You are merely—"

"The power flows within me," Lotan replied evenly. "Just as the athtar magic flows within Anat now. Neither of us have seen

God. Perhaps there's something to that." He crossed his arms over his chest. "You still haven't answered my question. Why are you here and what do you want?"

"To ask the boy I raised to return to the noxlands," Yaotl said. "Bring your human. We'll bring her into the fold and make her a sister in the pack. Anat's human can come, as well. All four of you can live out the rest of your lives happily in the noxlands and Ath-kur."

"Sadly, my human—her name is Cam, by the way—does not wish to become a nox, nor do I want her to join the pack," Lotan said. "Neither one of us likes what it's become."

"I suppose it's hard for a demon who's never spawned to understand," Yaotl said.

"No," Lotan said, turning to walk away but then stopping. "But I would offer you a word of advice. You only continue to breathe because I asked Anat to stay out of the noxlands and leave you be."

"How kind," he said. "What did I do to deserve such mercy from our prince?"

"Nothing, yet," Lotan said. "But you will promise on my mother's life that you will cease your alliances, cease your world domination plans, and get back to protecting the pack the way you should be. In return, I will keep the belu athtar from severing your head from your body."

"Do you proclaim to have such power over a fearsome creature?"

"I proclaim to be her friend, and she has thus far respected my wishes," Lotan said. "But if you'd like to test that theory, I can't be held responsible for her actions."

"And a word of advice back to you," Yaotl replied with a knowing smile. "Your athtar belu may not be as powerful as you think she is. One day, she might find herself in the same position as Bael. Nothing but dust and memory."

"There's only one problem with that," Lotan said. "Anya herself was the one to behead Bael. And I don't see anyone around here who can keep up with her now."

"So you say, boy. So you say." He took a step backward. "I suppose I'll leave you to it."

"Wait."

Yaotl stopped, a curious look on his face. "Yes?"

"If you promise me that you'll take good care of the noxes, and you'll keep them from harming too many humans…" Lotan paused, licking his lips. "I will ensure that once I find a way to rid myself of the power, it will pass to you."

Yaotl gave him a once-over. "How can you do that?"

"I don't know." Lotan shrugged and stuffed his hands inside his pants pocket. "But when Bael died, his power remained in his land, just ripe for the taking, I'm sure we could figure something out."

Yaotl eyed him. "I promise."

"You have until I figure out how to do all that to prove to me you will be a good steward," Lotan said. "I'll be watching."

Yaotl sniffed as he backed up across the border to Liley. As he turned, his body shifted into beast form, and he bounded away across the mountain.

"How'd it go?"

Anya was behind him, glaring at the space where Yaotl had left.

"Don't you know?" Lotan asked over his shoulder.

"I told you I'd give you space, and I meant it," she said. "Somewhat. I didn't listen." She cleared her throat as her cheeks reddened. "I did watch, though. Just to make sure he didn't try anything."

"Ah, Mother Athtar." Lotan turned and smiled. "How you dote on me."

The ghost of a smile appeared on her lips. "Only because Cam would kill me if something happened to you while she was away." But the smile faded. "I don't like that I can't See her and Jack. I haven't been able to since they crossed into the Nullius."

"So comfortable with these belu powers already," Lotan teased.

"I just like to know everyone is safe," she replied. "I don't know what they're going to find and I don't like them being out there alone."

"They're two well-trained, award-winning demon-hunting government agents," Lotan said. "I'm sure they'll be able to handle whatever the Nullius throws at them."

CHAPTER NINE

This journey into the Nullius was lightyears better than the last time. Cam felt nothing but the coolness of the air conditioner, the hum of the engine, and the rumbling of the tires as they drove over sand dunes.

"So this is it?" Jack asked, looking over at her.

"Basically. I remember it being a lot more..." She grinned. "Vomit-inducing."

"Lots of gastric issues in the Underworld," Jack said.

"So what's going on with you and Anya?" Cam asked as they crested another dune. "Are you just not talking to her or...?"

"Man, I don't know. Can't we just focus on the wide expanse of dirt in front of us?" Jack asked.

"Road trip convo. Can't avoid it." Cam grinned. "So? Spill. What's your plan with her?"

"No plan. Just avoid her until I die, I guess." He shook his head. "Which will be sooner than her. Much sooner."

"Is that what you're irked about?" she asked. "That she's immortal and you aren't? That you're going to die before her? That she's stronger than you are?"

"It's not any of that," he said. "And right now, it's Frank—"

Cam sighed. "Forget what Frank said. What do *you* want?"

"Honestly?" Jack shifted in his seat. "I want to be able to look at her and not wonder if she's lying to me. To be able to believe that when she acts like she cares that she actually does. To..." He sighed. "To feel confident that she won't go off the deep end when we aren't looking."

"I'm not worried about that," Cam said. "Because I know her. I know what's in her heart. And you do, too."

"Do we?" He shook his head.

"Think about it this way," Cam said as the SUV went over another large hill, "you met Anya as an athtar. She had this magic before, and she was still the same big-hearted wounded flower we've got on our hands now. The only thing that's changed about her is that she doesn't have Bael popping up to insert himself between you guys."

"But her going to threaten Doroteia and María..."

Cam cast him a sideways look. "You know she's got funny ways of showing her affection for people. I think it's saying something that her first act as an all-powerful being was to scare the shit out of my great-aunt."

"I guess." He tilted his head, smiling a little. "You know, when we were on the run in Richmond, she found the nox who killed Sara and asked if I wanted to kill him. As a... I guess that was her attempt to show gratitude for all I'd done."

"Sounds like our Anya," Cam said. "And Jack, she's trying. She's desperate to show you that she's not going to turn into some monster. Why not give her a chance?"

Jack was about to answer, but the wheel jerked beneath his hands. The engine began to smoke, putter, then died. The air conditioner went with it, as did the lights on her phone. Everything was dead.

"What's happening?" Jack asked.

"Looks like the Nullius doesn't like human engines," Cam said, opening the car door and getting blasted by a face full of heat. She walked to the front of the car and popped the hood, looking at the motor as Jack tried to turn the engine over. But it wouldn't even make a sound.

"Cam," Jack said, stepping out of the car. "We are a long way away from the border."

"Yep," she said with a sigh. "Guess we should head back in that direction."

"What about the car?"

She gazed sadly at it. "I don't think it's going to help us."

With a jug of water each, they followed the tire tracks back the way they'd come. Walking was as difficult as Cam remembered, except as a human, she didn't feel like her entire soul was being leached from her body. Jack's face grew red with heat and sun, and he soon stopped answering her questions.

"Hold up, let's take a break," Cam said, as they came to the top of another hill. "Just for a second."

Jack plopped to the ground, panting hard. His shirt stuck to his back, and everywhere that was exposed was red and starting to freckle. Cam handed him her water, but he waved it away.

"Keep it for yourself," he said, looking up. "Cam, I hate to tell you this, but there's nothing out here. Are you sure you saw something the last time you were here?"

"Pretty sure," she said. "I mean... I might've been hallucinating."

Jack groaned and sank backward into the sand. "So we're out here based on a hallucination?"

"I said maybe, Jackass," she said, taking a swig of water. "It's a big place."

"Does it get dark here?" he said, nodding to the sun. "Because if we have to walk all the way back, we're going to be in trouble."

The answer to that question was *yes*, it did get dark in the Nullius. The sun sank too quickly for Cam's liking and before long, they were bathed in darkness. And what had been abysmal heat turned icy in the blink of an eye.

"Camilla."

"Yes, Jackson, I know." The shadow that was her partner stopped, and she nearly ran into him. "What are you doing?"

"We can't just keep blindly walking in the dark," he said. "What if we get even more lost? I can't see the footsteps in front of me anymore and with the sun gone, I can't tell you which way we're going."

"So what do you suggest we do?"

"Stay put until morning," he said. "We'll cuddle."

"Oh, good."

Cam sat down next to Jack, grateful the sand was still somewhat warm. It wouldn't stay that way for long, especially with the cold wind blowing across the desert, shifting the sands. Their footprints would be gone by morning, but the sun, at least, would stay in the right spot.

"Stars are pretty," Jack said, looking up. "Look a little different here than in Seattle."

"You spend a lot of time looking at the stars?" Cam asked.

"Mm." He sighed. "Anya and I would sit on this overlook in Seattle while waiting for a job to call us back."

"That's so dorky." She poked his ribcage. "Talk to me, partner. What's holding you back? Why not just throw that woman onto a bed in a world she concocted and have your way with her?"

He was silent for a long time. "I don't know what I'd do if I found out she wasn't the person I thought she was."

Cam had to smile. This really wasn't about Anya after all.

"I think you have to start with a little trust," Cam said. "Allow yourself a small leap of faith with her. You have the chance to be happy in your grasp, and I'd hate for you to squander it because you're a chickenshit."

"I'm not a chickenshit."

"Prove it," Cam said, nestling next to him. He tossed his arm around her and pulled her close, resting his head on top of hers. Together, they made one halfway warm body. And with Jack's pulse in her ear, Cam allowed herself to relax and drift into a half-sleep.

"Cam."

"Mm."

"Cam, I heard something."

"There's nothing out here," Cam said. "That's why they call it No Man's Land. It's your mind playing tricks on—"

But the screech that echoed across the desert was unmistakable, and Cam's eyes shot open.

"You didn't tell me there were raptors in the desert, Cam," Jack said, getting to his feet quickly.

"Maybe it was just the wind," Cam said, craning her neck. But with no moon, there was nothing except darkness—and the sound of wings beating.

"Duck!"

Jack tackled Cam just in time to miss the *whoosh* of wings followed by the loudest screech Cam had ever heard. She could make out the outline of a human-sized beast squawking—just one, no, two. Were there more? Cam couldn't tell in the darkness.

"We have to run," Jack breathed. "Goddamn, why didn't I take my weapons?"

"Because we're not supposed to be fighting bird monsters in the desert, Jack!" Cam barked. "This place was empty. It *is* empty."

"Clearly," Jack ducked as a talon came within an inch of his head, "not. We're sitting ducks out here, Cam. We have to go."

"Where?" Cam squeaked. "There's nowhere safe for us to run!"

"Just go!" Jack practically dragged her forward until she found her footing then she took off after him.

A sharp, hand-like talon clamped down on her arm, and her feet lifted off the ground, but with one well-placed sucker punch to a feathery midsection, she fell back to the sand. Her arm was on fire, but she scrambled to her feet and kept running.

"There!" Jack cried, pointing toward the distance.

"What is it?"

"The car!"

Cam's heart leaped into her throat as she put on a burst of speed. The large white car was a beacon in the distance, and she'd never been so excited to see it. The winged beast behind them swooped in for another grab, taking a slice of her other shoulder with it. But Cam was too focused on getting to the car to pay much attention to the wetness pooling down her back.

Jack reached it first, flinging the passenger door open and diving into the front seat. Cam followed, slamming the door behind her and gulping breaths. Beside her, Jack locked the car and sat back in the chair.

"What. The hell. Was that?" he asked, looking over at her.

"I don't—"

Bam! Something landed on the roof of the car, leaving a large dent in the metal. *Bam!* Another hit the side, cracking the window. And yet another's black, clawed foot landed on the windshield in front of them.

"Fuck, fuck, fuck," Jack said, fumbling with the keys. "C'mon, you stupid thing."

The car began to rock as the monsters bombarded it from all sides. Unease crept up Cam's back as the car slid backwards on the dune. She buckled herself in and held on as the car landed on its side then rolled down the dune. Blessedly the car landed upright at the bottom, but the squawking continued nearby.

"I don't—"

The lights turned on, illuminating a man-sized monster in front of them. The monster screeched loudly and began to smoke before lifting off and flying away.

"*Go, Jack!*"

Jack turned the key and barely waited for the engine to warm up. He put the car in reverse, hitting something solid, then flipped it toward the way they'd come. The screeching became the most terrifying symphony Cam had ever heard, followed by the rocking of the SUV as one of the monsters dive-bombed them. At this speed, the car slid in the shifting sands, Jack struggling to keep it straight. Cam just hoped they were going in the right direction and not further into the desert.

"I think I see Ath-kur!" Jack said. He gave one terrified look at Cam. "Do you think these things will follow us there?"

"I don't want to find out," Cam said with a grimace. "Step on it."

Jack floored it, and the car zoomed ahead, rattling with every hit from the monsters. Cam screamed when the glass in the back window shattered, and a large, clawed foot reached inside. She grabbed one of the empty water canteens and slammed it against the creature. The leg disappeared.

"Almost there," Jack said, gripping the wheel so tightly his knuckles were white.

Three concurrent *booms* landed on top of the car, and to Cam's horror, the metal began to peel away. "Jack..."

"Almost there!" He glanced over at her and the son of a bitch smiled. "Never a dull moment, huh, partner?"

The roof over the trunk lifted, and Cam got a glimpse of a disfigured face with razor-sharp, gleaming teeth. "Fuck it all, Jack, if these things follow us into—"

But the face disappeared, as did the cacophony of squawks and screeches. In fact, the only thing Cam could hear was the rumble of the engine and her own pounding heartbeat. Slowly, she turned to the front, but instead of tall redwoods, there was dark, open plain.

"That doesn't look like Ath-kur," Cam said as the headlights illuminated the land ahead. "It's not the Nullius, but it's not..." A wave of lightheadedness washed over her, and she swayed a little. Her shoulder, which she'd ignored in favor of running from deadly monsters, started to burn. She couldn't help the moan that escaped her lips, and when she pulled her hand away, it was blood red.

"God, Cam," Jack said, his eyes wide. "Cam?"

His voice sounded far away.

"Cam!"

CHAPTER TEN

Cam fainted, and Jack slammed on the brakes, throwing the car into park and leaning over to check on his partner. She was bleeding, but there was something else—something dark—seeping through her veins. Her eyes had rolled to the back of her head, and she could only murmur.

"Fuck, Cam!" Jack said, jumping back into the front seat and throwing the car in drive. He took a calming breath, running through the list of options. They'd left the portal Anya had made for them back in Ath-kur—Anya thought it would dissipate in the Nullius. Not that it mattered; Jack's phone was still dead, as was Cam's.

Not that if Jack knew who could help Cam—not with that poison leaving black trails up her neck.

"Fuck, Cam, fuck," Jack said, panic rising like smoke in his heart. "C'mon, Anya, find us."

But he didn't even know where they were—certainly not in Ath-kur. The ground beneath them was rocky, and there wasn't a tree in sight. No trees also meant Jack could gun it, and that was what he did—pushing a hundred on the mostly smooth rock beneath him. He had no idea how long he was driving, but the black streaks up Cam's neck were growing more pronounced and were now trailing down her arms.

"Cam, stay with me," Jack whispered. "Don't you die on me."

He glanced down at the gas tank and his heart sank. He was nearly out.

"Fuck me," he whispered, reaching over to grab her hand. "Cam, I don't know how we're going to get through this, but we will. You can't just die here. It's not right."

She murmured and her brow furrowed as she turned. A light sheen of sweat had formed on her face as her skin turned sallow.

"Just stay with me." Jack whimpered, pressing the gas pedal as far as it would go. Maybe they'd run into a demon here. Maybe they'd get lucky. Maybe.

He flattened the gas pedal and gripped the wheel as he rolled over bumpy rocks and splashed in puddles.

He noticed the rather large body of water too late and slammed on the brakes. The car slid sideways before splashing into the water. Jack's whole body slammed against the steering wheel, and the airbags deployed, pushing him back. His head swam for a moment before he registered the sinking sensation. The car was going underwater.

"Nope," he spat out, unhooking his seatbelt and doing the same for Cam. Half-dragging her, he climbed to the back of the car where the winged monster had broken the glass and poked his head out. He was able to open the door and walk into the frigid water, stumbling as he carried Cam toward what he assumed was dry land.

With chattering teeth, Jack put Cam down on the shore and sighed, gazing around for something—anything. He squinted—was that a light in the distance? It was too far to tell, and he didn't know what he'd find when he got there. But based on the temperature of Cam's skin, he didn't have a choice. So he hoisted her onto his back and began to walk the coastline.

"Stay with me, buddy," Jack breathed, ignoring the blackness of her arm draped across his chest. It reminded him of the way Lotan's arm had looked under that talisman. But Cam wasn't a demon, so why was this magic killing her the same way? For someone who'd studied demons and demonic magic since he was a boy, Jack was hopelessly lost. He was starting to understand why Lotan was grasping at every thread he could.

Jack turned to look at the light in the distance and sighed. It didn't look any closer. He feared he was just walking parallel to it, not—

He blinked and squinted. Was that a smaller light coming his way?

Bracing himself, he put Cam down behind a rock. He couldn't trust that whatever was coming would be friendly, and while he had no weapons or talismans, he had his fists and hopefully, he'd be able to tell what kind of demon it was before it ensnared him.

He guarded himself, clenching his fists and running through the list of self-defense techniques. Elokos, listen for a bell. Noxes, that flutter of anxiety. Kappas, listen for water. Lilins—

The smell of flowers. It was unmistakable. They must be in the Lilin part of the Underworld. Better than the eloko part, but perhaps not the best place, especially if this lilin wasn't friendly. And based on the intense scent on the air, and the uncomfortable swelling in his pants, the lilin was ready for a fight.

"Who goes there?" came the booming male voice. "Why do you encroach on Lilin lands?"

"I need help," Jack called. "Do you come in peace?"

The light came closer, illuminating the face of the most beautiful creature Jack had ever seen. He was pale and tall, with broad shoulders and slim cheeks. His eyes sparkled even in the night, and as Jack stared into his beautiful visage, he almost forgot about the panic in his chest.

"You..." Jack found himself smiling then shook his head. "Please, I need help. My friend is dying."

"Humans." The man frowned. "Humans in the Underworld."

"I'm... I'm friends with Anya—Anat. She's friends with Freyja, I hope. Please—"

"Anat? You're..." The lilin nodded. "The human. The one we saved. Jake?"

"Jack," he said, sighing a little. "Please, Cam is dying."

"Cam? Lotan's Cam?" The lilin hurried forward. "My word... What happened to her?"

"We went to the Nullius," Jack said. "We were attacked by... I'm not even sure what to call it. Some kind of winged creature."

The lilin leaned over Cam and gently touched her face then reared back in pain. "This is not something I know anything about. I will take you to the belu." He turned behind him to a pair of creatures Jack hadn't noticed yet. They were like eels the size of boa constrictors, with a small chariot between them.

"What...the hell are those?" Jack asked.

"Nureonna," the lilin said, taking Cam in his arms as he walked onto the chariot. "Come, we don't have all day."

Jack swallowed his apprehension and joined the lilin on the chariot. He was starting to get the feeling he knew very little about the Underworld, despite having spent several weeks here. Then again, all he'd seen was the inside of Bael's castle.

But all of that was pushed to the side in favor of Cam, whose skin was turning an ashy green. Her eyes fluttered and she mumbled to herself, and Jack tried not to panic.

The eels pulled up onto the rocks and the beauty that greeted them blew the lilin out of the water. Jack had seen Freyja very briefly once before, but now, it was like seeing her for the first time. She had long, blonde hair and piercing blue eyes with porcelain skin that seemed the most delicate and softest thing in the universe. She wore a fur coat that was open to her navel, perhaps not the warmest choice, but it provided Jack a glimpse of her ample breasts.

"My..." Freyja's attention turned to Cam and her smile evaporated. "What happened?"

Jack told her as much as he could while the male lilin carried Cam into the dreary, stone castle. "I'm out of my depth here. I don't even know what could be wrong with her."

"I've never known anything to be alive in the Nullius," Freyja said. "But I've also never seen a human walk there, either. Come, let's get her somewhere we can look at her."

She led them into a room, and the male lilin laid Cam down on the bed. In the candlelight, the blackness had spread across her chest and down both of her arms. Her lips were turning purple even as she took deep, gasping breaths.

"What do we do?" Jack asked, his heart pounding in his chest. "We need to call Lotan and Anya."

"In a moment," Freyja said with a warm smile. "Let me try some things first. Stay here."

Jack paced, oscillating between stopping to put his hand on Cam's warm body and walking back and forth. He couldn't stop checking her, fretting with her, and praying that someone would have an answer. He hated feeling this helpless.

The lilin belu returned carrying a bowl. "I have no idea if this will work, but it's a healing poultice," Freyja said. "Turn her for me and remove her shirt."

Jack gently rolled Cam onto her back and pulled the shirt off her back. There were three gaping holes on her left shoulder and one in her right, all of them bright red and violent against the black of her skin. Jack's heart came to his throat.

"Hold her," Freyja said. "This may sting."

She smeared the purple goop onto Cam's back, earning a wriggle and a yell from his comatose partner. But once the poultice covered her back, the furrow in her brow lessened, and her breathing steadied. Once Freyja finished applying the poultice, Jack thought Cam did look a little better—but it could've been wishful thinking.

"Is it working?" he asked.

"It's too soon to tell," Freyja said. "But your Cam is a strong woman. I wouldn't bet against her. Right now, though, she needs her rest, so we should let her be."

He nodded. "Thank you."

"For Cam, anything." Freyja looked at her lovingly for a moment. "Now, as for Anat and sweet Lotan." She walked to the window where a large crow flew onto the perch, squawking. Jack jumped—it had three eyes. "Please go to the border and let Anat know to come here."

The bird snapped its beak, opened its wings, and flew away.

"She will know, as I did, that someone has come onto her territory. Perhaps with her Sight, she'll be able to see the crow and find you here."

"Thank you," Jack said, slowly feeling the beginnings of a headache.

"Now, while we wait, why don't you catch me up on what you and Cam are even doing here? Preferably over a stiff drink."

Freyja's lilin helper procured a large bottle of what appeared to be vodka, and the belu poured them both a drink as Jack waited silently. He wasn't sure she could be trusted; she'd fought alongside Anya in the nox battle, but Jack had also killed plenty of her spawn. That she'd even taken them in at all was a miracle —and that she'd helped Cam even more so. But Jack remained on his guard.

"So how did you come to be on my lands, Jackson Grenard, demon hunter?" Freyja asked, handing him a glass with a warm smile.

"Cam and I were in the Nullius," he said. "Lotan's idea—"

"Oh, my beloved nox prince," Freyja said with a smile. "Are he and Cam still wonderfully and absolutely in love?"

"Er... yeah," Jack said, taking a sip of the vodka. Almost immediately, warmth spread from the top of his head to his toes. "Anyway, our car broke down and—"

"And Anat?" Freyja said, her eyes fluttering happily. "Have you been taking good care of her?"

Jack wasn't sure how to answer that—especially since the demon before him was a belu. But the alcohol had already loosened the knot in his chest. "I've been doing my best but..."

"Oh, Anat," Freyja said with a sigh. "She has been distant, yes? Building walls and refusing to let anyone in?"

"Not lately," Jack said. "Not since she took Bael's power."

"She...what?" Freyja blinked and some of the etherial lightness left her voice. "She *took* Bael's power? How is that even possible?"

Jack gave her the long and short of it and Freyja's light blue eyes remained wide and disbelieving. When he finished, she released a slow laugh. "That is...something else. I've never... I don't even know what to say to that."

"Well, it's good to know it was a surprise to everyone," Jack said.

"I had seen the world change across the border, but I never imagined... What a magnificent turn of events," Freyja replied with a smile. "The prey has become the predator. I wonder if Bael himself could've imagined such a thing. Oh, it's a shame he's no longer around. I would've liked to have seen her lord over him the way he did to her."

"Let's not even consider that possibility," Jack said with a shake of his head. The weight of their near-death experience was starting to fall heavily on Jack's shoulders as the vodka made his head swim. "Those things... they were unlike any demon I've ever seen. I don't know any demon that has wings. Cam...well, Cam said before we were attacked that the last time she was there, she saw nothing."

Freyja tapped her finger to her lips. "I wonder if they were drawn to you because you're human?"

"What?"

"The demons, all demons, really, we have a healthy fear of the Nullius. It makes us ill, almost like one of those talismans that Cam was toting around. Even to think about it turns my stomach. So I wonder what kind of creature, what kind of demon, could survive there?"

"Not a demon?" Jack offered. "Cam said it looked like the whole place was a giant talisman the last time she was there."

Freyja put her hand to her lips, deep in thought. "Perhaps, indeed."

CHAPTER ELEVEN

Anya couldn't sleep, nor could she stop staring at the border where Jack and Cam had driven off. The sun had set long ago, and they were supposed to be back by now. They should've been back hours ago. Something was wrong.

But she could do nothing. She had tried—repeatedly—to walk toward the Nullius, but she couldn't take another step farther without every single cell in her body revolting.

"I should go," Anya said to Lotan, who'd been her silent companion for the past two hours as they waited for motion in the distance.

"You shouldn't. I should. I'm the one who told them to go."

"You have noxes who count on you. I'm just me. Diogo will survive." She grimaced. "I hope."

He swore under his breath and sat down on a nearby rock. "I don't like this."

Anya's head snapped toward the east. Something had crossed the border on the Liley side—one of Freyja's birds. The thing squawked and cawed and echoed into nothing before turning around and flying back into Liley.

"What is it?" Lotan asked.

"It's Freyja," she said slowly. "Sent a messenger, perhaps wants me to come."

Anya turned her Sight on Liley, crossing the dark, cold world Freyja inhabited until she saw the castle, the light, a fireplace, Jack drinking something clear—

"They're in Liley."

The words were barely out of her mouth before she brought them to the room where Jack and Freyja were talking. The glass tumbled from Jack's hand and he jumped up in surprise.

"Ah, sweet Anat!"

Freyja, looking as perfectly beautiful as always, crossed the room and took Anya in her arms, pressing a firm kiss to her lips. Anya took the welcome as she always did, uncomfortably, before Freyja noticed Lotan and did the same to him. Jack's brows had gone up to his hairline, and he reached down to pick up the glass he'd dropped.

"Where's Cam?" Lotan asked, practically pushing Freyja out of the way.

"Come with me," Freyja said, sounding not the least bit concerned. "I gave her a poultice, but she was in a bad way when she arrived."

Anya and Lotan followed Freyja to the room next door.

Anya stopped in the doorway when she saw Cam lying face-down on the bed. There was something unnatural, something that made Anya's demonic energy want to get as far away from her as possible. Perhaps it was the black magic seeping through her skin, turning it dark.

"Jack says they were attacked by something in the Nullius," Freyja said, looking stricken.

Both Anya and Lotan stared at her, incredulous. "What kind of something?" Anya asked.

Freyja shook her head, taking a bowl of purple paste that her helper had brought and handing it to Lotan. "I don't know. But this has been helping."

Lotan carefully applied the paste, wincing as Cam cried out in pain. "Is it working?"

"Slowly, yes," Freyja said. "The darkness had extended to her wrists before, and now it's only to her elbow."

"What do you think it was?" Anya asked. "This poison?"

Freyja shrugged. "It seems to me that if the Nullius is the source of the anti-demonic magic, then perhaps what has infected Cam is...that magic. And applying that which grows in the demon world seems to counterbalance the effects."

"I have an idea," Lotan said, looking at Anya and handing her the bowl. "Take this to each of the other four realms and grab something—anything—we can mix into this."

Anya nodded and as fast as her magic could move her, she was in Ath-kur, grabbing a handful of sand. Then she landed in Kappanchi—at the very edge—and dipped the bowl into the sludge. Another jump to Elonsi to grab the dust and a couple of tree leaves. Finally, the noxlands, for some dirt and water. Then she was back in Liley.

"Here," Anya said, handing the bowl to Lotan. "Best I could do."

Lotan mixed the goop then winced as he poured it onto Cam's back. But like a syringe pulling blood from a vein, the darkness retreated from Cam's back, leaving nothing but fresh, red wounds where the beast had cut her skin. She moaned a little, moving and wincing, then turned her head and stilled.

"Well, good to know that worked," Lotan said, after a long pause.

"That wound looks nasty," Freyja said. "And I worry with all that dirt, it might get infected. Humans have such slow healing." She brightened. "You could turn her?"

"No," Lotan replied. "She wouldn't want that. We should wait it out and see what happens. Only time will tell now."

You could help her.

That nagging voice was back, the one that had been dormant for the past couple of days. It was so loud Anya was sure the others had heard it, but they didn't react. Still, she couldn't ignore it, not with her mind racing toward different scenarios, different memories.

Bael had made time traps, small windows in the world where time would move at a different pace. He'd found it amusing to watch a kappa or lilin fall victim to the trap, and slowly waste away. But those time bubbles, they could be put around anything.

No sooner had that thought crossed her mind than she recalled her own youth, the moment when Bael had found her, and used one of those time bubbles to turn her from a child into the woman she was today. And deep in her veins, Anya knew she could use that same magic to help Cam.

"Can I...try something?" she asked.

"What?" Lotan asked.

"Just..." Anya approached the bed. "May I?"

Lotan got out of the way, and Anya gently sat down next to Cam. She pressed a hand to Cam's bare back, wincing at the heat that was still there. Freyja was right, this wound could lead to an infection that would do as much damage as the Nullius poison had.

"Let me know if this hurts," Anya whispered.

She focused on the skin around Cam's wounds, using her Sight to visualize her cells knitting themselves back together. And with concentration, she sped those little cells along faster until...

"Holy..."

Anya opened her eyes. Cam's skin was pink and scarred but healed. "Cam?"

"Mm. Go away." Cam rolled onto her back and curled into a ball. "Sleeping."

"That should do it," Anya whispered, pressing her hand to Cam's forehead.

Freyja motioned for the two of them to follow her. Once

they were outside the door, she let loose a loud squeal. "I'm so proud of you, Anat! That was absolutely magnificent."

"That was absolutely bizarre," Lotan said, still dumbfounded. "Can all athtars heal like that?"

"I don't know. I just...I just knew I could do it." She looked at her hands, an excited smile crawling onto her face. "Every day, I learn more about what this magic can do."

Thanks to me.

The voice sang in her mind, almost promising that it would require a sacrifice from Anya. Or perhaps she was just used to such bargains from Bael.

"The belu magic is..." Freyja said with a cautious smile. "Vast. I don't know that I've uncovered everything I could do with mine, but I have no use for it other than what I have." She took Anya's hands. "But you, my love, might just uncover all of the secrets, if you have a mind to."

"And in the meantime," Lotan said, running a hand over his face. "I need a drink. Did I see you drinking some of that lilin liquor? Is it in here?"

"Lilin liquor?" Jack said, rather loudly behind them. Anya hadn't even noticed his absence until now—and the pale, sweaty look on his face was concerning. "Is that what I've been drinking?"

"Better use that athtar healing again," Lotan said, patting Anya on the back. "Or else he's going to have a wicked hangover."

Deciding against the use of her magic, at least for the time being, Anya cautiously led Jack back into the room he'd been in before. If he'd been drinking the potent lilin alcohol that made even demons lose their minds, his human body would have no defense against it.

Her love-drunk human stumbled into the room, and she helped him find a seat on the bed.

"Jack?"

"Hey." The smile on his face was easy, and he looked genuinely pleased to see her. He must've been really drunk. "How's Cam?"

"I think she'll be okay. What happened?"

"Hit some snags," Jack said, walking to the bottle left in the room and pouring himself a glass. "Namely, the car broke down, we got a little lost, then when the sun went down, we were attacked by winged monsters—"

"You're sure that's what you saw?" Anya said. "You have been...drinking a little."

"I know what I saw. Can't forget those things," Jack said with a small laugh. "But here we are. Cam was..." He took another sip. "She looked better after Freyja got done with her. But she's not..."

"You should stop drinking that," Anya said, noticing Jack was going for the clear liquid again. "Lilin liquor is potent."

"I need potent tonight," Jack said, before casting a look at her. "You look good."

"Seriously." Anya stopped time long enough to pull the

drink from his hand. "You've had enough."

"Not of you," he said, his eyes growing heavy. "Not nearly enough of you."

His hands found her hips and pulled her close, and she could already feel the swell of his manhood against her. But as much as she wanted him, wanted this—it wouldn't be right in his state.

"I think you should go to bed," Anya whispered.

"We need to talk," Jack said, dancing her hips side to side. "Really talk. For real talk."

"We can talk tomorrow."

"I'm scared."

Her eyebrows shot up. "I'm sorry?"

"I'm scared. To love you. To be honest with you. To really get deep in that kind of love that I had with Sara." His words came out clearly, but the light was gone from his eyes. He was good and well suckered. "Man, it was so easy with her. I was just in love, and there wasn't any struggle. But with you, it's all thinking. It's all wondering about what happens if everything goes wrong. I don't know if I can handle that pain."

This seemed like a conversation Anya shouldn't have been having with Jack in this state, but she couldn't help herself. "What about what Bael did? You said it made you stronger."

"I dealt with my grief..." He smiled crookedly. "And I'm not sad anymore. But every time I get close to trusting you. Boop!" He hiccupped. "Something stops me. I'm afraid you're lying to me about everything. Your magic, what you can do, all of it. What if you're really Bael, and you're just stringing me along?" He shook his head. "I don't think I could deal with that."

"Jack," Anya whispered, cupping his face. "I need you to stop talking before you say something you regret."

"What was it you said to me?" He leaned in closer. "I've never regretted you. Not once. Not even when I was mad at you for telling Doroteia we were coming. Not even when you left a gaping hole in our house. And that's what makes this so damn confusing."

Before she could stop him, he closed the distance between them and kissed her. It was the first kiss they'd had since... Anya couldn't remember when. Perhaps since the night she'd found out her curse wasn't real. Even drunk, Jack was a good kisser, his lips sliding against hers slowly, sensuously, starting a fire inside her that would be hard to put out if it got going. His strong hands held her hips, pulling her closer, and it would've been so easy to let herself fall into this moment.

Easy, but wrong.

"To bed, Jack," she said softly. "We can resume this in the morning."

"Morning sex. I love morning sex," Jack said as Anya helped him over to the bed. "You know, I wake up almost every morning with a boner. Some days I think to myself, 'I should text Anya to come in here' but then I chicken out." She laid him down on the bed and he yanked her down on top of him. "Yeah, like this."

"In the morning," Anya said, unable to keep the smile off her face as she leaned in to kiss his forehead. "Good night, Jack."

"I love you," he said.

Something twitched in her heart as she reminded herself he was drunk on love magic. "We'll talk in the morning."

CHAPTER TWELVE

Lotan lay next to Cam, counting the seconds until she woke up. He would never forgive himself if something happened to her—especially if something happened to her while on a boneheaded mission to the Nullius. Seeing that black poison seeping through her veins had shaken him to his core, made him question this entire effort. He didn't care what happened to him —he could suffer, torture himself, nearly die. But Cam…

He ran his finger along her back, where the new skin had been knitted together. What kind of monster had she unearthed that could cause this much damage? And how the hell had Anya been able to use her magic to heal her? More questions, very few answers. But he supposed all that really mattered was that she was sleeping soundly next to him. Safe.

As soon as he lifted his fingers, she stirred, blinking heavily in the dim light and moaning. "Lotan?"

"Good morning, beautiful," he said with a gentle smile.

"What are you doing here?" She shook her head and blinked heavily. "Where is here? Why is it so cold?"

"You and Jack were attacked in the Nullius and escaped to Liley. You're in Freyja's castle." He ran his finger down her bare back again. "I'm here because I love you."

She furrowed her brow. "Right. We were attacked. Winged creatures." She cast a look over her shoulder. "What… I thought one of them got me?"

"They did," Lotan said. "Through teamwork and some neat athtar magic, we healed you. Now you're back to normal." He hesitated. "Are…you back to normal?"

"I mean, I think so," Cam said, laying back down on the pillow. "I don't feel any different. I didn't sprout wings or anything, did I?"

"Not yet," he said. "So I suppose we're safe."

She nestled underneath his arm and he pulled the furs on the bed over her. But her eyes remained open. "I have no idea what those things were, but I definitely don't remember them from the last time we were there. They only showed up when the sun went down." She chewed her lip. "It didn't like the light from the car, so maybe they're light sensitive."

"What else can you tell me about them?"

"They had wings," Cam said. "Roughly the size of a person, with clawed feet. Sharp teeth. Like bat people, but…" She made a face. "Grosser. Any idea what that might mean?"

"None at all, my love," Lotan said. "Except to say that we yet again know very little about the Nullius. And I'm afraid you aren't going back there ever again."

She sat up. "I mean, that's kind of rash. We just made a discovery. I think it bears repeating—"

"I think not."

She pursed her lips at him. "We just bring some fire next time, and they'll stay away."

"No."

"It's a smarter plan than you and your talismans," Cam said.

"You almost died, Cam," Lotan said, sitting up. "I'm not letting you go back there."

"Good thing you can't *let* me do anything," she said, poking his chest. Then she paused. "What do you mean, almost died?"

"The beasts injected you with some kind of poison," he said. "Your skin was decaying. It was..." He licked his lips and captured her gaze. "I don't ever want to see that again."

"Poison." Cam made a face and looked over her shoulder. "How did you save me, then?"

"As I said, teamwork," Lotan replied. "Freyja applied a healing poultice from herbs here in Liley, and I had the idea to perhaps use material from all five realms. Anya made the trip. It was...immediate."

Cam sat back against the headboard and crossed her arms over her chest. "Huh. It's almost like—"

"Like there's a demonic and anti-demonic magic," Lotan said. "We had the same thought."

"So..." Cam chewed her lip. "What if the talismans aren't

just symbols? What if they, themselves, are magic? What if the Nullius isn't just No Man's Land, but the source of a sixth kind of magic? One that counteracts all of your magic?"

"A theory I had myself, but..." Lotan smiled and rested his hand on top of hers. "It's not a thread worth pulling anymore."

"What if we could use that magic to suck the demonic energy out of your body?" Cam said in a matter-of-fact tone.

"It's not worth the risk," Lotan said.

"To whom?"

"To you," he replied, resting his head on her lap. "I've never been so scared in my life, Camilla Macarro. I don't wish to experience that again."

She threaded her fingers through his hair, sending chills down his spine. "Turnabout is fair play, butthead."

"Shall we just make love and not argue anymore over which of us is going to kill ourselves first?"

In the morning, Freyja had a spread of breakfast for them. The belu lilin clearly hadn't had much company of late, and she and her lilin friend Rainart had pulled out all the stops. It was a meal fit for a queen, and Freyja certainly looked the part in her long fur robes. But as was usually the case in Liley, the table was round, so they settled into their respective seats and dug in.

"Oh, but where is Jack?" Freyja asked. "You didn't wear him out last night, did you, Anat?"

"Hardly," she said, busying herself slathering a biscuit with butter. "You left him with a bottle of lilin wine. It was all I could do to put him to bed without him humping my leg."

"Well?" Freyja said, looking at her. "Why didn't you let him?"

"Because that's not right," Anya barked.

"You two are sleeping together, are you not?"

She took an angry bite of her biscuit and looked at Lotan and Cam. "They are. Bother them."

"Oh, good," Freyja said, turning in her chair to Cam. "Was it pleasant? I've been keeping my magic at a minimum, but I can't control all of it. Was your orgasm excellent?"

Lotan snorted as Cam choked on the orange juice. "It was fine, thank you."

"So." Freyja turned back to Anya. "Why don't you tell me what happened in Seattle?"

Anya's green eyes darted to her then away. "Be more specific."

"When you waltzed into Hobson's house, and he took pity on you."

Lotan looked at Anya, unfamiliar with the name. From Cam's perplexed expression, she was as well.

Anya licked her lips and put down her glass. "I miscalculated and got lucky. Anything else?"

"But why would you do something so silly?" Freyja asked.

"What sort of silly thing did Anya do?" Cam asked, glaring daggers at Anya. "And was this pre or post athtar-reversion?"

"My dear Anat wandered into a lilin orgy with naught but her little human heart," Freyja said with a sad shake of her head.

"If it wasn't for our very close relationship, she might've found herself a lilin—or worse!"

Lotan actually felt bad for how uncomfortable Anya looked, but luckily, she was saved by Jack's arrival. He looked like he'd just woken up from a four-day bender. His pale skin had taken on a yellowish tint, he looked clammy and sweaty, and the bags under his eyes were visible across the room.

"What. The. Hell. Did. I. Do?" he said, leaning against the doorframe and rubbing his head.

"Good morning, sweet Jack," Freyja said, jumping up from the table and rushing to his side. "I've prepared an exquisite breakfast."

"Toast," he croaked out. "All I need is toast."

"Oh." Freyja's face fell. "Well, I have that, too."

He plopped down and looked over at Cam, shaking his head in disbelief. "Why am I the one who feels like shit this morning? Why aren't you dead?"

"Because I know better than to drink lilin wine," she replied in a singsong voice.

"Fuck me, I thought it was vodka," he said, laying his head on the table. After a moment, light snoring came from him.

"Oh, let him sleep," Cam said with a smile. "This isn't the worst hangover I've seen him have. You should've seen him stumbling into training sessions at the Academy."

In a blur, Jack was gone. "I've put him back to bed in Athkur," Anya said. "With a plate of toast for when he wakes up."

"Well, good, now we can get down to business," Freyja said.

"I must say things aren't well in my world. ICDM seems to have it in their mind to just unilaterally destroy the kingdoms of my spawn."

Anya furrowed her brow. "What do you mean?"

"They've been taking down younger demons, but I fear it's just the beginning. Tabiko and I have been writing to each other, and we both find ourselves absolutely horrified by some of the things that are happening."

Lotan looked up, catching Cam's eye. "Tabiko? You've been in contact?"

"Indeed. We correspond all the time."

"Do you happen to know how Mizuchi was able to keep his line going after his demise?" Lotan asked.

"No, sadly, and I haven't asked." She shrugged. "I'm not planning on dying any time soon, and I don't believe anyone out there will try to kill me."

Lotan licked his lips and sat back. "Well, I want to give up this magic, so it would be nice if someone would let me in on the secret."

"Tabiko might, if you ask nicely," Freyja said.

Anya's gaze fell into her lap. Cam swiped her glass off the table and took a drink. "Unfortunately, she's not on speaking terms with us at the moment."

"Oh, I'm sure she'll come around. She's a lovely kappa." Freyja paused, as if remembering something. "Though you did kill her wife."

"Yep," Anya said.

"And I hear you threatened to kill every kappa in existence if she didn't hand over one particular demon who'd crossed you."

Anya looked at the ceiling. "In the village, but close enough."

"So perhaps not," Freyja said with a lighthearted shrug. "Anyway, who wants some more tea?"

"Please," Lotan said, offering his cup. "Say Freyja, would you say this ICDM problem is one weighing heavily on Tabiko?"

"I would," Freyja said.

"Enough that she might be willing to bargain with us if we were to solve it for her?"

"Nope," Cam said, putting her hand on the table. "That's not happening."

"You haven't even heard how I was going to solve the problem." Lotan smiled sweetly at her. "I was going to suggest that we use our combined efforts—namely, your and Jack's connections to the Council—to come up with a bargain that could be acceptable to all parties."

"And what, if they don't go for it, send in Anya?" Cam asked.

"You said it, not me," Lotan said. "I have a feeling they could be amenable precisely *because* Anya could step in. We don't have to say it."

Cam blew air between her lips, but Freyja spoke first. "It would be nice if we could resume normal relations with the humans. I know there's always been tension, but without Bael, I feel we could come to some kind of agreement. A quota of humans transformed and demons killed."

"They won't go for that," Cam said. "They're in an all or nothing mood."

Freyja's smile was a little hesitant. "I don't know if they're in a position to make those kinds of demands. Not to sound…well, tyrannical, but the humans aren't any match for demons."

"They're getting there," Anya replied. "They have the talismans, and they've been using them, but they aren't invincible quite yet. I think they might be able to live with some transformation."

"I'll tell you what María will say," Cam said softly. "That demons don't need to transform humans. There's no need for it other than their own predatory nature. They should control it and leave humans alone."

Lotan looked around the table and waited for the arguments, but none came. Freyja looked down at her food and pushed a small piece of egg across the plate and Anya took a long sip of juice.

"So maybe the proposal we make to them is that we agree no more transformations and the humans will leave the demons alone," Lotan offered. "The demons lose their population growth, and the humans will have to figure a way to live with demons. Both sides have to acquiesce somewhat."

"It could work, as long as we had buy-in from across the demon realm," Anya said. "And you could control your lilins."

"That's a hard thing to ask," Freyja said. "There are so many now."

"Then that's a stipulation," Lotan said. "If any topside demons break the treaty, ICDM is free to do with them as they wish with no retaliation from the belus or other demons adhering to the treaty."

"And I doubt Yaotl would agree to such a thing," Cam said, looking at Lotan. "You aren't in charge of the noxes anymore, so you can't make that determination for them. And it'll only take one demon race to muck things up for the rest of us."

Lotan bristled at her bluntness but tried to brush it off. "I still say it's a conversation worth starting with ICDM. We can figure out the details later."

CHAPTER THIRTEEN

Cam had worked for ICDM long enough to know that it would be hard to bring all the players to the table. The Council would balk at the idea of being in the same room as the belus after what Bael had done. On the other side of the table, the demons were used to doing whatever the hell they wanted, and the trio would probably get laughed out of every demonic castle. Yaotl was absolutely not going to be on-board, and Lotan wasn't anywhere close to recognizing that the *only* way to deal with him was to just lop his head off.

But at least it was something.

After breakfast, Cam, Lotan, and Anya said their goodbyes to Freyja, who made them promise they would invite her over for dinner and a tour of the new Ath-kur soon.

"We would be glad to," Anya said. "As long as Lotan doesn't cook."

"I'm getting better," he insisted.

"If memory serves, your father used to cook every meal for your mother," Freyja said with a soft smile. "I'm glad to see you've continued the tradition of cooking for those you love."

He glanced at Cam as if to say "See?" and she couldn't help but laugh. "We'll keep practicing. Perhaps with a little more supervision."

They left Freyja there, walking through the portal back to Ath-kur. Cam hadn't really noticed the difference between worlds, but a lightness left her heart when the portal closed behind them. It felt like leaving her grandmother's house after a long summer of fun.

"I suppose I should go check on Jack," Cam said.

"He's awake," Anya said quietly, her eyes taking on that darker shade. "But I wouldn't bother him just yet. He probably wants some privacy while he throws up everything he's ever eaten."

"Poor guy," Lotan said with a grimace. "I've been hungover on lilin wine, and it's not fun for me. I can only imagine his pain."

Anya glanced toward the back bedrooms. "I don't know what I could do to help him. Other than aspirin."

"You could try that time thing you did on me," Cam said. "Make the alcohol leave his body faster."

Anya demurred, shaking her head. "I don't think Jack wants anything to do with this magic. We'll just let him sleep it off. I'll see about retrieving him some medicine." Then she was gone.

"I have to say, it's convenient that she can come and go to the human world whenever she pleases," Cam said. "Because I'm not looking forward to returning there again."

"It sounds like we might not have a choice, my love," Lotan said. "But I would be happy to hold your hair back."

"True love," Cam said with a smile. "Speaking of, I think I'll go check on the drunkard. Can't go back to ICDM without him."

She ventured down to the other end of the hall. The bathroom light was on, so she knocked on the door softly.

"Jackie?"

A groan came from the other side.

"Do you need anything?"

"Death."

Cam snorted and cracked open the door. The stench of bile hung in the air, and Jack looked like he'd seen the bottom of a tequila bottle.

"This is unfair. How are you upright? You were bleeding out last night." He groaned and pressed his head to the side of the toilet. "I hate my life."

"Anya did some kind of whizbang magic," Cam replied, sitting down on the tub next to him. "Something about a time bubble. It sped up the healing."

"Can she do that to me?" Jack asked.

The corners of Cam's mouth turned upward. "She's under the impression that you don't want anything to do with her magic."

He winced and burped as he returned his attention to the toilet. "I might've said some things to her last night. I can't exactly remember what..." He groaned. "I definitely kissed her."

"I'm sure she knew it was the lilin alcohol," Cam said. "But you really should talk with her. Sober, preferably, but if you need some liquid courage—"

"Never again, Cam." He shook his head. "Never again."

It took three days for Jack to finally feel somewhat human again. Cam was forced to play nursemaid, as Anya seemed too chicken to deliver the electrolytes, aspirin, and crackers she'd retrieved from the human world.

"This is bordering on ridiculous," Lotan observed as he and Cam lay awake discussing their predicament. "They just need to fuck and get it over with."

"Preaching to the choir."

But fucking was seemingly off the table, as Cam and Jack made preparations to return to Geneva, where the Council was gathered. Jack sent an email to his grandfather, asking him if he could request a meeting with the full Council. But the response he got didn't engender a lot of confidence.

Come on by, Jackie. I'd love to take you and Cam to lunch.

"Lunch is not a full Council meeting," Cam said with a frown.

"Perhaps he just wants to see what we want," Jack said,

though Cam read the concern on his face.

Since Anya was in the other room, she asked, in a low voice, "What are you going to tell him about Anya?"

"Nothing," Jack said. "I never agreed to his request. I'm not spying on her or manipulating or doing anything of the sort for ICDM or Frank or any of them."

She sighed. Frank certainly wouldn't see it that way. "You need to be prepared for him to ask about it."

"And perhaps instead of lecturing me, you should be paying a visit to *your* relative on the Council," Jack retorted with a glare. "I don't think you've seen María since Lisbon, have you?"

It was Cam's turn to glower. She hadn't, nor did she think it worth her time to try. María had made her feelings quite clear and Cam wasn't sure she could be civil. "There's nothing I need to say to her."

Jack rose just as Lotan came back to the table, and Jack patted the nox prince on the shoulder. "All yours, buddy. I have to go find some antacids before making the trip to Geneva."

Cam glared at his retreating back. "I don't need *management*, thanks."

"You are being stubborn." Lotan reached across the table to hold her hand. "You have been hurt by your great-aunt, and you need to speak with her about it. Besides that..." He half-smiled. "It wouldn't hurt to have two Councilmembers on our side. We need fifteen votes, and if you can sway your aunt, that's one less we have to work on."

She growled. "María won't agree to our plan just because

we're related. Clearly, I'm not important to her."

"I think you're more important than you give yourself credit for," Lotan said. "It's worth a shot."

He turned those beautiful brown eyes on her, and Cam found herself struggling to argue with him. "*Fine.* But I'm only talking about the treaty. That's it. And I'm only going because I don't think you'd be a welcome sight. And Jack doesn't really know her. And—"

Lotan squeezed her hand. "I'm sure you will do what you feel is right in your heart. And I'll be counting the minutes until you return."

The trip to the human world was just as unpleasant as Cam had imagined, and even though she and Jack had taken medicine, they both spent fifteen minutes dry heaving in the alley they'd landed in.

"I'm so tired of this," Jack said, wiping his forehead.

"Maybe we'll get used to it eventually?" Cam offered, but she had little faith.

Once they'd righted themselves, they ventured out of the alley to orient themselves. ICDM headquarters was located in a large, glass building in Geneva, complete with museum, heavy security, and a large fountain out front where tourists milled around.

"So what's your play?" Jack asked, checking his watch. "I have...ugh...lunch in half an hour. Are you going to email María and request an audience?"

"I doubt she'd give me one if I asked," Cam replied, pulling her badge out from her back pocket. "I was going to see if my badges still worked, and if not, go from there."

Jack patted her on the shoulder. "Good luck, partner."

Cam didn't need much luck, as she was apparently still employed by ICDM and her badge still worked to get her through the first level of security. María's office was on the tenth floor, and it had its own level of access control, much like all the other councilors. Cam held Anya's portal in her back pocket, just in case, but she was hoping to not have to use it.

When Cam reached the tenth floor, the receptionist at the front desk smiled at her. "Hello, welcome to Councilwoman García's office. How may I help you?"

"Please let the Councilwoman know her great-niece is here to see her," Cam said.

The woman's smile faltered for a second. "I apologize, but the Councilwoman is quite busy. Do you have an appointment?"

"It's urgent."

"I'm sorry, but without an appointment—"

"Well, I tried," Cam said, dragging the portal out of her back pocket and sending it directly to María's office. The receptionist's shocked gasp and stuttering disappeared as Cam walked through.

María was on her feet, staring at Cam as if she'd seen a ghost. Pale, she sank back into her chair, exhaling loudly. "You certainly know how to make an entrance, Camilla."

"Your receptionist wouldn't let me in," Cam said, walking

toward the desk. "Clearly, family only goes so far."

"I have quite a large family, all of whom have come asking for favors," she said, returning to her computer and lifting her chin to read. "You aren't the first to show up unannounced."

"I think I get a pass, considering."

María's sharp eyes darted to Cam. "Considering what?"

"Considering you made an executive decision to leave me to die at the hands of the noxes," Cam said. "And considering that one of my best friends is now the most powerful demon in the universe, and I hear she paid you a visit to discuss said decision."

María removed her hand from her mouse. "Have a seat, Camilla."

"I think I'll stand, thanks."

"Very well." She sat back. "If we had attempted a full-frontal assault on the nox stronghold to rescue you, we would have lost agents. I made a calculation that your life is no more important than theirs—one I didn't make lightly." She actually softened. "I'm grateful you are unhurt."

Cam shifted on her feet, trying to maintain her anger when she could see the logic in her great-aunt's thinking. "I'm here because I want to discuss a potential treaty. We've been talking with Freyja—she's getting a little annoyed that her demon lords keep dying."

"And?"

"And we—all of us—are worried that it might escalate," Cam said. "Therefore, we've proposed a treaty. The demon belus will sign it if ICDM will."

María didn't look wholly interested, but she didn't laugh. "What are the terms?"

"The demons—at least the lilins, and I bet we could get the kappas and elokos on board, too—are willing to agree to transform no more humans. Should one of their spawn break that code, the perpetrator will be punished. Really punished, the way it ought to be."

María pursed her lips. "And meanwhile, we have to continue to live with these monsters."

"So?" Cam said. "They don't bother humans, we don't bother them. Boom—world peace."

"Are you that naïve?" María asked. "Or are you just hoping I am?"

"I'm hoping that instead of you starting a war you have no hope of winning, we can come to an agreement." Cam gestured to the office behind her. "I'll remind you who I have in my corner, and how very quickly she can do damage if she wants to."

"So you're threatening me?"

Cam rolled her eyes. "Now you're being obtuse."

"Considering your newfound friend, Anya or Anat or whatever she chooses to go by now, came here and..." She cleared her throat and adjusted her jacket. "Showcased what sort of torture she was capable of, I'm not quite sure I can trust her word—or yours."

Torture. Cam swallowed slowly. Frank had said Anya had merely threatened María, not that there had been any physical harm.

"What did she do?"

María actually looked uncomfortable. "Let's just say I've had more pleasant root canals."

Cam swore under her breath and looked in the other direction. Jack had once described the torture Bael's minions had inflicted upon him. He said it was like his entire body was being pulled apart. If Anya had done that…

"We are managing her," Cam said, after a moment. "She did apologize for losing her temper."

"The difference, Camilla, is when you or I lose our tempers, we say hurtful words. Your belu athtar could kill people. It's hard to believe she *can* be managed."

Another point Cam was having a hard point arguing with. "Jack—"

"Yes, your friend Jackson. What happens when he grows old and dies and she remains eternally young?"

"Lotan's looking for a way to rid himself of his magic," Cam said. "If he can, surely Anya can as well."

María leaned onto her desk. "And you honestly believe she would?"

"I think she could be convinced. I think Jack could convince her." Cam took a step forward. "But in the meantime, we can call a ceasefire. Just give everyone a moment to breathe without the chaos of demon lords getting offed every five minutes."

"As long as demons exist in our world, there will always be chaos." She folded her hands, her face a mask without emotion.

"My job is to protect humanity from the evils of demonic activity—whether they transform us or merely walk among us. Signing any kind of treaty that hamstrings us from protecting innocent lives is a non-starter."

"You would be protecting innocent lives," Cam said. "The treaty would only protect demons going about their business. The moment they transform or attack a human, they can be brought to ICDM's justice—real justice, not that fake shit we've been doing for years."

"Or," María said, "we can continue our efforts to eradicate this world of all demonic presences, and humanity can live in peace." She shook her head. "I'm sorry, but I fail to see how this treaty would help us be any safer."

Cam could've predicted this response, and she felt foolish for coming to María in the first place. "Then consider this my official resignation from ICDM."

María tutted. "I think that's hasty—"

"Do you know what I saw when the nox magicked me?" Cam said, looking out the window. "You, telling me I was fired. And all I felt was relief."

"Cam." María stood. "I know about your relationship with the nox prince."

"Do you?" Cam honestly couldn't care. "I hope the next words out of your mouth are 'congratulations' and 'I hope he makes you happy.'"

"I hope you'll consider the ramifications of such a match," María said. "And perhaps consider that his intentions aren't—"

Cam cut her off with a loud snort. "If you think I haven't already run through those scenarios, you don't know me. Lotan is honest. He's a good man. Better than anyone in this building, I'd bet. He's done nothing but support me. And considering he's persona non grata with the rest of his noxes, he has little power. Power that he's hoping to give up, in fact, so he can..." She cleared her throat. "So he can be with me."

"And you believe him?"

"I believe my eyes," Cam said. "And right now, they're telling me there's nothing more to discuss with you. I hope that Jack's having better luck with Frank, because clearly you have no intention of changing your mind."

She opened the portal behind her.

"Camilla," María said. "I care about you very much."

"You care that I don't embarrass the family," Cam said, looking over her shoulder. "But lucky for you, I'm a Macarro. You can just pretend I'm a stranger now."

She walked through the portal and left her great-aunt behind.

CHAPTER FOURTEEN

Since Jack had time to kill, he took a tour of Geneva, reminiscing about the last time he'd been here with Anya. On the run, looking for answers about Anya's curse (even though Jack had guessed there was no curse). They'd broken into the museum to look for clues, talking with a research assistant. They'd only barely escaped after an athtar showed up and Anya overpowered him.

Looking back, knowing what he knew now about the master-demon connection, Jack couldn't believe they'd been so blind. Bael had always known exactly where they were and had been content to let them believe otherwise. What might Anya have done had she known?

Probably thrown in the towel and gone back to him.

Jack found himself staring into a fondue restaurant and recalling the early dinner they'd had there. Seeing the look of enjoyment on her face when she ate the first melty bite, the joy it brought him to see that he could still surprise her after three thousand years of living. The moment when the first springs of more than just pity had emerged in his heart.

Now he was avoiding her at all costs, ashamed of the fragments of memories he recalled from his drunken night and unsettled by the truths it had revealed. The wine hadn't so much pumped him full of lusty emotions as taken away the fear surrounding his heart. He hadn't even known it had been there, hadn't been able to understand *what* had been stopping him all this time. But in those moments when it was gone, it was like gulping fresh air after being underwater. In some ways, it was a relief to know he could still feel that way. Perhaps deep down, he'd also been a little afraid he was broken beyond repair.

He had no idea how to fix things, and until he did, keeping his distance seemed the smartest plan. He was prone to saying the wrong thing, and Anya was such a flight risk that if he flubbed his delivery, she might go somewhere he couldn't follow. But in the meantime, leaving her hanging wasn't helping anything.

He sighed and found the table in the restaurant where they'd eaten all those months ago. He ached for those moments when he and Anya had thrown caution to the wind and started something new. One day soon, he hoped, he might find that bravery again.

His phone buzzed, reminding him that he was due down the street, and he left the memories behind.

"Good to see you, my boy," Frank said, taking Jack by the hand and pulling him in for a warm hug. "I hope things are going well."

Jack wasn't sure he wanted to let Frank in on *everything* he'd seen in the past few days, so he simply smiled. "Yes. And with you?"

"Yes, indeed," Frank said, averting his gaze as he resumed his seat. "Please, sit. I think we have much to talk about."

Jack settled into the chair across from him and took a sip of water. "You go first."

"Well, I suppose my most burning question is…how are things going with Anat?"

Jack shifted. "Are you asking as my grandfather or the Councilman?"

"Can't it be both?" Frank asked with an affable smile.

"Well, my grandfather, I assume, simply wants me to be happy, whereas the Councilman is asking for an update on the mission he gave me. A mission, I might add, that I didn't agree to."

"There's no need to be angry, Jack," Frank said.

"I kind of think there is," Jack said, a little sharply as he started to rise. "Look, I'll be blunt with you. I have feelings for this woman, and I'm struggling to understand what they are. You coming in here and making me do…whatever isn't helping. Now, whenever I'm with her, the only thing I think about is you asking me to spy on her. And that's not fair to either of us."

"It's not fair," Frank said. "But unfortunately, you are in the unenviable position of being the closest person to her. I hope you know I wouldn't be asking if I didn't think it was important. Please, sit down."

Jack sank back down into the seat, albeit reluctantly. "Has she done anything else?"

"No, not to our knowledge. But we can't trust that it won't happen again."

"I can," Jack said, looking out the window. "She was ashamed of what she did, asked for forgiveness. Cam..." He snorted. "Cam made her promise to keep her temper. And she wouldn't break a promise to Cam. Or to me."

"Well, that's good, at least," Frank said as the waiter placed salads in front of them. "I apologize, but I went ahead and ordered for us."

But Jack wasn't very hungry. Talking about Anya to Frank felt wrong, like he was sharing secrets that he shouldn't have been. Besides that, he had a mission.

"We've been in contact with some of the belus," Jack said. "Freyja, specifically. They don't like what ICDM is doing."

"I daresay they don't," Frank said with a snort. "We're finally fighting back."

"They'd like to propose a truce," Jack said. "An agreement between the belus and ICDM. The demons would agree to no more transformations as long as ICDM stood down and stopped killing off demons."

Frank put down his fork. "That's...an impossible order."

"The belus could make them do it," Jack said. "And any who step out of line would see justice."

"And the belus are in agreement on this?"

"Freyja is. Lotan, of course, is."

"Lotan isn't in charge," Frank replied. "And if the noxes have their way, he'll be back in the prison in Mexico City."

"Right now, he's safe in Ath-kur," Jack replied. "And I think the noxes might want to get in on this deal, considering the only thing keeping Yaotl's head on his body is Lotan's good graces."

Frank sat back and considered him for a long time. "Look in your heart, Jackie. Do you really think an agreement between ICDM and the belus would be enforceable? We've been doing that for thousands of years now, and the humans always end up on the short end of the stick."

"But now we have Anya," Jack said. "And she's not Bael."

"Are you sure of that?"

"Yes, I am."

Bael wouldn't have cared about his hangover, wouldn't have brought him crackers and soda water from the human world. Nor would he have created a portal for Jack to use without stipulation or demand for something in return. She was, at least, *trying* to do the right thing.

"You really do care for her, don't you?" Frank said. "Even after her betrayal? You were fairly steamed at her on the plane to Mexico City. Or are you simply bewitched by the power she has now?"

"She made a mistake and apologized for it," Jack said. "She's still...well, she's not human, but she's allowed to make mistakes."

"Except her mistakes are on a grander scale," Frank said. "And what happens in fifty years, when you look like me? Will your Anya still want to be with you?"

"I don't know," Jack said. "But if Lotan will give up his power for Cam—"

"Lotan is dying, or so you told me. He's simply choosing when." Frank tilted his head. "Anya, on the other hand, will remain immortal. And you, my dear grandson, won't, unless you opt to make a rather drastic life change." He paused. "Are you planning on becoming a demon?"

"Not in this lifetime," Jack said with a snort. "Why are you even bringing any of this up?"

"Because I want you to understand that despite what you may feel for this woman, she's moved to a place you cannot follow," Frank said. "And as you negotiate your own emotional connection, remember that you still belong to humanity."

"I know which side I'm playing for," Jack replied. "Which is why I'm here, trying to negotiate a ceasefire between all parties. I'm not saying it for any other reason than I think it's the right course of action—for everyone."

Frank sighed, looking right through him. "I can't say that the Council will entertain such an idea, Jackie. *However*, if you were to get buy-in from all the belus—and I mean all of them—I can get you in front of them."

Jack exhaled. "Fine. We'll make it happen."

"Oh, good," Frank said as the waiter reappeared with two plates. "Steaks have arrived. Dig in, Jackie."

After lunch, Jack took another trip around the city to settle his stomach and his nerves. He found himself back at the fondue restaurant, sitting on a bench across the street and reminiscing about the look on her face. Every look on her face, actually. The sadness, the excitement, the anger. The vulnerability she showed the moment he told her he wanted to take it slow back in Mexico.

Remember you still belong to humanity.

Jack had offered a variation on that idea to Cam when they'd been looking for Lotan. Then, things had seemed very black and white. Demons bad, humans good. Now, he was beginning to understand Cam's point of view. It was hard to believe someone as warm and welcoming as Freyja could allow her spawn to run roughshod over the world.

He was grateful he hadn't eaten much, because the trip back to Ath-kur was going to be painful. But as he stepped through, the rolling in his stomach wasn't as bad as it usually was. In fact, he felt mostly…fine.

"Was that better?"

Anya was in the kitchen, about to take another bite of a sandwich. She looked so normal it was hard to remember she had the ability to stop time, create portals, kill him. She was just Anya, the broken, strong woman who'd built so many walls around herself Jack didn't know what to do when they came down. The woman who'd enjoyed the hell out of some fondue while on the run from her abusive ex.

"What?" Jack said, after a minute.

"I asked if the portal trip was better," she said, putting down the sandwich. "I spent a little time trying to understand why things were so different between here and there, and if there was a way to ease the transition." She dropped her gaze. "I hope it wasn't as bad."

"It wasn't," Jack said. "Thank you. That steak was expensive. I'd hate to see it again."

She smiled, carefully closing all the bags she'd assembled on the counter. Jack felt the distance stretch between them, and that *fear* that kept him from opening his mouth. Having been without it for a moment was enough to make him acutely aware of it. But he still couldn't break through it.

"Is Cam back yet? Lotan?" he asked, walking into the kitchen.

"He said something about taking her out to dinner after her meeting with María, so my guess is…no." She shrugged. "Any luck with Frank?"

He stopped, unable to look at her again. "Ah, he said that if we got all the belus to agree to a treaty that he'd get us on the Council agenda, so that's good news."

She winced. "Kind of. We still have to get them to agree—and that probably includes Yaotl and Tabiko. I don't think either of them want anything to do with us."

"Then we'll need to make talking to us worth their while,"

Jack said. "And maybe start with the elokos first."

"I'll send a note to Biloko," Anya replied, wiping the counter.

They descended into awkward silence, and Jack wished he could be as brave in front of her as he was defending her against Frank's accusations.

"I guess we should wait until Cam and Lotan get back," Anya said, absentmindedly looking out the window. "I could search for them, but—"

"I wouldn't," Jack said, making a face. "It's bad enough they're making kissy faces around here."

She hid a smile. "Do you want to take a walk? There's something I've been meaning to show you."

"Walk instead of magic?" Jack asked with a raised brow.

"Sometimes the best things are worth working a little for." She quirked a brow. "But if you don't think you can keep up with me, I understand."

He grinned. "Challenge accepted."

CHAPTER FIFTEEN

Anya's body hummed with nervous energy. Jack seemed different. Perhaps he'd had an epiphany during his talk with Frank. Or perhaps he'd gotten another sip of lilin alcohol. Either way, he wasn't actively trying to avoid her, and for that she was grateful.

She'd wanted to show this to him for some time. Back in Seattle, when he wasn't around, she'd hike them solo, a chance to breathe fresh air and remember she was still alive. But deep in her heart, she'd always wanted him to join her. To experience the views that came with a hard-fought climb.

Her pace was quick, and Jack kept up, although his pale cheeks were growing rosy with exertion—and she tried not to internally gloat that she was finally the one with seemingly unending energy.

"Can we take a break?" Jack asked, after they crested a rather large hill. "Just for a second."

"Sure." Anya disappeared for a moment, returning to their home to fill a canteen then handing it to him. "Here."

"It kind of defeats the purpose of a walk if you can just come and go as you please," he teased, unscrewing the cap and taking a drink. "I daresay it's cheating, Anya."

"If you'd like me to take us to the top of the mountain, I can do it," she replied. "But it's not as much fun."

He put down the canteen and looked around, taking a deep breath. She took in his entire being, from the freckles dusting his forehead to the way his brown hair lay on his forehead. He was at once familiar and a stranger, and she wondered when she'd stop being so damn scared to speak around him.

"How did you do this?" Jack asked.

"What?"

"This—your magic." He gestured to the world around them. "How did you make all this? How did you *know* to make all this?"

She looked at her hands, unsure if she wanted to tell him the whole truth. They were in such a fragile place right now, but he was talking with her and she didn't feel like he was halfway out the door.

"It's hard to explain," she said, climbing on top of a rock. "Some of it comes from my memory, some if it comes from… I don't know. My heart, perhaps."

"Bael didn't tell you how to do any of this?"

"Diogo says…" Anya cleared her throat, debating if she

wanted to continue that thought. "He says Bael wasn't very curious. That he had the power he had, and that was all he wanted. So he never really explored what was possible."

"Makes sense," Jack said. "And he never told you anything?"

She slid off the rock, back down to the ground. "No."

"So what else have you figured out?" Jack asked. "That healing thing was pretty nifty. Not that I remember it."

"That's...not a new thing. Bael used the technique on me once upon a time." Anya looked up at the sky. "But I never saw him use it again. I wasn't even sure it would work, but... I'm glad it did."

"I hereby give you permission to fix me next time I drink too much," Jack said.

She beamed as they kept walking. Anya climbed with vigor, and Jack followed right behind. It was almost a race now, and Anya kept pushing the pace faster with every step, waiting for Jack to call uncle and ask for another break. But the challenge seemed to awaken something in him, and he lit up when she turned to check on him.

Finally, Anya reached the top of the mountain and stood, gazing out across the land. Unlike on their mountain, where Seattle could be seen, there was no city in the distance.

"Wow."

"What do you think?" she asked softly.

"I think this is incredible," Jack said. "Even more so that you...you were able to make all of this."

She grinned.

"I think..." His voice was quiet, and a little shaky. "Look, I think we probably need to talk about the other night. When I was...drunk."

"We really don't," Anya said, the words tumbling out of her mouth before she could stop them. "You weren't in control, you said some things, I don't even remember what they were."

"There you go again," Jack said with a sigh. "Apologizing for me when I don't deserve it. You really should break yourself of that habit. I'm perfectly capable of telling you I'm sorry without your help."

She swallowed, unsure what to say. "Do you remember any of it?"

"Some." He cleared his throat as he came to stand next to her. "I remember kissing you."

The memory of his lips on hers warmed her to her toes, but she shook it off. "You said you were afraid to be with me."

He turned to look at her, surprise on his face. Then he snorted and muttered to himself.

"Look, you were drunk," Anya said, desperate to move off this subject before things got worse.

"Maybe it wasn't just the alcohol."

She made the horrendous mistake of turning to look at him and found herself captured in his intense gaze. In his dark brown eyes that somehow looked different than any other human's she'd ever met before. She wanted to look away, to disappear into the aether, but she could do nothing except stay put.

"I think I am a little...afraid," he whispered. "But I'm trying not to be."

There was something under his words, something that felt raw and beautiful and forbidden. She turned to the front, her face warming with all manner of emotions she couldn't name. It was easier to stare at the land beyond than to realize how vulnerable he was being.

Her brow furrowed as an unpleasant jolt surged through her mind. Something had stepped onto her land from Elonsi.

"Anya?" Jack said. "What is it?"

It was one of Biloko's messengers. He wanted an audience with her. She hadn't even had a chance to ask to meet with him yet.

"Fuck," she swore, turning away from Jack, who looked concerned.

"Anya, I'm sorry if—"

"No, it's not you," she said. "Biloko's sent a messenger. He wants to meet with me in his little hovel."

"About what?" Jack asked.

"Who knows?" Anya said, putting her hands on her hips. "He's a sniveling little insect and he's always looking for someone to do his dirty work."

"Oh." Jack nodded and looked out onto the mountainside. "But we do need him. For the treaty."

"We do."

"So maybe we go talk to him?" Jack asked. "At least find out what he wants."

She hesitated. "I don't know if you should go with me.

Biloko's a belu, and going onto his lands… It might be dangerous."

"Then it's a good thing I have the belu athtar with me," Jack said, resting his hand on top of hers and squeezing it. "You'll protect me."

She smiled, heartened by both his faith in her and that he was no longer squeamish about her magic.

Within a heartbeat, they were across the Underworld, landing outside a large, one-story castle-like structure. Bricks matching the color of the clay under their feet made the structure, with windows wide open to the world beyond. It was a welcoming space, but most of the demonic houses were. Knowing what she knew now about how the belus could manipulate their world, it struck her as odd that Biloko remained in this primitive castle.

"We can't just go inside?" Jack asked.

"It's rude," Anya replied softly. "Biloko will know we're here and come out to meet us."

A few moments later, the front door slowly groaned open. A short demon with grass for hair and a long beard waddled out, his stomach protruding over threadbare pants. He didn't have his bell, but he rarely carried that outside his castle—only when he wanted to show off.

"My dear Lady Anat," he said, bowing at the hip. "How good of you to come see me. And your human is here, too. Quaint."

"What do you want?" she barked. "And whatever you say

had better come with an apology for taking up arms against us in the Great Demon War."

"A thousand apologies for my behavior, my lady," Biloko said, bowing again. "I'm your humble and loyal servant."

"Then speak," she said then, because Jack was nearby, added, "Please."

"I wanted to seek your favor, dear lady. The humans have completely lost their good senses and started assassinating my demon lords. Three in the past month, and I don't—"

"Who?" Jack said. "And where?"

The eloko athtar glanced at Jack and his brow furrowed. "Caspar in Belarus, Ethelyn in Russia, Lucius in Scotland. All of them dead by a sniper rifle with no evidence. Thousands of elokos reverted to human. There's chaos in Belarus right now, as they don't know who to turn to. Some have even resorted to..." He sniffed. "Becoming other demons."

"How do you want me to help?" she asked.

"Go to ICDM and threaten whichever human is in charge..." Biloko glanced at Jack. "Do you think we could have a private audience?"

"This is private enough," Anya replied with a half-smile. "As it stands, Belu Eloko, I won't be threatening anyone. However, we are looking to strike a deal with ICDM."

"A deal, hm?"

"The demons will agree to cease all transformations," Anya said. "And in return, ICDM will agree to stop killing demons."

"But it requires buy-in from all five belus," Jack said.

"My topside demon lords will refuse," Biloko said. "Their very existence relies on the ability to gain more power. How can they do that if they can't transform humans?"

"Would they rather ICDM hunt them down and kill them?" Jack asked. "That's the alternative."

"ICDM can try—"

"ICDM has new weaponry that's effective against demons," Anya said. "They're already making moves, as you've seen. Our only hope of staving off civil war is to try to broker peace. Yes, you will have to give up some sovereignty. But you'll get peace in exchange."

He rubbed his beard, tangling his bony fingers in the green grass. "This is a different plan than the one Yaotl was proposing."

That damned nox is trying to usurp your power.

Anya ignored that hissing voice in the back of her mind. Whether or not she claimed ownership over humanity, Yaotl continuing his schemes was something of a concern—more so that Biloko was considering them. Clearly, the belu eloko did not see her as the true successor to Bael, or else he would have laughed the nox out of his land. Perhaps it was time to lean into her baser instincts once more, if only to prove a point.

Yes, that's it. Show Biloko who you are.

She dug deep, burying her fear that Jack would think poorly of her, and took a step forward, channeling every bit of her that was anything like Bael.

"Yaotl is no match for me," Anya said. "Or have you forgotten the might of the belu athtar?"

"Of course not," Biloko said, glancing at Jack with a sidelong look. "If the Lady of the Mountain wants me to…er…not transform humans, I will oblige. My spawn, however, will need more convincing."

"Then I will convince them," Anya said, advancing on him again. "And if they all have to die because of your incompetence —"

"Anya."

She straightened and looked behind her, to where Jack stood. "What?"

"Calm down," he said. "As much as I'd like to see half the elokos die, I don't think it's what you want. And I don't think this is the way we sway them to our side."

Biloko chortled. "It seems your human believes he can control you, m'lady."

The human must be put in his place. No man can control the Lady of the Mountain.

Anya let the voice win, slowing the world around them except herself and Biloko. Then she carefully extracted her blade, examining it with careful curiosity as Biloko looked on.

"Would you like to see how well I can be controlled?" Anya said, turning to the eloko with fire in her veins. "You will speak with your demon lords and you will gain their approval for this treaty."

"And if I don't?"

"You know, when Bael died, his power remained at the bottom of Ath-kur, waiting for me," Anya said with a half-smile.

"Perhaps I'll just behead you and pick another eloko to take your place."

"Even Bael could not behead me," Biloko said with a haughty snort. "You have a lot to learn about the limits of your power, Anat."

She felt his magic pushing against hers, accompanied by the sound of a bell. It was an unfamiliar sensation she hadn't felt since becoming the belu. Perhaps Bael wasn't as strong as he'd made himself out to be.

"Fine," Anya said, stepping back. "Then I'll ask you nicely and remind you that ICDM is gearing up to eradicate demonkind as a whole. It would be beneficial for your demons to enter an agreement while there's still one to be had."

"And I will remind you, Anat, that the humans have been our subjects for as long as time has existed. Their feeble attempts to control us will be met with a wall of demonic miasma." He smiled. "And you, my dear, will not be the strongman your ex-lover was."

In the same movement, Anya sped up time for Biloko, and took herself and Jack back to the house in Ath-kur. Jack blinked, looking around for a moment as he regained his bearings.

"What happened?" Jack asked.

Punish him for his insolence.

Absolutely not, her heart was clear. But perhaps she could… explain a few things.

"You can't speak to me like that in front of the other belus,"

Anya said. "You can't contradict me. I'm the belu athtar."

Jack gave her a look. "You don't have to threaten people to get your way. I'm sure Biloko can be reasoned with."

"He can't," Anya said. "Believe me. He survives by aligning himself with whomever will protect him. His loyalty amounts to about nothing." She waved her hand impatiently. "It was all bluster, I promise. But with him, bluster is needed."

"There's a line between bluster and threat, Anya," Jack said. "You were threatening him. Were you really going to kill every eloko demon if he didn't comply?"

Yes.

She crossed her arms over her chest. "Maybe. They're demons. What do you care?"

"You care," Jack said, suspicion in his gaze. "Or you did. Didn't you promise me you weren't going to be this way?"

She had promised. Her bluster petered out like a balloon popping and the incessant voice in her mind drowned with it. Perhaps she had gotten a tad swept away in her own ego.

"I'm sorry," she said. "The only way I know how to handle the belus is through fear. If there's another way to get him to sign this treaty, I'm all ears."

Jack shook his head. "I just need to know what's really going on in that head of yours. I think I do. But then you talk like you're going to slaughter a continent, and I guess..."

Her cheeks reddened and she gazed down. "If you ever think I'm crossing the line, let me know. Just...not in front of an audience I'm trying to convince otherwise. Okay?"

He stared at her for a long time then exhaled loudly. "Look, there's something else I've been meaning to tell you. All I ask is that you listen before you react."

"Then maybe don't tell me." Anya looked away. "I probably don't—"

"No, I need to tell you this." He stood in front of her, taking her hands gently, his brown eyes sincere. "Frank asked me to... use our relationship to keep you from becoming..."

"Bael," Anya said quietly, releasing Jack's hands and turning away.

No wonder he's so eager to keep you in line. The voice was back. *He wants to control you.*

"Anya." He took a step toward her but didn't make any move to touch her. "Frank asked me, but I told him no. That's not what I'm here for."

"Then why are you here?"

"Simple," Jack said with a genuine smile. "I'm here because I want to be."

He lies.

Jack was many things, but a liar was not one of them. Perhaps a little clumsy with emotion, definitely stubborn, somewhat cocky. But he had never once lied to her. And somehow she didn't think he was starting now.

"Why didn't you tell me?" Anya asked.

"Part of me didn't want to tell you because...well, we're finally getting somewhere," Jack said. "And I didn't want to mess that up or make you feel like I was trying to manipulate you."

He shook his head, biting his lip in anger. "The last thing I want is to make you feel like you aren't in control."

"And the other part?" Anya asked.

"Wanted to tell you so we could stop tiptoeing around each other," Jack said. "Since we met, one of us has always been running toward the door. Sometimes it's you, sometimes it's me. But we're never in the same place at the same time." He met her gaze. "I wanted to head off this fight at the pass. Tell you now so we can get it over with and move on." He rested his hands on his hips. "So go on, yell at me. Tell me you hate me."

"I don't hate you." But she couldn't deny she was hurt by his lack of faith in her ability to control herself, that after her demonstrating she was trying to help, he was still wary of her intentions. But more than that, she was disturbed by how very easily she had almost fallen into the exact thing he was afraid of—and it was only by his presence that she'd not.

"Anya—"

"I'm going to go for a walk," she said quietly. "Please don't follow me."

CHAPTER SIXTEEN

Lotan stared at the Nullius in the distance, keeping an eye on the time. He should've gone to the human world to pick up Cam and take her to dinner, but he'd been unable to remove himself. Something in this place gnawed at his curiosity. Like the first wisps of a solution to his problem.

The monsters that had attacked Cam and Jack were completely foreign to him, and the magic that had been inside her—some perverted version of the talisman magic—was intriguing and seductive. Was that the missing piece to the puzzle? If he were to ingest some of it, would it allow him to leave his demonic magic behind?

Of course, he had bigger problems than that. Namely, how to get such poison. The way Cam had described it, the monsters couldn't cross the threshold into the demonic world, much the same way a demon couldn't go into the Nullius. But the damage had continued to spread within Cam even though she'd left the land. What did it mean?

More questions Lotan didn't have the answers to. But perhaps there was someone who might.

He turned on his heel, walking through the portal Anya had given him and landing in Diogo's very impressive library. The athtar looked up, a frown on his face, clearly annoyed to be disturbed.

"Evening, Diogo," Lotan said with a slight bow of his head.

"Evening." The athtar was considerably colder to him when Anya wasn't in the room, but at least he spoke. "My belu isn't here, if that's who you're looking for."

"No, actually, I was hoping to pick your brain, if you've got the time," Lotan said, amusing himself with his own pun.

Diogo didn't look enthused. "I'm not sure I can be of assistance."

"You're a very smart man," Lotan said. "I wanted to know what you've discovered about the Nullius?"

"No Man's Land?" He shook his head. "Nothing. Never had the urge to study it."

Lotan sighed, defeat threatening to take hold. "That's unfortunate. Nobody has, and I have so many unanswered questions."

"Why? It's a land where demonic energy goes to die."

"Except in the case of the monsters who attacked Cam and Jack," Lotan said. "It seems that instead of killing demonic energy, it's merely another kind. The opposite, if you will. I don't know if I'm making sense."

"You aren't." Diogo blurred and reappeared with two cups of tea. "Sugar?"

"Please," Lotan said, joining him at the table.

"Why would the prince of the nox demons want to know about the Nullius?" he asked, pouring the tea.

"Because I'm hoping to find some way to rid myself of this demonic energy," Lotan said. "And I was hoping the Nullius might help me do that."

"You would end the nox line?"

"Well, no," Lotan said, stirring the tea in the cup gently. "I was eager to find out how to avoid that as well. Bael was able to keep his line going after his demise. As was Mizuchi."

"Both had their heads separated from their bodies," Diogo replied, sitting back. "I don't think you can survive that."

Lotan shook his head. This was all so very repetitive. "I suppose I was just hoping you'd have some answers for me. Every other avenue I've gone down has been a dead end."

"It seems to me that in order to understand how the line was continued, you'd need to understand what happened when the belu died," Diogo said.

"Unfortunately, no belus are offering themselves up for my experimentation."

Diogo smiled. "Then perhaps you might ask our new belu athtar for some help."

The phone in his pocket buzzed; Cam was getting worried about him, it seemed.

"I will certainly do so," Lotan said, although he wasn't sure Anya would allow herself to be decapitated for his experiments, either. "Thank you, Diogo, for your time and the tea."

With a sigh, he pulled the portal from his back pocket and tossed it at the air, walking through to the streets of Geneva to meet his lady love for a bottle of wine.

"There you are." The frown lines on Cam's face set his heart aflutter. He'd never had a woman worry this much about him, save perhaps his dear mother. He was still getting used to the feeling.

"I'm sorry, dearest," he said, kissing her cheek. "I lost track of time."

"What were you doing?" she asked, her glare razor-sharp.

"Thinking." He picked up the menu. "What looks good here?"

She knocked the menu down. "Thinking about what?"

"Our various problems," he replied, pulling the menu back up. But just as quickly she pulled it down again.

"Such as?"

"Cam," Lotan said, a little annoyed. "I promise I didn't do anything except look at the Nullius and think about it."

"You aren't thinking about going in there, are you?" Cam asked, though she left his menu alone.

"I am not."

"Are you thinking of sending me?"

"Not at the moment."

"Lotan."

He lowered his menu and couldn't help but feel a little guilty for the way she was looking at him. "I'm sorry, love. I'm distracted this evening."

"No shit," Cam said, snatching her wineglass off the table. She was rather cute when she was mad. "You need to leave the Nullius alone. We have bigger problems to worry about right now. You becoming human should be the last thing on all our minds."

"I take it your meeting with María wasn't fruitful," Lotan said.

Her anger evaporated and she took another sip before gently placing the crystal back on the table. "I resigned."

Lotan couldn't say he was surprised. "How did she take that?"

"She told me she knew about our relationship," Cam said, avoiding his gaze. "I suppose Abuela told her."

"I wouldn't think so," Lotan said. "Abuela keeps your secrets. I suppose it filtered up through the noxes—and perhaps serves as an explanation for why you were taken."

"In any case..." Cam looked out the window, and Lotan took a moment to appreciate the lines of her profile. The way her nose had a slight upturn. The color of her lips. The turn of her eyelashes. "I don't think María is going to be in our corner. Frank might be."

"Then we'll have to come up with an offer they can't refuse." He picked up his wine. "Did she accept your resignation?"

Cam sighed. "Not really. And maybe I was hasty in giving it."

"You weren't," Lotan said. "Your heart hasn't been in this job for weeks now."

"Because I've been distracted by all this." She gestured to the air and to Lotan. "But what happens when the world settles down? What do I do when I need a paycheck?" She softened. "Who am I if not an ICDM agent?"

"You are and will always be Camilla Luisa Macarro," Lotan said. "A fearsome woman able to do anything she puts her mind to."

"I'll just apply for all the open fearsome women jobs," Cam said with a shake of her head. "Lotan, I'm serious. I've never been anything but a demon hunter. Ever since I was a little girl, this is all I wanted to do."

He reached across the table and took her hand. "Not to make you a kept woman, but I have money for us, if that's what worries you."

She shook her head. "I need purpose in life, Lotan. I have to have something to do. Something to work toward. If it's not saving humanity from demons, then what is it?"

"We will just have to find you something," Lotan said. "If you ask me, you would make an incredible researcher. Perhaps join Diogo in his pursuit of knowing everything there is to know about the world. You could write a few books. We could document the original demons and their emergence." He started counting on his fingers until Cam reached across the table to put her hand over his.

"I get it," she said with a genuine smile.

"But whatever you choose to do—even if it's to go back to ICDM—I support you. All I want is to see you happy."

She threaded her fingers through his. "How the hell did I get so lucky?"

"The question, my love," he kissed her fingertips, "is how did I?"

The grin that blossomed on her face warmed his heart considerably, and he considered perhaps asking her to sneak into the back with him for a pre-dinner treat. But before he could ask, the hair rose on the back of his neck.

A nox was nearby.

Dropping Cam's hand, Lotan turned in his seat, searching the restaurant and the windows outside for the offending creature. Nobody was there, but he'd felt a nox. Absolutely sure.

"Lotan?" Cam said. "What is it?"

"Hopefully nothing," Lotan said. But movement behind Cam drew his attention, and his pulse quickened. "Stay here."

"Lotan, what—" Cam turned, and her mouth dropped as she followed his gaze.

Before Lotan could leave the table, Yaotl strolled over to them, sporting his usual black suit and overly confident smile. Lotan didn't like that this nox was thousands of miles away from the pack, so close to ICDM headquarters. There wasn't another nox around for at least three countries.

"Evening," he said, gazing down at the two of them. "This

seems like a romantic date."

"One I hope you won't ruin," Lotan said, narrowing his eyes at him. "What are you doing here?"

"I was passing through and felt the presence of our esteemed prince, so I thought I would stop by and say hello," Yaotl said. "You're looking well, Camilla."

Lotan fought the urge to knock Yaotl out. There were too many humans around for them to have a clean fight, if that was what he was after. And he didn't want Cam out of his sight, just in case.

"You have said hello," Cam barked, clearly unafraid. "Now you're ruining my date. So fuck off."

Yaotl smiled. "I see why you like her, Lotan. She's so much like your mother. All fire and passion. She would make a good queen for you."

"I'm not interested in becoming a nox," Cam said. "If you're just here to gloat, you can do that somewhere else. We're having a good time."

"What are you doing in Geneva, Yaotl?" Lotan asked.

"I told you—"

"I know when you lie to me," Lotan said. "So you should save your breath unless you feel like speaking the truth."

Yaotl plucked Lotan's wineglass off the table and took a sip. "Excellent choice, boy. At least I taught you how to pick wine. Even if I did fail in everything else." He put the glass down. "I will leave you to it then. I wouldn't want a visit from your athtar chaperone for ruining your date." He strolled away, nonchalant and unconcerned like his appearance was nothing special.

"He's up to something," Cam said, once he'd left the restaurant.

"If he knows what's good for him, he isn't," Lotan said.

"What's that supposed to mean?"

"I told him I'd consider giving him the belu powers once I figure out how to cleave them from myself," Lotan said. "On the condition he proves to be an apt steward of our pack."

"Oh, Lotan." Cam sighed. "You can't actually believe that he's not—"

"I'm giving him a chance."

"He kidnapped us both. And tried to have me killed."

Lotan bristled. "I'm optimistic, but I'm not stupid. There are other noxes who might be a better fit for this title. But I'd hoped a carrot might tempt Yaotl away from his current plans."

She stared at him as if she thought him a child. "I guess who gets the nox magic after you doesn't really matter right now since we still are no closer to figuring that particular puzzle out."

"We have been distracted by other things." He reached across the table. "But if you'd like to help me get back on talisman research, I'd be happy to."

"I'll pass," Cam said, picking up her wine glass instead and sitting back. "Because as much as I would like to continue working on your little side quest, there's a civil war brewing between demons and humans. And it might be beneficial for you to retain those nox powers until that issue is resolved. Perhaps even to use them on those noxes to get them in line."

Lotan sighed. "I can't. I'm not able to sway them the way a belu can. Hence why Yaotl is able to waltz through here after his sins against us."

Cam's phone buzzed and she furrowed her brow, picking it up off the table before sighing. "Update from Jack. He and Anya went to see Biloko. Apparently, it did not go well."

"He's a tough nut to crack," Lotan said. "Perhaps still somewhat loyal to Bael."

Cam put the phone down. "Says that he has received a better offer from Yaotl."

Lotan ignored the way she glared at him, opting to stare out the window instead.

"Biloko's a no, Tabiko won't let us into Kappanchi. Freyja won't sign unless the others do. And Yaotl is clearly not interested in doing anything except taking control." She exhaled. "That leaves nobody, Lotan. This treaty is dead in the water."

"I say we take another crack at Tabiko," Lotan replied. "If we can get two belus, perhaps Biloko might be amenable."

"And the noxes?" Cam pressed. "Yaotl is clearly stirring up trouble still. We need to take care of him. Let Anya—"

"No." Lotan shook his head firmly. "This is my fight and I don't need assistance."

"Well, when you *feel like* fighting it, let us know," Cam snapped. "And in the meantime—"

"In the meantime, Tabiko and the kappas remain our lowest hanging fruit. We just need to get her the one thing she wants."

"What's that?"

"An apology from Anya."

CHAPTER SEVENTEEN

"Absolutely not."

Cam could've bet money on Anya's reaction, but she wasn't ever one to take no for an answer. "And why the hell not? You said you were sorry."

"Sorry to *you*," Anya snapped. "Doroteia fucked us, nearly got *you* and Jack killed, and all because she was being a little prick. Tabiko should've handed her over to me there and then."

Cam sighed and gestured to Jack and Lotan, sitting on the couch and looking as if they would rather not be in the room at all. "But Jack and I are fine, Lotan's fine, and all's well that ends well, right?"

"Not in my book," Anya said. "Justice still needs to be done."

"Or, alternatively, you can put aside your ego and apologize so Tabiko will sign our treaty," Cam said. "We struck out with

Biloko, the noxes are too far gone, and Freyja's only interested if everyone else is. We're running out of demons here."

"We didn't strike out with Biloko, I just need to convince him of my dominance," Anya said. "Which is hard to do when Jack is spying on me."

Jack grunted and looked at the ceiling. "I told you I wasn't telling Frank anything."

"And how can I trust you?" Anya said.

"Because I told you what he'd asked me to do."

"That logic makes no sense."

"Oh, my God," Cam muttered, pinching the bridge of her nose. "Anya, you really can't be mad at ICDM for being paranoid. You had your powers for two seconds and..." She sighed. "You did some pretty shitty things to my aunt."

Anya started, looking first at Jack, then back at Cam. "I told you I was sorry. I lost my temper. It won't happen again."

"*I* know that," Cam said. "But ICDM doesn't. So don't get mad at Jack for telling you that Frank is concerned about your behavior when you're the one who gave him something to be concerned about, mmkay?"

She sniffed and looked away, and Cam took that as a win.

"In the meantime, Tabiko needs your attention. Or somebody's attention. This treaty is dead in the water unless we get some other demons to sign."

"Then you go talk to her," Anya said. "She's more likely to listen to you than me, anyway."

Cam was nothing if not determined. "Fine. Then I'll go

myself and see if I can't smooth things over. And once I've done that, you *will* apologize if that's what Tabiko wants from you."

"Going to Kappanchi alone isn't a good idea," Jack said.

"I'm not going alone," Cam said with a mean smile. "Pack your kappa talismans, partner. We have diplomacy to do."

Cam drew four kappa talismans on her stomach, and Lotan helped her with a matching set on her back. It was probably overkill, but Anya had a good point. They had to assume that Tabiko would give them the same frosty welcome she had before—with added relish.

"I'm not going to convince you otherwise," Anya said, giving Cam a look. "But I will remind you that the Underworld is no place for humans. I've done my best to keep the magic at bay here, as did Freyja when she realized you were on her lands. But there's no telling what Tabiko will do when you show up."

"Then it's a good thing Mother Athtar is keeping an eye on me," Cam replied.

"Tabiko might be able to close the border to me if she chooses," Anya said. "Just keep that in mind."

"If you need rescuing, I'll come running," Lotan said.

"You two stay out of trouble while we're gone," Cam said, opening the portal.

She stepped through to the other side, the kappa magic brushing against her skin but bouncing off harmlessly.

"Marshy," Jack said, looking around. "Where are we going?"

"This is a different place than last time," Cam said with a

frown. "I don't remember that castle being there before."

"I'd guess that's where we'll find her," Jack said.

But, as in the village previously, they were stopped before they could get very far by a pair of angry-looking kappas.

"You are not welcome here," one said. "Our Sewanin was fairly clear last time you entered these lands."

Cam put her hands on her hips. "We come in peace without weapons and without Anya, as Tabiko so explicitly stated. What more does she want from us?"

"My wife back, for starters," Tabiko said, approaching them from the village. "But for now, I'll settle for an explanation."

"We have a proposed treaty," Jack said. "In the name of peace between demons and humans."

Tabiko lifted one brow, then motioned to her kappa guards to lower their weapons. "You are, of course, aware that your human demon hunters have been killing kappa spawn all over the world?"

"We are," Cam said. "Which is why we think a treaty might be the best bet to stem the bloodshed. If we can get all the demons on board, ICDM will sign it, too."

She considered them for a moment. "What are the terms?"

"ICDM will stop targeting kappas," Cam said. "If the demons topside will agree to stop transforming humans."

She barked a laugh. "Are you out of your minds? There's no belu in the Underworld who would agree to such a thing."

"Freyja has," Cam said. "Because the alternative is that ICDM just kills all the demons en masse. At least with this agreement, demons get to live."

"It's not much of a life if we can't grow our families," Tabiko said with a soft shake of her head. "And what of humans who want to transform? What about accidental transformation?"

"Maybe you should come to the table to discuss it," Cam said. "Because we'd love your input."

There was a long, tense pause, and Cam was sure that Tabiko would expel them from her lands. But the kappa demon just pursed her lips and shook her head.

"Even if I wanted to, it's not up to me," she said. "I'm merely the Sewanin."

"Well, Mizuchi can't make the decision either, unfortunately," Cam replied. "So it's on you. And if you don't make the decision, then ICDM might make what happened in Lisbon a walk in the park."

"As I understand it, you were the ones who killed the kappas there," Tabiko said, managing to sound pissed off even as she smiled.

"And ICDM asked us to finish the job," Jack said.

"They have talismans, Tabiko," Cam said. "The same ones we used against Bael. And they won't stop until every kappa is gone."

"We aren't trying to trick you," Jack said. "We just want what's best for demons and humans before more bloodshed happens."

"I understand your concern, but as I said, it's not up to me." Tabiko chewed her lip, looking at them with hesitation for a long time. "Do you understand what Sewanin means?"

"Caretaker," Cam said. "You're taking care of the kappas."

She walked toward Cam, her gaze so intense it made Cam cower a little. "If I show you something, I want you to promise, on the life of your beloved nox prince, that you won't use this information to hurt any kappas."

"Of course," Cam said. "You can trust us."

Tabiko turned and led them into the village. To be safe, Cam reached into her pocket to hold onto her talismans, but she felt no danger. Just the nervous looks of all the kappas around them, ready to jump in at a moment's notice.

"Why do I get the feeling we're better off not knowing what this is?" Jack muttered.

"I think it's a good sign she wants to show us," Cam replied under her breath. "Maybe?"

"Or she's taking us to a pond to drown us."

Tabiko walked toward a hut in the center with smoke coming out the chimney. She took a breath then opened the flap, leading them inside. Cam braced herself before following, ready for anything.

But there wasn't much of anything. Just a small bed in the center of the room with…

"It's…a baby," Cam said, shocked. An ugly baby. The ugliest thing Cam had ever laid eyes on.

"Like I said, I thought the continuation of our line should've been obvious to Lotan," Tabiko said with a smug grin. "Unfortunately, our kappa prince's mother was not strong enough and perished shortly after his birthday."

"Was the mother a kappa?" Jack asked.

Tabiko nodded. "Until this child is of age, I'm its Sewanin. He is the one who will decide what is right for our kappa spawn. Much the same way your Lotan makes decisions for the noxes."

Except he's not making decisions at the moment. But Cam didn't want to mention that just. "It's gonna be a couple decades until he's old enough to make choices. In the meantime, there are thousands of kappas in danger of eradication by ICDM. There has to be something you can do."

The kappa glanced up, and Cam felt a flicker of hope that she might help. But it was gone in a flash.

"I will take your request under advisement. Now leave us."

"She's lying," Anya said. "There's no way Mizuchi could've spawned that way. I don't know what you think you saw, but that wasn't... That's not possible."

They'd returned to Ath-kur and told Lotan and Anya what they'd learned. Lotan had been curious, but Anya's reaction was swift and decisive.

"It is possible," Cam said. "I mean, the noxes did it."

"They were both belus."

"You weren't," Lotan replied, his voice gentle. "And you managed to conceive an athtar child."

Cam winced, not sure they wanted to go there when Anya was already agitated.

Predictably, Anya's eyes flashed at the nox and she advanced on him. "Because I wasn't a belu, I had to *beg* God on bended knee to make it happen," she said, pointing at him with a level of fury that seemed overkill to the situation. "Unlike your mother, who just...fell pregnant."

"It still took them a few thousand years," Lotan said. "And, since we're sharing closely guarded secrets..." He winced. "My father wasn't a belu."

Anya shook her head. "Yes, he was."

"No, he wasn't," Lotan said softly. "He was transformed by my mother before she fell to the Underworld. He was the first... transformed demon."

She turned, her eyes wide. "That isn't possible, either. Your mother didn't know how to transform demons before Bael told her how."

"I'm sure that's...what you were told," Lotan said gently. "But it isn't the truth. My mother was the one touched by God, and my father was her first spawn."

Anya stared at him. "So you're telling me you were not born from two belus?"

"That is correct."

"And Mizuchi, a lesser demon—"

"There's no such thing," Lotan said. "He's a belu, as powerful as Bael."

Anya licked her lips. "Mizuchi was able to just...*make* a demon child with one of his spawn? As if it was no big deal?"

"I'd say it was a big deal," Cam said. "The mother died."

But Anya seemed lost in her own world, as if her entire

worldview had just been shattered. Then she was gone.

"I'll go find her," Jack said, rising from the couch. He opened a portal and disappeared through it, leaving Cam and Lotan alone.

"Oh, Anya," Cam said, leaning back on the couch. "It's a good thing she has Jack to help her sort through all this."

"I can't imagine why this information would be upsetting," Lotan said with a frown.

"She struggled to make a baby with Bael," Cam said. "And my guess is that...well, he'd probably told her that struggle was her fault. Yet another thread in a rich tapestry of bullshit she's having to wrestle with."

"Then yes, I'm glad she has Jack," Lotan said, turning to her. "But I wonder if Mizuchi's child could solve another problem for us."

"Oh, yeah?" Cam turned to him. "Which one?"

He wagged his eyebrows at her. "Why don't we make a baby? A little nox prince or princess who can take over for me."

"Couple reasons," Cam said with a laugh. "First of all, I'm not a demon. Second, I don't know if you and I *could* make a baby."

"Mizuchi did."

"And it cost that kappa her life, apparently," Cam said. "Point the third. It must have something to do with the age and strength of the mother."

"Do you want children?" Lotan asked, giving her a sideways look.

"I mean..." Cam swallowed. "In theory. But in practicality..."

Lotan pulled her into his arms, swaying her slightly. "Forget your practical self for a moment. What does Cam want?"

"Cam wants to get married before she has kids," she said with a wry grin. "I may be dating a demon, but I'm still a traditional girl."

"I'd marry you," Lotan said with a smile that melted her heart. "How about right now? I'll find us an officiant."

She had to laugh. "All my life, I've dreamed about having this big wedding surrounded by family. And it being chaotic and crazy and fun and filled with so much love I might burst. One of my cousins had three hundred people at hers."

"Fine," Lotan said. "A big wedding. Let's set a date."

She patted his arm. "I don't know if that's in the cards for me anymore, Lotan."

"Why not?"

"In the first place, I'm sure my entire family thinks I'm a traitor by now," Cam said. "And in the second..."

He waited for her to finish, but she wasn't sure she could without hurting his feelings.

"I would marry you wherever you wanted, my love," he said, twirling a lock of her hair "And give you a thousand children."

"Okay, okay." She pushed him aside. "You're getting ahead of yourself. I refer you back to the original three points I made."

"But what if we made sure you weren't in danger..." He smiled. "Would you give me a nox child to continue the magic?"

She sighed. "I don't know, Lotan. I've already been athtar. I don't know..."

"You would be the only one I've ever...spawned with," Lotan said, a little bashfully. "And I'd only ask it of you when I know for sure I can be successful, so *we* can be successful."

She looked at him, with his warm cheeks and eyes full of hope. And despite herself, she took his hands. "If the only way to continue your line is through having a baby, and if we can both revert to human afterward, then yes. I will think about having a nox baby with you. But let's exhaust all other options first."

He wagged his eyebrows again. "Want to practice now?"

She didn't have time to respond before he tackled her.

CHAPTER EIGHTEEN

For the second time, Jack found himself climbing the mountainside. He could've used the portal all the way there, but he didn't want to spook her. He didn't trust that she wouldn't disappear if she felt him coming. Besides, there was something to this climbing thing. It gave him time to think, to figure out what he'd say, to try to come up with a game plan.

All those ideas went out the window when he arrived at the top and saw her, curled into a ball with her chin resting on her knees as she stared out onto the land beyond. She was so small, so fragile. It was hard to believe she was the most powerful creature in the universe.

"I'm not in the mood for company," she said, her only acknowledgement of him.

"Then it's a good thing I'm not company," Jack said, coming to sit next to her. "But I'm not going to leave."

They sat in silence for a while, punctuated by Anya's soft sniffling. He didn't expect her to open up, not when she was still mad at him. But he also didn't want her to be alone after what she'd just learned.

"Are you going to tell Frank?" Anya asked. "Take a photo of me crying and show him I've retained my humanity?"

Jack shook his head. "You know, for someone who's lived as long as you have, you don't listen real well. I haven't told Frank a thing. And I don't plan to."

She drew further into herself, sitting in silence again.

"I'm sorry that I hurt you," Jack said. "But I thought honesty would be the best policy for us."

"Us?" Anya snorted. "Is there an us to speak of?"

Jack didn't respond, mostly because he didn't know how. Anya was in a rough spot, lashing out, and any overtures would be met with the same derision. It was a refreshing change from her usual attempts to please and placate him without regard for her own happiness.

After another long stretch of silence, she wiped her wet cheeks. "How many more times will Bael's lies continue to haunt me, I wonder?"

"He told you the noxes were both belus?" Jack asked. "Maybe he didn't know?"

"He knew," she said, wrapping her arms around her knees and pulling them in tighter to her chest. "He had to have known. There's no way he didn't. It's probably what drove him mad." She licked her lips. "It's why he knew to transform me when he found me. It wasn't happenstance. It was...it was intentional. Everything was intentional."

Jack wanted to take her in his arms, but he kept his distance.

"I remember..." She looked up at the sky, a tear leaking down her face. "I remember *begging* God for a child. But it wasn't because..." She closed her eyes. "It wasn't because I wanted one. It was to please Bael. To get him to stop reaching for me every *single* night—sometimes multiple times, no matter if I wanted it or not." She let out a watery laugh. "And when I became pregnant, I thought God had given me a miracle. That my penance had been rewarded. But it turns out, I could've had a child all that time. There was no miracle about her birth. Maybe I just... Maybe deep down, I knew what might happen if I brought a child into our chaos."

That wasn't what Tabiko had said, but Anya needed to get this out, so Jack didn't correct her.

"I've spent all this time thinking Bael killed her because she was..." Her face screwed up as more tears fell. "Because she wasn't good enough for him. But it turns out...my baby could've been more than him. Could've continued the line if he died. Maybe he felt threatened by that."

"There's no point in trying to understand why Bael did what he did," Jack said. "There's just...moving forward."

"I can't move forward," Anya said. "I've never been able to. Every time I get far enough away from the grief, something happens to drag me back down into it. Some new revelation about Bael that reminds me how fucking stupid I was to believe everything he said. To have continued to share his bed after..."

She could hold back her tears no longer and dissolved into sobs, burying her head in her hands. Jack couldn't help himself and slid his arm around her, resting his cheek on the side of her head. There really was nothing to be said, nothing he could do to make this pain go away. She leaned into him, stiffly at first, then slowly, relaxing into his arms. He tightened his hold, grateful she was no longer pushing him away.

"You aren't stupid, Anya," he whispered.

"I really am," she said. "Because you told me you couldn't be trusted and yet here I am."

"Do you really believe that?" Jack asked.

"Do you really believe I'm turning into Bael?"

Jack swallowed. "Do you want me to be honest...?"

"So yes."

"Anya..." Jack sighed, trying to find the right words. "Look, I won't lie. You scare the shit out of me sometimes. When you act like... When you act like everyone should come to you on bended knee. That's the person I saw when you were with Bael. I don't recognize you. And I... I don't like it."

She pushed him away and held herself, but it wasn't anger on her face. It was disgust—at herself.

"Do *you* think you're turning into him?" Jack asked.

"No, but..." She closed her eyes. "Before...I heard his voice. A lot. I thought it was just...just the nox magic that broke me." Tears began to leak down her face. "But then I found this power, and I don't know if this was his design." She shook her head, as if trying to convince herself. "That's impossible. He's dead. But at the same time... I can't be sure."

"He's extra dead, Anya," Jack said, his hand coming to rest at the small of her back. "And if you heard voices, it might have just been from the noxes and perhaps your own...your own fears. Perhaps even goaded on by my shitty behavior."

She looked up at the sky. "You have no idea."

His brow furrowed. "Enlighten me."

"Are you sure?"

"I want to know."

She swallowed. "In Lisbon, after our... After you left..."

Jack's stomach dropped. "Yeah?"

"Before Diogo found me, I was in a pretty dark spot." She became very interested in the small pebbles under her hands. "I'd never heard you speak to me like that...and I was sure that what we had was too far gone to..." She drew circles on the rock and her eyes had taken on a desolate sort of look, one Jack recognized from his own rock bottom. "I just didn't think I had anything left, so I thought I might do us all a favor."

His mouth hung open as he took her in, and all he could see was his own words flung in her direction. That he'd helped her reach this point, that he'd spoken so carelessly to her... He would never have forgiven himself if those had been his last words to her.

"You were going to kill yourself?" he asked, his voice quiet.

"When you put it like that," Anya said, with a watery laugh. "Sounds horrible."

"I never should've... That you felt..." He exhaled his fury at himself. "God, Anya. I'm sorry. I never wanted to make you feel that way."

"You were angry—"

"Don't do that," Jack said, wagging his finger at her. "Don't give me a pass. You were doing so well."

"You keep saying that," Anya said. "What do you mean?"

"I mean..." Jack sighed. "When I do something wrong, I should have to apologize and promise to never do it again. And you should...well, I'm not saying you should hold a grudge, but you should hold me to a higher standard. You should be allowed to call me out on my mistakes."

"Do you think you made a mistake?" Anya said.

"Yeah," Jack said. "I'm not perfect, Anya. But I never want to make you feel like you can't trust me or come to me or get mad at me. You used to do it so well once upon a time. And you did a great job being mad at me for what Frank asked me." He couldn't help the smile that came to his lips. "Kept bringing it up. It was almost a Macarro-level grudge."

She looked out onto the mountainside, seeming to digest what he'd said. "Maybe the Frank thing just hit a little too close to home."

"I know," Jack said, covering her hand with his.

"And maybe I was afraid to admit that...sometimes maybe I do need a reminder," she said. "Because I don't want to turn into Bael. I took these powers to help people, not to become the new ruler of the world. But sometimes... Sometimes it feels like it'd be easier to rule through fear than diplomacy."

"Easier but not better," Jack said. "Bael had to pop in every four years to remind the world he was watching them. But through diplomacy, when everyone has a stake in peace, that's lasting."

Anya sat back, looking out onto the mountainside. "What would we even do in such a world?"

"I don't think that'll ever happen," Jack said.

"But what if it did?" Anya asked, casting a long gaze at him. "What would you do?"

"Not sure." He looked down at their hands, pleased that she hadn't removed hers. "I suppose I always thought I'd end up like Frank. Married to the job after losing my wife. I thought Cam might find someone and have a couple kids I could play uncle to."

She snorted. "I'm sure Lotan is back in the house right now trying to convince her to procreate with him."

"I wouldn't doubt it," Jack said with a smile. "She might consider it, too."

"I'm so jealous of his…confidence?" Anya said. "I don't know what to call it. But he just… He loves without fear. He says what's in his heart and doesn't worry about what might happen. He saw Cam, knew she was the one, and did whatever he needed to in order to make her his. And now, he's confident that giving up his demonic powers will happen, and he can live happily ever after with her."

"Yeah, it's infuriating," Jack said with a small laugh.

"I wish I could be like that," Anya said. "But I'm too far in my own mind."

He brushed a stray hair from her cheek. "You were pretty honest with me just now. Confident that you were pissed at me, in fact. And you haven't accepted my apology yet, so that's progress in my book."

She cast him a curious look. "You want me to never forgive you?"

"I told you I wanted to earn it," Jack said. "Because you deserve that much from me."

Gently, and without expectation, he kissed her. It was a soft connection of his lips to hers, a tentative step forward into hoping she'd forgiven him enough to allow him to touch her heart the way she allowed him to touch her body. But he didn't want to try his luck, so he lifted his lips, opening his eyes into hers. Shock had replaced sadness in those vibrant emeralds, and she stared at him without saying a word. He wasn't even sure she was breathing still.

"Anya, I know we've never had an easy go of it," Jack said. "But since we're being honest with each other, I want you to know that even though you scare me sometimes, and I don't understand what you're going through, I'm here. And I promise you, from now on, I always will be."

She leaned in, pressing her forehead to his and closing her eyes. "I believe you."

"Just do me one favor."

She sighed happily. "Anything."

"Do *not* tell Lotan and Cam." He grinned. "Because they will be insufferable."

The grin that blossomed on her face was too irresistible, and he kissed her again, taking his time and making it count.

CHAPTER NINETEEN

Jack was beautiful when he slept.

Not that Anya was supposed to be in his room, but she couldn't help herself. Their mountaintop kiss had lifted her spirits in ways she hadn't thought possible. It was easy to forget Bael's lies when Jack was so open. When he admonished her for being too forgiving and demanded she hold him accountable.

It was enough to make a belu athtar swoon.

Although she could taste him on her lips, she didn't move to join him in bed. She'd asked, and he'd told her it might be better to take things slower. She was still raw, he'd said, and she'd somewhat agreed with his assessment of her. But he promised that they would have more time, more kisses, more... everything.

It wasn't a foreign concept to her, this idea of honesty. But Jack's brave confessions stood in stark contrast with Bael, who would lie and twist his way out of any perceived or actual misstep. It hadn't happened, or it wasn't that bad, or she was overreacting, or it wasn't his fault, or... or she'd deserved it.

But Jack... Sweet Jack was man enough to take ownership for his faults and insist that she hold a grudge. She couldn't believe she'd ever allowed herself to accept less.

Crossing the room, she leaned down to kiss his forehead.

"Mm..." He groaned, blinking in the darkness. "Night, Anya."

"Night," she whispered, sliding her fingers through his hair.

As if stepping into another room, she transported herself into Diogo's library. Her athtar confidante was wide awake and jumped to his feet when she arrived in front of him.

"My lady," Diogo said, bowing low. "To what do I owe the pleasure?"

"I have some questions," Anya said. "Do you have a minute?"

"For you, absolutely."

She smiled, remembering what Jack had said about boundaries. "If you're busy, I can come back later."

"I'm never too busy for you," he said, closing his book. "Tea?"

A few minutes later, Anya had a steaming cup of chai and waited for Diogo to finish making his and get situated. Her confidante smiled from across the table.

"Now, my lady, what can I do for you?"

"Were you aware that Mot wasn't a belu?"

"I'm starting to reassess my definition of the term," Diogo replied, stirring his tea. "Especially in light of...well, you. I didn't see God anywhere around when you took Bael's power, and yet, here you are."

She nodded. "But Mot?"

"I'm not surprised, but I didn't know, no." Diogo sat back. "The noxes have always been a secretive bunch. But Mot, as I understand it, was as powerful as his wife. Perhaps due to their similar ages." He tilted his head. "Why do you ask?"

Anya didn't feel like sharing her own emotional roller coaster with him. "Just curious."

"The nox prince was here the other day," Diogo said.

Anya blinked. "He came to you?"

"Yes, he seemed troubled and in need of help." Diogo half-smiled. "I hope it wasn't against your wishes that I helped him."

"Of course not." She waved her hand. "But what was he asking you about?"

"The Nullius, mostly. I can't say I know why. No demon has ever been halfway interested in that place."

"Lotan is," Anya said. "Did you help him?"

"I told him it might be beneficial if he could see what happened when a belu died," Diogo said. "And that you might be able to help."

Anya snorted. "Are you suggesting I allow myself to be beheaded?"

"Oh!" Diogo laughed. "Goodness, no. Merely that you could take him back to that time."

Anya blinked, not quite sure she'd heard correctly. "Um. I'm sorry, what?"

"You can use the athtar magic to visit a time when such an event occurred. Perhaps when Mizuchi was beheaded, or even Bael's death." He spoke so plainly, but the words coming from his mouth made very little sense.

"Visit a...what?" She licked her lips. "Of course, I was there, but I don't recall seeing anything that would lead me to give Lotan any more information than I have already."

Diogo picked up his tea. "I'm sorry, my lady, I don't know how else to explain it. You can use your athtar magic to observe a moment in the past. Simply venture to when Mizuchi was beheaded."

"Wait, are you saying I can *travel through time*?" Anya said with a look. "That's...ridiculous."

"Is it?" Diogo asked. "Our magic is built on the manipulation of time and space. While we cannot move forward in time, we absolutely can turn the clock back. Not to change anything, of course, but merely to observe."

There was a buzzing in Anya's ears. "Observe. Time travel. This is insane."

"The only thing that's insane is that you didn't know about this," Diogo said, putting down his cup. "I feel I've failed you. Bael was surely a master of the art. He would use it to..." Diogo licked his lips. "Ah, I think I know why he never told you."

"Why?"

"I believe he used it to spy on you," Diogo said, looking

pained.

Anya exhaled, shivering at the thought. She and Bael had shared a connection; what more could he have needed to know from her?

"Is there anything else you think I ought to know?" Anya asked, her mind racing with possibilities. "Any other powers you've uncovered that I didn't know about?"

"None spring to mind, but I will surely let you know if I think of any."

Anya walked through the quiet house, chewing on her lip.

Time travel. How ridiculous.

And yet, it was no stranger than the other revelations she'd had over the past day or so. Mot wasn't a belu, the kappas could make children. Her own struggle with making Asherah wasn't because, as Bael told her, she was unworthy. And her own child wasn't lesser than Lotan—she was exactly the same. She could've been as old as the demon prince, a beautiful, fearsome warrior with dark eyes and sharp cheekbones.

Anya stared at her reflection in the mirror. If Diogo was to be believed, Anya could venture back to Asherah's brief moments in this world and see her daughter again. Could she even… Her heart skipped. Could she bring her daughter back from the dead?

View the past, not change it. Diogo had been very clear. There was no way to go back and save her daughter's life. No way to stop Bael any earlier. She would simply be able to observe what had already occurred as if she were in a movie theater.

She'd asked Diogo how far back he'd gone. His powers were limited, and he was stopped from going further than five minutes before the present. But he seemed convinced someone like Anya, who had nearly infinite magic, could go back to the dawn of time if she chose.

She left the bathroom and ventured to the couch, sinking down into the cushions and closing her eyes. She dove deep into her powers, and the lower she sank, the more she felt it—the flow of time. The progression of seconds, like the smaller hand on a clock. Flowing forward, moving everything along. A current that could not be stopped.

And yet.

She could slow it, almost to a standstill, but never all the way. But in this state, could she push it the other way?

No, not push, but like a sailor navigating headwinds, she could reverse her own sails and glide against the river. In her mind's eye, she could see the world over the past five minutes, the conversation with Diogo, watching Jack sleep.

But these were all memories. She wanted to go.

She adjusted her mental sails once more and glided away from her own current, into that of someone else's. Tabiko.

Anya opened her eyes and found herself standing in the kappa village. It was daylight, and no one seemed to notice her. She took a step forward, then another, and strolled confidently down the street. She would've been noticed if they could see her.

But, as Diogo said, all she could do was observe.

Tabiko was in Mizuchi's mansion, and when Anya walked through the open door, she stopped short. Jack and Cam stood over a baby, both with perplexed and somewhat disgusted looks on their face. Anya couldn't blame them, not with the way that tadpole looked. Asherah, at least, had come out looking somewhat human.

"This is how our great belu managed to continue his line," Tabiko whispered, looking down at the creature with love. "Unfortunately, his mother was not strong enough, and perished shortly thereafter."

"Was the mother a kappa?" Jack asked.

Tabiko nodded. "One of the oldest, but not old enough."

Anya felt herself being pulled back to the present, but she adjusted her sails again—this time further into the past. Seven months.

She opened her eyes in Mizuchi's castle and her heart sank at the sight of the belu kappa himself. It was an odd thing to look at a man who would soon be dead, knowing that she could not stop what was to come. He walked with purpose, his green hands stuck under the flap of his robe. She followed him, wishing she could reach out and warn him.

He rapped on the door—odd for a belu—and was granted entry by a soft voice. He pushed open the paper door and a warm smile came to his face. The kappa on the other side was unknown to Anya, but still powerful. Her belly was swollen, and her skin had taken on an ashy look. She forced herself to smile and attempted to push herself up.

"No, please," Mizuchi said. "You need your rest."

She settled back down onto the bed. "My lord. How are you?"

"I'm quite well, but more importantly, how are you?"

"I will be grateful when this thing is out of me," she said with a half-smile.

The winds of Anya's mental sail pulled her forward, and the sound of screams came to her ears. The kappa was in labor, and from the looks of it, it wasn't going well.

"The child is not coming out," Tabiko said to the kappa next to her. "We may have to do surgery."

"It would kill them both."

She glared at the doctor. "Save the child. That's the only thing that's important."

Anya skipped ahead another hour. Tabiko held the child in her arms, tears leaking down her face. The kappa mother lay dead beside her, her belly sliced wide open. She could've recovered, had the child not taken such a toll on her.

"I will tell our belu," Tabiko said, handing the child off to a nearby kappa. "You will protect this child with your life. If anyone should find out about it, kill them."

"But why?" the kappa asked, cradling the baby. "Who could want to harm our belu?"

"That isn't something you need to know either," Tabiko said, her gaze softening as she touched the child's face. "For your own safety as well as the baby's."

Anya adjusted her sails once more, traveling backward in

time. She wanted to know more. How Mizuchi was able to conceive such a child, what it took for him…although the thought of watching the turtle hump someone was somewhat disconcerting.

But her grip on time slipped, and she was thrust forward, flailing and reaching for anything to hold onto. Her hands made purchase on a moment in time and she wrenched herself out of the flowing current.

Geneva. A year or so ago. She gazed upon her past self, trying fondue for the first time. Her eyes had rolled into the back of her head and she was very clearly enjoying the new experience. But time-travel-Anya couldn't tear her gaze away from the man sitting across from her past self.

Jack.

There was such affection in his eyes, a light she hadn't seen in a long time. He'd begged her to go out to dinner with him, to enjoy a moment of peace before they had to rush off to the next adventure. And enjoy it she had, never even noticing the softness of his gaze on her.

But something twinged the back of her mind. Someone was watching *her.*

She turned around slowly and her heart dropped to her stomach. Bael stood a stone's throw away from her, a ghost in the time river, same as she. He tilted his head in confusion, but as soon as she opened her mouth to speak, her grip on reality slipped again, and she could no longer grab anything solid. She lurched forward off the couch, landing in a heap on the floor.

The back of her neck was drenched in sweat, and she felt like she'd just fought off a thousand men. Shakily, she pushed herself to sit upright, gasping for air.

A smile crept across her face. She reminded herself she'd have to send Diogo something nice for his help.

CHAPTER TWENTY

Lotan frowned as he pulled the muffins out of the oven. They were black. He poked the timer on the oven, wondering if it didn't work the same as in the human world. Then again, he'd burned practically everything he'd put in the oven in the human world, too, so perhaps it was just him.

He glared at the offending muffins, but it wasn't their fault. While Cam had been preoccupied with Tabiko, Jack with Anya and vice versa, Lotan couldn't shake his concern for Yaotl's appearance in Geneva. It had, perhaps, been wishful thinking that Yaotl would take Lotan's offer to take power once he rid himself of it and settle back into the noxlands. And he could convince himself he was making the right call, but once he opened his mouth to explain it to Cam, his reasoning would fall apart.

The fact of the matter was Lotan had no idea what to do

about Yaotl. Even if he'd wanted to kill him... Lotan wasn't sure he would win in a fight. Yaotl was thousands of years older and had taught Lotan everything he knew. He could tell Anya to handle it, but the noxes would never accept him as their leader. He lacked the ability to sway his mother's spawn the way she would have. The only way he'd been able to get anything done was through charm and the goodwill the original fifty had toward his late mother.

If he could just *get* into the noxlands without alerting Yaotl, speak with some of those who he felt might align themselves to his cause, then maybe he might have a chance to mount an offense against Yaotl. But the moment he set foot in his lands, every nox would know.

"Oh, honey," Cam said, walking out wearing her pajamas. Lotan's gaze lingered on the shortness of her shorts, and the way her smooth stomach poked out when she stretched. "Why do you keep trying to cook us breakfast?"

"Because it's how I show my love for you," Lotan said, sniffing the black muffin. "Although I'm much better at other forms of affection."

She wrapped her arms around his midsection and pressed her cheek to his back. "I appreciate the attempt, but you should probably let one of us cook from now on. Or go get takeout from the human world." She batted her eyes. "I wouldn't say no to an espresso and a concha."

Lotan knew a direct order when he heard one, so he stepped through the portal to Mexico City and found Cam her requested pastries, along with some extras for the others. By the time he returned, Jack was awake and drinking a cup of coffee, but his eyes lit up when he saw what Lotan had brought.

"You're a saint," he said, diving for the espresso and a bear claw. "I'm so glad you keep my best friend happy."

"Is that because it means you also get danishes and coffee?"

"Perhaps." He took a big bite. "You're so good for her."

Cam snorted and settled in. "So you and Anya were gone for a little while. Is she doing all right?"

He swallowed his bite. "I guess so."

But Cam must've seen something in his face because she released a loud bark of laughter. "You son of a bitch. You slept with her."

"Why do you always assume that?" Jack said, throwing the rest of his pastry down with a grimace.

"Because I know you, Jackson, and you look like you got lucky last night," Cam said.

"We didn't have sex," he grumbled.

"But?"

He muttered something under his breath that even Lotan couldn't understand, but Cam just shook her head. "Jack, for crying out loud, you've already slept with her," Cam said. "Twice, I might add. What's the hold up now?"

Jack glared at her. "Reasons, Cam. Which I won't share with you."

"Where is she?" Cam asked, glancing toward the back of the house. "She's usually up by now."

"Maybe you exhausted her with your slow-moving advances," Lotan said. "Perhaps if you just took her to bed, she'd wake up."

"Real funny," Jack said with narrowed eyes.

But as soon as Lotan spoke, the door in the back of the house opened softly, and Anya padded out. The belu athtar looked...rough. She was paler than usual, with purple bags under her eyes. She blinked in the light of the living room and slowly ambled to the dining room table.

"Oh, thank God," Anya said, lurching for the espresso on the table.

"Up late?" Cam asked, wagging her eyebrows.

"No..." Anya said, looking at the table as if it confused the hell out of her. "I just..."

"Anya?" Jack said, leaning in. "What's wrong?"

Lotan held his breath, hoping the athtar's current state didn't mean she'd gone on a rampage or in any other way upended their already tenuous plans.

"I found out something last night," Anya said. "Something that might be hard to believe, but just... You're going to have to take my word for it."

Lotan glanced at the two humans, who seemed as perplexed as he was. "Well?" Cam prompted. "Don't keep us in suspense."

"Apparently, it's possible, with my athtar magic, to observe events that happened in the past," Anya said, slowly lifting her gaze to look at them, as if waiting for them to laugh at her. "Way in the past."

"Wait, wait, wait, wait," Cam said, waving her arms. "You can travel through *time*?"

"Not travel, not physically," Anya said. "It's more like being able to see what happened. I can't change anything or make anything different. But I can watch."

"Watch," Jack said slowly. "So like… Time travel."

"Not time travel," she said with a smile. "You didn't see me at Tabiko's hut when you saw the kappa baby, did you?"

Jack and Cam shared a look. "No."

"But I was able to observe you," Anya said. "And then go further back to when the child was born. See things outside my own memory." She grabbed the last pastry on the table and took a bite. "Diogo said it was one of the many ways Bael used to spy on me without me knowing."

Lotan looked up, an idea coming to his mind. "Can you take someone else with you?"

"Possibly," Anya said. "Why?"

"Cam and I saw Yaotl skulking around Geneva a few days ago," Lotan said. "It would be nice if we could, as you say, spy on him without him knowing. Find out what he's up to. Observe the noxes in search of allies."

"And do what with that information?" Jack asked.

"If we can identify those who've fallen out of favor with Yaotl, perhaps we might be able to sway them to my side."

A trio of dubious glances came his way. "What side?" Anya asked.

"The side that will sign a treaty with the humans," Lotan

replied, his face warming. "That is still our intent, is it not?"

"And what will you do with the noxes who won't listen?" Cam asked.

"We'll cross that bridge when we get to it," Lotan snapped, not liking their questions. "So can you do it or not?"

"Give me a few hours to recover," Anya said.

Later that day, the quartet ventured down to the laboratory, setting themselves up for the trip. Cam was given instructions to jot down anything interesting, and Jack wore a look of disapproval but didn't voice any concerns. After all, Anya was agreeing to this as much as anyone.

"So how does this work?" Lotan asked.

"Time is like a current in a river," Anya said. "Normally, we all just float forward. But with the athtar magic, I can adjust my sails to slow my pace in it, or speed it up. If I completely reverse them, I can move backward. But the flow is always there, and so it takes effort and concentration to remain in a period for more than a few seconds." She paused, looking up. "Make sense?"

"Absolutely," Lotan said, even though it absolutely did not. "So how do I hop on board this ship?"

"I'm not entirely sure, but we can try it," Anya said, walking over to him and laying her hand on him. Immediately, her magic reached out to him and, although his instinct was to withdraw, he met it with confidence. The world slipped beneath his feet, and he could feel the flow of time she'd been talking about. With her magic connected to his, he was able to keep his footing and move with her.

The trip was too short, and Lotan stopped abruptly. His breath echoed around him, the only sound he could make out. To his left, the belu athtar looked ghostly, like she wasn't there either. She caught his gaze and nodded to the front of the room.

"Things are moving along well." Yaotl was sitting in Lotan's seat at a large table. Seven of the oldest and most powerful noxes flanked him—the Nox Council he'd once sought guidance from. But the rest—they were new. Yaotl had built himself a whole new leadership group—presumably one that would do what he said.

Lotan tried to keep his optimism at bay. The fact that Yaotl didn't trust the old council gave him hope that there might be some sense to be had somewhere. People who'd once been in power could be persuaded to join Lotan if he promised to restore it.

"Biloko tells me the noxslayer has been making overtures," Yaotl said. "The prince is still with her and supporting this plan. They want us to sign a treaty saying we will stop transforming humans so that ICDM will cease their attacks against us."

A rumble of laughter echoed from all corners of the table. Lotan had to admit it was a ludicrous idea, but then again, he was time traveling, so his definition of ludicrous was changing rapidly.

"ICDM will be taken care of, brothers and sisters," Yaotl said. "Leave them to me. Soon, we will have all the humans we want as we expand our reach across the world."

"Go back further," Lotan said. "Can you follow Yaotl alone?"

Anya nodded, and the vision before them began to rewind. Those seated rose and walked backward to the door. Lotan found himself following Yaotl as he reversed through his life.

"More," Lotan said, over his shoulder to Anya.

She nodded, and the world sped up even faster. Lotan didn't have to move, the world moved for him. Yaotl walked all the way back toward Ixtli, one of Lotan's favorite noxes. The other nox was lying facedown on the ground, or rather, his head was. The rest of his body was facing upward.

"I want to hear what happened before this," Lotan said to Anya.

She nodded and Lotan looked away as the head drifted up toward the body and reattached itself. He and Yaotl had a long conversation, but Anya kept rewinding until the two began to walk away from each other.

"Here you go," Anya said. "Are you sure you want to watch this?"

"I need to hear."

"Evening, Ixtli," Yaotl said, walking up to him. "What is the meaning of this?"

"I could ask you the same question," he said. "It was one thing when you took our prince hostage, but I hear now you've claimed the nox pack for your own? Quetzal was killed, and you told Mazatl to take the reverted? What gives you the right to make those decisions?"

"I have earned the right," Yaotl replied. "Our prince has defected to the athtar's side and has persisted in his need to kill himself. But I have it on good authority that once he succeeds, the power will be ripe for the taking." He smiled. "And I plan to take that power for myself."

"But now you've told me," Ixtli said. "What's to stop me from taking it?"

Yaotl pulled his sword out, and before the other nox could stop him, Ixtli's head slipped from his body. Yaotl showed neither regret nor compassion for the man he'd spent the better part of a thousand years living and breaking bread with.

Lotan's heart sank. "Can we—"

Anya swayed and her eyes fluttered, and she and Lotan were flung back to the present. He arrived back in his body with such force, he took three steps forward, landing in Cam's waiting arms. She looked at him with concern on her face, rubbing his cheek and speaking to him. But he didn't quite understand what she'd said.

"What?"

"Are you all right?" she whispered. "God, Lotan, that was scary."

"What happened?" He turned behind him.

Anya was out cold in Jack's arms, her head lolling backward. Her skin was an ashen gray, not unlike the color it had been before she'd taken Cam as her spawn. Guilt settled in the bottom of Lotan's stomach, but he didn't approach too close.

After a moment, she blinked and moaned softly. "Perhaps I

should've waited another day before attempting that."

"I don't think you should attempt it again," Jack said.

"No, no." Anya gently pushed him away as she sat up. "I'm fine. Every time I do it, I get a little better at it. I think I just needed more rest."

"Anya..." Jack said with a sigh. "This isn't a good idea."

"No, actually," Anya said, looking at Lotan. "Did you see all that?"

"I did," Lotan said, gravely. "Yaotl's killing off the old noxes to solidify his power."

"But he didn't notice I was there," Anya said with a smile. "Or that you were. I think maybe this might be a good way to find out what everyone's up to over there. ICDM, the noxes—all of them."

"At the expense of your own health?" Cam said. "You look like shit, Anya."

"I told you, the more I do it, the better I get," Anya said, but her eyes fluttered for a moment and Jack was there to catch her.

"Okay Marty McFly, let's get you to bed," Jack said, hooking his arm under her knees and standing. He disappeared through her bedroom door and didn't come back out.

CHAPTER TWENTY-ONE

Cam listened patiently as Lotan told her everything he'd seen. She wasn't surprised that Yaotl was clearing house, but she was a little sad Lotan hadn't considered it a possibility. For whatever reason, he seemed to think the best of Yaotl, even after the nox had proven his colors time and time again.

"We need to go back farther," Lotan said. "Or spend a few days following him—"

"Lotan, this isn't a good idea," Cam said. "Every movie I've ever seen where people go back in time, something bad happens."

"My love, I've seen those movies as well, but this isn't the same. We aren't physically in the past. We're merely viewing."

He paused and smiled. "Like a movie, in fact."

"And spying on people is worth it to you?" Cam asked. "Because it doesn't look like it's worth it to Jack—and Anya will stop if he tells her to." She stroked his arm. "And I hate to tell you this, but we didn't learn anything new. Yaotl has taken control of the noxes, and we all just assumed that meant he would be offing anyone who disagreed with him."

"But we don't know if they all have," Lotan said. "If I could just *reach* one or two of them, maybe..."

"You can't go," Cam said. "You told me you can't set foot inside of the noxlands without everyone being alerted to your presence. And this time travel magic thing Anya does isn't sustainable."

"So am I to just give up?" Lotan asked. "What about this treaty we're trying to get signed? It won't happen unless every demon race signs it."

Cam pursed her lips. "And you think that by getting one or two noxes away from Yaotl, you might be able to get it done?"

"It's a start," Lotan said.

She exhaled loudly. She didn't think this would make any difference, but at least Lotan's scattered focus was in the right place. "Fine. If you truly believe that if you reached out, noxes would defect from Yaotl to you, and that would help you regain the noxlands..." She was probably making a mistake, but she nodded. "I'll go."

"That's ridiculous." Lotan scoffed. "They won't take an audience with a human."

"They won't have to," Cam said. "We'll write them a letter. It's a bit old-fashioned, but I should be able to sneak in and out, especially as a human."

He nodded slowly. "I suppose that could work. But how will you get there?"

"That's what we have Anya for."

The easiest, simplest solution would've been for Lotan to let Anya decapitate Yaotl. *Then* they could figure out who was loyal to whom. But Lotan hadn't yet reached his breaking point—though he was at least starting to see Yaotl as an enemy. Just not one he wanted dead.

Cam rapped on the door to the back bedroom.

Jack opened the door. "Yes?"

"May I see the prisoner?" Cam asked, saluting him.

"Very funny." He opened the door wider. "No more time travel."

"I told you, I'm fine. Jack, let her in."

Jack stepped out of the way and let Cam enter. Anya was lying in Jack's bed, a steaming cup of tea next to her, as well as a couple discarded books. She appeared in perfect health, although the ghosts of purple bags still hung under her eyes.

"Can you give us a minute? I'd like to talk with Anya without you breathing down my neck," Cam said.

"About what?"

Cam pursed her lips. "I'm in need of a portal to get me into the noxlands so I can deliver a couple letters for Lotan, you nosy little butthead."

"Wait, *what*?" Jack took two steps forward. "You want to go to the noxlands? Why?"

"I told you, to deliver letters," Cam said, looking at Anya, who seemed intrigued. "He never listens."

"Is the demonic post office not running?" Jack asked. "What possible reason could Lotan have to want to send *letters*?"

"Lotan wants to reach out to some of the underworld noxes, see where their loyalties lie," Cam said. "Why are you getting your undies in a twist?"

"Because if you're going to the noxlands, I'm going, too."

Cam had just been about to ask him to come with her but couldn't resist an opportunity to tease. "Are you sure you can leave your swooning lady?" she said, her eyelids fluttering as Anya snorted. "I hear she's absolutely useless. Like Scarlett O'Hara, fainting all over the place."

"Not funny."

"Jack, I'm fine," Anya said. "Except maybe a little hungry. Do you think you could get me something to eat?"

"Fine." Jack glared at Cam as he left.

Anya exhaled. "That should buy us some time."

"How are you, really?" Cam asked, coming to sit on the bed next to her.

"I've been leaving the room to sneak food," Anya said with a devilish smile. "Don't tell Jack. He's been very...sweet. And overbearing. It's somewhat nice."

Cam snorted. "You just like being taken care of, don't you?"

"Maybe..." She looked down at her hands, love shining on her face. It was a brand-new look—and it warmed Cam's soul to know who'd caused it. "What do you need?"

"I thought I'd ask if you could use your Sight to help make sure everything's clear before I jumped through the portal," Cam said. "That way we get in and out quickly."

"That won't work," Anya said. "You can use the portal to get into the noxlands, but it'll have to be far, far from the village or they'll be able to sense it."

"Oh." Cam suddenly didn't feel so confident about this plan. Success seemed to be based on expediency.

"But as long as you are covered in enough talismans, you can slip in and out of the place without being noticed," Anya said. "The original fifty all live near the castle, so you can cover a lot of ground in a short amount of time."

Cam nodded. "That's what Lotan said. But it would be easier if I could just drop myself into their bedrooms."

"Sorry," Anya said with a grimace. "But..." She chewed her lip. "I will warn you. If Yaotl is already amassing power, there won't be many who can stand up to him. The more spawn—"

"The more powerful he is," Cam said. "Yeah, I know. So is it hopeless?"

"Not with me by your side," Anya said with a smile. "Soon, I think, Lotan will see reason and he'll either take care of this himself—or let me."

"Why don't you just..." Cam looked around, making sure no one was listening. "Why don't you just kill Yaotl?"

"Because it's not what Lotan has asked of me."

"So?"

She pursed her lips. "It's hard to explain. It's not... It's not my business nor my place to make decisions about who should be leading the noxes. Lotan *is* the heir to that throne, and he *should* be able to control them."

"Why doesn't he?"

"Probably doesn't believe he can," Anya said. "But don't worry, I've got my eye on him and so far, the waves he's making are small. If he does get out of line, I will step in."

Cam surely hoped so. "Look, I don't want to make you nervous...but when we saw Yaotl, he seemed confident he had a way to deal with you."

"They are always confident," Anya said. "Yaotl especially. But he's never gone toe-to-toe with the belu athtar, and I think he'll find himself wanting."

That athtar pride was in her voice again, and Cam poked her in the thigh. "You just remember that even Bael was defeated eventually. So don't get too cocky."

With nox talismans drawn on every available inch of her arms, legs, and stomach, Cam stood in the living room as she and Jack went over the plan of attack. Lotan had drawn them a map of the village and circled the houses of noxes most likely to be friendly. The plan was for Cam and Jack to portal in somewhere far from the village, walk there, deliver the messages, return to the rendezvous point, and get back to Ath-kur.

Lotan reached for Cam's hand but pulled back in pain. "I should've kissed you before you drew all that nonsense on yourself."

"You kiss her enough," Jack barked.

"Jealous?" Lotan asked.

"Lotan," Cam said. "It's not Jack's fault he's a chicken."

Jack glowered at them both, and Anya ducked her head to hide a smile.

"Be careful, and don't dawdle," Anya said. "Those talismans will protect you from touch, but that doesn't mean they can't shoot an arrow through your heart." She glanced at Jack. "I'll have my eye on both of you."

"We'll be fine," Cam said. "Don't come after us unless we need it. I'd rather Yaotl not know we were skulking about."

Cam opened the portal, revealing the lush green jungle of the noxlands. She looked up, catching Lotan blowing her a kiss and smiling at him, then stepped through to be hit by the muggy, steamy air of the jungle. Like when she'd visited Kappanchi, she could feel the nox magic permeating the air, but it remained separate from her mind.

"This place is…interesting," Jack said, as the portal closed behind them.

"That's right, you've never been to the noxlands," Cam said. "It's pretty much this jungle."

"Where are we on this map?" Jack asked, pulling the map from his back pocket.

"I think we're here," Cam said. "I asked it to put us to the south."

There were four houses on the eastern side, and three on the west, so Cam told Jack she'd take the east.

"Meet back here in an hour, right?" Jack said, pulling his phone from his pocket to check the time.

"Yep." Cam did the same. "See you then."

Cam moved quickly through the jungle, keeping herself low and trying to make very little sound. It didn't take her long for the sounds of the village to be audible, and she slowed, carefully moving leaves to unveil the village beyond.

She pulled out her map, trying to orient herself. The first house was described as a nice size by Lotan, with open windows, patterned curtains, and a telltale reddish tint to the roof. Cam scanned the houses until she saw one that matched the description.

Stuffing the map back in her pocket, she searched the immediate area for any passersby. The village seemed active, but no one was paying attention to the outskirts. So she took a breath and dashed toward the closest house, pressing herself against the rough, clay walls. When no one sounded the alarm, she darted to the next one, ping-ponging off the houses until she reached the one she wanted.

She peered in through a glassless window into an empty room. After hoisting herself up, she slid through the opening to land on the ground. There was a desk in the corner, neat and tidy without as much as a paper out of place. Cam slipped the envelope under the fancy paperweight that looked like El Ángel back in Mexico City.

The next house was across the way, and she made sure no one was looking as she skirted across the empty street. Much like the previous house, she checked to make sure no one was around before crawling through the open window. This house lacked a desk, but she put the note on the nicely made bed before scampering to the next house.

The third house was similarly empty, but something on the desk drew her attention. It was a list of properties from Mexico City, all in human parts of town. That was odd—noxes stayed in their vast neighborhood near La Madriguera, and because El División had given them such a wide berth there, they had been fairly strict about letting them own property outside the perimeter.

Cam pushed the property list aside and kept digging, suddenly intrigued. What could this nox want with properties in the human side of town—and why would El División condone such a thing? If they had at all.

"What are you doing here?"

Cam froze. "Shit."

"Turn around. Show me your face."

Slowly, praying this nox might be one of the friendly ones, Cam turned around to face her.

"You," she said with a small nod. "You are Cam, Lotan's lover."

She called me by my name. That's a good sign. "I am."

She smiled. "What in the good belu's name are you doing here?"

"Er..." She reached into her back pocket and held out a letter. "A note from the prince."

"A note?"

The nox stalked closer, and Cam fought the urge to back up. Her talisman markings were doing their job, but genuine fear of this powerful creature was taking over. She was beautiful, but the power around her was palpable.

She took the envelope from Cam and smiled. "You are brave to keep your footing. I can see why our little Lotan has fallen so hard for you."

"I hear that a lot."

The nox read the letter and Cam held her breath. "This is unsurprising. But because I love our little prince, I will give you a message in return." She caught Cam in her steely gaze. "Yaotl's plan will succeed, and there is nothing you can do about it. If I were you, I would counsel your lover to make you a nox and bring you back to our pack. Yaotl can be benevolent if Lotan apologizes on bended knee."

"Noted," Cam said, stepping back. "Except for we have the belu athtar on our side."

She glanced at Cam and shook her head. "If you say so. But Yaotl seems to think he's solved that problem, should she show her face."

"They are always confident."

Cam wasn't sure who to believe, but she did know she

needed to leave before anyone else saw her. "So... are you going to call the cops on me?"

"No. Out of respect for our prince, I will let you leave."

Cam turned to go, but then stopped. "Will you... Are you interested in joining forces with Lotan?"

"Perhaps if he'd shown himself strong enough to defeat Yaotl," she said. "But he is, and always will be, a lesser belu. And that is why we must align ourselves with Yaotl."

CHAPTER TWENTY-TWO

Having now visited all five demonic realms, Jack was quite sure the noxlands were his least favorite. The plants, purple and foreign, seemed poisonous, and there were mutant mosquitoes that bit him. He trudged through the world, wishing he hadn't thought about splitting up. Cam, presumably, had gotten the easier route. He couldn't imagine anything worse than what he was doing now.

This seemed like an idiotic plan, but Jack was trying to be supportive.

Finally, voices. He crouched low, pushing aside large, flat leaves as he moved closer to the sound. Through the thicket, smoke was rising from a fire on the ground, and shadows moved through the filtered light. He waited until the conversations had ceased before moving closer.

He compared his map with the houses in the village, spying the three he was set to visit. Making sure he had the letters in his back pocket, he crept toward the houses, keeping his ears out for people. But most of the village seemed to be elsewhere.

He reached the first house, which was very easy to break into as there weren't any doors or windows. There was a small kitchenette with a few papers on it, and Jack double-checked the name with the one on his letter. After confirming they were the same, he placed the envelope on the desk. Then he scrambled to the window and hopped out, crouching low to the ground and waiting.

One down, two to go.

He avoided a pair of noxes walking by, who took no notice of him. After waiting a breath, he peeled himself off the wall and crossed his way to the second house, finding the desk right under the window, so he dropped the letter there. And the third house, he was in and out in less than thirty seconds.

"Well, that was easy," he whispered to himself.

He darted back toward the jungle, sighing in relief as he pushed through the leaves to make his way back to the portal. But the longer he kept walking, the more concerned he became. This was taking a little longer than before. Or was it? He couldn't remember.

Turning around, he listened for the sound of people. If he could get back to the village, maybe he could orientate himself enough to—

Something snapped a twig nearby. Someone else was coming.

"Cam?" he whispered, albeit hopefully.

"No." The voice was low, dangerous. Tinged with fear magic.

Jack froze. Perhaps the monster wouldn't find him if he stayed perfectly still.

"There's no use in hiding. I can smell you. It will be worse if I have to find you."

"Fuck," Jack whispered, walking toward the sound of the voice. He had his knives, so he wasn't completely useless—especially with the nox talismans drawn on his body. But he wasn't looking forward to going toe-to-toe with a demon from the Underworld by himself.

Jack stepped out into a clearing, finding the source of the voice and doubly cursing his luck. The nox was familiar—the same one who'd taken Cam back in Lisbon. Anya had called him Mazatl.

Definitely not a friendly.

"What are you doing here?" the nox asked, narrowing his eyes at Jack. "You're the one who travels with the nox prince now, aren't you?"

Jack took a step backward, wondering if he could make it back to the portal in time, or if this nox was as fast as he feared.

"Just a lost human," Jack said, adjusting his footing.

"Why have you come?"

"I told you. I'm lost. It happens." Jack stepped another inch backward. "Know the right way to Albuquerque?"

The nox grinned, taking a step forward. "I'd watch that fear, human. Any nox within scenting distance will be able to find you."

"Thanks for the tip," Jack said. "You wouldn't be kind enough to let me walk out the door, would you?"

"Depends on whether you answer my question," Mazatl said. "Why are you here?"

"Isn't it obvious?"

"No."

Fuck. "Spying for the prince, obviously. Easier for me to walk around unnoticed."

"Hardly. You stick out like a sore thumb."

Jack inched backwards again. It was growing close to the time when he and Cam were meant to return to the portal, and after that time passed, Anya would turn her Sight on them. He didn't want to jeopardize Lotan's mission so quickly.

"And for what reason are you spying?" Mazatl asked. "Is he hoping to start a coup? Because I daresay he'll lose. He was no match for us when we plucked him off that island, and he'll be no match for us now."

"What can I say?" Jack said, testing another inch backward. "He's stubborn. And he really wants everyone to play nice."

Mazatl cracked a smile. "We'll be sure to send him your severed head as a response."

That was enough for Jack, and he bolted back toward the

portal. But he didn't get five steps before the transformed hellbeast landed in front of him, teeth bared and drooling. Jack pulled his knives, but he was pretty sure they'd be no match for the thick nox flesh—and even if they were, the thing was too big for him to decapitate with his short blades. The most he could hope for was incapacitation, perhaps if he could get to the hamstrings. It would buy him enough time to run back to the portal and close it.

But as that thought crossed his mind, three more noxes showed up behind him, eyeing Jack with curiosity. They were still in human form, but for how much longer, Jack wasn't sure.

"Prince Lotan has sent a messenger," Mazatl announced, looking back at them with something like glee in his wolfish eyes. "Shall we show him what we think?"

Jack swore under his breath as the three noxes transformed, advancing on Jack. He was surrounded.

The noxes jumped and looked up, Mazatl glancing behind his shoulder. Something was coming from the forest.

"Mazatl. Zuma. Antony. Eurico. Enough."

Lotan walked out from behind the jungle leaves, human and furious. Jack inched back toward the portal, caught between wanting to stay to help Lotan and knowing he was well out of his depth. Now if he'd had a talisman launcher, that would've been a different story.

"Have you tired of skulking with the noxslayer?" Mazatl asked. "I'm surprised you were brave enough to show your face." His smile widened. "Then again, you never did have much sense, boy. Now why don't you turn tail and run home before we embarrass you again."

Lotan smiled. "I am home, you son of a bitch."

The prince turned into a giant wolfbeast in a second, fearsome and large, but somehow less intimidating than the other three. Jack didn't know much about noxes, but this wasn't going to end well.

It happened in an instant, four on one, and Jack jumped forward to join the fray. But someone, whether it was Lotan or one of the other noxes, kicked him backward. He tumbled, landing on his stomach with an oomph. Slowly, he got up, shaking his head and blinking stars out of his eyes.

One of the four noxes stepped back and reverted to human. Her gaze turned on Jack in a devilish, hungry way. "Are you feeling left out, little human?"

Jack jumped to his feet, swinging his knives. "Not particularly, but if you need attention, I'd be happy to oblige."

The nox pulled out a club similar to Cam's macuahuitl and exposed the teeth. Jack couldn't help but grin; he'd spent most of his youth ducking those damn teeth, and he was intimately familiar with the way it swung.

Her hand clamped down his shoulder, and she let out a scream of pain as she fell to her knees; she'd landed on one of his talismans. Jack took his shot, crossing his knives and slicing her head off with a single move. A howl of pain echoed from one of the other three, and the gleaming, yellow eyes landed on Jack.

"You'll pay for that, human." It was Mazatl. "She was my

favorite spawn."

"Sorry," Jack said, panting a little. "I can help you join her if you want to come down to human-size and fight me like a man."

The nox on the ground—Lotan, Jack assumed—reached up and snapped, but the other two tackled him, pressing him to the ground without much effort. Perhaps they'd just been playing with him up until now.

"Jack," Lotan's voice came from the large beast. "Just go."

"Listen to the boy, human," Mazatl said, padding toward Jack in all his monstrous glory. "You are no match for us."

Jack felt the incoming rush of Anya's magic on the back of his neck, and dread filled him. He should've just run when he had the chance.

"I'm going to need you to get away from my human."

She was beauty, fire, and confidence, the epitome of the Lady of the Mountain. She made no move to draw her sword, but then, she didn't need to. She could kill everyone in this village before they knew what was coming.

"You are not welcome here," Mazatl said.

"That's funny, your prince gave me express permission," Anya said with a bit of a laugh. "It's you who aren't welcome here, Mazatl."

"Aren't I?" Mazatl smiled. "I'm not the one hiding behind the demon who killed our belus. He dishonors their memory."

"The only one dishonoring their memory is you," Lotan said from the ground. "Do you even know what Yaotl is doing? He's killing the fifty—one by one."

"Only those who won't stand with him," Mazatl said. "It's been a long time coming. He'll be pleased to know that we've reclaimed our wayward prince once more." He glanced to Anya, narrowing his eyes. "Now get out of my village unless you plan on killing us."

To Jack's surprise, Anya looked at Lotan. "Well? By your command, prince."

"You don't fool me, boy," Mazatl said, looking at the nox prince pinned to the ground. "The athtar is the one in charge now, not you. You hide behind her magic because you're too weak and too scared to face me yourself. You're a c…o….w…"

Mazatl's words became slower, dropping several octaves as the world slowed. Jack looked at his hands, watching them move in the time stoppage. Anya had put the three of them in a small bubble of time.

"What the hell are you doing?" Lotan said, pushing Mazatl off him and reverting to human. Blood dripped from cuts and bruises all over his face. "I had this."

"You were pinned," Anya said. "And I was tired of hearing Mazatl talk. Doesn't it grate on you?"

"I told you to stay in Ath-kur with Cam," Lotan said. "Now it's all ruined."

"What is?" Anya asked. "If you were concerned for your reputation, I hate to tell you that it was ruined the first time they snatched you."

"The *point* of this whole thing was to look for allies," Lotan snapped, looking at Mazatl and the others with disgust. "If I don't win this fight, if I walk away under your wing, no one will ally themselves with me. It will be a completely lost cause. The noxes won't sign the treaty."

"Then we will figure something else out. In the meantime, you can walk away with your life and freedom," Anya said. "That's worth more than their respect."

"Is it?" Lotan turned to her. "They have never forgiven you for my parents' deaths, and if they see me choose to leave with you, tail between my legs… There will be nothing left for me to fight for here." There was a sadness in his voice, perhaps knowing his fate was already sealed.

"Then *take control*," Anya said, glaring at him. "You are the son of the belu—"

"Exactly," Lotan said with a half-shrug. "Their son. Not them. I could no sooner control time."

Jack looked at Anya. Frustration radiated off her form, but she shook her head. "Fine, but I won't let you get yourself killed or captured. So if you won't take control, you are coming back with me. And there will be no arguments about it."

Lotan sighed, looking at the forest village around him as if for the very last time. But slowly, painfully…he nodded. "Promise me, Anat, you won't kill him. Promise me you won't kill any of them."

She exhaled slowly through her nose. "Until they give me a reason otherwise, they may live. Now let's go. This place smells of dog."

CHAPTER TWENTY-THREE

Anya knew—very acutely—the internal struggle Lotan was wrestling with. That didn't make it any easier to be on the other side of it.

Lotan had convinced himself, much as Anya had with Bael, that he was powerless against Yaotl. He believed that his own magic was the only thing keeping the noxes in existence, but he believed himself merely a conduit. Anya had a feeling his power went much deeper than that, that he'd never tapped into the true powers given to him as the son of the belu to control spawn. Until he figured it out for himself, she could talk until she was blue in the face and he wouldn't get it.

It wasn't just his lack of confidence, though. The love the

boy held for Yaotl was clouding his judgment. Any rational person would've asked Anya to deal with Yaotl weeks ago. But, just as it had taken learning of Bael's most unspeakable acts to break Anya from her own spell, it would take something equally soul-shattering for Lotan to recognize his own strength.

In the meantime, the nox prince had been rage-baking nonstop since they'd returned from the noxlands. First, a dozen blueberry muffins that tasted of too much baking powder. Once he'd finished that, he'd moved into making dinner, a charred chicken dish that probably could've been cooked ten minutes fewer and still been burnt. Finally, he'd attempted to make dessert before Cam shooed him out of the kitchen so she could tackle the mess of dishes and flour that was practically everywhere.

Lotan had retreated to the laboratory, scribbling in his notebook and muttering to himself when Anya came to check on him. She had no illusions that she could talk some sense into him, but she thought she might try.

"Lotan, we need to talk about—"

"I would like to see the day Bael died," Lotan said, taking her by surprise.

"What?"

"Two belus lost their lives in that moment," Lotan replied. "And that is where I would like to go." He cleared his throat. "If you feel up to it. Please."

Anya nodded slowly. "I may be able to do that. But first, I think you should talk about what just happened."

"Don't think so," Lotan said, shaking his head. "Nothing to say."

"If I'd let that fight continue—"

"I'm well aware of what the outcome would've been."

Well, Anya couldn't say she hadn't tried. "What would going to that moment in time accomplish?" she asked, after a moment. "I'm not saying no. I just want to know where your mind is."

He tapped his pen on the notebook, looking furious at nothing in particular. "I feel like... I feel like I want to know exactly how the magic left their bodies. And where it went. Much like when you followed Yaotl the last time we went back in time. But instead of following a person, follow the magic."

She furrowed her brow. It wasn't something she'd tried before, but it didn't seem too far off what her powers were capable of. "To where?"

"I'd just like to see what happened," Lotan siad. "Because maybe whatever happened to Mizuchi's magic is the same that happened to my mother's. There may be some hint...some sort of clue as to how it all works. And then..." His eyes grew dark. "Then I just rid myself of this stupid magic once and for all. Yaotl can have the pack."

Anya sighed, sensing she wouldn't be able to change his mind just yet. "Very well. But only if you promise not to tell Jack."

"I think he'll notice," Lotan said with a growing smile. "You looked quite rough before. It's going to be hard to hide this from him."

"I've been...practicing without anyone knowing," Anya said, feeling like she was divulging a dark secret. "Jumping back, resting, jumping back. I've gotten quite good at it, I think. I can hold a position for a few minutes."

Lotan's brow furrowed. "Where have you gone?"

Where hadn't Anya gone? She hadn't wanted to go crazy with it, so she'd kept it within the past week or so. She revisited herself on the mountain when Jack kissed her, gone to check up on Frank and María, even spent some time watching Yaotl. None of them had done much of note. Frank and María's meeting had been a monotonously boring debate about some policy change regarding the number of leases demons could hold within a city limit. Yaotl had spent the week visiting the spawn of the nox he'd killed and convincing them to become his. He'd grown by twenty demons in the past week—and those demons were given the green light to grow their fiefdoms again.

"Many places," she said finally. "But I think I've gotten the hang of it. Going back further in time might cause more trouble, but I'm much stronger than I was previously."

"Then, shall we, m'lady?" Lotan asked, holding out his arm for her to take.

She rested her hand on it and closed her eyes, tapping into the river of magic, and almost by instinct now, she reversed the direction of her metaphorical ship and she and Lotan slipped backward in time.

She spotted the moment in her mind's eye, and dread

blossomed in the bottom of her stomach. She perhaps hadn't considered all the ramifications of this request—namely what she would see. And who.

But she steeled herself and kept pushing toward that end goal, reminding herself she'd survived it once before. She could do it again.

The movement slowed and they landed in the middle of a chaotic scene. Kappas, lilins, elokos, noxes, athtars, all fighting each other, and it was hard to figure out who was winning.

"There," Lotan said, pointing to an outcropping.

Anya's breath caught in her throat seeing Mizuchi up there, along with Tabiko and the rest. Soon, Mizuchi would be dead. Anya wasn't sure she could stomach it a second time.

No. She shook her head. She was strong, she could do this.

As they made their way up the rock, two figures were coming up the other side—Jack and Cam. The latter was still athtar, and Anya smiled at her ferocity. She was supposed to take Jack back to the human world, but clearly she'd had other plans.

And Jack, fresh from his captivity with Bael. Anya remembered the moment she saw him, the relief she'd felt that he was safe.

"Ah, Agent Macarro," Mizuchi said with a wide smile. "I see you've found your human."

"Yeah," Cam said. "Jack, this is Mizuchi and Tabiko."

"P-pleasure," Jack said, clearly having never seen a kappa before. His innocence was somewhat adorable.

"Has Bael arrived yet? Where is Anya?" Cam asked.

Tabiko pointed at a spot in the distance. "Over there. She's leading the tip of the spear. The elokos and athtars have discovered our talismans and retreated further into Ath-kur. But even without the talismans on the ground, our weapons still bear the markings, so we are at a stalemate."

"You're pretty far away from Liley, Mizuchi," Cam said, frowning. "Isn't it dangerous for you to be out here?"

"We are all in danger, but there's been no sign of Bael," Mizuchi said. "I believe he's waiting for—"

Mizuchi's eyes bulged, then his head slid off his body. A bright light blinded Anya and the rest, and when the spots faded, Bael stood above Mizuchi's body, his sword still raised and his eyes wild with vengeance.

"I always hated that old frog."

"Stop," Lotan said, holding up his hand. "I want to see where this magic goes."

Time slowed, but Anya couldn't take her eyes off Bael. He was beautiful, deadly, confident, the embodiment of every fear she'd ever had. He had no idea what was coming for him in the next few moments, how she'd finally accept that he was the monster she'd told herself he wasn't. How much pain it would cause her to finally take up her sword against him. How much she'd suffer and continue to unravel the world of lies he'd built for her.

"Anya." Lotan's ghostly hand was on her shoulder. "We need to follow Mizuchi's magic. That's why we're here."

Numbly, she nodded and looked at the ground where the

kappa magic was seeping into the rock. Much as she'd done with Yaotl, she locked her focus on it and moved them through time and space. The magic dripped down through the rocks in Athkur, falling through small cracks. Down, down, down, down... It wasn't stopping.

Anya kept on it like a moth to the flame, the rock turning to sand turning to...

"Holy shit."

They were in the Nullius.

"Stay on it," Lotan said. "It's not gone yet."

Anya nodded, and they kept moving with it as it slid through the desert, a green blob of magical energy that struggled and crackled against the world. Above them, a pair of winged creatures cawed in the dark sky.

"Look!" Lotan said, pointing ahead. The magic was slinking toward a cave that was illuminated with a soft light. They walked down the craggy path, following the green blob, which was moving quicker the closer it got to its destination.

"What the actual fuck?" Lotan gasped, taking a step back.

Anya could've said the same thing. In the center of the cave was a large, glowing...*thing*. It had bulbs and extensions like some kind of grotesque monster cloud. The green kappa magic floated toward it, speeding up as it grew closer, and the thing reached a white arm out and grabbed the blob, absorbing it back. There was a shimmering of green across the creature then it returned to white.

"It...*ate* Mizuchi's magic?" Lotan said. "But then how—"

A moment later, a dark blue magic floated by. Anya recognized it as Bael's—the very same magic she'd taken for herself.

"I don't understand," Anya said, watching the blue magic get absorbed. Her grip on the time river was starting to falter and she refocused her attention. "If this magic was absorbed, how did I—"

The answer came as the white blob vibrated, and a new bulb appeared. The blue magic broke free from it like a chicken hatching then floated upward.

"So... magic returns to this...thing when the belu dies," Lotan said quietly. "And it's rebirthed."

"Mizuchi's didn't," Anya said.

Lotan nodded. "Because of his child."

"So how did Diogo keep his magic?" Anya said. "This is giving me more questions than answers, Lotan."

"We have to go back further," Lotan said. "All the way back."

"All the..." She swallowed. "To when the belus arrived?"

He nodded. "I feel like we're close to figuring all this out. But we just need to—"

Her grip on the river snapped, and she and Lotan were flung forward in time, landing in a heap on the ground at the bottom of Lotan's laboratory. Anya was drenched in sweat, her body shaking from exertion. She looked up at the ceiling and couldn't quite square what she'd seen with what she knew to be true.

The belus were supposedly touched by God.

"I'm starting to reassess my definition of that term."

When Diogo had said it, Anya had just thought… what, that she was special? That perhaps Bael had left his magic for her to take? So he could manipulate her from beyond the grave?

It was too much to process all at once.

"We need to go back," Lotan said. "Perhaps not that far, but just to see if that…thing still exists."

Anya nodded, looking at him as he got up. "Where are you going?"

"To tell Cam," Lotan said. "This is a major discovery."

"Don't," Anya said before she could stop herself. "Look, I know you and Cam are good, but if you tell Cam, she'll tell Jack and I'll get an earful."

"If you want my advice, Mother Athtar, keeping small secrets leads to keeping larger ones," Lotan said, giving her a look. "And you and Jack have only recently gotten to a point of trust. It would be troublesome to break that so quickly." His gaze on her softened. "Whatever it is that you fear, I'm confident he won't react too poorly to it. He's nothing like Bael. You should stop treating him as such."

Anya licked her lips and nodded.

CHAPTER TWENTY-FOUR

"That was so dangerous. What were you thinking?"

So Lotan might've misjudged how much Jack didn't want Anya traveling back in time, based on the concern on his face. The belu athtar pursed her lips at Lotan, glaring at him for goading her into speaking and silently demanding he fix the problem.

"Jack, it's fine," Lotan said, waving his hand. "She's been skipping all over the place over the past week—"

"What?" Jack turned to Anya and she scowled at Lotan, who looked at Cam for help, who sighed.

"Jack, calm your tits," Cam said. "Anya's a big girl, and she knows her limits. You don't have to worry about her, as much as

I know it gets you off to do that."

He grunted. "That's not true."

"And Lotan, you can't be telling Anya's secrets. Anya, you shouldn't have secrets, because that's not fair to us. There, are we all taken care of?" She glanced around the room. "Now, you were saying something about a discovery you made in the past?"

"Y-Yes," Lotan said, a little proud of how easily his lady love could settle the room. "We went back in time to the Great Demon War, to the moment when Mizuchi was killed. We followed his magic."

"Followed his magic?" Jack said. "What does that mean?"

"I can pinpoint a person," Anya said. "Or in this case, Mizuchi's magic, and follow them forward or backward in time. We were able to follow this magic to the Nullius."

"And neither of you suffered any ill effects?" Cam asked.

"The time travel aspect seems to work differently," Lotan said. "Which we'll get to in a minute. But we followed the magic through the Nullius to..." He sighed. "I'm not exactly sure how to describe it. Anya?"

"It's a...thing." Anya couldn't think of how to describe it. "And somehow I can't help but think...it's the source of all demonic magic in the world."

A heavy silence descended on the group as they processed what Anya had said. "The source?" Jack said. "But I thought God—"

"We may have to put a deity aside for the moment," Anya said. "Because I'm proof that it doesn't always happen that way.

God was nowhere to be found when I became the belu athtar. Just... Just the magic it regurgitated after Bael died."

"Regurgitated?" Cam made a face. "So it's alive?"

Lotan shared a look with Anya. "It appears to be."

"What about those creatures, those monsters who almost killed Cam in the Nullius?" Jack said. "What the hell are those?"

"No idea," Anya said.

"But the both of us were able to stand in the Nullius without suffering any ill effects," Lotan said. "Which means that if we go back again, we may be able to learn more."

"Are you kidding me?" Jack exclaimed. "Absolutely not."

Anya sighed. "I can step back in the river a minute and it doesn't exhaust me the same way. It's going back years, centuries, even—that's when it takes its toll. But Lotan's right. If we step back a second, we can spend some time in the Nullius to really understand what we're looking at."

"And what are you hoping to learn?" Cam asked.

"Not entirely sure," Lotan said. "But that's why they call it an experiment."

The next morning, the four of them meandered down to Lotan's laboratory again, two to partake, and two to observe. Anya told Jack that they wouldn't really be seeing much other than the two of them standing around but didn't tell him to leave. Perhaps Lotan's comments had gotten through to her.

"The plan is to venture back in time a few minutes, then find that...blob thing in the Nullius and watch it for a bit, right?"

Lotan said.

Anya nodded. "We should be able to spend some time in this space, perhaps even walk around for a while."

"Be careful," Jack said, squeezing her hand.

She smiled and looked at Lotan, now familiar with this process. With little effort, she stepped backward in time only a moment, staring at herself and Jack as they were mere seconds before.

"Be careful," Jack said, squeezing past-Anya's hand.

"Such a caring soul," Lotan cooed. "Shall we?"

She nodded, and the world slipped beneath their feet. Athkur flew by them and the Nullius was coming up fast. Anya held her breath. But they glided over the border between the lands, flying over dunes and large craters. Lotan didn't feel the least bit uncomfortable; the time river negated any effects from the anti-demonic magic.

"Up ahead," Anya said.

As soon as Lotan and Anya landed at the mouth of the cave, the glow was visible on the cave ceiling. Carefully, they walked down the rocky path as they'd done before, the surroundings nearly unchanged from the last time they'd visited.

"There it is," Lotan said. "The blob."

It was still grotesque, white, bulbous, but without demonic magic coming in and out of it, it was mostly stable. Anya stood apart from it, staring at it with a disgusted look on her face.

"What is it?" Lotan asked.

"I can't believe something that came out of…that thing is

inside me."

"It's inside us both," he said with a laugh. "I think, anyway."

"Don't ask me. I'm rethinking everything I ever thought about magic," Anya said.

Lotan walked up to the thing, reaching his hand out to touch it, but his etherial form went right through it. "Ah. Well, that complicates things."

"So what now?" Anya asked, keeping her distance.

"I suppose we just watch it," Lotan said. "Perhaps we could go back to when Mizuchi's baby was born and see if anything happened here."

Anya already seemed paler than before, but she nodded and the world before them sped up. The blob remained more or less the same—perhaps shrinking a little—then Bael's blue magic sped past them, followed by Mizuchi's.

"We must be close," Anya said, a drip of sweat falling down her chin.

But they waited and waited. It was hard to know from watching the motionless thing in front of them how much time had passed, but Anya's hands had begun to shake.

"This is two years," she said. "I don't think anything happened."

"So it really did come from Mizuchi himself," Lotan said with a nod. "Can you go back to—"

Anya's eyes rolled back into her head and the scene dissipated, flinging them forward in time until the present day. Lotan came back into his body and this time had the wherewithal to keep himself upright, although he was panting hard. Anya, on the other hand, was yet again unconscious in Jack's arms.

"You two have to stop this," Jack said. "Whatever you're uncovering isn't worth all this."

"But it was," Lotan said. "I—"

"This is clearly not a healthy obsession," Jack said.

"I'm fine," Anya said, weakly.

Jack glared at Lotan. "Enough. Don't ask her to do it again."

"We're only just—"

"Lotan," Cam snapped, giving him the "don't-say-another-word" look. "Take her to bed, Jack. She probably just needs to rest."

Lotan paced in the living room, digesting what he'd seen, trying to determine *what* he'd seen, and how it fit in with the world as he knew it. There was no *new* connection forged, so that meant Mizuchi had simply transferred his own connection from that blob to his child. And presumably, that meant Lotan had the same from his mother.

He released a loud sigh, looking at the ceiling and putting his hands on his hips as he walked to the window. Was it possible he just hadn't unearthed his own strength? And if so, did he just need someone to show him the way?

"Well, I think the patient will be fine," Cam said, walking out of the back bedroom. "Jack, on the other hand—"

"We should go see Freyja," Lotan said, cutting her off.

"Freyja? Why?"

"I just… I have questions," Lotan said. "And she's the only original demon who's speaking with us right now."

"Look, Lotan…" Cam cleared her throat. "I think you might need to cool your jets on this whole time-travel thing. You're like a man obsessed, and it's not… Honestly, honey, it's not helpful. We have problems in the here and now that are more important."

He took a step back, hurt by her bluntness, and she shook her head.

"I'm sorry. Why do you want to meet with Freyja?"

He grew silent again. "I suppose I've been lying to myself about certain things. About what's possible and not. Things I know I have to do, but I don't want to." He took a long sigh. "And fear that I might not be able to do them at all."

"Such as?"

"I don't think I can kill Yaotl."

"No kidding."

"Cam." He gave her a rare admonishing look. "I mean I don't… I think he would kill me first if I engaged him in battle. Or at the very least, I'd end up back in that basement."

She remained silent, waiting for him to continue.

"After what we saw in the time river, there should be absolutely no difference between what my mother could do with her spawn and what I can do. But there is." He looked to Cam. "Our foray into the noxlands was—"

"A clusterfuck."

"Yes," Lotan said, walking over to her. "And after what happened in the noxlands, I was convinced that perhaps I wasn't the connection between the noxes and their magic. How could I be and still..."

"Get your ass handed to you?"

He chuckled. "Yes, my love. But what we just saw—when Bael died, the magic was almost immediately regurgitated. When Mizuchi died...nothing. And we ventured back nearly two years to see if the magic had manifested when the baby was born—nothing. So that means that Mizuchi gave the magic to his child. There remains a connection."

"Yes, which is why all the kappas maintained their magic and the land didn't disintegrate like Ath-kur," Cam said, taking his hand. "This isn't new information. It's why Yaotl won't kill you. You are the connection between the noxes and their magic."

"Connection, conduit—not *controller*," Lotan said, wishing he could articulate it better. "Freyja, Biloko—even Anya to an extent—they can control their spawn, if they wish. That ability has never been available to me." He paused. "Or so I assumed."

Finally, Cam nodded. "So you want to learn how to control your mother's spawn?"

He exhaled, a relieved smile coming to his lips. "Yes, exactly. If I have all the powers my mother does, perhaps it's just a matter of me never knowing how to use them. My parents died so young, and we kept our distance from the other belus. But if I can learn, perhaps I can revert Yaotl to human. That way I don't have to kill him, but his power will be gone."

Cam licked her lips. "And you think Freyja will be able to help you?"

"I don't think Biloko would be interested in becoming my belu tutor," he said with a half-smile. "And Anya seems a bit tired of my antics, so she's out of the question. Besides that, I don't think she knows all she's capable of—or at least the kind of control I'm hoping to exert. Freyja, at least, would have some fun with it, I think."

"Fine," Cam said, after a moment. "I think it might be good to get out of Ath-kur for a while anyway. Jack needs time to cool off, and probably time alone would do him and Anya some good."

CHAPTER TWENTY-FIVE

Cam and Lotan departed for Liley as soon as the Underworld sun rose over the trees the next morning. Anya and Jack didn't come out to say goodbye, but Cam left them a note so they didn't think she and Lotan had been kidnapped. She could only imagine Jack's reaction.

"Good. Get him away from Anya for a while."

In truth, Cam was getting a little worried about Lotan. Cam was worried he was going to hurt himself—or Anya—all for something she wasn't sure he would ever figure out. Now he seemed to be doing a complete reversal, and she hoped he wasn't planning anything stupid. She was just grateful Anya had said she was keeping an eye on things.

They stepped through the portal and the dark, tall Liley castle appeared cold and uninviting from the outside, but the warm heart inside was always welcoming. Freyja, having felt them arrive, was at the front steps in minutes, wearing her traditional fur robe open to the center and an ear-to-ear grin.

"My loves!" she called, running down the front steps so quickly, Cam was sure she would see a nipple. "Welcome back. I'm so pleased you've come for a visit. Come, come, inside. You'll catch your death of cold out here."

Inside the large wooden doors, Cam warmed considerably, thanks to the roaring fires. Freyja was all a-twitter, promising that if she'd known they were coming, she would've prepared a large feast, but all she had today was a medium-sized one.

"I'm sure it'll be fine," Lotan said, following her. "We came here to ask for your help, actually—"

"Business later," Freyja said, waving her hand. "First, let's drink!"

The "smaller" feast was still way too much for three people. Ten cuts of meat, large dollops of potatoes, a velvety gravy, steamed vegetables of every shade—it was enough to feed an army. Freyja procured a bottle of lilin wine for herself and Lotan but managed to rustle up human wine for Cam.

"I felt so bad about your friend Jack," Freyja said, pouring the wine into a large glass. "So I scrounged in my basement and found this."

"It's appreciated," Cam said, taking a hesitant sip of the wine. It was a good vintage, and she didn't immediately feel like stripping her clothes off, so she felt safe to continue drinking it.

"Where are Anat and Jack?" Freyja asked. "Have they finally managed to smooth their thorny relationship?"

"They're getting there," Cam said with a glance at Lotan.

"Oh, poo. They do care an awful lot for each other," Freyja said. "And now that Bael is gone, there's no one left to get between them."

"Except each other," Cam said.

Freyja tittered and poured more human wine into Cam's glass. "I do love your wit, Cam."

"That makes two of us," Lotan said, grinning at her across the table.

Freyja rose as a beautiful female lilin brought a large cake into the room, clapping and praising her baker with a firm kiss on the lips. The baker beamed and bowed, rushing out of the room, blushing.

"Such a love," Freyja said. "She came to me two Demon Springs back and has been doing her best to feed my sweet tooth."

Cam had to admit, the lilin was an excellent baker, and the cake was one of the most delicious that she'd had—coconut, pineapple, and some kind of creamy delicious icing. She was already full from the meal, but managed to polish off the entire slice before she could stop herself.

"Now, I suppose we should discuss the unpleasant business," Freyja said. "Your lovely Yaotl has come to visit me."

"He has?" Lotan said, his face darkening. "For what

purpose?"

"I believe he's doing much the same thing you are," Freyja said. "To unite the demons to a singular cause. Except—"

"He wants to enslave humans," Cam finished for her.

"Yes," Freyja said. "And I'm not interested in that, but unless ICDM stops these attacks, I may have no other choice." She tapped her spoon on the plate. "How is that treaty coming along? Have you managed any other buy-ins?"

An unsettled feeling ate at Cam's stomach as silence descended between the three of them. Freyja probably wasn't the only demon considering alternatives; Biloko had already said as much. And Tabiko probably was as well.

"Yaotl is part of the reason I wanted to speak with you," Lotan said. "Or rather, how to bring him back under my control."

Freyja turned to him, curious. "Oh?"

"I'm the child of a belu, but I've never thought I had the same level of power my mother did—or that you do, especially over your spawn. But after some new information has come to light, I was hoping… I was hoping you might help me learn what it is to control the noxes."

Freyja's mouth popped open in surprise and a little laugh came from her lips. "This is not the request I anticipated, but it's a good one. I'm not sure how much help I will be—noxes are so very different than lilins."

"They all come from the same source, though," Lotan said.

She smiled. "They do. God bestowed the powers we

currently have. Your mother, like me, was chosen to bear the burden of sin for all humanity."

Cam had heard the same story growing up, and found it woefully inadequate even then. But she didn't feel like bursting Freyja's bubble by telling her it was actually some blob in the center of the Nullius who gave her power.

"And because of that," Lotan continued, "I thought it was only a belu who could control their spawn. It made sense, you know. But as I said, we've discovered some new information—"

"What kind of information?" Freyja asked, tilting her head.

Lotan hesitated. "Speaking with Tabiko," he said, catching Cam's gaze for a moment so she wouldn't correct his lie, "she indicated that Mizuchi's spawn would be able to control the kappas."

"I see."

"So how do you do it?" Lotan asked.

"Well, it's not a power I use often," Freyja said with a little laugh. "My spawn are my loves, and I wouldn't ever want to force them to do anything."

"But you have used it before?"

She nodded slowly. "Once. I had a lilin who was acting out of line. So I… Well, I suppose we should start with whether or not you feel the connections."

Lotan looked perplexed. "In what way?"

"I feel every spawn I have, more or less," Freyja said. "The ones I've directly sired, I feel more palpably than others. It's like a million threads running from my heart to theirs."

"Lotan," Cam said. "You seem to be able to sense Yaotl when he's near, don't you?"

"I felt his magic. That's different," Lotan said. "It's a signature."

"It's all part and parcel of the same thing," Freyja said. "Their magic comes from you, and so being able to feel someone's magic acutely is different than being able to just sense magic in general. You probably know when a lilin is near based on their magic, but do you know which lilin specifically?"

Lotan shook his head. "But I didn't know it was Yaotl either. Just a powerful nox."

"You'll learn to tell them apart," Freyja said. "Let's give it a try. Close your eyes."

He did as he was told, and Cam held her breath, watching the two of them as Freyja told him to clear his mind and reach out.

"Do you see them? The threads?" she asked, closing her eyes as well. "I can feel the baker in the kitchen, her joy at my praise. She's so grateful to be here."

Cam glanced at Lotan, and frowned as he squirmed. "I don't…" He opened his eyes. "I don't feel anything."

Freyja, though, didn't seem bothered. "You will. Give it time."

Lotan tried all afternoon and still didn't get anything out of the sessions. Cam wished she had some guidance to give him, but this was out of her wheelhouse. She could tell, though, that

Lotan was growing frustrated, especially as the afternoon faded to evening.

"Stay for dinner," Freyja said. "Stay the night. You can return to Ath-kur in the morning."

Lotan didn't seem in the mood, and Cam was still full from lunch, but it was hard to say no to the goddess of love, so they sat down for another meal of different meats, different vegetables, and another cake that was out-of-this-world delicious.

After dinner, Lotan confessed his exhaustion and padded up to the bedroom Freyja had set aside for them. Cam watched him go, her heart breaking for him.

"He will get there, I promise you," Freyja said. "I've never met a more determined soul."

"That's for sure," Cam said. "Thank you for helping him. He's running out of options."

"Perhaps that's his problem," Freyja said. "He has every option available to him, but he has to believe they are his to own. I've never known Lotan to want or desire anything other than a simple life. To ask him to become the true nox prince will take some readjustment."

Cam nodded and looked down as Freyja put a small vial in her hand.

"A very, *very* small amount of lilin wine," Freyja said. "For you. Perhaps you can cheer him up with a little lovemaking."

Cam pocketed the vial and said her goodnights, but she was fairly sure she wouldn't be imbibing. Her scant memories and Jack's recent experience were enough to keep her far from it. But her resolve softened when she found him sitting on the edge of the bed, his shoulders slumped as he stared out the open window.

"I suppose I'm not good at much, am I? Terrible prince, terrible belu nox. Can't even bake right."

"Stop that self-pity shit," Cam said, coming to sit next to him. "You know that's not going to fly with me. You are great at a lot of stuff."

"Name one."

"You're brave. You jump headfirst into danger. You're very smart."

"Excellent qualities. Still doesn't make me able to do the one thing I need to do."

"Maybe because you're sitting around feeling sorry for yourself?" Cam asked. "Be confident, and confidence will follow. That's how I usually operate."

"We can't all be as amazing as Camilla Lucía Macarro," Lotan said, taking her hand. "But I'll certainly try. Perhaps in the morning, I'll feel better."

Cam stood and faced him, reaching into her pocket and pulling out the lilin wine. "I know one surefire way to make you feel better."

"Is that lilin wine?" Lotan asked with a quirked brow. "What are you up to, my love?"

She popped the cork and downed the liquid. It was barely a shot, but almost immediately, her core lit up, and everything about Lotan looked good enough to eat.

"Making you feel better," she said, her voice low as she approached him. "Now come here."

CHAPTER TWENTY-SIX

The house was quiet, and if Jack tried hard enough, he could believe he was back in Seattle, and not in the demonic underworld. He held his coffee and looked out onto the woodsy front yard, expecting to see a deer or birds. But no such animals existed here.

Behind him, Anya stirred. "Morning," came her sleepy voice from the darkness. "Did you bring me coffee?"

"I can make you some," Jack said. "I didn't think you'd be up yet. How are you feeling?"

"Absolutely fine." Anya sat up. "You shouldn't worry like this over me. I just needed a good sleep to recover my strength."

The dark bags under her eyes told a different story. "You

look like you did in Europe."

"Pssh." She took a sip. "I'm not that bad."

"I was the one looking at you." Jack smiled, but there was a serious note to it. "You're supposed to be stronger now. Belus aren't supposed to be like this—get weak."

Anya snorted. "That's what Bael wanted you to think. But after every Demon Spring...he was wiped. Slept for months afterward." She narrowed her eyes. "Hm."

"What?"

"I've been wondering...It hasn't been any great feat to make a portal," Anya said, sitting back and holding her mug between her hands. "Diogo was able to do it quite easily—and keep it for a couple hundred years. I wonder if something else was zapping Bael's energy. Like maybe going back in time when he was topside. It would make sense how he seemed to know so much." She narrowed her eyes. "Time works differently here, so maybe...maybe he couldn't tap into the time in the human world unless he was physically there."

Jack watched her muddle through the scenarios and was reminded of her comment on the mountain, and how Bael's lies seemed to continue to be uncovered. He was just happy that this time she didn't seem completely devastated by the new information.

"I'm sorry," she said, rising. "I should be discussing this with Diogo."

"Why?" Jack said, looking up at her. "I'm interested in this, too."

"Are you?" Anya asked. "It's all very…weird."

"Yeah, but I like weird," Jack said. "And I told you, I don't want any more secrets between us. Whatever's on your mind, I want to know."

She glanced up at him with those glowing emeralds then looked down at her coffee. "Cam and Lotan have left, I take it?"

"They have," Jack said. "I wouldn't expect them back until tomorrow, at the earliest."

"So we're alone?" Anya said, putting down her cup. "That's…nice."

Jack didn't disagree. "I'll let you rest."

"No," Anya said, a little quickly. "By the way, where are you sleeping if not in your own bed?"

"Yours," Jack said.

"You could put me in my own bed, you know." Anya licked her lips and looked up at him, a little suggestively. "Or you could join me…?"

He did want to, but not yet. He'd stolen a kiss here and there, but they hadn't had much more than that. Jack had kept looking for the right moment, the right situation for him to make his move. But with all the distractions, there hadn't been a chance.

He sat back and smiled. "Why don't we go somewhere?"

"I'm sorry?" She furrowed her brow. "And do what?"

"We could go back to Richmond?"

She grinned, and he liked that she knew exactly why he'd chosen that spot. "And do what?"

"Enjoy each other's company," Jack said, taking her hands and helping her out of bed. "I believe some people call it a date."

It was midday in Richmond, and Cary Street was bustling with activity. The first time they'd been here, months ago, Jack had been too chicken to take her hand. Now, he easily threaded his fingers through hers, and she seemed brighter for it. No one paid much attention to them, and after a moment, Jack realized he could barely feel her power.

"Where's your magic?" he asked.

"I've tamped it down," Anya said. "Diogo showed me how."

"When?"

"Ten minutes ago."

Jack snorted, looking down. "So you could disappear on this date a thousand times and I wouldn't know, would I?"

She turned to him, smiling. "I won't. I'm happy to be fully present with you."

They spent the afternoon and early evening leisurely exploring the shops and buying nothing, but they didn't need anything except each other's company. Anya lingered for a moment in front of a children's clothing store, but when Jack asked if she wanted to go inside, she shook her head.

"I know you miss her," Jack said, taking her hand as they walked down the street. "Do you want to talk about it?"

Anya looked behind her at the shop, then turned forward, as if conflicted. "There are times..."

Jack waited for her to finish, but she seemed unable or

unwilling to share her thought. At the risk of pushing her away, he squeezed her hand. "You can tell me."

"There are times that part of me wants...wants another child," Anya said, looking as guilty as if she'd just confessed to mass murder. "But I wonder if that's... I can't help but feel like that's..."

"You wonder if, by moving on, you're dishonoring her memory."

She nodded, relief in her gaze. "Exactly."

"You aren't," Jack said. "I know your head's been in the past lately, but there's so much to look forward to in the future. You have infinite possibilities at your fingertips, and if that includes another child, then that's what you should do." He looked forward. "I don't think Asherah would want you to linger in sadness forever."

She looked at him. "Is that how you feel about Sara?"

He nodded. "I'll always love her, but..." He smiled at her. "I'm happy where I am today. And I know that's what she would've wanted for me."

Anya looked down with a smile on her face, her hand still tightly inside of his. "Knowing Mizuchi was able to procreate so easily, and that Mot wasn't a belu himself...it's given me a little hope that the impossible isn't so impossible."

Jack started; was she thinking *he* would want to become athtar? So far, he'd been able to avoid thinking about what might happen once the world calmed down and the treaty was signed, but he was sure it didn't include him becoming a demon.

But he couldn't bring himself to pop her bubble, not when she was looking so light and airy.

They wandered up and down the main street until the sun set, then Jack treated Anya to a romantic dinner in an open-air garden restaurant. It was refreshingly normal to talk about none of their usual concerns and just reminisce about jobs and clients they'd had back in Seattle.

Jack was riveted to hear the stories from her perspective and couldn't believe they'd lived together through it all and never shared their thoughts like this. Anya's smile was free, and as the bottle of wine between them dwindled, Jack got the check and they continued their walk.

"Where would you like to go next?" he asked.

"I have the perfect spot," Anya said with a knowing grin.

She took Jack's hand and the world slipped beneath them. His eyes adjusted to the darkness around them, the cool air on his skin—and he blinked. They'd gone back to Ath-kur, except they hadn't. There was the gaping hole in the side of the house.

"Our house?" Jack said, turning to her.

His gaze landed on the living room, where the couch had been turned back over. A bottle of fancy champagne sat in an ice bucket with two flutes and two dozen roses. Down to the exact placement of his one attempt at romance.

"I thought we could try this again," Anya said, a little bashfully. "And I'll try not to freak out this time."

Jack let her guide him to the couch, and he set to opening and pouring the bubbly. She picked up her crystal glass and held it aloft, waiting for him.

"To second chances," she said with a smile.

He tapped his glass against hers. "To getting that hole fixed before we move back home."

She started, before taking a sip. "Move back home? Even though we have this exact house in Ath-kur?"

Once again, Jack realized he and Anya had two different mindsets. He'd always thought of this demonic transformation as temporary. Lotan would find a way to rid himself of his powers, and he supposed he always assumed Anya would as well. After all, Diogo had kept his after Bael's death, and there were no other athtars to concern themselves with. Anya wouldn't *need* this power after a certain point.

"Jack?" Anya asked, looking a little concerned.

"Sorry, got to thinking," he said, offering what he hoped was a comforting smile. It still wasn't the right time to ruin this moment. "This is good champagne."

"I remember," Anya said, looking at her glass. "I remember downing it after you'd gone to bed and having a wicked headache the next morning." As if to prove a point, she took a big gulp. "No danger of that today."

Jack looked at his champagne, mesmerized by the bubbles for a moment, but then couldn't hold back any longer. "Do you think you'll keep it forever?"

"Hm?"

"The athtar magic," Jack said, looking at her. "If Lotan reverts himself, would you...consider doing it as well?"

"I don't... I don't know." She held herself. "When I was human I felt... useless. Like I couldn't do anything to help you. I was just there."

Jack debated whether telling her that her mental state contributed to that more than her physical one, but that didn't seem a helpful thing to add. "But if you didn't feel that way... If you could revert to human and be as happy as you are right now. What would you do?"

"I don't know," Anya said. "Why?"

"I know you took this power to save us, but it seems like..." Jack sighed. "I don't know."

"Do you want me to give it up?" Anya asked. "Even though it's the only thing keeping the world from descending into chaos?"

"Well, hopefully this treaty will do that," Jack said with a smile. "If we can get Yaotl to play along."

She pursed her lips. "Treaties need to be enforced."

"And so that'll be your job? To forever enforce a treaty between humans and demons?"

"I mean..." She swallowed. "I'd do other stuff."

"But what if you just let demons and humans keep each other in line? What if you didn't have to hold the world together?" He turned to her and took her hands. "What if you did something else?"

She smiled. "Like?"

He leaned in and kissed her, taking his time and lingering for a moment. She released a soft sigh and her eyelids fluttered when she looked at him. There was a softness there that tugged at his heart, and a somewhat triumphant feeling that he'd brought this powerful creature to her knees with a kiss. But as soon as he thought it, he hated himself a little. She wasn't the belu athtar right now. She was Anya. His Anya.

"Why do you do that?" she asked.

"Hm?"

"Kiss me and stop?" She leaned back. "Are you still holding back?"

"Maybe I'm trying for a bit of romantic suspense," Jack said, taking her hands and pulling her close again. "Attempting to woo you. You know, that sort of thing."

"I'm already wooed, Jack," Anya said. "Now I'm just getting impatient."

He smiled and leaned in, capturing her lips again, resting his hand against her cheek. She opened her mouth to his, gently sliding her tongue along his lips. He leaned in closer, his hand resting on her back and holding her close.

She shifted, climbing onto his lap and straddling his hips. Gently, she pushed him to lie back on the couch, never breaking her kiss. There was something so easy about it, something so natural about them getting physical like this in the home they shared. A part of him wished they hadn't wasted so much time, but mostly he was just grateful for the current moment.

"Jack," Anya said, fluttering her eyes sarcastically. "Do you think we're ready?"

"Oh." He slid his hands over her hips. "Only if you are."

She grinned and drifted her fingertips down his stomach until they found the button on his pants, sending his breath into his throat. There was a deep urge inside of him, one that had been tamped down for months as he kept his distance. But she was too close now, and he was desperate to relearn her.

He moved to kiss her again, but she started, lifting her head as if she'd heard something.

"What is it?" Jack asked, brushing the hair from her face.

"Someone's calling for me. Fuck." She turned to him, leaning in to kiss him deeply. "To be continued?"

"Wait, Anya—"

Before he could stop her, she was gone.

CHAPTER TWENTY-SEVEN

It seemed Anya's curse was that just as she was getting somewhere with Jack, some asshole would walk into Ath-kur. And she had a feeling this wasn't going to end well.

Tabiko stood on the edge of Anya's land, having crossed all the way through Liley herself.

"Good evening, Tabiko," Anya said, bowing her head slightly.

"I have convened a council of kappas. We have agreed to sign your treaty on one condition," Tabiko said. "That you prove to us that you're willing to keep the humans in check as much as the demons."

Anya blanched. "How do you expect me to do that?"

"I have it on good authority that the humans are targeting the kappa lord in Los Angeles. They've already taken out ten of his top lieutenants, reverting two-thirds of the city's kappas to human—thousands of kappas." She sniffed harshly. "Many of the demons killed have been there for hundreds of years. But I believe their main target is the kappa lord Farr, and I fear they will find him in the coming days. I would like you to—"

Anya moved quickly, finding the kappa sitting at his desk and dragging him to the present moment, tossing him at Tabiko's feet.

"There," Anya said, crossing her arms over her chest. "Happy?"

"What the fuck just happened?" Farr said, blinking wildly. "T-Tabiko? Where am I? Is this Kappanchi?"

Tabiko's nostrils flared. "And *also*, I would like you to show the humans that targeting demons will not be tolerated."

Anya didn't think that would be as easy. "How?"

Tabiko looked at the bewildered kappa at her feet. "Who is in charge in Los Angeles?"

He blinked. "I am?"

Tabiko blew air from her nostrils. "On the human side."

"Oh, uh..." Farr turned to Anya. "John Kuehnbaum. He's the director of the LA Division."

"Then I want his head," Tabiko said, catching Anya with her gaze. "You're good at decapitation. It shouldn't be too hard for you."

Anya stared back, unwilling to rise to the bait. "I don't have to kill them to get them to toe the line."

"If you aren't willing to kill humans, it's clear you are more loyal to them than to us," Tabiko said, as she turned away. "And therefore—"

"Wait," Anya said. "Fine. If I bring you this John Kuehnbaum's head, you and the kappas will sign the treaty?"

Tabiko nodded, and a drop of water slipped from her head.

Anya paced the living room in the house in Ath-kur, chewing on her thumb, unsure what to do. She didn't want to return to Jack, not when she wasn't sure what he'd say. They'd just come so far; how badly would it ruin things if he found out what Tabiko had asked her to do?

What she was *considering.*

She hadn't killed a human in a few hundred years, not since she was cursed. Demons, sure. But humans always seemed so weak. Fragile. Killing a Division Director might ruin any chance at negotiation with ICDM. But not doing it would close the door on negotiations with the kappas.

She stopped and looked out the window. She should get back to Jack, who by now was probably wondering what the hell had happened. But she knew what he would say, and she didn't want to listen to him. What she wanted was for someone to tell her what she wanted to hear.

Kill the human.

Anya went stick-straight. That voice, the one that sounded like Bael and herself, echoed between her ears. It had been some time since she'd heard it so clearly, so very temptingly. It was like a north star that seemed to lay her path out before her.

Kill the human, prove to them that she was every bit the terror Bael had been. Prove to the kappas and other demons on the fence that she wasn't a pushover. Bring the world to the table through fear and iron-fisted rule.

But if she were the catalyst for peace, it would require her constant presence. And any dreams of being with Jack would evaporate. He surely wouldn't condone killing anyone.

"Anya?"

She'd felt him step through the portal and had hoped he'd go anywhere but here.

"What the hell happened?" Jack asked. His cheeks were still somewhat flushed, and his clothes wrinkled from when Anya had pulled them off. "Where did you go?"

Lie to him. He doesn't need to know your business.

But Anya had learned that lesson once before, and it had nearly ruined everything. She and Jack had just come so far, she couldn't jeopardize it.

Telling him will jeopardize it. At least if you lie, he may never find out.

"Anya?" Jack was now in front of her; she couldn't escape. Nor could she stop herself from speaking.

"Tabiko reached out. She wants me to..." Anya swallowed. "ICDM has put a target on the demon lord in Los Angeles and she would like me to handle it."

"How?"

She inched backward a little, waiting for the fight to begin. "She wants me to bring her the head of the LA Division Director."

"The head of the LA Division?"

"No." Anya ran her finger along her neck. "The head."

"Ah." Jack blinked. "Did…you?"

"Of course not," she said, almost too quickly, then added, "I mean, not yet."

Jack stepped closer to her. "But you're thinking about it?"

"I don't know," Anya said, turning away from him to sink down onto the couch. "Nobody seems to be listening to us. Sometimes I think violence might be the way to get things done. If one person has to die, but the rest of the world would be spared civil war, maybe it's worth it."

She felt Jack's eyes on her. "You can't believe that. It'll be the LA Director today, the Atlanta Director tomorrow. Soon, they'll want you to take out a Councilperson."

"Then the kappas won't sign the treaty," Anya said, turning to him. "There's nothing left for us to do."

"Yes, there is. We get ICDM to back off," Jack said. "And once we have it in writing that they are, we can go to Tabiko and let her know that we don't do loyalty tests."

Anya's heart perked up a little at Jack's confidence. "Do you think that'll work?"

"I think it has a better shot at working than you going around decapitating directors." He took her hand. "You said you don't want to do business the way Bael did."

Yet again, Anya realized just how close she'd come to breaking her own promise—but this time, all she felt was gratitude toward Jack for the reminder.

"You're right," Anya said. "Let's give it a try."

Anya and Jack appeared in LA, standing at the bottom of the ICDM building and staring up at the art deco building that stretched into the sky. Anya still wasn't sure what was in Jack's mind, but she trusted him to know how to manipulate and work in the bureaucracy.

Jack pulled out his phone and searched, snorting. "Yep, Director John Kuehnbaum. He's the same guy we met when we were here for Demon Spring a couple years ago."

She loosed a breath. That Demon Spring, like every one before it, Anya had made sure to be as far away from the action as possible. But it had been wasted effort. Bael could feel her just as strongly as she felt Diogo through their portal. He'd never lost track of her, no matter how far she'd run.

"Hey." Jack's voice brought her back to the present. "What is it?"

"Nothing." She shook the memories off herself like snow from her back. "Should we knock or just walk in?"

"I don't think you or I would get past the front desk," Jack said with a smile. "But his office light is on, and directors like him always work late. I'd guess he's alone up there. Why don't we pop in for a chat?"

Anya nodded, and the world slipped again, bringing them

into an expansive office. She'd Seen the director sitting at his desk before they arrived, and his surprised gasp echoed as the air stilled around her.

"W-what the hell?" John Kuehnbaum scrambled out of his chair. He had no weapons anywhere on his person or nearby, but Anya still moved to the door to bar it in case he had the ability to call for help. But a scan of the building told her there was minimal security—perhaps not the smartest for a man who was in the middle of pissing off every demon in the city.

"Evening, Director," Jack said, stepping forward in that affable, calm way he had.

"J—Jack Grenard? Is that you?" He glanced at Anya and licked his lips. "Is that who I think it is?"

"Don't worry," Jack said, waving his hand in the air. "We're not here to hurt you. Just want to have a chat about—what's the demon lord's name?"

"Farr," Anya said, crossing the room to stand next to Jack. "We hear you've decided to kill him."

Kuehnbaum cleared his throat. "What we do in ICDM is none of your business, Grenard. You're retired, from what I understand."

"It becomes our business when it impacts what we're trying to do," Jack said. "Namely, prevent all-out war. What do you think Farr's lieutenants will do when they find out you've decided to kill him?"

"Not much, I'd say," he said, slowly sinking into his chair. "As we've nearly taken them all out. Just a handful left—and

Farr himself. Soon there won't be a kappa left in the city." He half-smiled. "I hear you almost accomplished the same thing in Lisbon."

The tops of Anya's cheeks warmed as she tried to keep her face expressionless, but Jack wore a mask of indifference and confidence.

"You won't find him," Jack said softly. "He has gone to the Underworld."

"Then he'll be a demon lord without an empire," Kuehnbaum said. "Which, as I understand it, is a fate worse than death to them."

"And how long until a lilin or a nox shows up to take the kingdom?" Anya asked gently. "Or an ambitious kappa from the pod in San Francisco decides to come down the coast?"

"Then they'll suffer the same fate," Kuehnbaum said. "We are no longer in the business of tolerating demonic creatures in our city."

"And you're prepared for the consequences of that?" Jack said.

"What consequences?"

Anya glanced at Jack, unsure what he was talking about, but his gaze was even.

"Tabiko—she's the kappa boss since Mizuchi died—she's placed a bounty on your head," Jack said. "And I'd guess that if you manage to eradicate the kappa population here, the pod in San Francisco might just feel the need to make good on that request so she'll look kindly on them."

Kuehnbaum clicked his tongue. "Are you threatening me, Grenard?"

"Warning you," Jack said.

Kuehnbaum snorted and sat back in his chair. "Seems the rumors were right. You've decided to play for the demons." He glanced at Anya. "Don't blame you. She's pretty."

Jack's smile widened. "She is, but she's merely here to give me a ride. I'm here to tell you that we're trying to work a treaty between demons and humans so that all this killing can stop—and your little vendetta makes it difficult to make the demons believe that the humans are willing to play ball."

"These orders aren't mine," Kuehnbaum said. "I'm getting direction from the top. If you have a problem with it, you should speak with your grandfather, Grenard."

Jack's mask slipped. "Frank gave you this order?"

Anya watched him, hating the look of disbelief on his face and the smirk on the director's. This human thought he was impervious?

Show him what real fear looks like.

She marched up to the director and pulled her sword, pressing it against his neck. "You listen and you listen well, human. You exist in this world because I allow it, do you understand?"

He swallowed. "I'm not afraid of you."

"Then you're even more of an idiot than I thought," Anya said, pressing the blade harder to his neck. "You will cease all activities against demons in this city until *I* tell you otherwise.

And if you disobey me, I will show you just how torturous it is to defy the belu athtar." When he didn't flinch, she cracked a smile. "And when I'm finished with you, I'll find your family and do the same to them."

That earned her a hard swallow.

"Do not cross me," Anya said, stepping back. "And don't underestimate my cruelty either." She picked up a blank piece of paper and placed it on the desk. "Now write me a letter that says you'll stop killing kappas and I'll make sure your head stays on your body."

"That was certainly..." Jack cleared his throat when he and Anya slipped back down to the streets of LA. "Egregious."

"I told you, sometimes threats work," Anya said, casting him a look. "I didn't... I didn't mean it."

"Didn't you?"

She turned to him fully. "What would you have me do, Jack? I'm losing my grip on things. If these humans can't see reason, I may just have to bully them into compliance. At least for now, Tabiko won't have anything to complain about in this city." She looked down at the hastily handwritten letter in her hand. "Hopefully, we can hold him to his word."

Jack stared at her for a long time, tilting his head, and she almost thought he didn't believe her. But finally, he nodded. "Just... Maybe take it down a notch next time. Threatening a guy's family...?"

She blushed, looking at her sword. "I'll be sure to seek your approval before I threaten anyone else."

His fingers came to her chin and tilted it back up so she'd meet his gaze. "You don't need my approval, Anya. I'm just trying to help."

She actually smiled, but the voice in the back of her mind was clear.

He's holding you back.

CHAPTER TWENTY-EIGHT

Lotan awoke, bleary-eyed and unsure where he was, but his hands found Cam, and he was comforted as his mind sped up. They were in Freyja's castle, they'd gotten too drunk on lilin wine (he, two bottles, and she, a small sip that had made her an unusually attentive lover), and they'd spent the night making the most unique love he'd ever had. His head pounded, but he sat up anyway, taking care not to disturb his lady love.

He put his feet on the furry rug and rose slowly. Freyja would have a lovely pot of coffee and a large breakfast, and by mid-morning, he'd be right as rain.

Cam, on the other hand…

"Kill me," she murmured.

"Do you want me to get you some painkillers?"

"Mmph."

"Okay," Lotan said, kissing her pale forehead. "Stay here."

He found Cam's pants on the ground and retrieved the portal from the back pocket. He whispered his instructions into it and stepped through to an alley in the middle of Mexico City near a tienda. He adjusted his shirt and smoothed his pants before making a beeline for the small shop.

When he returned to Cam, laden with provisions, she was already up and consoling a teary-eyed Freyja, who was sobbing into her hands.

"What's wrong?" Lotan asked, putting the bag down on a nearby table.

"They've killed another one," Freyja said, wiping her cheeks. "Colette, my beloved demon lord in Paris. Thousands of demons are now without a home, and I fear…" She wiped her cheeks. "I fear the elokos in Versailles will be moving in to take the city for themselves." She snorted. "Can you imagine it? An eloko demon lord in charge of the city of love?" Her face darkened. "This will not stand."

"Okay, let's all take a breather," Cam said, sitting up slowly as some of her color returned. "Are you sure ICDM was responsible?"

"Of course I'm sure," she said with a scowl before turning to Cam. "Anya gave you a way to travel to the human world, did she not?"

Cam swallowed hard, looking at Lotan for a moment. But

Lotan knew lying would be much worse.

"Yes, she did," he said. "But is your presence what is needed in such a time? Perhaps Cam and I can visit the city and assess what happened. It's been centuries since you've been seen in the human realm. It might cause more chaos than you anticipated."

"But my poor demons..."

"Any who wish to return to Liley will be able to," Cam said. "We'll leave the portal open for them, and they can come here to become lilins again."

"I need to go," Freyja wore a mask of determination, and Lotan knew there would be no swaying her. "If only to show my lilins that their belu does care for their well-being and bring calm to the chaos."

"A belu showing up in Paris is going to be anything *but* calm, Lotan," Cam muttered once Freyja had left them. She popped three antacids and downed an entire blue bottle of electrolyte drink in one gulp and still looked unsettled. "We should get in touch with Jack and Anya. And maybe contact Frank so he doesn't scramble the jets when a belu demon shows up in a massive city."

Lotan sighed quietly. "And what's to say that Frank wasn't behind the killing of the demon? You said yourself they wanted you to eradicate the kappas in Lisbon."

"That was then, this is now," Cam said, but her tone lacked her usual conviction. "But regardless, better to be prepared. These guys have anti-lilin talismans. If they worked on Bael, they can work on Freyja."

She opened the portal and stepped through, returning a moment later with a black bag that jangled. Talismans.

"For whom?" Lotan asked.

"Lilins—and elokos," Cam said. "Might as well draw a couple more on before we get going."

"Freyja may be mistaken about the elokos coming to town," Lotan tried, taking the marker and drawing on her skin.

"And if she isn't, things are about to get rough there," Cam said, shaking her head. "And while I bet they were armed to the teeth against lilins, they probably have nothing to defend against elokos."

Lotan hoped that wasn't the case. Nevertheless, he helped her draw the anti-eloko talismans on her body, and, after a quick jump to Shanghai to "borrow" some anti-eloko weaponry and gear, they were ready to go. He put a sword on his hip that had anti-eloko talismans drawn on it, but he didn't think he'd need it. Cam had insisted, and since Lotan had rarely seen her this unsettled, he didn't argue.

Freyja returned shortly thereafter, wearing the same armor she'd worn during the Great Demon War. Her long, pale hair was swept back behind her pointed ears, and her sharp blue eyes had lost their mirth.

"Are we ready?" she asked.

Cam pursed her lips as if she wanted to argue more about Freyja coming to the human world, but perhaps even she knew it would be a futile effort. So she opened the portal once more, and asked it to send them to Paris.

Without waiting a beat, Freyja walked through, her sword clanging against her metal armor. Cam adjusted her satchel of talismans and macuahuitl and followed. Lotan, muttering to himself for strength and patience, brought up the rear.

Paris had always been a city full of life, but today, the streets were eerily empty. The cafes and shops down the street were boarded up, and the only movement seemed to be trash blowing from the sidewalks.

Freyja walked down the street, her shoulders back and gait confident, but there was confusion on her face. "Are we not in Paris?"

"We are," Cam said, looking at Lotan. "We should head toward ICDM headquarters. Maybe there we can get some answers."

But Lotan slowed, turning his head to the west. There was a powerful nox in the city. The power hummed the way it always did, made more prominent by the lack of other noxes in the surrounding hundred miles. And if Lotan could feel the nox, it could feel him—and perhaps come looking.

"Lotan?" Cam asked.

"There's a nox nearby," he replied.

Cam frowned. "Should we check it out?"

"No, I think it's best if we split up," he said. "You two head to ICDM and see what you can find out. I can deal with this nox myself."

Cam hesitated, but then nodded. "Fine, be careful."

Lotan nodded and kissed her gently. "You as well, my love."

And as she turned away, he transformed and bounded away down the street.

It was usually best to meet challenges head-on. One of the many lessons Yaotl had imparted to Lotan as a young boy. He wasn't sure why he was thinking of that particular one at this point, considering he'd been avoiding conflict for the past few weeks.

But things were beginning to spiral out of control. ICDM wasn't to be trusted—Lotan had assumed that from the beginning, but now they were actively trying to undermine this treaty effort. And if a nox was in Paris, most likely at the behest of Yaotl to stir up trouble, Lotan would see to it that it didn't happen.

He hoped.

But he was walking slowly, taking the opportunity to test out this new theory about his mother's magic. If he concentrated, the power he felt from the other nox wasn't just a feeling, it was almost a thread—the very same one Freyja had spoken about. He could do nothing with it except notice it, but even noticing it seemed like a win.

He found the source in the middle of Park Manceau. The expansive park would prove a spacious battleground for them to conduct their business. And thankfully, the humans had already been sheltering in place.

Mazatl stood in the center of the park, his hands clasped

behind his back as he waited for Lotan to approach. Lotan transformed back into his human form and walked slowly toward this nox, marveling at how much more power he seemed to have now. He and Yaotl had been busy.

"I'm surprised you came," Mazatl said. "And that you still find it within your taste to use your nox magic. I thought it was beneath you now."

"Not quite yet," Lotan said. "What are you doing here?"

"Passing through."

Lotan clicked his tongue. The same answer Yaotl gave when Lotan had found him in Geneva. Somehow, it didn't seem like a coincidence.

"This city is in turmoil. It doesn't need your interference."

"I think it does. The humans seem to think it's their job to police us, to decide who is in charge and who isn't," Mazatl said. "They need a re-education."

"And how many innocent lives will be lost in the process?" Lotan said. "How many noxes have you killed to take their power for yourself?"

"They wouldn't have had to die if they'd just accepted Yaotl as their leader. But they stupidly maintained their allegiance to you." His smile widened. "Deaths that could've been avoided had you shown deference to the true leader of the noxes."

"Then perhaps it's time I regain control of the pack," Lotan said, allowing his anger to feed the magic in his veins.

"You wish to fight me again?" Mazatl said. "After it went so poorly for you the last time?"

"Perhaps now I'm willing to try."

Mazatl chuckled and took a step forward. "I hope you aren't expecting your athtar pet to come for you again." He pulled a necklace filled with coins from beneath his shirt. "I doubt she can even see us right now."

Lotan swallowed his fear, regretting not staying with Freyja and Cam. They should have counted on Yaotl getting his hands on anti-athtar talismans—and Mazatl had enough to keep Anya at least a block away.

He was on his own.

"I don't need her," Lotan said, his power growing as the wolf inside him itched to come out. "Not to deal with the likes of you."

His transformation happened not a moment too soon, as Mazatl had done the same and launched his wolf form onto Lotan's. Lotan struggled to get the upper hand, but as soon as he pushed himself on top, Mazatl would push back, and they'd tumble. Mazatl wasn't just stronger physically, but his magic pressed in around Lotan's.

"Just like back on that island," Mazatl said,

"Not exactly," Lotan said, swiping his leg against Mazatl's to break the hold.

Mazatl wasn't fazed, and his snapping jaws landed on Lotan's shoulder, ripping a chunk out and spitting it into the street. Lotan's whole body shook with pain, and the exertion of keeping his wolf form in the face of Mazatl's ever-strengthening hold. As a nox, Lotan wouldn't succumb to the fear magic, but his would lose its strength, and with it, his wolf form. Mazatl would easily be able to capture him then.

"You are a cheap imitation of a belu," he snarled. "Destined to never be quite good enough."

Lotan struggled, reaching for that thread that existed between him and Mazatl. It was so strong in his mind's eye, but it was just a thread. Lotan could still do nothing with it.

But he was running out of options, so with all his strength, he reached across the connection. As spots danced in his vision, he thought he saw something tangible, something he could hold onto. Unsure what it was, he latched onto it and yanked it back toward himself.

Even in wolf form, Mazatl's eyes bulged as Lotan pulled. The magic was powerful, but it was familiar to Lotan. He yanked harder, finding strength with every inch of Mazatl's magic that made its way back to him. Lotan pushed Mazatl off of him, his body growing larger as the nox magic swelled in his veins, and Mazatl's growing smaller until he reverted to his human form.

"W-what are you doing?" Mazatl cried. "How is this possible?"

Lotan didn't respond, slimming down to human and walking up to Mazatl. The anti-eloko sword hung from his hip, and Lotan pulled it out slowly. The talismans wouldn't help, but Mazatl was so weak, the blade itself would be enough.

"You have betrayed our kind and your prince," Lotan said softly. "And this is your punishment."

He swung, the sword connecting with Mazatl's flesh and

severing the connection. There was no release of energy, no massive rush of power that came back to Lotan. He had taken most of it for himself, anyway.

But as he stared at the body of a demon he'd grown up with, one who'd been like a brother to him, and yet had taken him captive and made his life miserable, he found a deep sadness growing in his chest. He'd never killed a fellow nox before, and he hoped he never would again.

Looking up at the sky, he didn't think he'd be that lucky.

CHAPTER TWENTY-NINE

Cam hurried along the streets, cognizant of how quiet everything was and how *wrong*. It felt like the weeks after a Demon Spring when the city had been overrun and most of the humans had left.

"This certainly isn't what I was expecting," Freyja said with a frown. "Where are all the people? What is that?"

She pointed at a streetlight that hung above them.

"When's the last time you were topside?" Cam asked.

"Hm..." She tapped her finger against her delicate chin. "I don't recall. But it's been a few hundred years. Bael didn't like the belus stealing his thunder." She snorted. "Petty fool."

Cam plucked a newspaper out of the trash and struggled to

decipher the French. But based on context, she got the gist. The city had enacted Demon Spring protocols—the first time in over 300 years. Everyone who could should've evacuated. And those who couldn't needed to shelter in place.

"They're preparing for an onslaught," she said, tossing the newspaper back in the trash.

"I'd say so," Freyja said with a frown. "They brought this upon themselves. Colette was a gentle soul who never hurt a fly."

Cam had to bite her tongue. She didn't know too much about the Parisian demon lord specifically, but if she was lord of a city as large as Paris and was old as Freyja said she was, then she was no angel. There were probably thousands of lilins who'd been coerced into transforming against their will, and thousands more over the years who'd just been killed. But somehow, Cam didn't think Freyja would want to hear that right now.

Cam slowed her pace as she came to the Paris Division headquarters, a beautiful glass building that shone in the sun like a beacon. But in the plaza directly outside, there were hundreds, if not a thousand, ICDM agents, armed to the teeth and wearing full body armor.

"Well?" Freyja asked, looking at Cam and reaching for her sword. "Do we fight?"

"No," Cam said quickly. "Look, I'm going to go in and...see what I can find out. Why not find the lilins—"

"There are none in the city," Freyja said, her eyes flashing. "Which is why I'm here."

Cam sighed, trying to find the words to convince Freyja that walking into the heavily armed group of Division agents, most of whom were probably armed with anti-lilin talismans, wouldn't go well. And if she thought things were rough with the Paris lord gone, Cam could only imagine the chaos if the belu lilin were killed.

And what ICDM might do if they realized they could do such a thing to a belu.

"I believe we can reason with them," Cam said. "At least find out who ordered the mission."

"What will that do for us?"

"We can tell *that* person not to kill any more lilins," Cam said, thinking quickly. "You've got a large community in Amsterdam, don't you?"

Her smile warmed, as if thinking of them. "Yes."

"Then we need to ensure that *those* lilins aren't harmed," Cam said. "We can control the snake if we can get to the head. Let me handle that."

"And if you can't?"

Cam swallowed, unwilling to admit failure. "I'll handle it. Just stay back. Ten minutes, that's all I'm asking for."

Freyja sniffed. "Fine. Ten minutes."

Straightening her shoulders, Cam turned to walk toward the crowd. She wasn't even halfway across the square before the guns rose. The agent spoke in rapid-fire French, and Cam held her hands up, waiting patiently for him to finish, hoping Freyja didn't see this as an opportunity to intervene.

"Director Macarro," she said, pulling her badge from

beneath her shirt. "Institute for Advanced Weaponry."

They shared a look then stepped away and allowed her to pass. Cam was glad they didn't have scanners, because she wasn't sure her badge still worked. But in a time like this, protocol was bottom of the list of things to worry about.

She found the command-and-control tent and, yet again, showed her badge to those guarding it, who had to check with those inside before granting her access. She waited with what she hoped was the impatient look of someone who should be there before they came back and let her in.

"Director Macarro," an agent came to greet her. "We are in the middle of a crisis. What do you want?"

"I'm here because of the crisis," Cam said. "On whose orders did you kill the demon lord?"

The man shifted. "I thought you were a Director. If you don't know, then it's not your—"

"It was the Council, wasn't it?" Cam said with a soft sigh under her breath. "You have no idea what you've started."

"I think we have a pretty good idea," he said. "The lilins from Luxembourg are amassing on the French border."

"And what about the elokos?" Cam asked. "Are you ready for them?"

"Elokos?" He blanched. "Why would elokos come here?"

She ran her hand over her face. "The elokos are coming to claim the city. And you might also have a nox running around, probably with the elokos. Are you ready for all that?"

A lieutenant came jogging up, a worried look on his face,

and spoke to his superior quickly. The agent looked at Cam then turned away abruptly, barking orders. All around Cam, the agents hopped into action, grabbing their guns and gear and—

"Oh, shit."

Cam turned and darted out of the tent, her heart sinking. Freyja stood in the center of a group of agents, holding her sword aloft. Luckily, no one had been killed yet, but she looked ready to start.

She spoke in French to the agents, her blue eyes fiery and unforgiving. It was easy to forget that she was the goddess of love, and consider her more the goddess of wrath.

Cam pushed through the crowd, muttering curses to herself about the brilliance of bringing an irate belu to an already tense situation. When she finally broke through to the center, she took a hesitant step forward.

"Freyja," Cam said, her pulse pounding at her throat. "I told you—"

"I am the belu lilin, sweet Cam," Freyja said, wearing none of her usual patient smile. "There is nothing these humans can do to hurt me."

"There is," Cam said. "They have the talisman magic."

She scoffed. "Pathetic attempts. I—"

Something hit her in the arm, sending a spray of blood from a fresh wound. She stared at it curiously for a moment, her brow furrowing as if she were in pain. Then she pulled a knife from the folds of her armor and popped the offending item from her body. It landed with a clang on the ground.

"Now," Freyja said, straightening. "I would like to speak to the person responsible for killing my beloved spawn. They will pay for their crime, or I will make them pay."

A cacophony of cocking guns echoed from all sides, and Cam's heart leapt to her throat. One bullet, sure. But they were armed to the gills. Freyja wouldn't survive this. And somewhere, deep inside, Cam had a feeling that if the Council knew they had the ability to wipe out an entire demonic race in one fell swoop, they would.

"Freyja," Cam said, inching closer. "This is unwinnable."

"They are humans," she said, catching the gaze of the leader who was barking orders. "They should fear me."

A whoosh of energy drew the hairs up on the back of Cam's neck, and Anya appeared in the middle of the circle of agents. "All of you, stand *down*."

Her power radiated in waves, sending an ill feeling to the bottom of Cam's stomach. The look on her face was eerily similar to the one Bael had worn just before he began slaughtering people. For a brief moment, she worried more for the hundred or so Division forces standing around them.

But Anya turned to the belu lilin; the intensity was perhaps a show for her. "Peace, Freyja. This is no place for you."

"They have murdered my spawn, Anat," she said. "This is my fight, and I will not have you interfering."

"This is no one's fight," Anya replied. "Have you forgotten the treaty we're working toward?"

Freyja pointed at those gathered. "They clearly have. There

was no reason for killing my spawn other than spite and evilness. If you won't prove your loyalty to us, I will have to take matters into my own hands."

Anya's face flashed, and Cam swallowed as she took a step toward the belu lilin. "I am *not* to be tested. I am the belu athtar, and no demon, least of all a lesser demon such as yourself, should demand a loyalty test of me. I am here so this world can know peace, and if you aren't going to help me, perhaps I will have to replace you with someone who will."

Freyja's eyes grew wide. "How *dare* you? You are not Bael."

"I am the one with his power," Anya said. "And you've done enough today."

Whatever Freyja said was lost on the wind as Anya's magic sent her back to Liley. Cam had a feeling the lilin would be spitting mad when she realized what had happened, but it was better than the alternative.

"As for you," Anya said, turning to those gathered.

Cam started. "Anya, don't—"

But before she could finish, every single gun had been removed from the hands of the ICDM agents and broken in half. Their gear, too, had been removed and thrown into a pile on the other end of the square—and set on fire.

"Leave my sight," Anya snapped. "*Now.*"

Bewildered, the agents took hesitant steps backward, nervous chatter rising from the ranks. The agent-in-command Cam had spoken to in the tent pushed to the front, his armor and helmet missing, barking orders to the retreating army. Cam guessed he was telling them to stay in formation—but they were clearly more interested in self-preservation.

"I think you're losing your army," Anya said, nodding behind her with the ghost of a smile. "You have earned mercy from me today. But if I hear of you killing any more demons in this city without my permission, I will not be so kind. Understand?"

Whether he did or didn't, Cam didn't know because he disappeared from sight, perhaps back inside the building. Anya stared at the space he'd just vacated for a moment before turning around, her expression resuming the familiar sort of discomfort that Cam was used to.

"How was that?"

"A bit heavy-handed but passable," Jack said from behind.

Cam jumped, turning. "Where did you come from?"

"We were coming to find you to let you know that LA is in turmoil, but it appears so is Paris," Jack said. "Where's Lotan?"

"He said he was looking for eloko activity on the edge of the city," Cam said, running a hand over her face.

Anya furrowed her brow as her eyes turned black. "Looks like he found some kind of activity. Doesn't look eloko, though."

Before Cam could ask, she was whisked across town to a large square. There she saw two figures on the ground, one in a pool of blood with his head separated from his body, and the other…

"Lotan!" she cried, running over to him. He was a mess,

covered in blood with his clothes ripped in places. But he opened his eyes into hers, and smiled.

"Fancy finding you here, my love."

"What the hell happened to you?" Cam asked, checking him over head to toe as Jack and Anya looked on.

"Mazatl," Lotan said, sitting up.

Jack swore under his breath then looked up as the sound of a helicopter echoed over the square. "Unless we want to have this discussion with a few hundred of our closest ICDM friends, we should probably return to Ath-kur."

"C'mon," Anya said, looping Lotan's arm around her shoulders. "We'll get you home and healed up, then we can try to figure out what sort of clusterfuck we've got on our hands."

CHAPTER THIRTY

Jack had never seen Anya heal someone, and even after he watched every scrape and bruise on Lotan's body rapidly turn from grotesque to invisible, he still wasn't sure he believed it. But when it was done, Anya sank down on the couch next to him, leaning into him for comfort.

"We have a problem," she said.

"I'd say," Cam said. "ICDM should not have approved that kill."

"They're approving kills all over the world," Anya said. "Tabiko just asked me to bring her the head of the LA Division Director because he's targeting the demons, and she thinks he's going to kill the demon lord."

"You didn't, did you?" Cam asked, looking somewhat horrified.

"No," Jack said. "But he told us that his orders to kill the demon lord came directly from Frank."

Lotan made a noise as he sat up. "Mazatl was not forthcoming as to why he was in Paris, but my guess is that he was taking advantage of the chaos to recruit people to Yaotl's cause."

"Which is?" Jack asked.

"Unclear, but my guess is that he's still looking to take Bael's spot as king of the demons," Lotan said.

"He'll have a hard time doing that," Anya said with a scoff.

"The noxes have the anti-athtar talismans," Lotan said, meeting her gaze. "Can you See Yaotl right now?"

"I'm sure," Anya said, but as her eyes darkened, her lips parted in surprise. "Wait... Where is he? Where is La Madriguera?"

"Probably surrounded by talismans," Lotan said. "Mazatl had a whole necklace full of them."

"He what?" Anya said. "How did they get their hands on anti-athtar talismans?"

"There were plenty of them after the Great Demon War," Lotan said. "It wouldn't surprise me if Yaotl managed to secure a few for himself.

"But Freyja didn't seem bothered by the lilin talisman," Cam said. "They struck her with one and she shrugged it off like it was nothing."

"One," Anya said. "It's a good thing I got there when I did."

Jack waved his hand. "We have some serious issues: Tabiko wants to declare war on the LA Division, Freyja is ready to massacre everyone in Paris, and who knows what Biloko is up to, but my guess is Yaotl isn't far behind. Meanwhile, ICDM is giving the order to eradicate demons around the world. So I'd say our little treaty idea is on its last legs, if not already dead."

He waited for someone to say something, but the grim faces around the living room said enough.

Anya sat back and sighed. "I should go talk with Freyja. I'm sure she's pissed. Last thing we need is for her to defect to Yaotl's side."

"And we should go to Geneva," Cam said to Jack. "At the very least, get some assurances that the bloodletting will stop. Maybe ask for a six-week moratorium until we can get things under control. Unless they want all the belus showing up and starting shit."

Jack sighed. "I don't think we'll get that, but it's worth a shot. I don't think we have any other options."

"You're going to have to take the train," Anya said, looking up at the ceiling. "Because they've surrounded Geneva with talismans. My portals won't work. The closest I can get you is…" She winced. "An hour outside the city."

"Great," Cam said. "That doesn't bode well for us."

"Nothing does, lately." Jack rose gravely. "But the only way we can get any kind of peace in this world is if we drag all these parties to the table—willingly or otherwise."

Jack stood on the train station platform, acutely aware of how privileged they'd been with Anya's magic to flit to and from places instantaneously. Beside him, Cam kept checking the time on her phone and tapping her foot against the ground.

Jack nudged her gently. "We'll figure this out—"

"No, not about that. About Anya," Cam said, looking to Jack. "She looked terrifying when she arrived. Like Bael. And the way she spoke to Freyja. They were supposed to be friends."

Jack licked his lips. When they'd arrived at the scene, Anya had made him wait in the alley and told him she'd handle it—and she had. But he couldn't shake the image of her anger spiking when Freyja demanded a loyalty test, and the words she'd all but spat at her closest ally. It was the second such demand for loyalty that Anya had received in as many days, and Jack was getting the feeling Anya had grown tired of them.

The train arrived, saving Jack from having to answer, and they hopped on board. Cam fidgeted, as she did when she was nervous, and Jack stared out the window, worrying.

"But what if you just let demons and humans keep each other in line? What if you didn't have to hold the world together?"

What had seemed like a foregone conclusion a mere day ago was now slipping away. He'd been stupid to assume Frank wouldn't continue to pursue ICDM's eradication goals, but he'd underestimated how ready they were to live in a world without demons. As much as he didn't want to admit it, he was starting to fear that Anya was the glue that was going to keep this world together.

And if she was…what did that mean for them?

ICDM headquarters was surrounded by a cadre of agents,

much like Paris had been. Cam flashed her badge to get them through the perimeter, but once they got to the building, they were stopped at the front desk.

"Your badge doesn't work," the clerk said. "Says expired."

"Clearly not," Cam said, looking at the expiration date on the card.

"System says your account was terminated."

She sighed and looked at Jack. "Guess that means I've been fired."

"Fine," Jack said, pulling out his phone. "We'll call Frank."

He reached Frank's assistant, who was apologetic and promised to be down in a moment to retrieve them. The clerk was wary but allowed them to stay in the lobby until they were retrieved and gave them a pair of visitor's badges—but asked Cam to surrender her badge.

"This is ridiculous," Cam said, handing it over. "I'm sure it's just a mistake."

"I mean, you did offer your resignation," Jack said with a half-smile. "So maybe María accepted it."

Cam shook her head. "Jack, none of this is good."

"No, it's not."

Frank's deputy arrived, greeting them more warmly than Jack was expecting. He offered no explanation for Cam's lack of access, but merely engaged Jack in conversation about his parents and their health. Jack, who hadn't called home in a couple of weeks, offered the latest he knew and swallowed his guilt about not calling his parents more.

The elevator doors opened to Frank's level, and the deputy led them past the security guard and into the US Division Councilman support staff offices. There was a hum of activity as the computer screens showed aerial views in different cities around the world—including LA and Lisbon. Jack even saw one newsreel featuring Anya and Freyja's showdown.

They reached the conference room, and the doors opened to reveal not just Frank but María and several other Councilmembers. Not enough for a quorum, but enough.

"Ah, Jackie, Cam," Frank said, rising to greet them but without his usual jovial smile. "Good to see you. I hope you didn't encounter too much trouble downstairs."

Cam glanced at María for a moment but forced a smile onto her face. "None at all. Thanks for meeting with us."

"Of course, of course," Frank said. He introduced the others in the room as Councilman Lavinge from Europe and Acting Director Shu from the Weapons Division in Shanghai. To her credit, Cam didn't flinch when they mentioned the current vacancy at the director job.

"There have been some developments," María began after all were settled.

"Yes, there have," Cam said. "And none of them have been good. ICDM has been picking off demons, and the belus are starting to notice. They aren't happy."

"Demon lords die every day," María replied evenly. "What do the belus care?"

"They care because it's against the previously established

rules of engagement," Jack said, his voice taking on an edge. "And I think you know that. It's the same as what happened in Lisbon."

"Lisbon is fine," Frank said. "The kappa population is a third of what it once was. Our local Lisbon division is keeping tabs on things and so far, transformations have been way down."

"Unwilling transformations," Cam said. "I bet every single one of Solomao and Edite's demons have been re-transformed."

"Not to our knowledge—" Levinge started.

"And your knowledge is all-encompassing?" Jack asked.

"It's as good as yours, I'm sure," Frank said, brushing off Jack's accusatory tone. "Perhaps a little better."

"Ours includes the present kappa leader, Tabiko," Jack said. "And Doroteia herself, who, last time we saw her, was practically brimming with power. I'd guess she's probably as strong as Gualter was before he died in the Great Demon War."

"And is safely in the Underworld," Frank said. "Which brings me to our proposal."

"Proposal?" Cam quirked a brow at Jack. "You mean the treaty."

"I think all parties can agree that this treaty was ill-advised," Frank said.

"Because you keep doing things to ruin it," Jack said. "Freyja was on board, but as you probably saw in Paris, she's furious with ICDM. If it wasn't for Anya, you would've had three hundred dead Paris agents."

"Or, we would have eradicated an entire demon race," María

said. "Which has become our goal."

Jack sat back, sharing a look of shock with Cam. "They won't let you."

"I've been waiting for this havoc that your athtar promised, and clearly, nothing of it has happened. Cities haven't been overrun with demons. The lords have stayed dead. And the thousands of reverted humans have accepted their fates."

"Or have you just killed any who felt otherwise?" Jack asked.

"No," María said with a swift shake of her head.

"That's a lie," Cam said. "Freyja told us you were killing reverted demons who'd sought out a new sire in Paris."

María cleared her throat. "Then perhaps they shouldn't have sought out another demon."

"You know Anya's not the only one with the ability to traverse worlds," Cam said. "If Freyja allies herself with Yaotl, you'll really be in trouble."

"She, like all other demons, is susceptible to the talisman magic," Frank said, gently. "You told us yourself that even Bael felt their effects."

"Felt, yeah, stopped, no," Jack said. "He still managed to kill Mizuchi."

"And speaking of that, why have you put athtar talismans all over the city?" Cam asked, tilting her head to the side. "Do you not trust us or something?"

"No," María said. "Because your alliances have shifted. Your athtar is a danger to this world as long as she sets foot on it. And she would be well-advised to stay in her own world if she knows what's good for her."

Jack shifted, the hair on his neck standing up. "Is that a threat?"

"We're not threatening anyone," Frank said, holding up his hands in something that looked like peace, but no one else at the table seemed to agree with him.

"You're just giving the order to kill belus," Jack said.

"And why is that bad?" María asked. "They've been responsible for suffering since the moment Bael appeared in this world."

"It doesn't have to be all or nothing," Cam said. "If you can give us six weeks without another murder, and we can get the belus on board—"

"I think, perhaps, it's time for you to step back from this effort," Frank said. "ICDM is capable of protecting humanity without your help."

Cam sat back, looking at Jack and shaking her head. But before she could say anything, there was an urgent knock on the door. Frank's deputy was back and based on the wide-eyed look, whatever he had to say was important.

"You need to take a look at this, boss," he said. "May I?"

Frank nodded, and the deputy walked in turning on the television. News choppers hovered over Lisbon, which seemed to be on fire. Thousands of people flooded the streets, but it was hard to tell what had happened to send them outside.

"What's going on?" Frank said, looking to his deputy.

"It looks to be an army of kappas and elokos," he said. "They appeared out of nowhere and started destroying things."

"Get the Portugal Division head on the phone, as well as the Lisbon Division head," Frank said, rising out of his seat. "I want to know everything that's going on and what we've got to fix the problem."

He hurried out of the room, leaving Cam, Jack, and María to watch the quiet havoc on the television. Jack swore under his breath, and Cam could barely tear her eyes away. The scene was something out of Cam's worst nightmares. Civilians ran for their lives, some of them barely getting five steps before a kappa or eloko jumped out of an alley. But they weren't interested in transforming the humans—at least not from what Cam could see. This was a slaughter, plain and simple.

"So you were saying…?" Jack said, breaking the silence.

"Don't be snide," María snapped. "These are merely growing pains. We will quell this little uprising and bring things back to normal."

"Alternatively," Jack said, rising, "you could've done as we asked, taken a knee, and let us get things in order. I doubt it's a coincidence that it's elokos and kappas down there—they probably got the go-ahead from their belus."

"And who brought them to Lisbon?" María asked. "It looks to me like—"

Whatever she said was lost in a large explosion, and Cam's entire world went black.

CHAPTER THIRTY-ONE

Anya attempted to reach Liley but was stopped at the border between their worlds. She wrote a letter and tossed it across, waiting for one of Freyja's messengers to retrieve it, but they never did. Clearly, Anya was no longer welcome in her dear friend's homeland. One day, perhaps over a bottle of wine, Anya would apologize and try to get Freyja to understand the gravity of the situation she had found herself in, and why it had been so important for her to leave. But for now, there was just hurt.

She replayed the words she'd said in a quick fit of anger. They'd come from somewhere deep inside, and she'd almost watched herself say them.

You were correct. No loyalty test is required of the athtar belu.

"Hush."

The voice had been whispering in her ear since Jack and Cam had left over an hour ago. Lotan had returned to his room to sleep off his ordeal, saying little. The boy clearly hadn't killed many people in his life, and the haunted look in his eyes was almost innocently sweet. Anya could've offered some platitude about how it got easier, but she didn't really think it did.

With nothing but time, Anya rose to pace the living room, looking at her phone and hoping for an update, as it was the only way to communicate. Anya couldn't See Jack or Cam, and if anything went wrong, she'd be blind to it. ICDM had begun playing by their own rules lately, and she didn't trust that her humans wouldn't end up in prison.

"Heard anything?" Lotan was up.

"No," Anya said. "Hoping no news is good news."

They stood in silence for a moment before Lotan spoke up again. "Do you think I might ask you a favor? While we wait for news?"

"Depends on what it is."

He smiled. "We have ventured back in time plenty, but I would ask...perhaps, if you're up for it, and if you're not, I understand—"

"Out with it."

"I would like to see the moment my mother was given her powers."

"Why?"

"Perhaps it might hold the secret to finding out how to rid

myself of it," Lotan said. "Or maybe... Maybe I just want to see her as a human."

"I don't know if I can go back that far," Anya said with a dramatic sigh. "But we might as well attempt it while Jack isn't here to bitch about it."

She rested her hand on his shoulder and time began to move backward. She surfed the time river until she found Xo's magic five hundred years ago then she adjusted the proverbial sails and went even farther back. The events of history passed in a blur, too fast for her to process, but once the magic moved to the human world, she abruptly stopped.

"Where are we?" Lotan asked, craning his neck. Jungle trees crowded the canopy above, and humidity was thick on the air. Birds chirped in the distance, and rustled the trees, but otherwise, it was quiet.

Anya didn't answer right away because the answer would show itself. A young woman walked out of the forest holding a basket in one hand. Lotan's breath hitched in his chest, and Anya's heart twisted at the way he stared at her.

The human Xo was clearly in search of something. "I hear you. I hear you," she whispered in a language that was long dead. Anya's heart went into her throat. Was Xo hearing the voice calling to her, the same way Anya had heard Bael's voice?

"Hear what?" Lotan asked, looking at Anya.

Before she could answer, Xo took a wrong step, and the world collapsed under her feet. Anya drew them down into the crevasse where she'd fallen. She was injured, but alive.

"What—" Lotan began, but Anya held up her hand.

Mot, Lotan's father, appeared at the top of the crevasse. Then, full of concern, the still-human shimmied down to the bottom of the hole to find his love. He gently cradled her head, whispering her name as she moaned incoherently.

Anya watched Lotan drink them in like a man in the desert.

"I'm glad I could show you this," she said, after a moment. "They loved each other very much."

"Have you ever..." Lotan turned to her. "Have you ever gone back to see your daughter?"

"No," Anya replied with a heavy shake of her head. "I'm not... I don't think I could handle that."

Lotan wrenched his gaze from her. "What is that?"

There was a darkness beyond Xo's body. It was faint at first but began to glow—the black nox magic. It crept toward Xo, as a frightened Mot looked on, waving at it with his hands. But it slipped through her fingers, up her arm, absorbing into her body. The magic pulsed inside of her, transforming her into the fearsome nox demon who would one day give birth to Lotan.

And as Mot held her, they both disappeared from sight—to the Underworld.

"Follow them," Lotan said.

Anya rested her hand on his shoulder and they slipped forward in time, albeit slowly enough that Lotan could watch his mother and father explore and build the world they had made for themselves. Xo was just as caring as Mot, and they were a beautiful team. Years passed.

But then, Anya slowed time to real-time.

"Bael."

Lotan looked to where Anya was pointing and narrowed his eyes as Bael appeared in the forest. He looked raggedy, with longer hair and a beard, but his eyes were as sharp and calculating as always. He walked into the clearing as if he owned the place.

"Hello," Bael said in a language Anya only barely understood. "Can you understand me?"

Mot rose, defensively standing in front of Xo. "What do you want?"

"Merely to check on my lovely noxes," he said. "My name is Bael, and I'm the one who gave you these powers."

Xo glanced at her husband, distrust on her face, then back at Bael. "You gave me these powers?"

"How?" Mot asked.

"I'm the belu athtar," he said, bowing. "The all-powerful being and demon lord of the five realms, including this one."

"That's odd," Xo said, rising to her feet. "We've been here for years and haven't seen you."

"Well, I have been keeping my distance, allowing you to enjoy these gifts I've given you."

"It was not your gift," Mot said with a steely look. "I do not recall seeing you in the cave where Xo fell."

Lotan stifled a laugh when the corner of Bael's lip turned upward. "You have simply forgotten."

"No, I didn't," Mot said. "I remember exactly what

happened the day my wife was consumed by the magic."

Bael cleared his throat and clicked his tongue. "So your wife was the chosen one? Then how did you come into this magic?"

"I gave it to him," Xo replied. "Why?"

"How did you do it?"

She smiled. "I thought you said you were an all-powerful God?"

Bael clenched his fists. Anya's red flags went up, even though she was just a ghost in the past and Bael couldn't hurt her. But old habits died hard.

"*How*?"

Xo narrowed her eyes, clearly not liking Bael's tone. "I think it's time for you to leave, stranger."

Bael made a noise and reached for the sword on his hip, but before he could advance, he took a step backward. Then another. Then another.

"What is...happening?"

"I've told you that you are no longer welcome," Xo said, giving him a smirk. "And thus you are being expelled from our land."

Bael's cries of protest were lost on the breeze then there was silence as Mot and Xo resumed their daily activity.

"No wonder he hated my parents," Lotan said. "Anya—"

But Anya grabbed his shoulder and sent them further back in time. Bael had always said *he'd* been the one to give the belus their powers, and Anya had always thought it was his usual bluster. But there was something in his voice, in his eyes. A truth that she hadn't really seen before.

Anya steered through the years, past the moment where Xo took the magic, and back to when it appeared in the Underworld. Back to wherever it had come from.

She stepped out of the river into an unfamiliar world. The jungle was gone, replaced by a marshy river that resembled Kappanchi, except for the bright blue sky and desert surrounding them. The water rushed from horizon to horizon, an unending stream of crystal-clear glass.

"Where are we?" Lotan asked, looking around.

"The noxlands." Though it certainly didn't look like the noxlands she knew.

"This is..." Lotan began but stopped when movement appeared in the reeds. A man with dark, smooth skin ran through them, wearing a strip of cloth around his waist. He splashed into the river and rushed across, glancing behind him in terror as he did.

"Who is that?" Lotan asked.

"This is... This is the creature who had the nox magic before your mother," Anya said, the words coming from her mouth, but making no sense. The belus were the originals. So who or what the hell was this?

Before the man could take another step, Bael appeared on the other side of the river, wearing much the same clothes—or lack thereof. His hair was long and unkempt, and his beard extended past his chin. But those same piercing eyes that had captured Anya on the first day they'd met were furiously watching the man in the river.

"There is nowhere to run, nox," he said in a language Anya understood—perhaps thanks to her athtar magic. It was ancient.

"You are a murderer," the nox said, stepping backward. "I saw you kill the lilin and eloko. Did you kill the kappa too? We have lived together these many thousands of years—"

"And your time has come to an end, just like the nox before you," Bael said.

"Why? Because we've seen through your lies?" he snarled. "You have no ownership over this magic."

"See, that's where you're wrong," Bael said, walking into the river. "When I strike you down, I will be able to hand-select the human who will take it after you. And I will find someone much more..." He smiled. "Amenable. A new group who will swear fealty to only me. Who will be grateful for the magic I give them."

"You?" He scoffed. "You are no better than us."

"Yes, but they won't know that."

The nox jumped backward. "The only way you'll get this magic is if you kill me. But what if I don't let you?"

"What are you babbling on about?"

The nox took another step backward onto land, and Anya recognized the other side as the Nullius. "You can't follow me here, can you?"

Bael's eyes darkened. "What are you doing? It will kill you."

"Perhaps." But he smiled and closed his eyes. "But at least you won't get my gift."

The nox took another step backward, and the magic rippled from his body in a way Anya had never seen before. It was akin to the way the magic had come into her own body, the accepting of this gift. But it almost seemed...

"I give this gift back to the Gods," he said, before a light flashed. And as he slumped to the ground, he was human.

On the other side of the river, Bael watched the ball of nox magic fly backward toward the Nullius, back to the source of demonic magic. Within minutes, it would be regurgitated and appear in the human world for Xo to stumble upon.

The human stirred, blinking in the bright sun and looked at Bael. "Who are you?"

But the strain of holding them there in time finally got to Anya, and she lost her footing. She and Lotan lurched back to the present time. She landed on her knees, heart pounding as she processed what she'd seen.

She was no longer fatigued by the journey, the questions swirling in her mind. Bael was older than all the original demons, who weren't even original demons. How many had there been before Mizuchi, Xo, Freyja, and Biloko?

"So that's it, then," Lotan said. "I can just...choose to give it up."

She looked at him, taking a moment to realize what he was talking about. "Your magic? It can't be that simple. You've been trying for weeks."

She jumped when she felt Diogo arriving. Their connection was agitated, and he was scared—honestly scared. When he arrived, Anya could almost predict what he was going to say.

"Demons are overrunning Lisbon. We need your help."

CHAPTER THIRTY-TWO

Lotan's head was still spinning from his time in the past. Based on Anya's perplexed expression, she was similarly confused.

"What? Demons have overrun Lisbon?" Anya said, blinking at Diogo.

"Noxes, elokos, kappas," Diogo said, giving Lotan a look as if he were to blame. "They came from everywhere, almost crawling out of the walls. They've taken the humans' little demon-hunting headquarters, and it wasn't pretty. And worse still—they have talismans." He looked at Anya. "Those that work against athtars."

"Yaotl," Lotan said with a furious shake of his head. "So this is his play? Lisbon."

But Anya's eyes had gone dark and her brow furrowed. "It's not just Lisbon. Cities around the world have gone dark. Mexico City, Los Angeles, Paris." She swallowed. "Unless ICDM has blanketed the world in anti-athtar talismans... I think we can safely bet that this is Yaotl's doing."

"What about Cam and Jack?" Lotan asked.

Anya licked her lips. "Geneva is a black hole to me. But Yaotl would be a fool to attack them there."

Would he? Lotan disagreed but didn't want to say so.

"We need to split up. Jack and Cam are capable of handling Geneva," Anya said, though the concern on her face said otherwise. "The other cities, though, they're defenseless."

"What do we do?" Diogo asked.

"You stay here," Anya said, smiling at him like a mother might to her frightened child. "You are not a warrior, so you might just get yourself hurt."

"They have the talismans, though," Lotan said. "You won't be able to use your powers against them."

"I can still wield a sword," Anya said, looking much like the Lady of the Mountain from lore. "And that will have to be enough for today."

Lotan rose, feeling a sense of dread and responsibility. "I will find Yaotl. This needs to end today."

She stared at him, her brow furrowed. "Are you sure you want to fight him alone?"

"There is no other way," Lotan said, gravely. "If I'm

successful, the noxes should fall. That should take care of at least a third of the attackers."

"The kappas will have to be put down," Anya said. "Tabiko cannot control them. And I doubt Biloko will listen to reason at this point."

"He will if Yaotl is dead, and you are the scariest demon on the playground," Lotan said with a half-smile. "Now go."

Anya nodded at him once, gripping his shoulder. "Good luck. And remember..." She licked her lips. "You are your mother's son. Don't ever let anyone tell you differently."

Lotan stepped through the portal to Mexico City—as close as he could get with the anti-athtar talismans covering the city. The scent of burning wood reached his nose first. It was like a Demon Spring, but so much worse. As Diogo had said, there was a mix of noxes, kappas, and elokos, and they didn't seem interested in transformation. This was a bloody revenge on humanity for their perceived sins.

Lotan quickly transformed into his wolf form and bounded down the street, stopping to save humans he came across who needed help. But as soon as he'd saved one human, twenty more would cry for help down the street. At this rate, it would take him all year to save the city. What he needed was to put a stop to all this—to kill the demon who was pulling all the strings.

He slowed his gait and closed his eyes, searching for the connection he'd had with Mazatl. Although that particular one was frayed now, he was able to see others—thousands of them, in fact. Many of them severed, thanks to Yaotl. But one very clear strand that pulsed with power in the dead center of the city.

Lotan dashed through the city, following the connection. There, in front of the Mexican ICDM headquarters, he found the source, sitting in what appeared to be a throne, gazing out upon the city with an ownership he hadn't earned.

"So you've come," he said, his voice carrying across the open square. "I confess, I thought you too afraid."

"You left me no choice," Lotan said, transforming back into his human form and walking toward Yaotl with shoulders back, gaze steady. "The world is on fire. Are you happy?"

"Very," Yaotl said. "My vision is finally coming to fruition. The humans are finally recognizing what happens when they lose the protection of the mighty noxslayer."

"They have other talismans, though," Lotan said. "They have the weapons to destroy noxes as easily as Anat."

"But they have been so concerned with her, they haven't prepared in the slightest," Yaotl said with a smug smile. "As they took out demon lords, they sprinkled talismans around the city. But only for her, not for the chaos that's unfolding now." He smiled. "They have brought this upon themselves. I wonder if the noxslayer will be able to stand it, her precious humans in danger and her unable to help."

"She'll find a way," Lotan said.

"I doubt it. She has burned every bridge possible. Even sweet Freyja has turned against her completely. I've never seen someone so eager to switch sides before."

Another issue that would have to be dealt with later. "And what will you do once the world is yours?" Lotan asked. "Kill all the humans who won't comply?"

"If I must," Yaotl said.

Lotan lifted his gaze, allowing his anger to fill him with confidence. "And what if I defy you? Will you kill me?"

Yaotl didn't respond, and Lotan only just transformed back into his nox form before Yaotl's massive wolf body landed on top of him. Yaotl took advantage of the surprise, pressing a thick paw against Lotan's throat.

"I wonder if I'm powerful enough to maintain my own connection," Yaotl said. "Shall we test the theory?"

Lotan found a foothold and kicked him off, gasping for air and feeling the wetness of blood on his throat from Yaotl's claws. "Are you so blinded by your ambition that you'd risk it all?"

"Merely studying new theories around belus," Yaotl said. "Tabiko was quite helpful. She told us that an athtar managed to survive after Bael's death. No living child required. I'm willing to gamble the same thing will happen when I destroy you."

Something like dread sank into Lotan's stomach. He'd come here under the impression that Yaotl would never risk his own power by killing Lotan. Maim, hurt, torture, sure. But he was too fond of his kingdom to risk it.

Not, it seemed, anymore.

"You're hesitating, boy," Yaotl sneered. "Are you now second-guessing your decision?"

"No," Lotan said, steeling his resolve. There would be no

walking away from this if he failed. And Cam would absolutely never forgive him if he died before saying goodbye. "It's time I do what needs to be done."

Lotan lunged, snapping at Yaotl's neck, but was easily knocked away. Yaotl landed a good swipe, leaving a searing pain down Lotan's left shoulder as his claws dug in. Lotan sank his teeth into Yaotl's arm and the other nox retracted, hissing in pain. But it was merely a glancing blow. A mosquito bite.

"I'm surprised you came to me first," Yaotl said, his large black eyes gleaming in the fire around them. "I would have thought you would've gone to your Cam instead of coming to face me."

Lotan started. "What did you do?"

Yaotl took the opportunity and landed another claw right in the wound he'd made before. Lotan couldn't help the cry that came strangled from his throat when Yaotl swiped him with his other claw. Again, the pressure was too much and Lotan fell backward, Yaotl's massive weight crushing him.

"Geneva was particularly easy to infiltrate," Yaotl said, pressing harder on Lotan's ribcage as Lotan saw spots. "They were so scared of your athtar they didn't even notice the elokos and kappas amassing nearby."

"If you hurt her," Lotan gasped, but he was slowly losing his ability to breathe.

"You should worry about yourself."

Lotan struggled against the weight on his chest, but strength to strength, he was no match for Yaotl. The other demon had made himself too powerful for Lotan to overcome. Realization that he might not win this fight began to trickle into his subconscious, sending shoots of fear and remorse through every inch of his massive body. But if he was going to die, it wouldn't be as a coward.

"You are your mother's son. Don't ever let anyone tell you differently."

Anya's words came back to him, haunting him with their irrelevance. And yet... He had defeated Mazatl, not with brute strength, but through the connection he'd forged with his mother and she'd forged with them. And Lotan had used that connection with Yaotl to find him.

"Please tell your parents I will take care of their pack," Yaotl said, raising his clawed hand.

Lotan closed his eyes, but not in resignation. He pinpointed that connection between his magic and Yaotl's, and—just as he'd done with Mazatl—he pulled. Hard.

"What are you—"

The harder he pulled, the stronger Lotan became, absorbing the magic Yaotl had bloodily obtained. And then, like a dam breaking, the connection opened fully, allowing Lotan to reap the benefits of Yaotl's hard work. It washed over him, finding the magic that had been lying dormant in the bottom of his bones and bringing it into the bright sunlight. The magic was like his mother's scent, like his father's smile, and warmed him as fully as spending evenings nestled in their arms. It was safety, and familiarity, and the knowledge that if he tugged a little harder, he could take the magic from this creature who did not deserve it.

"You... This is impossible."

And just as innately as he knew Cam was the woman he wanted for the rest of his life, he knew how to pull the rest of the magic from Yaotl's body, routing every connection the nox demon had made and keeping it for himself, the way he should've done hundreds of years ago.

The pressure on his chest lessened, and Lotan opened his eyes to see Yaotl slide off Lotan's barrel chest to the ground. By the time his body hit, Yaotl had reverted to human.

Lotan got to his feet slowly, adjusting to the full majesty of hundreds of thousands of demons routing directly to him. He took several calming breaths, reveling in this power that he'd had all along, but, for all his curiosity, had never even questioned.

As Yaotl stirred on the ground, Lotan transformed back to his human form and knelt down beside him. He was frail now, a shadow of the man who had set the world on fire.

The human opened his eyes, slowly coming to terms with the world, then looked up at Lotan in fear.

"Who are you?" He spoke in a long-dead language that Lotan understood.

"I'm the belu nox," Lotan said, looking at his hand as it trembled with power. "Do you not know me?"

"I know nothing," Yaotl said, rubbing his face. "I was in my village. There was a man who promised me power if I went with him."

Lotan stared at him with pity. Yaotl's memory would return, in time, and he would be faced with the reality that not only had he failed, but he'd lost everything. He would age and die, all the while living with the knowledge of what he'd gained and lost.

The merciful thing to do would be to kill him now.

"It is no good to linger over dying prey."

Yaotl had said the same thing when Lotan was a boy. He had helped him learn how to hunt, how to shoot a bow. To carry a sword. To become the man he was. Despite everything he'd done, Yaotl had still been a father to Lotan after his own had died. And for that, Lotan would be grateful.

But not merciful.

"I will send ICDM for you," Lotan said. "So that you will face justice for your crimes."

Yaotl shook his head. "I don't understand."

"You will, in time. And you will remember what it felt like to watch the son of Xo walk away with your kingdom."

"Where are you going?"

"To find Cam."

CHAPTER THIRTY-THREE

The first thing that came back to Cam was that something was burning. She coughed, and her lungs hurt, perhaps from the smoke. She blinked in the light, the sound of sirens and yelling echoing from all sides.

"Jack," she whispered, reaching her fingers out. They made purchase on a warm, familiar, calloused hand, and when it squeezed back, she sighed.

He grunted. "I'm here. I think."

"The fuck happened?" She sat up and rubbed her bleary eyes. A wind was blowing through the opening in the wall.

The opening in the wall?

Cam shook her pounding head and concentrated, not quite

believing what she'd seen. Beyond the overturned office desks and rising smoke, the front half of the building was completely gone. Collapsed, either by a bomb or some other explosive.

"Jack..." Cam whispered. "Frank? María?"

"Here."

Jack was already on his feet, pushing the conference room table off María. She was dazed, but alive. And despite everything that had happened between them, Cam was grateful.

"Where's Frank?" Jack said. "He was..."

Jack bounded past her, calling Frank's name as he rummaged through the chaos. Cam was slower to get to her feet, checking her body for bruising or any other damage. Her ears still rang, but she was mostly okay.

"I'm fine, Jack, I'm fine." Jack reappeared with a bloody Frank hanging from his shoulder. The old Councilman gingerly sat down beside María, holding up his hands in surrender.

"Stay here with María," Jack said. "I'm going to look for other survivors."

Frank sat back against the wall, clutching his side and breathing heavily. "I suppose we should've expected this."

"A little late for hindsight," Cam said.

"Sure would be nice to have an athtar right about now," Frank said with a half-smile before it wilted into a grimace. Cam tried not to notice the large red splotch on the right side of his body.

"Hey, Cam..." Jack stood at the edge of the building, holding onto a piece of rebar that jutted out from where the wall used to be. "You need to look at this."

She limped over, finding her body more stunned than hurt, and joined him at the edge of the building. When she followed his gaze down to the ground, her heart came to her throat.

The whole city was in flames, and, down below in the square, the carnage was in full swing. Demons had swarmed the square, overtaking whatever forces ICDM had left after the initial explosion—and there weren't many.

"What's our play, partner?" she said, her voice hoarse from the smoke.

Jack shook his head. "We need to find some weapons and get out there. Nobody's..." He swallowed, shaking his head. "I don't think we're going to get any backup."

Not from Anya, at least. Cam pulled her phone from her back pocket, but it was smashed to oblivion. Jack's was as well. They were truly on their own.

"Surely reinforcements are coming," Cam said. "This is ICDM headquarters."

"If it's happening here and in Lisbon," Jack replied with a grave shake of his head, "it's happening all over the world. There aren't enough agents to fight this."

Cam shook off the hopeless dread that was threatening to swallow her. "Then we give ourselves all the help we can get. C'mon, I think there's a stash of weapons on the third floor that we shipped here a few months ago. I just hope there's enough to make a difference."

Cam and Jack raced down the stairs, finding survivors hiding in the stairwell. It was, perhaps, the safest place to be, as the building was surrounded. Cam didn't want to think about what would happen if the demons got inside and started picking off people.

They reached the third floor, and Jack made no bones about breaking glass and opening locked doors until they found the weaponry Cam hoped would be there. She audibly released a breath when she saw the crates marked with her familiar logo and opened them to find long black rifles and rounds of ammunition.

"Who's down there?" Cam asked, pulling the guns out and checking them for defects. "All of them?"

"Hard to tell, but we should be ready for every type, save the athtars," Jack said, digging through the crate and cursing slightly to himself. "Which is all they've sent. Every bullet in here is an anti-athtar talisman. There's only one athtar, Cam. Was all this for Anya?"

Cam looked down at the crate and shook her head. "I don't know. It seems rather short-sighted, if so."

"Everything is fucking short-sighted," Jack said, walking to a cabinet of armory in the corner. He audibly sighed when the doors revealed a line of swords, knives, and other anti-demonic weaponry. "This is gonna have to do."

Working quickly, Cam and Jack gathered as many weapons as they thought they could carry, drawing talisman symbols on every inch of the blades to give them maximum efficiency.

Despite not having any ready-made talisman bullets, Cam drew some tiny symbols on ten or so bullets and loaded them into a small handgun that she put in the waistband of her pants.

"Gangster," Jack said with a half-smile as she handed him another gun loaded with the same.

"Use sparingly," Cam said.

Cam missed her macuahuitl, which was back in Ath-kur, but found a broadsword that would do fine. Jack had two swords and a pair of knives that were half his usual size but seemed satisfied. Before they put the marker away, they took time to draw symbols on their own bodies. The miasma would be thick in the fight, and they needed to keep their heads about them.

"Ready?" Jack asked, adjusting the knives on his belt.

"Do we have a choice?" Cam asked, turning to walk out of the armory.

They hadn't even reached the stairs yet before an ear-piercing scream echoed from the door beyond. Jack bounded to the door, cursing the whole way, throwing it open and looking up and down the stairwell.

"Up there," he said, running up the stairs.

Cam was ready to follow him when a loud banging down below drew her attention. A motley crew of demons poured inside, climbing the stairs with hunger in their eyes.

"Jack..." Cam glanced up and realized he was out of earshot.

She was on her own.

"C'mon, you bastards," she said, grabbing her sword off her back and holding it ready.

The first demon, maybe an eloko, locked gazes with her and grinned evilly.

"Move aside, human," he said, his voice laced with a thick Spanish accent. "It's time you learned your place."

Cam stepped toward him, grateful she had the upper level, but knowing that once she killed this one, there was a whole crowd behind him. She cracked her neck and adjusted her grip as the demon drew closer. Just a few more steps.

"C'mon, asshole," she muttered. "Try me."

She heard the telltale sound of bells in the background, but thanks to the symbols drawn on her body, it was merely annoying instead of entrancing.

"Eloko, hm?" Cam said. "Can't say I'm surprised."

The eloko's eyes widened. "How are you—"

Whatever he'd been about to say was lost when Cam's talisman-powered weapon sliced his head off, sending his body down the stairs.

"One down, ten million to go," Cam said, continuing down the stairs with purpose.

Cam dispatched five more demons on her way down the stairs—an eloko, two noxes, and, disappointedly, a lilin. After what had happened in Paris, perhaps Freyja wasn't interested in playing nice anymore. Jack had been smart to load her up.

They were all human enough, and it was only by the feel of their magic on her tongue that she knew the difference. That, and they were advancing toward her with the intent to kill her.

The only humans she'd found were already dead.

She considered retreating and finding Jack, but no sooner had she taken a step in that direction than another demon would appear. Her advance continued until she reached the bottom of the stairs, and with a deep breath, she opened the emergency exit door to the alley. Three steps beyond, five humans lay dead on the ground, their ICDM badges covered in blood. Cam swallowed as she walked by Frank's assistant, his green eyes staring up into nothing.

"Oi! Another one!"

Cam looked up as a pair of demons jumped down from the scaffolding above. They carried bloody weapons, clearly the ones responsible for the carnage here.

"Who sent you?" Cam asked, inching toward them cautiously.

The demon on the left didn't respond, coming toward her with a raised weapon. He wasn't even using his magic, it seemed, because Cam was able to parry his blow easily. She swung her elbow into his cheek, sending him falling backward for a moment. His partner jumped to his rescue, and Cam shot out her foot to meet his middle. The first demon grabbed her shoulder then howled in pain.

"What the—?"

"Yeah, don't touch me," Cam said, swinging the broadsword to slice through his neck.

She whirled around to see the second demon holding a human with his knife to her throat.

"Put down the weapon," he said. "And this human will live."

"Forgive me if I don't believe you," Cam said. And with a single movement, she reached into her waistband and pulled the gun out, shooting the demon in the head. He fell backward, dead before he hit the ground.

"Get up there," Cam said, looking at the frightened human. "Find a place to hide."

"What's the point?" she whispered, her voice shaking. "There's no escape."

"Then find a weapon and fight," Cam said. "Or get out of the way."

She left the human in the alley and walked out into the square. The scent of blood was thick in the air, and something inside Cam began to agree with that desolate human about their odds of survival. Without Anya, without Lotan, without help. Nine talisman bullets and one broadsword. Jack nowhere to be found.

And what appeared to be tens of thousands of demons crammed into one square.

"Welp."

She stepped into the fray, finding a demon fighting against an ICDM agent who was quickly losing steam. With a swing, she took care of the demon then pushed past the exhausted agent to help another. One then another then another. The muscles in her arms were starting to protest after months of disuse, but she kept going. The way she'd done in Demon Springs in the past.

Ten demons down, and Cam wasn't even past the periphery

of the fight. She kept at it, working at it.

"Look who it is. Lotan's whore."

She stopped, sensing the fear magic crawling up her spine. Turning, she didn't recognize the demon, but that didn't matter. He was a nox.

"Are you in charge?" Cam asked, cautiously approaching him. "Or is Yaotl slithering around here somewhere?"

"Noxes don't *slither*, despite what your cowardly lover might've told you," he replied. "And no, my belu is on his throne in our stronghold." He smiled. "I'm sure it looks something like this right now."

Cam swallowed her fear for her family and friends; that was just what the nox wanted. "Then who do I need to kill to get all these demonic bastards to heel?"

"Don't you understand?" he said, inching closer. "There is no central person, no singular control. The belus have given their blessing, but even they can't rein in this anger. The humans have brought this on themselves."

Cam couldn't argue with that—but she couldn't think about that. Not when the nox seemed to be trapping her against a building on the edge of the square.

"I've watched you," he said, his canine teeth growing longer. "But I wonder how you'll fare against a fully-transformed nox?"

Cam would wager not all that well, but there was nothing she could do as the monster grew larger before her. Suddenly, her broadsword seemed a toothpick in the face of teeth the size of her leg. She readied herself to fight, even though she knew, in her gut, that it was hopeless.

The nox seemed to know it as well, walking toward her and throwing all his magic at her. Even though her anti-nox talismans held up, her knees shook. This fear was real. She was outgunned and, as the nox opened its monster jaw to swallow her whole, out of options.

"Stop!"

The nox's teeth halted inches from Cam's body. She swallowed, trembling as the nox took two steps back, clearly furious, but obeying the disembodied voice. Cam glanced between the nox's legs and her heart soared to the skies.

Lotan.

"Turn to your human form," he said, his voice booming with all the authority of a belu. The power radiating off him was awesome, more potent than Cam had ever sensed from him. It was the first time she'd ever felt afraid of him.

The nox transformed and walked to Lotan. "I don't understand, how—"

Whatever he was going to say was lost as Lotan took his head off. He looked visibly upset to have done it, but when his gaze met Cam's, it melted into those familiar brown pools that she'd so often gotten lost in—and her fear vanished as well.

"Cam..."

She pushed herself off the wall and ran to him, flinging herself into his strong arms.

He hissed and put her down, rubbing his arms. "You have talismans on you, don't you?"

"Crap, sorry," Cam said, wanting to touch him but not wanting to hurt him again. "How did you get here? What are you doing here? What's...different?"

"A lot, but too much to explain now," Lotan said, looking out onto the square. "This is insanity."

"How did you find me?" Cam asked.

"I feared the worst when I saw the building," Lotan said, turning his gaze to the chaos. "But I figured the noxes might be searching for you, so I looked for someone who was more gleeful than the others."

"What the hell does that mean?" Cam asked.

He shook his head, his focus still on the fighting. "Like I said, too much to explain now. I can't...I don't know if it's possible to stop this, Cam."

"Then we just have to fight," Cam said. "And save as many lives as we can until..." She licked her lips. "Until."

Lotan nodded and flashed her a smile. "Nowhere else I'd rather be than by your side."

CHAPTER THIRTY-FOUR

Drawn by the sound of shrieks and cries for help, Jack ascended the stairs two-by-two. There were too many innocent civilians in the building, and a handful of demons could do a lot of damage.

He came to the fourth floor of the building, pushing past the door hanging off the hinge. The office was in tatters, both from the initial explosion and what appeared to be ransacking. Jack pulled one of the swords from the sheath on his back and walked carefully into the room, listening for the sounds of shrieks. It was eerily quiet now, and it didn't take long for him to find out why.

Five demons stood over a pile of bodies—humans, all of them—reveling in their bloodthirsty accomplishment. One of them spotted Jack and turned, his too-human smile growing.

"We got another one."

"What do we have here?" Jack asked, gripping the sword with a smile on his face. "Elokos? Noxes? Kappas aren't usually this grotesque."

"Wouldn't you like to know, human?" the ringleader answered, walking toward Jack. "Should we have a bit of fun with him before he dies? He looks too cocky."

Their magic brushed against his skin, but thanks to his painted-on defenses, it did little except make him smile. "Elokos it is. Doesn't matter. I can handle all of you."

He didn't give the eloko a chance to argue, running toward him with his sword up. It cut through like butter, leaving the demon in tatters on the floor. The other demons growled, advancing and brandishing their bloody weapons.

"Come on," Jack said with a nod. "Show me what you got."

One, two, three, four. Dead before they could land the first blow.

Jack looked at the sword with appreciation, and decided he'd keep talismans on his weapons from now on. It certainly made things go faster.

But his appreciation was short-lived, as his gaze fell on the human victims on the ground. They were all young, staffers for the Middle Eastern Councilman, based on the flags hanging from the walls.

Jack could do nothing for them now, but he could make sure the rest of the building was safe. He sheathed the sword and turned to the stairwell, where a shadow was running up the stairs. He kicked up his heels and dashed to the door.

"Oi!" he called. "Where are you going?"

The demon turned to him with a smile, pulling a gun from his waistband. "Gonna kill some humans. Guess I'll start with you."

Jack hesitated for a moment then remembered the talisman gun that Cam had given him, yanking it from his waistband and cocking it.

"I have one, too," he said.

The demon laughed. "Human weaponry can't hurt me. I'm filled with the magic from Mizuchi—"

Jack fired, and the demon fell backward, landing against the railing before disappearing down the center of the staircase.

"Shut up," Jack said, putting the gun back in his waistband. He didn't like using the bullets as he only had nine left now, but he couldn't deny they were useful.

He kept climbing the stairs until he reached the fifth floor, where, yet again, the door was off the hinges. This time, he heard nothing—no demons, no humans—but that didn't mean anything. He stepped on a pane of broken glass and heard a gasp coming from an open conference room.

"Hello?" Jack called. "Anyone there?"

No response.

"I'm here to help," he said, inching closer. "I'm Frank's grandson. Jack Grenard."

He slowly opened the door with the tip of his sword and

looked inside. The conference table had been flipped over, but Jack didn't think it was from the initial explosion.

A pair of dark brown eyes peered out from above the table. "J-Jack Grenard?"

Somewhere in the back of his mind, the face was familiar, but he couldn't place it. "Yeah, it's me."

The woman stood, and when Jack got a good look at her, his brain caught up with him. A lifetime ago, on the run in Amsterdam with Anya, he'd saved her son and his friends from an encounter with a lilin.

"Where's your Councilman?" Jack asked.

She gestured toward the front of the building that was gone. "Down there somewhere. We haven't been able to find him up here."

Jack nodded. He probably wouldn't be the only one. "Are y'all all right? Are there any more demons on this floor?"

"Not that we know of," a young woman in a ripped blouse said. "But they're everywhere."

"Has anyone called for backup?" Jack asked.

"Before our comms went out, we were monitoring demonic attacks on cities around the world," she said. "And even if there was backup coming, I don't know how we'd know where or how to rendezvous with them."

Jack exhaled. They wouldn't last long in this building, and he couldn't continue to play whack-a-mole forever. Cam was probably out in the fray, and he didn't want to leave her hanging.

"I have a signal!" an older woman shrieked, running over from the edge of the building. "France is sending military aid. Troops, equipment—all of it."

"Great," Jack said, the first bit of hope he'd felt all day. "When will they get here?"

She hesitated. "They're trying but…there are too many demons. They can't get past the perimeter of the city on foot."

Jack watched as dismay fell on the faces and dug deep to find those leadership skills he'd barely learned at the Academy. "Can you get them back on the phone?"

She nodded.

"There's a parking garage behind the building," Jack said. "Tell them we'll send survivors and injured there, and to send as many helicopters as they can."

"But we'd have to get there."

Jack sighed. He needed to find Cam, but if he left these innocent humans, they would certainly die. "Tell them I'll take you. But first you'll need to arm yourselves."

"We aren't fighters," said a mousey-looking man. "We're staffers. Policy wonks."

"Then defense it'll have to be." Jack found a piece of paper and hastily drew the anti-demon talismans. "Draw a couple of these on your body. They'll protect you against demonic magic, but not demonic blades. So if anyone feels like wielding a blade, it might be helpful."

Two of the staffers shakily raised their hands, and Jack told them where to find weapons in the armory, giving them one of his swords to take with them in case they ran into company.

"Finally, I need someone to do a sweep of the building, especially the seventh floor. Frank Grenard and María García are there. Frank is badly injured, and there are probably others who are as well. I'll take this group first, then I'll be back for them, and anyone else."

When the civilians were appropriately covered in symbols, Jack led the group of eight toward the stairwell, walking out first to listen for demons. He wouldn't be able to protect those in the back if they were attacked from above, so it was imperative that they moved quickly. At the third floor, they picked up the two staffers who'd gone to retrieve more weapons.

"I found these guns," she said. "Will they help?"

"Against these demons, no," Jack said with a shake of his head. "Long story."

With the two armed staffers holding up the back, Jack finally felt somewhat secure leading the group down the rest of the stairs. When the door below slammed open, Jack held up his hand to silence the group and pulled his sword from its sheath.

The demon—a lilin by the scent of flowers on the air—spotted them immediately and ran up the stairs, knives out and ready to kill. Jack took care of her easily then pushed her body off the side of the stairwell.

"I'm glad you're on our side," came a weak voice behind him.

"I've got you," Jack said. "Let's move."

They continued down the stairs, this time a little faster than before. Jack didn't want to waste all his time and energy getting out of the building when there would be so much more to deal with after they got outside.

They reached the bottom floor, and Jack carefully opened the door, revealing an alley. He poked his head out, looking around to assess the situation. Fighting was heaviest in the square, but their path to the garage was similarly packed. In the distance, he registered the sound of a helicopter, which strengthened his resolve.

"Let's go," Jack said, grabbing the second sword from its sheath and walking into the alley. The parking garage was close, across the street, but it could as well have been miles away.

His pulse quickened and sweat broke out on the back of his neck as he drew closer to the throngs of demons fighting tooth and nail against woefully under-equipped humans. Getting ten humans through this was going to take a miracle.

"How do you want to go about this?" one of them asked from behind Jack.

"Carefully," Jack said. "Everyone stick together."

He walked out into the chaos, swinging his sword at whatever came at him first. He wasn't even sure if the blows were killing, or if he was fighting the same creature or five different ones. The only thing he knew was that he had to keep himself, and everyone with him, alive.

"*Help!*"

Jack turned. One of his ten humans had been grabbed by a

lilin. But as the demon pressed the human to his chest, he let her go with a hiss of pain.

"Don't touch them," Jack said, pulling one of the small knives he'd hidden and throwing it at the lilin. It struck him in the neck, and with a swift swing, Jack hacked his head off.

"Jack! Help!"

"Fuck me," Jack said, turning to the other side. Now three of his humans were in demonic clutches—too far for him to do anything except…

He pulled the gun from his waistband and fired three shots. The demons released their captors and fell backward.

"I thought you said the guns didn't work," one of the saved humans said.

"I brought a special kind," Jack said, looking at the barrel. "And now I only have six bullets left."

"What do we have here?" came a slithery voice to Jack's right. "A pack of humans, all alone."

Jack could've cried; they seemed to have attracted the attention of almost every demon in the square.

"New plan," Jack said to the humans. "*Run like hell!*"

They didn't need to be told twice, breaking in ten different directions as they ran toward the garage. Jack hacked and sliced where he could to keep them off the humans' tail, but when one fell, another took its place.

The humans dashed into the parking garage, running as fast as they could up the concrete ramps. Jack hung back to take out demons, but even he was starting to grow weary. He couldn't keep this up forever.

Thankfully, as Jack hacked through the last two demons with two more of his bullets, no more seemed to follow. He caught his breath, leaning on a nearby luxury car, before turning and continuing up the ramp where the sound of the helicopter had grown louder and louder.

By the time he reached the top, the sound was deafening. Opening the door, he saw the civilians getting loaded onto a large black helicopter, surrounded by military in full body armor—at least twenty who stood around the perimeter of the roof. Several raised their weapons at Jack and he held up his hands until one of the civilians could peg him as human. An older officer jogged over, gesturing for Jack to follow him away from the helicopter.

"There are injuries in the building across the street," Jack began before the officer could speak, "and no real way to get them out except by hacking through. What weapons have you brought?"

"We're military. Not equipped to deal with demons." He straightened. "But we have some things that might help distract them."

Jack sighed heavily. "It's important that we get the councilmembers out. I'm going back for them."

"We'll do what we can."

Jack paused, unsure if he wanted to give up his ace in the hole, but these soldiers might need it more than he did. He reached into his waistband and handed the gun to the officer.

"This has anti-demon bullets it, but only four left," Jack said. "Use it in emergencies only. And if a demon comes up here, aim for the head."

The helicopter lifted off, and Jack took some solace that ten humans were safe—and that the twenty soldiers would remain to secure the parking garage. Jack gave them instructions on how to add talismans to their bodies, just in case, but their bullets wouldn't do much against the demons. Yet again, Jack was on his own.

He walked down the ramp, the sounds of fighting echoing in his mind as he struggled against hopelessness. When he and Cam were preparing for Demon Spring in Los Angeles, they'd been told that overwhelm was common and to focus on one thing at a time. One block, one fight, one demon, if it came down to it.

Jack's focus was Frank. His grandfather had made some mistakes, but the world would be worse off if their entire council was taken out. Jack pictured his father and mother, and the pain they'd feel if Frank were never to sit at their table for dinner again. He recalled the summers in Geneva, learning from Frank even when he didn't want to. The way Frank had spoken up for him when he'd come back from Bael's torture and made sure Jack had a generous retirement package.

As he came to the bottom of the stairs, where the demons had begun to outnumber the humans two-to-one, he took a deep breath and pulled his weapons, stepping into the chaos once more and hoping he would be enough.

CHAPTER THIRTY-FIVE

Anya watched it all as tears poured down her face.

Unable to reach the city, she could only stand one second behind the world in the river of time, powerless to stop any of it. And it was torture.

At least thirty major cities around the world were on fire—including Mexico City, Charleston, Los Angeles, Lisbon, Shanghai.

Geneva.

Jack, who'd saved ten civilians all by himself, was now fighting to get back to the building to save more of them. Including, Anya assumed, his grandfather, who was growing weaker by the moment.

Cam wore a look of exhausted fear that their best efforts wouldn't be enough, even after Lotan appeared to fight by her side.

And Lotan, now the powerful belu Anya always knew he could be, was finding himself unable to stem the tide. While he'd managed to cow the noxes in the crowd, the rest were out of his reach and too many to fight off.

"You have to stop watching this," Diogo said, standing next to her. "There is nothing you can do to help them."

Not for lack of trying. Elonsi, Liley, Kappanchi, and, of course, the noxlands were off-limits to her. She couldn't even set foot in them. Her frantic messages to the belus had gone unanswered. They were content to let the human world burn, not caring how many innocents died in the process on either side.

"My lady," Diogo tried again.

"There has to be something," Anya said, reaching toward the sword Jack was fighting against and sighing as her hand went right through the blade. "There has to be something. Bael must've known something—"

"There's a reason Bael didn't want the humans using the talismans," Diogo said. "He knew they were the only way to defeat him."

"And *you* said there was so much more he didn't know," Anya said, turning on him. "You said—"

"I have no more knowledge to impart," Diogo said, though his eyes were sad. "If there is yet another mystery of your magic, you are the one to find it."

He left her there, and she couldn't blame him. There was no stopping this—not unless she stepped into the present time. And then, she'd be no better than the humans themselves—and perhaps find herself weakened enough to be killed by them.

She exhaled slowly. She would be weak, but she'd still have her sword. And she wasn't helping anyone sitting here like a coward.

The anti-athtar magic touched her skin and weakness came over her immediately. Almost too late, she saw a blade swinging down at her. She found the strength to raise her sword and bring it down on the demon, but it only cast a glancing blow. She had a fraction of her demonic power now, but she still had her skill.

She swung her leg out and kicked the creature in the kneecap, then struck the killing blow as he fell. But he wasn't even completely dead before another had taken his place, and Anya was back to fighting. She did her best to ignore the way the magic seemed to be slipping from her body as she drew closer to the center of the fray.

All she wanted was to find Jack, to fight alongside him. To do something to protect him. To do *anything* except watch.

Finally, like the sun peeking through the clouds, she spotted him, fighting for his life. His shirt was slick with sweat as he swung the sword, his arms covered in nicks and scrapes. There was a large gash on his shoulder he didn't seem to notice. But he fought as well as any warrior she'd ever seen in her life.

"Jack!" Anya called, but her voice was drowned by the chaos.

She tried to take another step toward him, but the talisman energy was too strong, and she couldn't even manage that.

No, she thought to herself, *I'm stronger than this.*

With a cry of pain, she lifted her foot and put it an inch closer to Jack. If she had to crawl, she would reach him somehow.

But her world began to slow—and not thanks to her magic. Jack's sword, his only remaining weapon, was knocked from his hand. Another demon picked it up and ran off with it before he could retrieve it. Jack reached into his waistband, perhaps looking for that gun Anya had seen him give to the army on the rooftop.

The demon grinned, knowing Jack had nothing left, and Anya struggled against the talisman magic, praying to God Himself that He would give her some extra strength so she could save this man. The man who had given her a reason to live again, the one who'd stayed by her side.

The demon's blade came for Jack, and he straightened, perhaps knowing this was the end.

"*No!*"

Something broke free in the bottom of her chest, something powerful and deep, something old and commanding. It was as if the magic in her bones awoke from a ten-thousand-year slumber, radiating out of her like a shining beacon in the darkness.

And just like that, the world stopped.

The entire world.

Every butterfly, every breath. Every drop of water stayed

exactly where it was in the moment Anya stopped time.

As Anya looked around the square, blades were halfway to striking, blood spurted in mid-air, and the retreat seemed to be permanently halted.

Even more shockingly, the Underworld had stopped, too. Freyja, in her castle. Biloko smoking a pipe outside. Tabiko, rocking the babe, stopped in mid-motion. The noxlands were currently empty, but even the birds were stuck in flight.

And this control was absolute. She'd been able to slow time, down to the most infinitesimal increments. But never had she been able to stop it completely—and never manipulate time in the human and demonic worlds together. It seemed the anti-athtar magic was no match for this new plane of existence.

This control, like everything, wouldn't last. Eventually, she would have to let go and the world would start turning again. But for now, she had work to do.

With care, Anya sent every demon in Geneva back to their respective Underworld lands. She could've killed them, and might've even been justified, but it didn't feel right. The streets were already red with blood; adding more would just make things harder. This was an act of mercy. The only one they would get.

When she was done with Geneva, she moved on to Paris, then London, then New York, Charleston, Denver, Los Angeles, Mexico City. Across the Pacific to Tokyo, Shanghai and on and on. Every city that had a demonic attack was touched, and every demon returned to the Underworld.

By the time she returned to Geneva, her body was exhausted and her soul unsettled. This would be a temporary measure only. And as much as she wanted to pretend otherwise, there would always have to be a force in this world to keep the two sides from killing each other. And she was the one blessed with the job.

She plodded up the square, passing the humans still stuck in fighting mode with no one at all, until she found Jack. The look in his eyes said he knew his time had come, and it broke her heart to see no trace of fear there. He wasn't lacking bravery, but what would he say when he knew what Anya would have to do?

She could've lived in this moment forever, watching his beautiful face and avoiding what would happen when the world began to spin once more. But she allowed her control to slip from her tight hold, and slowly, the humans began moving.

Jack reared back, still expecting the now-nonexistent blade that would end his life, but when it didn't come, his brows knitted together. He straightened, looking around the square until his gaze landed on Anya.

"Anya!" Jack's eyes widened. "Get out of here! What..." His gaze melted into confusion. "What are you doing here? Where did..." He spun around. "Did you...?"

She nodded, but the talismans and exhaustion were starting to get to her, and she swayed on her feet. "Everything is fine, Jack. I promise. All the demons have been returned to the Underworld. All the humans are safe."

Jack walked to her, taking her into his arms. "You...you did that?"

She nodded. "Don't ask me how, but..." She half-smiled as she cupped his face. "I saw that demon about to kill you and I guess I just... did it. I was able to stop time completely and..."

She lost her train of thought as his eyes searched hers and he snaked one arm around her. He leaned down and kissed her, first gently then more desperately, as if he was realizing how very close he'd come to never seeing her again. She released a sigh as he pressed his forehead to hers, squeezing his eyes shut.

"It's all right, Jack," she whispered, holding him tighter to her. "Everyone is safe now."

His eyes opened, and he looked up at the remains of the ICDM building. "No, they're not. We need to find Frank."

Using magic was out of the question for Anya, but she kept pace with Jack as he rushed back into the building. He climbed the concrete stairs where dead demons and humans alike were scattered. Jack paused, looking at two young women, before shaking his head and walking past them.

They reached the seventh floor, and Anya got the full scope of the attack. A gray sky was visible; perhaps half the building was missing. How many had died in the initial explosion? Anya felt a growing sense of dread that they'd only begun to get a sense of the damage.

Jack made a beeline for the back of the room where Frank was leaning up against the wall. As Anya drew closer, she stopped in her tracks. Frank had been old, but she'd never have called him frail. Now, however, his breathing was labored and his skin was pale. A large red blotch marred his left side, and blood tinged the edges of his lips and dripped from a wound on his head.

"I told you I'd be back," Jack said, kneeling down beside his grandfather. "Now, we have to get you out of here."

"Jack..." Frank said, blinking in the darkness until he saw Anya. "What... How is she here?"

"That doesn't matter right now," Jack said, reaching under his grandfather to try to lift him. But the old man cried out in pain, so Jack put him back down, concern etched on his face.

"Frank!" Cam called out across the room.

"Over here," Anya called back.

Cam ran over, her face streaked with blood and sweat, but she looked otherwise fine. She took one look at Anya then seemingly decided that her questions could wait. Behind her, keeping a respectful distance, Lotan stood with his hands clasped in front of him. Anya nodded to him then turned back to Jack.

"We need to get him to a hospital," Jack said. "Something. They were sending medevac helicopters here. Are there any more?"

But Frank held up his hand and shook his head. "Save it for someone who needs it."

Jack released a breath and looked back at Anya, tears in his eyes. "Can you do something? Please."

Anya knelt beside the two of them and closed her eyes. But when she searched for an injury to heal, she found too many. He was too far gone for even her to save.

"I'm sorry, Jack," she whispered.

"It's all right," Frank replied weakly. "I've had a good life. It's time for me to pass on the torch to someone else." He shifted. "Tell your dad I love him. And your mom, too." He smiled. "And you, too, Jackie. Thank you for coming back for me."

Jack's breaths came in short spurts, his chest heaving as his gaze darted from his grandfather to Anya and back again. "I love you, too, Frank. Grandfather."

Anya hesitated then slipped her fingers into Jack's, expecting him to pull away. But he gripped them tightly, keeping her in place next to him.

"Frank." Cam knelt next to Jack.

"Ah, Cam." He smiled. "Is María...?"

"I'm okay," came the weak voice in the corner. María was bruised but sitting on a chair, her cheeks wet with tears.

"Frank, I'm so sorry we couldn't..." Cam whispered. "We should've known this was coming."

"Don't blame yourself for our mistake," Frank said, his breathing becoming more labored. "We let our fear guide us to the wrong conclusion and were unprepared, even though you told us otherwise." His blinking became slower. "Will you attempt the treaty again, Anya?"

Anya jumped, not sure she was allowed to speak. "I believe we can try."

"Then consider the North America vote in favor," Frank

said. "María—"

"I will record it," she replied, wiping her cheeks. "And you will have my support as well."

Anya turned back to Frank to say more, but his eyes had closed, and his chest no longer rose and fell. Cam's shoulders shook, and Lotan swept over to her, taking her in his arms as she cried into his chest. María covered her eyes with her hand, her shoulders trembling, but her weeping mostly silent. The others who'd gathered bowed their heads in respect.

Beside Anya, Jack released a sob but then wiped his eyes with his free hand. He nodded to himself, bowing his head a moment and perhaps saying a few silent words over his grandfather. Then he rose, bringing Anya with him.

"We need to sweep the building for survivors," Jack said. "The military should be sending more troops in, especially now that the demons are gone. This building might not be very safe, and there could be people buried under the rubble. Whoever needs medical attention should be prioritized, and whoever can walk should try to get out on their own."

Anya nodded, but a spell of lightheadedness came over her and she swayed, falling into Jack's arms. "I'm fine," she murmured, feeling like a rag doll. "Just need rest."

"She needs to get out of this talisman-infested place," Cam said, looking at Lotan. "Can you get her back to Ath-kur quickly?"

Lotan nodded and took Anya gently into his arms from Jack. "I will be back to help as soon as I can."

"We'll be fine," Jack said with a half-smile that warmed Anya's heart. "Thanks to you, Anya."

The last thing she saw before she fell asleep was his dirty, bloody, beaming face, full of pride and love for her.

CHAPTER THIRTY-SIX

With Lotan's newfound nox power surging through him, the nox form he took was three times bigger than before. Everything was heightened, from his sense of smell to his sight to the feeling of a million little strings connecting him to the noxes around the world. He was able to get out of the city quickly with Anya gently held in his jaws. She was fast asleep, and Lotan would have to ask how she managed to overcome a city full of anti-athtar talismans.

As he carefully padded through the streets, the full breadth of the demonic attack unveiled itself. The center of the attack had been on ICDM, but demons had stretched out far and wide. The further he walked from the square, the fewer dead demons and more dead humans he saw. Young, old, man, woman, it didn't seem to matter. It was just carnage for carnage's sake. Even in Lotan's most sympathetic thoughts, there was no excuse for this. These humans had no control over what ICDM had done and shouldn't have been punished.

But Anya, it seemed, had done a thorough job of removing every demon in the city. Lotan sensed most of them back in the Underworld, a fact he was going to verify in short order. But the amount of power that had taken, especially if she'd managed to replicate it across the entire world...

Finally, Lotan reached the outer edges of the city where the anti-athtar talismans would no longer prevent him from opening a portal. He placed Anya on the ground and reverted to his human form, pulling the portal from his back pocket and flinging it in the air. She stirred when he picked her up, her magic already returning with the connection to Ath-kur. With care, he stepped through to the living room, making a beeline for the couch.

"What happened to her?" Diogo jumped up from a chair on the other side of the room and rushed over, displaying more concern than Lotan had ever seen the taciturn athtar show.

"She's merely exhausted," Lotan said, gently placing her on the couch.

"I'm fine," Anya said, her eyes fluttering open. "Get me back to Jack—"

"He told me to put you here to recover," Lotan said. "And there's nothing more for you to do there. I daresay you've done enough for a while."

"I'll say," Diogo said with a haughty look. "Thousands of demons returned to the Underworld. They will sing of this for decades."

Lotan had to smile. "You certainly saved a lot of people today, Anya."

She exhaled. "I couldn't save Frank."

"You saved so many more," Lotan said. "How in the world did you manage it? There were talismans everywhere."

She looked at the ceiling, as if she weren't exactly sure how she'd done it either. "I desperately wanted to stop time, so I did. Perhaps it was the act of stopping time completely... I'm not sure. But once time started again, the anti-athtar magic was there. I'm still feeling it."

"But how did you *do* it?" Diogo asked, coming to sit on the edge of the couch next to her.

"There was something..." Anya said, rubbing her face. "Something deep within me. Something I'd never..." She licked her lips. "There's so much more power at my fingertips than I ever knew possible. You were right, Diogo. There are so many..." She shook her head. "I'm not making much sense. I must still be tired."

Lotan knelt beside her, taking her hand. "You're making sense to me."

"What happened to Yaotl?" Anya asked quietly. "I didn't find him in Mexico City."

"He's been reverted," Lotan replied. "I had a similar experience. A realization of my true power, as it were."

Anya smiled, settling back onto the couch. "About time."

"I feel the connection with every nox," Lotan said, looking at

Anya's hand in his. "It's...overwhelming at times. I can only imagine how intense it must feel with just one. And the abilities I have to..." He shook his head. "I can't believe Yaotl never told me. Or I never asked."

Anya smiled. "I don't think the man who wanted to control you wanted you to know you could actually control him. Much like Bael never..." Her smile faded. "Anyway. I'm glad you've found your way. You will be an amazing belu."

Just in time to give it up forever. Lotan patted her hand as Anya released a loud yawn. "You rest. Jack will return as soon as the situation in Geneva has calmed down somewhat. I'm sure you'll have much to catch up on."

Soft snores were his only response, and he had to admit that even the Lady of Destruction looked somewhat innocent while sleeping.

"I will keep watch," Diogo said. "But being in this land should help her more than anything."

Lotan nodded, feeling the noxlands across the Underworld in a way he'd never felt it before. It had always been home, but now, it was so much more than that. It was a part of him, as much as it was a part of his mother. And now he would have to destroy it.

"If Jack and Cam return before I do," Lotan said, pulling the portal from his back pocket again. "Please let them know I'll be...back in some time. But not to worry."

"Where are you going?"

Lotan half-smiled. "To deal with my pack."

With a heavy heart, Lotan opened the portal to the noxlands and stepped through to the dark night. The familiar power washed over him like a warm blanket, a homecoming to top all homecomings. He imagined his mother and father walking these woods, alone in their love for thousands of years. He placed his hand over his heart, recalling the look on his father's face when he'd seen Xo hurt, and the fierce way she'd told off Bael. It was a parting gift he hadn't realized he was receiving at the time. Their voices would remain imprinted in his memory for the rest of his days.

He felt more connected to his mother than he had in his entire life. Xo never would've approved of what the noxes had become. Oce had once said that she hadn't even wanted the noxes using her portal, but Yaotl had lobbied hard for the noxes to see their homelands once more, and when Xo perished, there was no one left to prevent them from coming and going as they pleased.

Now, Lotan felt his parents' ghosts at his back as he walked toward the sound of a large crowd in the center of the nox village. He didn't even have to announce himself before loud cheers and fearful cries echoed from the masses where Anya had put them. It had been a mercy that she hadn't just killed all of them, but Lotan wouldn't be so merciful.

"It's him!"

"Belu Lotan!"

"Here to save us!"

Lotan had to shake his head. They hadn't been so eager to listen to him in the human world, but perhaps his anger was carrying his power farther than up there.

"Quiet."

His voice and power reverberated over the crowd until there wasn't a peep amongst them.

"You have betrayed me," Lotan began. "You have allied yourself with those who would kill and destroy for the sake of blood. Yaotl filled your minds with falsehoods and delusions, but you allowed yourself to believe them. And when given the opportunity, you chose violence."

A cry of disapproval rose from the noxes, and one brave nox in the front stepped forward. "Belu Lotan, we were misled. Please, do not punish us for our crimes."

"I watched you walk into towns around the world and kill without mercy," Lotan said, glaring daggers at him. "It's become clear to me that this race of demons needs cleansing. A reset of our very core selves and what it means to be a nox." He breathed slowly. "None of you are worthy of the magic anymore."

And like poison from a wound, Lotan took the strands of magic and pulled them to himself. The first few struggled, but the others lost their grip out of fear and chaos, and their magic was easy to pull back. And one by one, the noxes fell to their knees, stunned and knocked out as they reverted to human.

Lotan stood at the helm of a crowd of unconscious humans, watching over them and testing his connections. But there was nothing—no nox remained in the human world. Yaotl had convinced every single creature with his mother's magic to take up arms against the humans, and those who refused had been killed. It was almost poetic that Lotan was the last nox in existence, and that he would put an end to the line his mother started.

Lotan used Anya's portal again, but it would only bring him so far. He pushed aside branches and leaves, the Nullius magic already a warning bell in his head. But he paused to touch the leaves, smell the air, remember this world that his parents had built from nothing. It was a reflection of her heart, just as Anya had made Ath-kur resemble the home she'd shared with Jack. Just as Mizuchi had made Kappanchi look like the home he'd left. Freyja. Perhaps even Bael. There was no fate with any of them. And Lotan's existence was merely another in a long line of happenstance. That made this decision somewhat easier to follow through.

He stepped over the small crack in the ground, the one created when Anya had taken his parents' lives. The result of the connection slipping from Xo to Lotan.

Bending down, Lotan laid his hand on the ground and closed his eyes. Anya had been right; the knowledge of how to manipulate the world was innate. The earth knitted together between his fingers, healing the rift that had marred the land for centuries.

He rose and kept walking until the trees began to thin, and the unsettled feeling of the Nullius was now making him nauseated. As he pushed away a large, flat leaf, a desert of white dunes and nothingness lay before him. The small river, more like a creek, flowed between the sand and the edge of the mossy jungle floor. All Lotan would have to do was set foot on the other side.

He turned around, imprinting this place on his mind. He had no idea what would happen if he managed to become human, what he'd remember and what he wouldn't. But just in case, he wanted to remember everything about the place he'd called home.

Cam's face appeared in his mind, and his smile softened. Out with the old, and in with the bright future waiting for him once this transformation was complete. And he couldn't wait to see what happened next.

Inhaling deeply, Lotan turned back to the Nullius and took a large step across the creek, landing on the soft, white sand. The feeling was instantaneous, a sensation that he shouldn't be here. He should turn and walk back to his lands and live out his life as a belu.

There was something else, too. It was such a simple concept, but so clear to him now. Unlike every other belu, and very much like the nox in Anya's vision, Lotan was finally willing to let this magic go. But not just this magic—his desire to preserve the world he thought had belonged to his parents. Deep in his heart, he'd wanted to maintain their magic as a tribute to them, and what they'd accomplished together.

Now, however, he saw the truth. His mother might've been

chosen, but she wasn't any more special than any other unlucky human who stumbled upon the demonic magic. To move forward, to focus on the beautiful future waiting for him on the other side, *that* would be a better service to their memory. And to rid the world of the monsters who had perverted what it meant to be a nox.

The magic in his bones rattled and shook before rising to the surface of his skin, releasing into the air. He cracked open an eye to watch it leave—a magnificent color so black it was almost purple.

He exhaled, a tear rolling down his cheek as the warmth and familiar feeling slipped from his grasp. It wasn't painful, but his body trembled as it lost the strength it had come to know. He fell to his knees as his legs gave out from under him, his fingers sinking into the warm, white sand.

His senses began to dull, but he thought he heard the sound of beating wings. Too late, he remembered those beasts who'd so viciously attacked Jack and Cam. The ones who had taken magic and absorbed it from the center of the Nullius.

He struggled to get to his feet, but by now, the process was nearly complete. The monster landed on the sand near to him, black, soulless eyes staring him down.

"Why do you give up your magic?" The voice was disembodied, and Lotan wasn't completely sure that he hadn't imagined it.

"Because those who had it no longer deserve it," he whispered. "The world needs a cleansing."

It nodded, and Lotan blinked as its face faded in and out of view. "You're the nox."

"I was."

"How?" Lotan's tongue was starting to lose feeling.

The monster, still patiently perched on its claws. "Bael has powers none of us understood. And a thirst for revenge none of us can stop."

Lotan opened his mouth to ask what he meant by that, but he fell backward onto the soft sand, his mind going blank.

CHAPTER THIRTY-SEVEN

Cam sank down on a bench, lowering her head into her hands as exhaustion threatened to overwhelm her. She and Jack had evacuated survivors and the most horrifically injured early on in the day and were now working with the various ICDM offices who'd come to offer aid. But they all came from smaller cities and lacked large-scale disaster management. Anyone who had any experience was dealing with the fallout in their own city.

At least a hundred cities had been attacked around the globe—including every city that housed an ICDM Councilman office. Charleston had been attacked, but luckily Jack's parents were okay. Jack had called them as soon as he'd been able to find a working cell phone to convey the news about Frank, and Cam had to walk away, as she couldn't stand to hear the sobbing from the other end of the line. She'd managed to fire off a text to her mom, safe and sound in El Paso, but she couldn't handle talking. Not now. Maybe not ever.

When Jack hung up, he looked at Cam, and she hadn't seen him so low since Sara's funeral. But for once, she had nothing to offer him. She barely had enough for herself.

"Anya saved…so many people," he said. "Dad said they've gotten reports that all the demons disappeared at the same time. A few hundred thousand. Gone in a moment." He rubbed his nose with the back of his wrist. "She said it was because I was… She thought I would die, and she said she just did it."

Cam nodded. She would find that heartwarming later. "Where did they go?"

"My guess? The Underworld." Jack gave the phone back to the man who'd let him borrow it. "She's too soft to have killed all of them in cold blood."

"She should have."

Jack nodded. "How is María?"

"No idea." Cam had no words for her great-aunt. Not when she'd been one of the masterminds of the escalation. Had she and the rest of ICDM just *stopped* for five minutes, Frank might still be alive. Hundreds of thousands of humans might be, too.

"You should check on her," Jack said. "Do it as a favor to Juana."

Cam scowled at the overt manipulation but turned on her heel and walked to the medical tent where she'd last seen María.

Her great-aunt was seated on a bed, hooked to an IV with a sling around her right arm. Her eyes were closed, but she was alive.

"It is a mess."

"Yep," Cam said, crossing her arms over her chest. "How are you feeling?"

"I'm talking and can stand on my own," she said, cracking open one eye and looking at the IV. "They insist upon this, but I don't need it."

Cam nodded, fighting the urge to scream *I told you so* at her. "Have you been briefed?"

She sighed, shifting in the bed as she tried to sit up more. "If you are here to tell me that you predicted this, please, save your breath. I understand the grave mistake we have made." She stopped struggling, and Cam noted the wince as she sank back down. "But if you are here with a proposed peace treaty with the demons, I'm willing to entertain it."

"The thing is…" Cam began, looking at the ground. If it had been just Yaotl and a handful of demons who'd caused all this havoc, that would've been one thing. But based on what she'd seen, this was a worldwide, coordinated attack. Freyja, Biloko, and Tabiko all shared responsibility for the deaths they'd caused. They might've been provoked by ICDM, but the response wasn't anywhere near the same. A treaty might not be in the cards anymore—because the demons didn't deserve one.

María opened an eye. "Yes?"

"Feel better soon," Cam said. "I'll be back if I have anything for you."

Cam was almost to the edge of the tent when María softly called her name. She turned slightly, not willing to give María her full attention.

"I'm very proud of you," María said. "That's all."

Cam turned and walked out of the tent, wishing those words meant more to her.

Cam found Jack speaking with the de facto commander on the ground. Somehow, he was still on his feet, even though they'd both been going for hours. But when he turned to her, his eyes were dim.

"I think I've had about as much fun as I can stomach today," Jack said. "What about you?"

She nodded. "Tell me we don't have to go all the way to the edge of the city to catch a ride. I don't think I can handle it."

"You're in luck, partner," Jack said as a large armored truck came rolling up.

"I could kiss you," Cam said. "But that might make someone jealous. And considering what she did around here, I don't think I want to do that."

They climbed into the SUV, and Cam finally allowed herself to relax next to Jack. The driver took Jack's direction without comment, and they were on their way. Cam closed her eyes to the carnage, grateful, at least, for the help from outside the city. She didn't want to be a part of having to identify and contact next of kin.

"I don't want to sign a treaty anymore," Cam said quietly, as

Jack put his arm around her and rested his head on top of hers. "They crossed a line."

"Agreed," Jack said. "But what other choice do we have?"

She sighed. "I don't know. I just don't know. But this… there's no coming back from this. And we're just going to have to convince Anya of that. This can't be allowed to happen again. There must be consequences."

The armored vehicle pulled up at the edge of the city, and Jack and Cam jumped out, thanking the lieutenant who'd driven them and assuring him they could manage from here. Once the vehicle was out of sight, Jack turned back to Cam and pulled the portal from his pocket, tossing it in the air and directing it to Ath-kur. They stepped through to the living room at Ath-kur, and Cam was yet again grateful Anya had managed to figure out how to make the transition between worlds less discombobulating. She didn't think her stomach could take another roil.

Anya was sleeping soundly on the couch, some of her color returning. Diogo was sitting on a chair across from her, perhaps trying to read his book, but his gaze was on his belu. The attentiveness was somewhat endearing, and Cam found it ironic that the only demon she wasn't completely sick to see was an athtar.

"How is she?" Jack asked, his stoic face softening markedly as he approached her.

"She's fine," Anya responded, opening an eye. "You, on the other hand…" She sat up, pausing for a moment to find her balance, then stood and walked over. "Are you two hurt at all?"

"No," Cam said. "Thanks to you."

"That was..." She exhaled, rubbing her face. "That was."

"Where did you put all the demons?" Jack asked.

"In the Underworld," Anya said. "Back in their lands. It seemed the most expeditious way to deal with them without inflaming tensions more."

Cam couldn't help the snort that came from deep within her.

"What?" Anya asked.

"They just massacred hundreds of thousands of humans, and you're worried about pissing them off," Cam said, too tired to have a filter. "The fair thing to do would've been to punish them. Take their heads off."

Anya looked at her hands and didn't respond right away. Cam expected Jack to jump in and continue, but he just took Anya's hand in his and kissed it gently.

"It's been a long day for all of us," Jack said. "I need a shower and to sleep for the next... ten years." He half-smiled at Anya. "Join me?"

Cam looked around, finally noticing someone was missing. "Where is Lotan?"

"He said he was going to deal with his pack," Diogo said, now back to his book.

"His..." Cam looked at Jack, her eyes wide. "Damn it all. Why would he do that?"

"Because he's now their belu," Anya said. "He was finally

able to reclaim the magic his mother gave him. The way he should've done when he came of age."

Cam pursed her lips. That certainly explained a few things. "So what? They're all going to bow to him?"

"He didn't give them a chance to," Anya said, her eyes growing dark.

"What?" Cam shook her head. "Take us there."

Anya's power had clearly returned, because in a moment, she, Cam, and Jack were standing in the middle of a crowd in the noxlands. Some of them had woken up, but others were still passed out on the ground. Most of them looked absolutely confused as to why they were there, talking to each other in a mix of languages nobody seemed to understand.

"What did he do?" Jack asked.

"Belus can reclaim their power from their spawn," Anya said, looking out across the crowd. "And it looks like Lotan exercised that option. They're all human."

"So where is Lotan?" Cam asked.

"I can't..." Anya narrowed her eyes. "I can't find him. But that means he's in one place."

The world moved beneath Cam again, and the three of them stood in the middle of a jungle. It seemed no different from anywhere else in the noxlands, but Lotan was still nowhere to be found.

"Where is he?" Cam asked, worry starting to burrow into her stomach.

"I can't get any closer," Anya said, bracing herself against a nearby tree. "But he's in that direction. I think."

Jack went to her, gently guiding her back a few paces. "Don't push it, please."

Cam ignored them and kept walking, throwing leaves and branches out of her way. She had a very bad feeling about where they were, and what Lotan had done. It would've been extraordinarily stupid to have done this alone. But she wouldn't put it past him.

She reached the end of the jungle, and her gaze immediately drew to the figures across the small creek. Lotan, on his knees as purple magic evaporated around him. And one of those winged bastards who'd nearly killed her, lying in wait for Lotan to fall.

"Oh, hell no," Cam barked, pulling the sword off her back and jumping across the creek. The winged monster stared at her, unfurling its wings and baring its teeth. Cam ran as fast as the sand would let her until she was between the monster and Lotan, who blinked at her heavily.

"C-Cam?" The words left his lips before he fell backward onto the sand.

"Shit, Lotan!" Cam said, turning to him. The winged monster let out a bloodcurdling scream and swooped toward her.

But Jack had whipped out his phone and turned on the bright flashlight, still working this close to the border. The monster screeched in pain, backing up but not flying away.

"C'mon!" Jack reached down to hook his hands under Lotan's armpits and dragged him backward toward the border with the noxlands. The creature screamed as it came back toward them and Cam took out her phone and shone the flashlight at it, keeping it at bay.

They crossed the border and the monster gave up, sitting on the border and squawking in frustration. Jack huffed, his cheeks red. "Are you going to make me carry your boyfriend all the way back to Ath-kur?"

Cam jumped and ran to Jack, taking Lotan's other arm and helping Jack drag him. They took three more steps before the world shook. A fresh crack appeared a few feet from where they stood. Another earthquake—this one nearly sent Cam to her knees.

"Oh, shit." Cam looked at Jack, then back at Lotan. "We need to—"

But just as the ground began to crumble under their feet, it slowed once more. Anya walked out of the jungle, her eyes dark as she held onto the time river. They barely had a moment to speak before she swept them away to their living room in Ath-kur.

"Fuck," Jack said, releasing Lotan's arm with an unceremonious thump. "Any more dangerous situations we want to get into today?"

"Lotan?" Cam slapped his cheek. "Why isn't he waking up?" She pressed her hand to his chest, relieved at the steady heartbeat there. "Lotan?" She turned behind her to Anya, whose eyes were wide with disbelief.

"The son of a bitch did it."

"What do you mean?" Cam said, her heart sinking.

"He's human," she said. "He really did it."

Cam knelt next to Lotan and turned him over. Already he felt…different. The rush of energy that came with his touch was gone, even though his chest continued to rise and fall.

Relief washed over her as his beautiful black eyelashes fluttered, and his gaze came into focus, on her.

"Who are you?" he asked, looking from Anya to Jack then back to Cam.

Cam's heart cracked a little. Had Lotan really gone this far only to lose all his memories? Would he still be Lotan? "My name is Cam. You and I—"

"You are… You are so beautiful," he whispered. "You are the most beautiful thing I've ever seen."

She had to laugh as tears fell down her cheeks. "Lotan…"

"Is that my name?" he asked, blinking. "I don't remember…" He furrowed his brow. "I remember my mother. Xo. She was magnificent. And my father… And a jungle…"

"I think he'll be fine," Anya said, reaching across Lotan to grip Cam's shoulder. "Just give him time to come back to himself."

CHAPTER THIRTY-EIGHT

Jack helped Anya carry Lotan back to Ath-kur, though he was pretty sure she could've handled it alone. Cam was still pale and in disbelief, and Jack himself was having a hard time processing what he'd just heard. After all the effort and experimentation, Lotan had just…figured out how to relieve himself of this burden. Once his memory returned, he would have more of an explanation, but for now, he was babbling about memories of his childhood in the noxlands and how beautiful Cam was.

They put him in the bedroom he shared with Cam, and Jack had had about enough of this day. His body ached, he smelled of blood and sweat, and all he wanted was a long shower. He walked into the bathroom, yanking his filthy shirt off, and finally got a look in the mirror. His face was a mess, his hair stuck up at odd angles. But something about his visage reminded Jack of Frank, and the pain came back fresh. He leaned on the sink and closed his eyes, letting the emotion well to the surface.

A pair of warm arms encircled him, and a soft cheek rested on his back. Anya said nothing, but he lifted a hand from the sink to clasp hers in a show that he wanted her there. Slowly, he lifted her knuckles to his lips and kissed them softly, before walking to the shower.

When he turned to strip the rest of his clothes off, she was naked before him, her long hair spilling down her shoulders. She was magnificent, completely free of injury, her skin glowing with health and vitality. But the look in her sparkling emerald eyes was one of concern. She walked past him and stepped into the shower, pulling him inside with her.

She took the washcloth and ran it across his body, wiping away every trace of battle she could find. As she passed a gash or a cut, she paused and used her magic to heal it. It was an odd sensation, a little itchy as the skin knitted back together, but he was entranced by the care with which she tended to him. This was a side to her he rarely saw, that vulnerable heart that had captivated him so many months ago.

When she finished, she turned off the water and looked at him. They stood in the steam and tile, and he found himself drawn to her. With a soft sigh, he slipped his hand behind her head and pressed his mouth to hers, resting his other hand around her lower back and pressing her naked body to his. She responded gently, at first, but then became more desperate, gripping his face.

They spilled out of the bathroom, stealing kisses and touches from each other before landing on the bed. Jack was desperate for release, the urge rising up from the bottom of his soul like a ghost. She was all he craved, all he wanted, and finally—*finally*—nothing would get between them.

She slipped her fingers around his manhood, stroking as he closed his eyes. He snaked a hand down to the tender space between her legs, finding her already wet with anticipation. She sighed as he toyed with her then removed his hand.

"I think you've done enough today," she whispered against his lips, pushing him onto his back and climbing him. He gripped her hips as she settled onto him, a welcome feeling like coming home. She moved slowly, and they found their rhythm. She rested her hands on his shoulders as she rode him, her cheeks growing red.

Her motion was deliberate, slow sending him close to his edge, but he resisted. She wore a smile as she whispered his name, and he let himself fall back into the pillow, gripping her hips.

She moaned in pleasure and clenched around him, her nails digging into his skin and he thrust once more into her and releasing everything. She tilted her head back and relaxed her grip on his chest.

Finally, she tilted her head down to him, an exhausted smile on her face. "Was that good?"

He nodded, resting one hand on top of hers. "Why did we wait so long?"

"Let's not wait again," she whispered, drifting down to lie on top of him. She fit perfectly against his chest, and he wrapped his arms around her, holding her tightly in place.

This was heaven right here. And as he drifted off to sleep, he could've sworn she whispered, "I love you, Jack."

Jack had no idea how long he slept, but he awoke wishing he could sleep for hours more. But a pair of emerald eyes staring into his kept him from falling back into his dreamless existence.

"How are you feeling?" Anya asked.

"Like I've been having a wonderful dream," Jack said, threading his fingers through hers. "You?"

"I haven't been able to sleep at all," she replied, gazing at him with a smile. Her fingers danced down his chest, down his ab line. "Waiting for you to wake up again."

He growled and leaned in to kiss her again, but a loud rapping on the door made them both jump.

"We need to talk." Cam's serious voice broke whatever spell they'd had over each other, and Anya grumbled.

"We do, though," Jack said, as yesterday's events came back to him. "C'mon. We'll continue this later."

"Promise?"

He kissed her gently. "Wild horses couldn't keep me away."

They got up and dressed quickly, Jack's muscles still stiff

from the day before. But he and Anya held hands as they walked down the long hallway. There, Lotan was sitting on the couch holding a cup of coffee.

He looked up and smiled at them. "Hello. You're the same couple from yesterday, aren't you?"

"Well, shit," Anya said, looking at Cam. "Has any more of his memory returned?"

"No," Cam said, glaring at him. "But that's not the pressing issue."

"What's wrong?" Jack asked, walking to the kitchen and retrieving a pair of cups for himself and Anya.

"Right now, the human world is what's wrong, thanks to the demons."

Jack sighed and brought a cup to Anya, kissing her on the forehead, and sitting down next to her. "I think the first thing is to explain to each other what the hell happened to everyone yesterday. Starting with Lotan."

"I'm not sure he's in much of a place to tell us anything," Cam said. "But as far as I can tell, he's been completely reverted to human."

"The noxes did not deserve my mother's magic," Lotan said, looking somewhat lucid for a moment. Then he squinted. "I think. What's a nox again?"

"And the humans in the noxlands?" Jack asked, albeit a little nervously, looking at Anya. "Are they still there?"

Anya shook her head slowly. "There's nothing there, Jack. It's all gone. Everyone who was there perished."

"What about those in the human world?" Jack asked. "Diogo retained his power after Bael died, didn't he?"

"Because Bael wanted it so," Anya said. "But I guess Lotan decided he wanted all the noxes gone. There are none left."

Jack looked around. "Where is Diogo anyway?"

"He's found himself a new place to stay until the talismans are cleared out of Lisbon," Anya said with a smile. "Which, I hope, will be soon."

"Don't count on it," Cam said.

"Why not?" Anya's brow furrowed. "I'm the reason the demons aren't terrorizing humanity right now. The least they could do is realize I'm not the enemy and remove the talismans."

"You also could have killed the demons yesterday," Cam said. "Instead, you left it up to the belus, I guess. There are no consequences for their actions unless the belus decide otherwise."

"They are unable to return to the human world," Anya said. "Xo's portal was destroyed when the noxlands collapsed. The only other way would be through me, and I won't allow it."

"Or," Cam said, rubbing her hands together, "you could do what Lotan did and give up your magic. Then the demons are stuck in the Underworld forever. Problem effectively solved."

Jack glanced between Anya and Cam, unsure which one to focus on. Anya's mouth had fallen open in shock, and Cam wore a look of fury that he knew better than to argue with. The small voice in the back of his mind said that she had a point, that if the bridge between the human and demon worlds was broken, it wouldn't be the worst thing.

Anya licked her lips. "If I'm not here, who will prevent the world from falling into chaos? I moved only the demons who were fighting. Not all of them chose to engage."

"Then those demons can enter into a treaty with ICDM or be destroyed," Cam said, her face stony. "But the time for coddling the demons is over. They massacred innocent humans, Anya."

"And I removed the guilty ones."

"Good, then let's permanently leave them where you put them, and you give up your magic."

Anya rose. "I can't believe you're asking me this."

"I can't believe you aren't on board," Cam replied, jumping to her feet as well. "You *just* got your magic back like a month ago. It's not as if you've gotten attached. And the only person who thinks you need to keep the peace is you."

To Jack's horror, both women turned to him, fury on their faces. "Well, Jack?" Cam asked.

"I..." Jack looked to Lotan, who seemed confused by the whole situation. "I..."

"Speak," Cam barked.

"Jack, you can't believe this is the only option," Anya replied, her eyes nervous.

"Not the only one, sure, but—"

She threw up her hands. "Are you serious?" She shook her head, her face melting into disgust. "But I guess I'm not surprised. You'll always take her side over mine."

"That's unfair," Jack said. "And not true. I'm looking at this objectively. We have a moment now where the factions are separate. ICDM is in a position to sign a treaty, and whoever remains topside might be willing to do so if their only bridge to their belus is gone. And you..." He swallowed, preparing himself for her wrath. "Cam's right. You don't need this power. You are plenty powerful on your own."

Anya's upper lip twitched as she balled her fists. Cam's movements slowed, and Lotan's mug stayed at his lips. Jack swallowed; she'd slowed time for a *private talk*. He was in for it.

"Bullshit," Anya said. "I was a ghost when I was a human. I wasn't... Jack, I wasn't happy."

"You are happy now," Jack said. "And I don't think it has anything to do with this magic."

"It has *everything* to do with it," Anya said. "Because I'm no longer dependent on you for everything. Does it not matter to you that I just saved *the entire world* with it?"

"Of course it does," Jack said. "And the world owes you a debt. But that doesn't mean..." He wasn't exactly sure how to phrase it. "I'm not sure that means you should keep it."

She clicked her tongue. "No? What about all that talk about staying with me?"

"I meant it," Jack said. "But, Anya, this isn't about us. This is about the rest of the world. There is no need for an athtar anymore. If you keep these powers, Freyja or Biloko might come to you one day and ask you for a favor. What's to say you'll remember the gravity of what they did? What's to stop you from wielding your power the way Bael did?"

"You will, Jack," Anya said, her eyes filling with tears.

"I may be dead by then," Jack said.

"Then let me turn you," she whispered, taking his hands. "We can be together forever."

This wasn't the time for this conversation, but he could avoid it no longer. "Anya, you know..." He swallowed. "I love you."

She half-smiled. "I love you, too."

"But as much as I love you, I don't... I don't want to become a demon. I want to be with you, but not like that."

"But what about what I want?" A tear spilled down her cheek. "Doesn't that matter?"

He opened and closed his mouth, wishing he could find a more artful way to say what he needed to. "Anya, this...staying athtar... It's not necessary. You would only be doing it to..."

"It was necessary when I saved your life just now," Anya snapped, removing her hands from his.

"But the danger has passed."

"There will always be danger—"

"Not if the demons can't reach the humans," Jack said. "You said yourself you're the only way they can get between worlds, so if you no longer have magic..." He took a step toward her. "You don't need it anymore, Anya. It's not who you are, and it doesn't define you."

She stepped back, her lip trembling as she stared at him. "Then you clearly don't know me at all, Jack."

And then she was gone.

"Wh...Where did she go?" Cam asked, blinking. "What happened?"

Jack stared at the space Anya had left, hoping that maybe something of what he'd said had gotten through to her. Because otherwise...

CHAPTER THIRTY-NINE

When she arrived atop her mountain, Anya let loose a guttural growl of frustration. How dare Jack ask her to give up her powers? How dare he presume to know who she was and what she wanted? He had no clue the dangers that could be waiting in the world.

He wants to slow you down.

The voice was back, and this time, Anya leaned into it. After all, she'd only scratched the surface of what was possible as an athtar. The whole world lay before her, and she had eternity to explore every bit of it. And along the way, she could be feared. She could demand control from those who would tremble at her feet. She would truly become the Lady of the Mountain, striking fear into the hearts of every human and demon around the world. They would listen and adhere to every word.

It would be as it used to be. She would wield absolute power over the belus, and they would have to do whatever she said in order to earn her favor. To have access to their topside demons and the human world.

You can find some other human for company—one who won't try to hold you back.

Another human?

She stopped, her heart sinking at the thought of never seeing Jack again. As much as she could pretend otherwise, he wasn't someone she could simply replace. She'd met thousands—hundreds of thousands—of humans in her lifetime, and not one had managed to grab hold of her heart and mind the way he had. There was something about him she could never let go of, something unique about the way he was put together. And she could live another three thousand years and not find another who managed to capture her so completely.

Don't be weak.

She hissed, quieting that voice in her head. Loving Jack had never been weakness—it had been strength. Unlike Bael, he'd never intended to keep her as his prisoner. He freely admitted his fears to her and promised her he would work to overcome them.

The world needs its belu to protect it.

It doesn't have to be me.

A new voice rose to answer in her mind, this one clear and

confident and decidedly her own. The world had been set right, and if she bowed out now, it would remain that way. Another athtar would perhaps gain her magic one day, but for now, things would be fine. And Anya could put this burden on a mantel and step into a new life, one where she was human, and this time, ready to love Jack with all of herself.

He is asking you to change for him.

"No," Anya whispered, wiping her cheeks. He wasn't asking her to change for him, he was asking for the greater good. Because even as she sat atop this mountain, the temptation to wield power over the other belus and humanity was tugging at her. Given enough time, she would give in.

And she *had* nearly given in. Many times. With the LA director, with Biloko. Freyja. It was only thanks to Jack's calm presence that she remembered who she had wanted to be. If he was no longer with her, could she say she was strong enough to resist the temptation?

Or could she be even stronger and choose the greater good even if it meant she'd be back to square one?

You can be great as the belu athtar.

"I won't become Bael."

Besides Jack, besides ultimatums, besides everything—that was reason enough to step into the Nullius and become human. She had promised herself that she would use this gift for good, to help instead of hurt. And now was the perfect opportunity to make good on that promise.

But first…first, she needed to do one more thing.

The current of time was strong in her hand, and she navigated it expertly through the centuries. Her heart pounded in her chest as she neared the time, the events that remained so clear in her mind. She closed her eyes as she passed them then stopped some time before.

She stood in a large room, filled with wooden toys and a small bed. She couldn't smell it, but the memory remained as she took in the sight of it. Everything was perfect, from the wooden floors to the curtains on the wall.

Her pulse quickened as little footsteps echoed down the hall, and Asherah, her precious little girl, bounded into the room. She was perfection in every way, with ringlets rivaling her mother's but her father's brown eyes. She carried a real sword on her belt, which she pulled out and slashed around the room.

"I am Asherah, Princess of the Mountain," she announced, slicing at nobody.

Hot tears fell down Anya's cheeks as her shoulders shook. It was as hard as she'd thought it would be, to come here and see her beautiful child locked in a moment in time. She would grow no older, never come into her powers. But Anya desperately needed this. To remember every inch of her, to hear her voice and carry it with her for the rest of her days.

She was so focused on the sparring child that she felt neither the rush of magic behind her nor feel the presence of someone watching her until a voice rang out across the time portal.

"Hello, Anat."

Anya's whole body went stick-straight. Her past self was nowhere to be found, and neither was Bael. Perhaps she'd just imagined it.

"Will you not turn to say hello? Or are you too proud?"

She squeezed her eyes shut. It was only a dream. Only a vision—a fear. Not real.

But something familiar slid itself around her hip and her whole body electrified. Slowly, she turned, and her heart stopped in her chest.

"B-Bael?"

He was a faded version of himself, much as she was in this time river. An athtar out of place. Out of time. Perhaps the same one she'd seen on her very first trip into the time river.

"Will you not say hello?"

"I don't have to say anything to you," she said, without much conviction. "You're…"

She didn't want to tell him he was dead. Because, she realized, this Bael was a time surfer as she was, but from sometime in the past. He had no idea what lay ahead for him.

"You have killed me, haven't you?"

She couldn't stop herself from reacting, earning a soft chuckle from Bael.

"It was inevitable, I suppose. One day you would grow tired of me." He turned to the vision of their daughter. "I have seen you peruse this river," he said. "Have you given up your human in favor of the nox prince who travels with you?"

Anya swallowed. This was Bael from recent history—he

knew about Jack. "You're the one who saw me. In Geneva." Realization dawned. "You used to time travel to spy on me, didn't you? I would have no idea… It's how…"

"How I watched you all those years?" He smiled. "You really have grown into this power, haven't you? I knew you would."

"You…" Anya shook her head. She needed to get away, but she was stuck. "This isn't going to work the way it did before. I don't believe your lies."

"I have never lied to you," Bael said without any remorse. "I love you too much."

"Bullshit," Anya spat. "You never loved me. You tortured me."

Bael shook his head. "You are merely upset—"

"That doesn't work on me anymore, Bael," she snapped. "After three thousand years, I see you for who you are. A weak, pathetic creature who manipulates everyone around you to think you were some sort of god. But you're just a man. A man who happened to get lucky and find some power."

Bael seemed unfazed by her comments. "What fire you have now, my lady. Can I thank your human for all this newfound confidence?"

"You can thank my soul-searching after I beheaded you," Anya said, anger pulsing through her.

"I see." Bael nodded. "Then you took my power for yourself."

Anya felt the tug of the athtar pride. "It was…a mistake. It's caused more harm than good. I plan to rid myself of it soon.

There is much more to be gained from losing it."

He smiled. "Did the magic call to you?"

"What?"

"Did it call to you?"

She took a step back, again unable to hide her emotions. "Y-yes."

"That's because it was yours," Bael said with a smile. "I have pondered my own death for centuries, knowing that the day may come when you no longer cared for me. So I made arrangements." He glanced at her. "Did Diogo find you?"

She shivered, even though there was no breeze in this world.

"And yet, after I moved heaven and earth to ensure *you* alone would get this gift, you would simply...give it up?"

"Yes," she said, though her resolve was slipping. She wrenched her gaze away from Bael and to the child still dancing in the periphery. "Because if there's *any* chance I could turn into you, that I would be capable of the things you did..."

"What did I do that was so horrible?"

Anya turned to him, fire in her eyes. "You killed my daughter."

"The noxes did that."

An incredulous laugh came from her lips. "You're such a liar. She was a threat to you, and you killed her." Anya swallowed, taking a step back as her defenses came back up. "She could have one day replaced you and taken the athtars for herself."

Bael smiled; she wanted anger, but all she got was amusement. "Such an imagination you have."

Anya could take no more of his lies and shifted herself forward in time until she lost the past Bael. Asherah was still in her bedroom, crying over a baby doll. Anya's heart broke at the sound.

"Mama!" she cried, tilting her head back and screaming. "Mama!"

"What is it?" Anya's past self appeared in the room, concern etched on her face. "My love, what is it?"

"I've killed the wrong doll," Asherah sniffed, her eyes wet with tears. "I was careless and wrong."

"Ssh, my sweet child," past-Anya said, holding her tight. "Your dolls will heal. They are athtar, are they not?"

The child nodded.

"And their heads are still on their bodies, are they not?"

Again, she nodded.

"Then there is nothing to fear," past-Anya said, brushing the hair from her child's face. "As long as their heads remain connected to their bodies, their magic will heal them." She took the sword gently. "But perhaps we should train more with our instructors before we wield our sword, hm? You know how Father doesn't like it when you play."

She nodded.

"That's not true," Bael said, breaking present-day Anya's attention. "I loved it when she played."

"Leave me," Anya snapped, instead of engaging with his version of reality. "You've already taken so much from me. Give me this moment alone with my child."

"Do you think I don't also return to this time?" Bael asked. "To see our precious girl? The noxes—"

"If you *dare* tell me the noxes were responsible, I will cut out your tongue," Anya snarled. "Because I can return to that moment. Your lies don't hold up in video replay, I'm afraid."

Bael stared at her, and for a moment, she thought he would continue the falsehoods, but he turned back to Asherah, slowing the time before them.

"This child would never have been able to take the throne from me, because like her mother, she was too soft. She would've been a loyal foot soldier, never questioning. The same as you."

There was something hurtful about his words, something that cut to the core of her and stung worse than finding out he'd been the one to take their daughter's life.

"She was perfect in every way," Anya said. "And I wasn't so weak that I didn't destroy you when the time came. You are dead, Bael. And I can't wait to *never* hear your voice again."

Her grip on time slipped, and her mind went blank as she floated back to the present. Her heart broke that she would never see her daughter again in the flesh, but she was grateful she'd been able to have a few more precious moments. No regrets, not now. Not when she had so much more waiting for her once she rid herself of these atrocious powers.

She landed in the present, opening her eyes to the ceiling and exhaling deeply. Now, for—

"I like what you've done with the place."

A jolt of fear coursed through her body. Bael—in the flesh,

real, whole—stood in her living room in Ath-kur, adjusting the cuffs of his shirtsleeves. He smiled at her, sending shoots of dread down her spine.

"How—"

"My love, there are so many things you don't know about this magic," Bael said, walking over to her and crouching. Her entire body went cold when his warm hands touched her face. "Thank you for showing me my own future. I now see what I must do."

And before she could stop him, he was gone.

To be concluded in

RECLAMATION

DEMON FALL TRILOGY

Book Three

ACKNOWLEGMENTS

First and foremost, thank you to my husband, without whom this book and my sanity wouldn't have survived. I do not know what possessed me to think I could draft a book while in the throes of the first trimester, but together, we did it. Thank you for picking up the slack when I couldn't even pick myself up off the couch.

Special thanks to Dani, my line editor, for catching my grammatical mistakes and non sequiturs. And thanks to my typo checker Lisa, who somehow always finds things I miss.

Finally, thank you, dear reader, for continuing on this journey with me. I hope you are ready for a wild ride in Book 3.

ALSO BY S. USHER EVANS

THE MADION WAR TRILOGY

He's a prince, she's a pilot, they're at war. But when they are marooned on a deserted island hundreds of miles from either nation, they must set aside their differences and work together if they want to survive.

The Madion War Trilogy is available in eBook, paperback, and hardcover. Download the first book, The Island, for free on all eBookstores.

Empath

Lauren Dailey is in break-up hell, but if you ask her she's doing just great. She hears a mysterious voice promising an easy escape from her problems and finds herself in a brand new world where she has the power to feel what others are feeling. Just one problem—there's a dragon in the mountains that happens to eat Empaths. And it might be the source of the mysterious voice tempting her deeper into her own darkness.

Empath is a stand-alone fantasy that is available now in eBook, paperback, and hardcover.

ALSO BY S. USHER EVANS

The Razia Series

Lyssa Peate is living a double life as a planet discovering scientist and a space pirate bounty hunter. Unfortunately, neither life is going very well. She's the least wanted pirate in the universe and her brand new scientist intern is spying on her. Things get worse when her intern is mistaken for her hostage by the Universal Police.

The Razia Series is a four-book space opera series and is available now for eBook, paperback, audiobook, and hardcover. Download the first book, Double Life, for free on all eBookstores.

The Lexie Carrigan Chronicles

Lexie Carrigan thought she was weird enough until her family drops a bomb on her—she's magical. Now the girl who's never made waves is blowing up her nightstand and no one seems to want to help her. That is, until a kind gentleman shows up with all the answers. But Lexie finds out being magical is the least weird thing about her.

Spells and Sorcery is the first book in the Lexie Carrigan Chronicles, and is available now in eBook, paperback, audiobook, and hardcover.

ABOUT THE AUTHOR

S. Usher Evans was born and raised in Pensacola, Florida. After a decade of fighting bureaucratic battles as an IT consultant in Washington, D.C., she suffered a massive quarter-life-crisis. She decided fighting dragons was more fun than writing policy, so she moved back to Pensacola to write books full-time. She currently resides with her husband and two dogs, Zoe and Mr. Biscuit, and frequently can be found plotting on the beach.

Find her on the internet:

www.susherevans.com

www.facebook.com/susherevans
www.twitter.com/susherevans
www.instagram.com/susherevans